CURRENCY OF WAR

by
Melinda M. Snodgrass

The Currency of War was first published by Prince of Cats Literary Productions in 2021

This second edition contains some minor updates.

Thank you for Reading!

Credits
Cover Design: by Fakel Barros

It's been two hundred years since the Solar League faced an alien threat. Now aliens have attacked with horrific force. And only the Empress Mercedes de Arango can inspire and lead her people, even as the alien menace rains death on the League worlds.

She desperately needs competent military officers to battle the aliens, so Mercedes reaches out to her secret love Thracius "Tracy" Belmanor. She begs Tracy to return to active duty – taking the risk that Tracy will uncover the truth about her son and a long ago encounter she and Tracy agreed to forget.

In the midst of a losing war against outside invaders with no mercy, civil war looms. Mercedes' son and her youngest sister face execution and worse as pawns in this game of thrones.

Unable to save them, Mercedes once again calls upon Tracy and his unorthodox smuggler's skills to rescue her sister and her son. But can any of them survive the revelation of a devasting secret, one that will forever undermine the stability of the throne?

DEDICATION

This book is dedicated to the memory of
Dr. Michael Engelberg.

Physician, movie producer, science fiction fan, philosopher, and my friend. He was brilliant and passionate, kind, and caring. He dreamed of the stars, and he loved the writers who brought them to him. Ad Astra, Michael.

CURRENCY OF WAR

THE IMPERIALS SAGA • BOOK 4

NEW YORK TIMES BESTSELLING AUTHOR
MELINDA M. SNODGRASS

1

THE TRUMPET'S CALL

"DON'T KNOW WHEN I'm ever going to get to sell these," BK Bower was saying as he watched his assistant load the crates of luxury goods onto a flitter van. "With a war on, nobody's much interested in Sidone jeweled handbags and fans."

Jahan Sirani, now captain of the trading vessel *Selkie* since the departure of her human captain several weeks before, glanced down pointedly at her credit spike holder.

Bower sighed. "Guess it's not your fault that I ordered this shit just before a war started, and you did haul it here, so … would you consider giving me a discount?"

"Let me check with our accountant," Jahan replied. She stepped aside and radioed Jax, the plantlike Tiponi Flute who kept them running at a profit. She relayed the request and heard all of Jax's fronds shivering so hard they were probably creating a breeze.

"Tell him we can knock twelve percent off the cartage fee," came the response.

The transaction was concluded, and Jahan decided that they had enough fuel to wait until San Pedro to refill. Prices were better on that station than here on Kronos, which was the financial hub of the Solar League. Especially now that the League was at war. The big cargo ramp was whining closed when her nephew Kielli's voice came over the ship's intercom.

"*Tia* Jahan." He was her sister's middle son, and he never called her aunt unless something was wrong. Jahan felt her fur begin to stand up on end. "I just intercepted a message from the orbital buoys that unknown ships have just emerged from Fold. They're light minutes out from the planet." He ended on a bit of a squeak.

Jahan didn't wait for the lift to take her to the bridge. Instead, she raced up the access ladder using all four appendages and her tail to increase her rate of climb.

On the bridge she took the command chair from Kielli, who jumped into the comm and scanner post. Panicked radio chatter filled the airwaves. Apparently, a lot of other civilian craft were also eavesdropping on the *Orden de la Estrella*'s communications, for there was a sudden scramble of ships trying to lift off without authorization.

The intercom was still on, so the remainder of the crew heard the frantic messages from the port authority to the ships whose engines had started. Too many ships and too many engines. Even inside the skin of the *Selkie* they could feel the ground shuddering.

"Well, this ain't gonna end well," Ernie Gantz, their new engineer, grunted.

Jahan jumped to the navigation station and bought the engines online. Her nephew was monitoring the commands she was inputting to the computer.

"You're only taking us up two kilometers?" he asked in

disbelief.

"Watch and learn," Jahan snapped back.

They got into the air just as Ernie's words proved to be prophetic. Two ships collided before they reached the mesosphere, and the resulting explosion had fiery debris raining down across part of the city and the port, destroying more ships who were still trying to lift, thus doing some of the work for the attackers.

There was no dodging in the chunky, unlovely little ship. Jahan just had to hope nothing big enough to hurt them hit them as she guided the ship toward the enormous lake around which the capital city of Olympus had grown. Several of the graceful skyscrapers were on fire, and one building began to collapse as alien fighters burst through the cloud cover and began firing on the city.

Jahan knew the wash from their engines was burning the buildings beneath them. The only good news was that the port was surrounded by warehouses and machine shops rather than houses, apartments, and businesses. She just had to hope that the stevedores had heeded the blaring alarms and gotten away or into basements knowing the spaceport would be a prime target.

The ship was wallowing, listing from side to side as she used the maneuvering jets to try and steer them. She sent up a prayer that the vessel would hold together. Spaceships were designed to keep air inside, so adding pressure *outside* wasn't a great choice, but it wasn't like they were going all that deep. They just had to hunker down until the bombardment ended and hope the invading enemy force didn't scan all that closely or wasn't bent on occupying the planet. *And please*

God let the engines restart, she added in a hurried afterthought.

"On my command do a hard kill of the engines," she called down to engineering.

"What? Why?"

"Just do it!"

"When?"

"Now!"

She dropped them into the lake.

✦ ✦ ✦

"Quiero pastel amarillo," Prince Cyprian Marcus Sinclair Amadeo de Arango lisped as he made his preference known to his father. "With chocolate icing," he added.

Beauregard Honorius Sinclair Cullen, Vizcondé Dorado Arco, Knight of the Shells, Shareholder General of the Grand Cartel, the 20th Duque de Argento y Pepco, Consort to the Empress, and father of the heir to the Solar League, Prince Cyprian Marcus Sinclair Amadeo de Arango, hugged his son closer. The child's pale brown hair tickled his chin. "I don't think there is a yellow cake, *cariño.*"

The little boy's face screwed up for a massive howl, and Boho reminded himself that his son wouldn't always be three. In fact, his fourth birthday was fast approaching. But in the meantime, he had to learn to behave. Boho pushed Cyprian off his lap and held him at arm's length. "Is that how a prince behaves? Hmmm?"

A small sob like a hiccup escaped, then Cyprian said, "No," so quietly that Boho barely heard it.

"All right, then. We'll go over to the buffet and see what kinds of cake are available."

They were in the palace gardens where fountains dotted the sweeping lawn. In addition to those elegant waterworks there were two bouncy castles, a large swing set, slide, and jungle gym, an aboveground pool and water slide, a carousel, and, for those who preferred the real thing, ponies from the royal stable saddled and waiting with their alien grooms to offer rides. Some of the older children had started an impromptu *fútbol* game.

Hayden McKenzie stood on the sidelines watching the play. At thirteen he was coltish, but he had clearly inherited his mother's beauty. More than a few of the older girls were eying him, but he was oblivious to their scrutiny. He also had an expression that was too somber for a boy. Understandable considering that he had survived the alien attack on the star base commanded by his mother. He had witnessed the death of his father and sister, his mother's injury, and her subsequent refusal to see him. The royal family had taken him in, and Cyprian had immediately attached himself barnacle-like to the older boy. Boho thought about calling him over, then decided Hayden might like a break from his royal shadow. Cyprian adored Hayden and followed him about like a puppy.

A large pavilion held an outdoor kitchen where hamburgers and hotdogs were grilling, French fries were boiling in grease, and human servants stood ready to fill plates with coleslaw, potato salad, fruit salad. The alien servants were relegated to emptying trash cans and bussing tables. A table held a giant sheet cake and a smaller cake with eight candles.

There was a table off to the side with culinary choices more to the taste of the parents, predominately mothers, who were chasing, scolding, and comforting their children who flitted across the greensward like brightly colored butterflies.

Boho felt like the troll at the fairies' ball. The only other man apart from servants who was present was Yves Riccardo Petek, Duque de Telqual. The hot August weather had him sweating, and his prodigious belly was bouncing as he tried to keep up with his six-year-old twins. Like every other FFH child under the age of twelve and still present in Hissilek, they had been invited to the palace to celebrate the birthday of one of Cyprian's royal cousins.

The little girl, daughter of Mercedes's half-sister Dulcinea, was turning eight today, and in addition to the children of noble families several more royal cousins littered the palace grounds. After the attack on an O-Trell spaceport and the near destruction of the Blue fleet, Mercedes had gathered her sisters and their children close. At least those who weren't in prison for having taken part in a coup attempt three years earlier or those currently serving aboard military vessels. Which left Boho with five sisters-in-law and their spawn who were too young to be either at The High Ground or already aboard a warship.

Personally, he thought Mercedes was crazy for bringing them all together. He had argued stringently that they try to find a hitherto unknown planet and retreat there to safeguard the succession. Granted, it wasn't easy to find a Goldilocks world, but they could put a number of ships onto the task and find a safe haven. Mercedes had vetoed it in a most unpleasant fashion, saying they needed ships to fight, not find a royal bolthole. Boho had thought about commandeering civilian vessels for the task, but decided he would wait until after Mercedes had left. For leave she would. It was required that the ruler of the Solar League be a military leader, and that wasn't going to change now that the League had its first Empress. Which would leave the Consort and the heir behind on what had to be a prime target for the enemy.

Boho tried to comfort himself with the thought that Ouranos was well guarded with O-Trell ships and missile batteries and there was a deep, heavily shielded bunker beneath the palace, with more being built elsewhere on the planet. But it was a toss-up which would be worse: being aboard a warship likely to see combat with this new and deadly enemy, or waiting for hell to rain down on the planet he was presently occupying. He tightened his grip on his son's shoulder enough that Cyprian gave a small mew of protest.

His present situation as primary caregiver to his child was galling, given that Mercedes was off holding high-level military meetings. Boho didn't particularly want to fight, but he did want to be included in the planning for those upcoming battles.

Before they reached the outdoor kitchen, Cyprian was distracted by the carousel, and he ran off to ride one of the painted ponies. Boho lifted him onto the horse of his choice—a black one with a tossing mane. Yves was seated on a bench alternating between fanning himself with a handkerchief and wiping sweat off his round face. His twin boys were just ahead and leaning off their horses to punch each other. Boho joined the other father.

"I just got the first set of them out of the house and now I'm starting all over again," Yves said mournfully, watching his sons.

"You didn't have to breed again after your divorce," Boho said.

"Alan wanted a family," Yves said. "And I had thought it might lessen the tongue wagging if I did my duty."

"I gather it didn't work." Boho had to raise his voice over the jaunty calliope music.

"Hardly. The kids I had with Michelle weren't happy that I married Alan after I divorced their mother, but it was the boys' birth that left them apoplectic."

"So, who is the mother?"

"We found a surrogate who looked a lot like Alan. My sperm, of course. After all, I'm the Duque." Yves gave a sigh that seemed deep enough to dislodge his soul.

"You going to stay on Ouranos?"

A headshake. "Alan is scared. We're thinking Earth. It's a backwater with nothing to recommend it. Maybe it will stay off the alien's radar."

"Just the home world of humanity. If they wanted to make a statement about humans, they could burn it to a cinder."

"Thanks, Boho, I really didn't need to hear that," Yves muttered as the music and the carousel slowed, the ride ending.

"Just making sure you consider all the options," Boho replied, and gave the other man a clap on the shoulder.

They went to recover their respective offspring, and Boho reflected on a culture that was built around children and the idea that the humans had to outbreed the aliens under their rule. A daunting task since there were more alien species than there were humans. All of which made it tough for humans to outbreed them in a demographic arms race.

The pressure to breed meant birth control and abortion were illegal, childless, or single-child families were fined, while subsidies were paid for every subsequent child after the first born to a family. Even the priests and nuns bred. It meant that a gay man like Yves was under tremendous pressure to stay in a heterosexual marriage. The pressure was even more intense since Yves was not only a member of the FFH, but of high nobility.

As Boho lifted his sole child off the carousel horse, he wondered if he and Mercedes were being fined for failing to add to their family. Considering it had taken them twenty-four years to get one kid, they weren't likely to get another. And would the office of Taxation and Revenue really be willing to fine the crown? He chuckled at the thought, and Cyprian gave him a questioning look.

"Daddy have fun?"

"Yes, Daddy had fun."

"Cake now?" Cyprian asked hopefully.

"I think we can do that."

✦ ✦ ✦

HER PRAYERS HAD been answered. The ship hadn't been crushed, Ernie had managed to get the engines back online, and they rose from the lake like a broaching whale trailing water plants, mud, and a couple of confused fish.

Olympus was burning, as were many other cities on Kronos, and the royal governor had sent out a desperate call for doctors and medical supplies. The ones on the planet who hadn't died were struggling with a deluge of patients.

Jahan had informed the frightened young clerk who had taken over the port authority that she was taking her ship to New Hope where hospitals and medical care were the primary industry, and they would return with doctors. He had shakily approved their launch.

Now they were docked at the orbital station above New Hope, and shuttles were on continuous turnaround from the surface below, delivering people and supplies to the ships and, once empty, returning for another run. A big troop transport ship had also arrived to augment the bevy of trading vessels who had volunteered to bring help to Kronos.

Jahan waited for the *Selkie* shuttle to dock. It was carrying their friends Doctor Michael Engelberg and his wife Kathy. Because of the League's resistance to women in positions of authority, Kathy was officially designated a nurse. In truth, she was a brilliant researcher. With them were three other young doctors for whom Engelberg had vouched, saying they wouldn't cavil at traveling on a ship run almost exclusively by aliens.

Jahan's fur still felt like it was standing on end in terror even though they had escaped from the death and destruction on Kronos three days before. Just before they had entered Fold, Jahan had sent a message to their friend, Doctor Michael Engelberg, telling him of the attack and asking for help. Jahan had not been alone in making the request. Mercedes Adalina Saturnina Inez de Arango had also put out the call for ships to bring medical personnel and supplies to the ravaged planet and its suffering citizens. As expected, he had mobilized the hospitals and now help was on the way.

As if her thoughts had summoned him, the doctor stepped through the door of the shuttle. The heavy duffel he carried gave him an odd swaying gait like a sailor just returned from a long stint at sea. His significantly younger wife was right behind him with an even larger duffle. The three young male doctors carried even larger duffels. It was an increase in scale that seemed be based on age and gender and the seemingly universal male need (even across species) to measure dicks.

Jahan hurried forward and, after a brief tug-of-war, took the duffle away from Engelberg. He frowned down at her from his six-foot two height. Since she wasn't quite five feet tall, the duffle rested on the ground even with the strap over her shoulder.

"You going to drag my delicate medical equipment?" Engelberg growled. "And where's Oliver? Tell him to get his lazy ass out here and help."

"Right. Oliver. That's a long story. So, we'll save it for later. As for your delicate equipment …" She swung the bag up until it rested across her shoulders like a power lifter partway through a clean and jerk exercise. Her smile bared her canines and Engelberg just shook his head. "Shall we?" She jerked her head toward the gangplank leading into the *Selkie*'s cargo bay.

"What about the big stuff?" Kathy asked.

"Jax had the stevedores alerted; they'll have it loaded in

the next thirty minutes." She glanced over at the three young doctors. "I'm Jahan Sirani, Captain of the *Selkie*." That made their eyes widen and she took a perverse pleasure in their reaction.

Inside the cargo bay, the rest of her crew was waiting to assist in settling their passengers. Jax held a TapPad in two of his fronds while a third held the stylus so he could check off items as they were delivered. Kielli was grinning, his fangs bright against the darker red fur around his face. The golden fur that covered his body was pretty much covered by his utility coveralls. Jahan gave a mental sigh; her nephew was still at the age where he found tumultuous times to be exciting. Dalea, their ship's doctor, was a Hajin. Taller even than Engelberg, she had a black and red mane that owed more to the bottle than nature given her age. The final member of the crew was a human, a grizzled old veteran who was too old and infirm to be called up back to active duty. Ernie Gantz was short and bandy-legged with a prodigious paunch. He was also a wizard when it came to mechanical equipment, and he had the *Selkie*'s engines purring. He moved forward immediately to take Kathy's duffle.

"Ma'am, welcome to the *Selkie*. We've got you and your hubby in the captain's cabin." His eyes raked the three young doctors who were staring at him with the air of shipwreck victims spotting a rescue vessel. "You *vatos* have our cabins."

"We don't want to put you out of your rooms," Kathy objected.

"It's fine. I sometimes sleep in the engine room anyway and the pony here"—he jerked a thumb at Dalea—"will bunk in the infirmary when one of us is bunged up so she don't care. That just leaves the squirrels, and they can hang a hammock and fuckin' sleep *anywhere*."

Jahan noted Kathy's flinch as Ernie casually threw around the speciesism slurs. She patted the human woman on the arm. "It's okay. We know Ernie is a bigoted asshole, but he's *our* bigoted asshole."

Forty minutes later the supplies were loaded, they were cleared to disengage from the station, and were boosting toward a safe Fold point. Engelberg set the young docs—Gregory, Ethan, and Cyrus—to organizing the crates. They had just thrown together supplies and Engelberg wanted quick access to whatever might be needed. Dalea joined in to help.

"Okay, they're out of the way," the human doctor said. "Now get me a coffee and tell us what the hell happened to Oliver."

They took the lift to the central level on the ship, which housed the med bay, galley, and cabins. Engelberg and Kathy sat at the table while Jahan prepared tea for herself and Kathy and strong coffee for her husband. Jax came rustling in and settled into his soaking pool.

"Oliver Randall was a made-up person," Jahan said as she handed out the beverages. "His real name was Thracius Ransom Belmanor, and he was a disgraced O-Trell officer."

"What had he done?" Kathy asked.

"Nothing. In fact, he was the living embodiment of the old adage that *no good deed goes unpunished*," the Tiponi Flute said.

"So, what was the good deed?" Engelberg asked.

"It's a long story. Bottom line, he protected a bunch of

half-alien, half-human kids—yeah, yeah, we know that's illegal, but it happened—and Oliver … uh, Tracy, he opened fire on the human troops sent to kill them." Jahan realized her claws had extended when she tried to spin her mug. She retracted them quickly, not wanting to alarm the human guests.

"The crown wanted to cover it up, so they buried him under bogus charges and cashiered him," Jax continued.

"Okay, but that doesn't explain where he is *now*," Engelberg growled.

"Hello? Big ugly aliens attacking… well, I guess they're ugly; we haven't seen any of them yet. Anyway, they're attacking us. Trained military officer, graduate of The High Ground. Of course, they pardoned Tracy and recalled him to duty," Jahan said.

"He's now joining his ship in orbit around—"

✦ ✦ ✦

"CAPTAIN THRACIUS BELMANOR requesting permission to come aboard."

The title still felt strange in his mouth. The *fusilero* guarding the access tube snapped off a salute which Tracy returned. The collar on his dress uniform seemed suddenly too tight and he quashed the impulse to run a finger around it. This was the first time Tracy had said *Captain* himself while wearing an O-Trell uniform. Others had used the title as he had made his way to Hellfire where he was to take command of his ship. Each time he'd had to curb his desire to look around and see who they were talking about. Now he had spoken the rank out loud and the sense of being an imposter had not lessened by one iota.

The only thing that didn't feel surreal was the *lanza de fuego fragata* he was about to board. As the big transport ship had glided past the station in orbit above Hellfire, Tracy had been able to observe the elegant beauty that was his fire lance frigate. Her name was emblazoned across the side in shimmering blue—*Swiftsure*. There had been a clutch in his chest as he'd observed her. Heavily armed and blindingly fast, the fire lance was the most advanced warship in the imperial fleet. The one downside was that to achieve the speed she was relatively lightly armored. And as every League citizen now knew, particularly the inhabitants of an O-Trell star port and the citizens on Kronos, their enemy possessed fearsome weapons.

Tracy had been in Fold when the attack on Kronos had occurred. Paranoia had fleet headquarters on Hellfire ordering every arriving ship to drop out of Fold on the outskirts of the system, which meant it took several weeks to reach the planet. Tracy supposed there was some logic in that the enemy (he really wished the high command would come up with a damn name for the bastards, not that the rank-and-file troops didn't already have plenty of vulgar and scatological terms already) tended to drop into real space deep inside a planetary system. Having military vessels on the outskirts might be helpful for a flank attack, and avoided any chance of friendly fire, but it did make for a long damn time in transit.

His musings were interrupted when a young woman with nearly white, blonde hair and dark blue eyes stepped forward and saluted. Her uniform looked as new as Tracy's, but she seemed to wear it more comfortably. "Sir, Lieutenant Lady Christina Flintoff. It would be my honor to escort you to the Captain's Mess. Commander Marquis Valada-Viers has assembled the officers to meet you."

"Excellent. Lead the way, Lieutenant."

As they moved through the corridors personnel stepped to the side and saluted. Tracy began to wonder if just leaving his hand at the bill of his hat would be simpler and less wear on his elbow.

"You don't have a batBEM, sir?" Flintoff asked him.

"I didn't have time to employ one prior to reporting."

"There are a number on Hellfire whose officers have been killed or wounded and are unable to return to duty for the foreseeable future. We can arrange for you to interview some before we Fold."

"Excellent, please do so."

"Do you have a preference as to species?" the young woman asked.

That raised a jumble of conflicting emotions, unpleasant memories, and a secret fear that Tracy had expressed to no one. Unconsciously, his hand went to touch the *Distinguido Servicio Cruzar,* the League's highest military award, given for extreme gallantry and risk of life in combat with an armed enemy force. Tracy had won it during his first year at The High Ground and given it into the keeping of his then batBEM just before he had been arrested.

Donnel was a smart-mouthed alien who was a physical horror because he was a member of the Cara'ot, an alien race that delighted in trading in DNA and tailoring bodies to fit worlds and tasks. The batBEM had three legs, four arms, a round head that seemed to sit directly atop his squat body, and four eyes that gave him 360° vision. Donnel had been assigned to Tracy when he entered the academy but had vanished with all the rest of his species on the day Tracy had been cashiered and convicted. Presumably the medal had vanished with him.

But then Tracy had found just such a medal sitting on his bunk back on the *Selkie* the day he learned he would be returning to active duty. Coincidentally, the Sidone Spider who had been a member of the *Selkie* crew had, like the long departed Donnel, also vanished. Since that day Tracy had harbored a secret fear that maybe Graarack wasn't actually a Spider, but instead Donnel in a new body with a new sex. Which implied that perhaps the Cara'ot hadn't actually disappeared but had simply altered their forms and were living secretly within the League plotting God knew what.

Of course, he hadn't dared to voice this mad idea even to his crew, much less central command, for fear of looking like a raving lunatic. Tracy tried to comfort himself with the thought that sometimes even very rare medals could be found in pawnshops, and this medal could not *possibly* be his *actual* medal. His crew had known about the award. This was probably just Graarack's way of wishing Tracy Godspeed. To believe otherwise would give him nightmares. *So why then had she vanished?* Unfortunately, for the state of his sleep, he hadn't been able to shake the fear.

"Sir?" the lieutenant prodded.

"Sorry. I have no preference. Pick four or five who come well referenced."

"Very good, sir."

They entered a lift and Flintoff pressed the button for deck level three. "Flintoff. I had a classmate who I believe married a Flintoff. Sumiko—"

"Yes, sir. My foster mother." There was an imperceptible emphasis on the word *foster*.

"Ah, yes, quite. That would make sense," Tracy said, feeling awkward.

He should have realized the girl was a child from a Hidden World just from her coloring. For generations, citizens of the League had been intermarrying so that now true blondes, blue eyes, and pale skin were rarities. Tracy himself with his dishwater blond hair, grey eyes, and dark ivory skin was a bit of an oddity and a genetic throwback.

As the lift rose toward the officer quarter's level, Tracy mentally reviewed the personnel files he had been sent. Valada-Viers, Cassutt, Lal, Washington, and Afumba. All of them held titles ranging from caballero to condé to marquis. Tracy hoped the fact that the captain didn't wasn't going to become a problem. *You have the one that matters,* he reminded himself, *captain.*

He snorted faintly. The irony was that his false identity had been granted a title of nobility. Oliver Randall, late of the trading vessel *Selkie*, was a caballero, the title granted for his service to the crown. Once Tracy had resumed his *actual* identity, he had gone back to being a mere *intitulado. Who is the captain of the most advanced ship in the fleet.*

He returned to his mental review. Cassutt had impressive scores in mathematics, so it made sense he oversaw weapons and navigation. Afumba was the ship's physician and had been educated at the medical school on New Hope, a powerful recommendation. Lal seemed to have found a way to coax three percent more speed out of the *Swiftsure* when they weren't in Fold, which could make the difference in a firefight. Washington had seen combat during the attempted coup three years before. He had held the governor's mansion on Dullahan. All in all, an impressive bunch.

The elevator sighed to a stop, and there was a moment of awkward dancing where Tracy tried to let the girl precede him and she tried to have the captain go first. He quickly realized his mistake and stepped past her, allowing her to hold the door. This deference was definitely going to take some getting used to. Once that nonsense was resolved, she took the lead again, and led him to the door of the Captain's Mess. Two *fusileros* flanked the door. Salutes were exchanged, the door was opened, and Tracy entered. Flintoff did not follow. The door slid closed.

2

WARS COME & GO, POLITICS IS FOREVER

"PLEASE, CIPRI, DON'T ask me for this," Mercedes Adalina Saturnina Inez de Arango, Empress of the Solar League, pleaded.

"But I am. And I'm doing more than asking. I'm *insisting*."

Mercedes studied her friend's ravaged face. Captain Lady Cipriana Delecroix-McKenzie's wounds and burns were still too fresh for her to have an artificial eye implanted, so she wore a black patch. That side of her face was a mass of twisting burn scars and slick skin where the grafts were starting to take hold. The other profile displayed the breathless beauty that had been one of her hallmarks. Her hair had been burned away. It was growing back as short black fuzz. Mercedes had a feeling it was going to stay that short. Cipriana had always been a cynic with a smile. Now the smile was burned away along with half her face. There was a grimness that shadowed her, and that made Mercedes feel very anxious. Mercedes wasn't sure what her old friend might do to avenge the deaths of her husband, ten-year-old daughter, and the thirty thousand plus inhabitants of the

Estrella Avanzada Cipriana had commanded.

They were walking on the white gravel paths in the palace garden. The mica flakes in the gravel caught the sunlight so it seemed like walking on stars. The smell of lavender and gardenia filled the air, and the laughter and excited shrieks of children floated over the top of a high box hedge that separated the knot garden from the grass of the croquet court.

"Hayden needs you," Mercedes pleaded. "He hasn't seen you for five months while you were being treated. Now you're going to just leave again? And without seeing him? Cipri, that's just wrong."

"He doesn't need to have any more nightmares," Cipriana said with a vague gesture toward her ruined face. "Besides, he's right where I want him. At the side of the prince. After what happened on Kronos, I know you'll put Cyprian someplace safe. I want Hayden with him in that safe place."

"Cipri, I'm not sure *any* place is safe from these monsters."

"He'll still have a better chance if he's with your boy."

"And he'll want you with him."

"No, I must try to protect him. Assign me to a ship, Mer, I'm begging you."

"Please don't take this wrong, Cipri, but you were a bureaucrat."

"Well, *meeeow*."

"I'm sorry, but there is no good way to say it. You've been running a space station. You've never seen combat, and you haven't served on a ship since your initial tour of duty after graduation. You wouldn't be an asset. In fact, you're dead weight."

"Then let me get back up to speed. I'll go to The High Ground, do refresher courses. And ships need bureaucrats, too. I could be a supply officer. I have to do *something*." She turned away; hands clenched at her sides. Mercedes put a gentle hand on the other woman's shoulder. It was shaken off. Cipriana whirled to face Mercedes. "They killed my daughter. They killed my husband. They killed my people. I will make them *pay*."

Studying the ruined face, Mercedes saw a value to having Cipriana at The High Ground. It was likely that a number of the sons and daughters of the FFH hadn't fully grasped the severity of the situation. Cipriana was a shocking object lesson.

"All right. You head up, and work directly with Captain Baron Tarek El-Ghazzawy. He'll tell me when or if you're going to be ready. After that, we'll find you a ship. But I'll only do it if you agree to see Hayden. Deal?" She held out her hand.

Cipriana took a step back. Her expression was murderous. "No! I will not be blackmailed. I'm walking out. Either to go to The High Ground or to look for a trading ship that's mounting guns or a corsair who slipped past you, or I'll enlist under a false name, but I'll be *damned* if you'll force me with blackmail, emotional or otherwise."

"You're his mother!"

"I was. Now I am Erinys. I have no room for any softer feelings."

It took Mercedes a moment to place the reference. *Erinyes, the furies out of Greek mythology. Female deities of vengeance.* There was no response to that. And looking at the wild expression in the remaining eye, Mercedes decided that perhaps Cipriana was right. She had no comfort to offer to her child.

She sighed and nodded. "All right. Take the next shuttle up. They're practically leaving on the hour."

Cipriana nodded and headed for the door into the palace. She stopped just before the threshold and looked back. "Take care of him."

"I'll love him as if he's my own."

"But you won't be here, will you?" Cipriana said. "So, it's better that he face the reality now rather than later. We're born alone and we all die alone. All the rest is just enduring."

"Cipri!" Mercedes began, aghast, but she was talking to her friend's back.

Shaken by the exchange, Mercedes settled onto a bench where her youngest sister found her some quarter of an hour later. Carisa was back in uniform sporting a commander's bars. She settled on the bench next to Mercedes, and they both watched Earth bumblebees' flit from blossom to blossom. The lazy droning buzz and the splash of the water in the fountains had replaced the children's laughter. It seemed they had all been spirited away by their nannies.

Carisa finally spoke. "I gather it didn't go well."

"No. She's not a person anymore. Just an avenging force." Mercedes sighed and ran a hand through her hair. "I'm still not sure I should let you deploy. If I'm killed, Cyprian will need a regent."

"He has a father, Mer, and the parliament would rather have a man in that role than a woman. You know that. It's better if you let me serve. It will help mollify the parents of daughters. Everyone expects you to fight. If I go, too, it helps drive home the point when you do start conscripting women."

"I hope it won't come to that."

"Hope all you want, but it's going to happen."

Mercedes shifted until she could study her sister's profile. Carisa was the most beautiful of them all, but right now that flawless jaw was knotted with tension and there was a line etched next to her mouth. Mercedes suspected it had a twin on the other side. "That's very pessimistic."

"They destroyed a space station, nearly destroyed the Blue; I saw the video from Kronos. We haven't faced anything like this since the Expansion Wars, and the Cara'ot didn't attack civilian targets. They were aliens, but they had some sense of honor."

"So where do you think I should assign you?"

"To the Gold."

"Beatrice is already there commanding an *explorador*."

"Yes, but you're taking command of the Blue and one empress trumps two princesses. Add us together and we might add up to your throw weight."

"You make me sound like a bunker buster bomb," Mercedes said with mock indignation.

"Think of it more as a way to spread around that sweet, sweet Arango charm," Carisa added with a smile.

"I don't want you charming. I want you alien ball busting."

"Aye, aye, First Lord, Fleet Admiral, Empress, and overall grand poobah." Carisa gave her a salute.

They shared a laugh and a hug, then Mercedes sobered. "Do you think you're ready to have a ship?" she asked.

Carisa looked down, scuffed at the gravel with the toe of her boot. "Not yet. Let me get my feet wet as an XO first. Then if I don't cock up you can promote me."

"All right." Mercedes gazed into her sister's brown eyes and suddenly gripped her in a tight embrace. "Oh, God, Cari, be careful. I couldn't bear it if anything were to happen to you."

Carisa gripped Mercedes even tighter. "Same to you and *double*!"

✦ ✦ ✦

HE HAD SEEN far more opulent dining rooms. Tracy's first posting had been aboard the *Triunfo* and the Captain's Mess echoed that captain's elegant tastes. It was also a peacetime navy where such fripperies were acceptable. This room was wood-paneled, but lacked the usual mirrors, paintings, and crystal chandelier. Instead, an attractive but simple brass fixture hung over the table, and beneath the white tablecloth Tracy could see the lines where the table could be quickly broken down for storage during combat. The chairs were metal and quite utilitarian.

Unable to delay any longer, Tracy turned his attention to the men awaiting him. It disappointed him that even after twenty-five years since FFH ladies had been required to serve, all of his senior officers were still male. Perhaps on some of the larger ships women were better represented. They were at attention, hands at the brims of their hats. "At ease," Tracy said, and they relaxed. Tracy removed his hat and the others followed suit. He wondered if he hopped on one foot if they would mimic that as well.

The silence was like a yawning chasm. Tracy allowed it to continue while he studied the faces of the assembled men.

Valada-Viers had curling black hair, rich coffee skin, and tawny eyes. Attractive without being handsome, just comfortable in his own skin in that way that people born to wealth and power so often were.

Cassutt was smaller and reminded Tracy of a Whippet or Italian Greyhound. His left hand was beating out a quick tattoo against the crease on his trousers. He had green eyes and a coffee and cream complexion. His greying dark brown hair set an odd contrast to his youthful face.

Afumba was a powerfully built, ebony-skinned man. He sported an impressive black beard, black hair, and black eyes. Overall, he gave the impression of a bear in human form. Not at all what one pictured in a healer.

Lal was a stunningly handsome man with smooth cocoa-colored skin and deep brown eyes. His hair was that iridescent black that sometimes seemed shot through with blue and purple streaks. It was perhaps a bit longer than regulation allowed.

Washington, the commander of the small contingent of *fusileros*, was heavily muscled, with a nose that had been broken more than once and a shaved head.

Tracy searched all their faces for the dueling scar. Only Valada-Viers sported one on his right cheek. He wondered at the lack of a scar on Lal, then saw the man smooth his hair and thought he understood. Lal had not been willing to mar what he clearly viewed as perfection. Tracy realized that Valada-Viers's eyes had narrowed, and he was studying the scar that pulled up Tracy's left eyebrow, giving him a sardonic air. Tracy resisted the impulse to touch it. *Something in common, or another point of competition?* Tracy wondered. He was a bit surprised that no chaplain was present. They were usually at the captain's table. Perhaps ministering to his flock? There were fifteen hundred men aboard the frigate. It was likely that at least one of them had a relative on Kronos. After this obligatory social event, he needed to view the pictures from Kronos. Know your enemy even if that meant having to watch that enemy kill your own people.

Tracy moved to the chair at the head of the table and gripped the back. The officers took their places and there was one empty spot, so clearly there was a missing person. No one sat down; they were all waiting on him. After a brief glance down at his white knuckles, realizing the metal edges were cutting into his fingers, Tracy released his too-tight grip and cleared his throat.

"I'd like to clear the air right up front. Most—probably all—of you went looking for my military records when you found I was being given command. And you didn't find much. You discovered that I'd managed to reach Captain Lieutenant, then an expunged record, then … nothing. So, you're all thinking who the fuck is this guy and why is he being given our ship?" He gave them all a long look then softened it with a small smile. "Believe me, I'd feel the same way."

There was some nervous foot shuffling, but no one risked

a chuckle. "There was … let's call it some confusion … between O-Trell and myself that led to me being cashiered." That got a reaction. Quick indrawn breaths, and someone murmured *fuck*. Tracy ignored it. "I struck out on my own. For the past fifteen years I've been the owner and operator of a small trading vessel. Needless to say, I haven't seen a lot of space combat. Didn't see any when I was serving. Those were peaceful times. So, I'm going to need your help. Show me the newest bells and whistles. Send me articles on combat techniques. I won't be offended. We all have a job to do. Protecting our people. Egos and hurt feelings can have no place in this effort. So, are we all going to be okay?"

Long glances were exchanged. Afumba was smiling and Valada-Viers was giving him a look that was almost approving. A chorus of *Yes, sirs* was raised.

"Then let's have some dinner." He pulled out his chair. He gave a nod to the steward waiting with a bottle of wine held in white-gloved hands. Glasses were filled and they stood for the toast.

"The Empress," Tracy said.

"The Empress," they all echoed.

✦ ✦ ✦

"OH, THAT FEELS good." Mercedes punctuated the sentence with a groan of pleasure as Boho massaged her foot.

She was collapsed on the sofa in their shared bedroom. To either side of this room were their private bedchambers maintained for the rituals of royalty—places where they could show favor to various noble personages by making them ladies-in-waiting or gentlemen-of-the-bedchamber. This was their shared place, their private refuge from the constant stress of being Empress and Consort.

"Wish you had gotten back to the private quarters sooner. Cyprian tried to stay awake, but ..." Boho shrugged and picked up her other foot.

"I know. I'm sorry. We got in the casualty reports from Kronos." She closed her eyes, both wanting to see that stark line of numbers as actual human beings and also wanting to keep them as mere statistics.

"I saw the images." He hesitated, then added, "I found myself picturing Cyprian covered in plaster dust, blood staining his face, that uncomprehending glazed look in his eyes."

"We're not discussing this again. You can't leave. I need you to stay here."

"Why?"

"Because the people look up to you. You rallied them during the coup attempt. In some ways you're more real and approachable to the citizens than I am. And I have to prove to the doubters that I can lead. Especially after ..." Her voice trailed away. She shook it off and continued. "So, I go to war, and you keep the home fires burning and the supplies flowing, and protect our child. There's no one else I can depend on."

He was silent for a few moments, and she hoped she had mollified him, and apparently, she had as he changed the subject. "What's your itinerary?"

"First to Hellfire to talk to the joint chiefs in person. Then Cuandru to check on the shipyard. Then to Yggdrasil where the remnants of the Blue are gathering."

"Say hello to your mother and stepfather for me."

"I'm not sure a war leader should be seen visiting their mommy," she murmured.

"I think any war leader would," Boho countered. He then asked, "So, how did it go with Cipriana?"

"Terrible. She won't see Hayden and she's already left for The High Ground."

"For Christ's sake, he's her son. The kid is hurting! And why the hell is she going back up to the academy?" Boho said.

"I told her I couldn't put her on a front-line ship since she had been a desk jockey for so long. I thought that might convince her to stay here, continue to recover, and take care of her one surviving child, but she refused; said she'd do a refresher at The High Ground. What could I say? No? And we do need every able-bodied soldier."

"On that subject … I know you picked Gelb to replace me as the commander of the Gold, but I'm not sure he's the best choice."

"Who would you have in mind? And how do I yank it away from Gelb without insulting him and making an enemy?" Mercedes shifted around until she could put her head in his lap. He stroked her hair.

"Give Gelb the command of your flagship. Make him feel like you value his counsel and he'll take this as a mark of honor."

"That could work. But who replaces him?"

"Jasper Talion. He's mean as a snake and I think that's what we need right now."

"I thought he specialized in leading *fusileros*?"

"He did, but he is one tough *hombre*, and since his father is still alive and in charge of Nephilim, he can easily leave the planet."

"How long has he been out?"

"A while, but a man like that doesn't forget, and I know he's been called up."

"Like everybody else," Mercedes murmured.

"Except me."

Mercedes sat up and faced her husband. "My darling, believe me, I would love to have you at my side. Either literally or in the ship next to mine. But somebody must stay here, and I've *got* to be the one on the front lines."

"This isn't just tradition and expectation that's driving you. This is because of Kusatsu-Shirane."

She tore herself out of his embrace and stood, breaths coming in short bursts. "Of course it is! The populace may have forgotten, but you can be damn sure the military hasn't. I've *got* to have a victory."

She covered her face briefly with her hands. "It made me feel dirty to even be thinking about the throne when my people were dying."

"Wars come and go," Boho said. "Politics are forever."

3

BREAD, BUTTER, & BULLETS

"COME."

Tracy was grateful for the soft door chime. It meant he could turn his attention away from the horrific images he was watching from Kronos. Unfortunately, they gave little hint of how to counter the enemy's tactics. The melancholy truth was that in an era with space flight people at the bottom of a gravity well were sitting ducks. He forced himself to stop picturing his father at the receiving end of just such an attack and tried to arrange his features into what he hoped would appear grave and dependable. A leader's face, in short.

The door irised open and a man walked in. Tracy's proper demeanor vanished as he leaped to his feet crying, "Father Ken!" It had been nearly sixteen years since he had last seen the priest, and he voiced his thought.

"Okay, you must have a goddamn painting hiding somewhere. You haven't changed a bit." Tracy embraced the much smaller man. Even though Father Kenneth Robin Herbrand Francis Russell, formerly the Duke of Bedford before putting it all aside to enter holy orders, was now in his forties, his face was barely lined, the black hair untouched by grey. The pansy brown eyes were still warm and humorous. "But how? You weren't on my crew list."

"I saw the posting of your assignment. I had thought you dead after you left Hissilek and vanished. I was relieved to discover that was not the case, so I asked to be assigned to the *Swiftsure*. It only happened a few days ago so the list probably hadn't been updated."

"So, you're my chaplain?"

"I am."

"But you weren't at dinner."

The smile faded. "One of your *hombres* learned that he lost his entire family—wife and eight children were killed on Kronos. I was with him."

Tracy's hands closed into fists. "Bastards!" He gestured to a chair in front of his desk. "Please. Would you like a brandy?"

"I wouldn't say no." Ken dropped into the chair with a sigh and the years seemed to appear, etched on his face.

Tracy filled a couple of tumblers. He made a note to get proper snifters before they departed from Hellfire. The niceties had to be observed. More so because he was an *intitulado* and people would be looking for any sign of his low birth. He handed Father Ken the glass, moved to his own chair, and dropped into it with a gusting sigh. They each took a long sip before either spoke again.

The priest gestured at the utilitarian office. "Love what you've done with the place," he said, irony icing every word but a quick smile removing any sting.

Tracy studied his Spartan surroundings. There were none of the memorabilia that would normally accompany an O-

Trell officer. No commendations, family photos or holograms, no art collection. The only personal things that were presently in the room were his dueling saber that was leaning in a corner and a clear Lucite cube on his desk that held a small spider-silk weaving created by Sidone artists. It had been with him since he was eighteen. He was now sophisticated, or cynical, enough to now know the reason he had been able to afford it was because he had been standing with the heir to the Solar League, and the shopkeeper had been currying favor. In his youth it had bothered him. Now it was a treasured memory along with a treasure trove of other memories of times spent with Mercedes … He reeled in his unruly thoughts. That was a mental path down which he dared not go.

"That was an interesting reverie," the priest said softly.

"What?"

"You wear your emotions on your face, Tracy."

"So, they tell me. It's why I never play poker." He went to refill his glass. Tracy gestured with the bottle at the priest, who held up a restraining hand.

"Thank you, no. I fear I will have more grief counseling sessions before we deploy." Ken gazed down into the amber liquid as if scrying. He finally looked up. "How bad is it?"

"Bad."

"Are we going to win?"

The liquor burned its way into Tracy's gut. The glass hit the surface of his desk with more force than he had intended. "The Cara'ot were the toughest opponents we faced during the Expansion Wars. They never delivered the kinds of defeats we've experienced with this lot. So, no, I don't know if we're going to win. I just know we have to try."

"Ironic. Finally, all those ancient Earth movies where evil aliens invade the Earth and try to kill every human have come to pass." Ken gave him a humorless smile.

Memory surfaced of an iconic photo from the wars. It had been in one of his military history textbooks and it showed a line of Cara'ot ground troops kneeling on the ground. Even kneeling, they were taller than the human soldier who stood before them brandishing a rifle. With their serrated mandibles and the four arms that ended in multiple pincers, they were terrifying figures, yet they cowered before a single human. Not for the first time, Tracy reflected that for the Cara'ot, Isanjo, Tiponi Flutes, Sidone, and Hajin, his kind had been the evil invading aliens.

"Well, so far, they seem pretty indiscriminate about killing our alien subjects, too. Which is probably a good thing. Otherwise, we might end up with a fifth column behind our lines," Tracy said.

"Well, that's a terrifying thought. How do we avoid that?" Ken asked.

"Make sure the civilized species know we value them and try to protect their home worlds as diligently as we protect predominately human worlds." He tossed off the rest of his drink, coughed, and added, "Problem is I doubt the high command views things the same way I do."

"Then I wish you were on the high command."

"Believe me, that's more of a curse than a compliment," Tracy said dryly.

The priest slapped his hands on his thighs and stood up. "Well, I'd best return to it." Ken had almost reached the door when he looked back. "So, Tracy, when was your last confession?"

"Oh, Father, you really don't want to know."

"That's what I thought. I'll expect you on Saturday."

✦ ✦ ✦

"I MAKE SCOOPRINGS and media equipment. What possible use could I be to the military?" Lin Wa Jacobson returned to Boho carrying a pair of crystal highball glasses. The scotch reflected amber through the glass.

"Military vessels and battle armor use highly sophisticated electronic equipment. We'll send you experts. Retool your factories to manufacture that equipment," Boho said.

"And do I and my employees get paid?"

Boho looked through the large window that offered a view of the clean room on the factory floor. It was mostly complex robots that were assembling the devices overseen by humans in clean suits.

"Yes, I'm sure those robots are worried about their next lubrication," Boho said, but threw in a flash of a smile to lessen the sting. "But I do understand. You have people relying on you. So do the Empress and I have people relying on us … In short, *all of them*." Jacobson's eyes dropped, unable to hold Boho's gaze. "And you will be paid."

"Forgive me, but with what? The cost of rebuilding on Kronos is going to rise into the billions, and when they hit the next planet?" His voice trailed away.

"There is money in the treasury, and more will be coming in as we begin selling war bonds. And because you are a patriotic citizen of the League, I'm confident you will be buying a large number of them."

"So, I'm paying for all of this out of my own pocket."

"How is that any different than what you do now?"

"There's some profit in there for me and mine."

"After the war is over, you'll be repaid with interest." Boho drained his glass and stood. "And if we don't win, you'll have bigger problems than worrying about a return on your money. Now, those experts will be arriving in two days. I'm certain you'll make them welcome."

His security detail was waiting just outside of the office. Boho found himself momentarily light-headed, and he realized that he hadn't eaten since early that morning and had been offered alcohol at every meeting he'd attended. Once that reality set in, his stomach decided to comment and sent acid backing up his throat. He choked, coughed, and pressed a handkerchief to his lips. The nausea passed but left his throat raw.

"You all right, sir?" the leader of his detail asked.

"Yes, just tired, and I need something to eat."

"Tell me what you would like and we'll have it waiting at the shuttle."

"A club sandwich and a glass of milk. No, a milk shake. Vanilla."

"Very good, sir." The *Servicio Protector Imperial* officer murmured into his throat mic as they left the building.

They were in summer on the third and largest continent on Geneva. The planet wasn't heavily populated and had chosen to go with low-impact manufacturing in order to keep the air and water of the world pristine for tourists. It was a pretty world, though the native trees were odd; they were like overly tall mushrooms with multiple caps on the top of their branches. As with most planets, the Earth plants were doing a good job of supplanting the local vegetation.

Rather like the humans have done on the aliens' home worlds.

"What's next?" Boho asked his chief of staff, Anselmo Moran, who had waited in the flitter. The younger man had begun as Boho's communications officer, but over the years had taken on more and more duties until he was now indispensable.

Anselmo checked his ScoopRing. "The CEO of an appliance manufacturer on the other continent. Dinner with him."

"Lovely. First no food, then two meals back-to-back. Brief me on this *pendejo*. And I need to talk with Rafe during the bounce."

As promised, the sandwich and shake were waiting at the shuttle. The CEO of the appliance company was also untitled and, based on Anselmo's briefing, likely to be less accommodating than Jacobson.

Boho sat chewing, trying to focus on the flavor of the bacon, ham, and turkey, the crunch of lettuce, the smooth sweetness of the shake, rather than gaming out his upcoming meeting, but it wasn't working. His mind played with scenarios, rehearsing various lines of dialogue based on possible reactions from Señor Alphonse Nikkolai-Waulda. He was also having a hard time banishing from memory the tears of his child as he had departed. Even the presence of Cyprian's beloved *Tia* Estella hadn't stemmed the waterworks. He realized rather bitterly that Mercedes's argument that she needed him to stay home hadn't been true. In order to cajole and strong-arm industries, he had to travel, and even in Fold it took time to travel between star systems, time away from his son. Space was big, as one of his old profs used to say.

The floor beneath his feet trembled as the engines spun up. He fastened his harness as the shuttle launched into low polar orbit on its way to the continent on the far side of the planet. He was just finishing his milkshake when the Foldstream call from Rafe Devris came through.

"So, how did it go?" the Chancellor of the Exchequer asked. For the first time since Boho had met the young man, Devris looked rumpled and there were shadows beneath his eyes.

"Got another reluctant captain of industry to at least pretend to be a patriot," Boho said. "When are those bonds going on sale?"

"Tomorrow. And, by the way, your recorded sales pitch is terrific. Tell Anselmo well done."

"Will do."

"Sir, have you heard from the Empress?"

"No. I expect Mercedes has her hands full."

"Well, you might want to reach out to her. Give her a heads-up."

"And what is this heads-up?" Boho asked.

Rafe's eyes dropped, looked up, then looked away again. "It hasn't gone unnoticed that we are deficit spending like mad. We've doubled the debt in just three months and it's going to get worse."

"Yes, not exactly a news flash," Boho drawled.

The blush was evident even on the holographic image. "The problem is that the *Financial Times* and the *Economist* have taken notice. They are publishing echoing articles about how destructive this level of government debt will be."

"Perhaps they would like to see how destructive an attack on the worlds that house their offices would be," Boho suggested with acid sweetness.

"I know it's infuriating, sir. And yes, they are being jackasses. The problem is that they've gotten some jackasses in Parliament to listen to their solutions."

"And what are their solutions?"

"Cuts, of course. To family child subsidies, ending basic payments, and cutting pensions. They are also proposing that Kronos handle its own rebuilding without disaster relief from the capital."

"Idiots," Boho snapped.

"Oh, it gets worse. They're also proposing a special tax to be paid by our alien citizens."

That brought Boho out of his couch and set him to pacing the length of the shuttle. "Oh, that's fucking genius. Let's create an active fifth column behind our lines that might decide they have more to gain by throwing in with the aliens rather than sticking with us." Boho regained control of his breathing and settled back into his couch. "Okay, clearly, I need to get back to the capital and knock heads together. Hold the fort for the next three days while I'm in Fold."

"You got it, sir." The holograph flickered and vanished.

Boho stared at the dregs of his sandwich and discovered he had lost his appetite.

✦ ✦ ✦

"WE ARE COMMANDEERING this ship." The young O-Trell officer was already looking past Jahan as she stood on the gangway of the *Selkie*. He was flanked by two *fusileros* with pulse rifles.

They had just finished off-loading the doctors and their equipment and had picked up another urgent delivery order. She was tired, sad, and didn't have even one fuck to spare for this mincing martinet, so she snapped, "'Fraid not, bucky."

That got his attention right quick, and his hand went to his sidearm. The rifles were slid off shoulders, and Jahan really wished she hadn't been quite so flippant. Especially when Kielli extended his claws. Fortunately, Jax came rustling forward, and he was holding a TapPad filled with a great deal of impressive legalese, things like section 35a, subsection 23d, and lots of parties of the first part and parties of the third part. Jahan laid a hand over Kielli's and shot him a warning glance. He retracted his claws.

"Ah, Commander," Jax said, bumping the young man an entire rank in an effort to ingratiate. "We understand the desperate need for ships, but our vessel is in fact the property of Captain Thracius Belmanor of Her Majesty's Star Command. We are merely crew and we run the ship on his behalf, and his specific instructions were to render all possible aid. Here are his instructions." Jax handed over a printed flimsy. "And here is the ownership record." Another printed sheet followed. "We've just brought physicians and medical supplies from New Hope and are about to lift and pick up a cargo of electronics on Reichart's World to be delivered to the shipyards at Cuandru." The human was frowning at the pages, eyes flicking between them. Jax gave that peculiar sound that passed for a cough from a Flute. "I do hope this can be handled expeditiously. It would be a shame if we missed our launch window, and those parts were delayed."

"I have to check this," the soldier growled. "Don't move this ship."

"Fine," Jahan said. "We're just going to keep—"

"No! You'll stay right here where my men can keep an eye on you. I don't trust you BEMs."

It took three hours, and they did lose their departure slot, but eventually the lieutenant returned, grudgingly returned the papers, and gave them permission to leave. Once the military had cleared the ship and they had buttoned up, Jahan rounded on Jax.

"Where the ...? How the ...?"

"You're welcome," the plantlike alien said. "I had a feeling a ship crewed predominately by aliens might be at some risk, so I had new ownership papers drawn up that show Tracy as the sole owner."

"So, our shares are gone?" Dalea asked.

"Great, you just cheated my aunt out of her—" Kielli exploded, only to be cut off by the Tiponi Flute.

"No, of course not. The *real* ownership papers are being held in trust in a bank on Geneva. These are forgeries."

"Obviously damn good ones," Ernie grunted.

"I went to the people who created Oliver's ... I mean, Tracy's false identity."

Ernie's eyes narrowed. "Still doesn't explain how they

didn't catch that the ship has two ownership titles."

"I have a feeling a certain person in high places is keeping an eye out for us," Jax said primly.

"I expect that certain person has a lot more on her plate to worry about than us right now," Dalea countered.

"Yes, but she has aides, and I expect one of them is trained to look out for any whispers about the *Selkie*, or Tracy, or any of us."

"So, who is this friend in high places?" Kielli asked.

"Yeah, I'd like to know that, too," Ernie added.

"You wouldn't believe us if we told you," Jahan said.

4

PURCHASE ORDERS & INVOICES

THE TWO MEMBERS of her honor guard preceded her through the door and took up positions to either side. Mercedes swept into the conference room aboard the imperial flagship the *San Francisco de Asis* as the *fusileros* announced, "Her Imperial Majesty, First Star Lord Empress Mercedes Adalina Saturnina Inez de Arango." The waiting men leaped to their feet, saluted, and then bowed. She returned the salute and moved to her chair at the head of the large oval table. The two *fusileros* departed and the heavy door rolled closed behind them.

Even standing rigidly at attention, she noted the men's eyes flicking nervously around the now utilitarian space and getting the pointed message she was sending. Most of these top O-Trell officers were familiar with the room. They had seen it when her father sat upon the throne of the Solar League. Then, it had been a luxurious space filled with mirrors, chandeliers, paintings, and portraits of notable members of the Arango family, elegant furnishings, bric-a-brac. Underfoot, a plush carpet woven by Sidone Spiders, but in a traditional human pattern, had cushioned the feet of the officers and muted the clip of Hajin footfalls or the rap of boots when human servants had been utilized. Mercedes had ordered it *all* removed. The room was now a coldly efficient and functional space. Battle armor and a weapons' locker were against one wall. Computer screens and view screens had replaced tapestries and paintings on the other. The only furnishing was the large oval table that could seat twenty without undue crowding. There were TapPads now embedded in the surface that could control the flow of data.

Gelb, newly installed as her flag captain, stood behind the chair at her right. Boho had been correct. The man had not viewed losing command of the Gold as an affront but had been nearly speechless over the honor being granted to him. They had known each other for a long time. He had been a third year when she first arrived at The High Ground, and they had served together aboard the *Nuestra Señora de la Concepción*. The dueling scar on his receding chin had begun to blend with his wrinkles. She wondered if that bothered him. Perhaps not. With age came wisdom, and a terrifying enemy tended to focus the mind and put in perspective the nonsensical games of youth.

There was nothing to disguise the mass of scars on the cheek of the man on her left. Reputedly, the scars had been bestowed by Baron Jasper Talion's own father, the royal governor of Nephilim, who had held the post for almost fifty years. No other noble had wanted the harsh, remote world despite its wealth in the form of lithium.

Talion was now at an age where his hair, that had gone grey in childhood, now looked normal. Unlike some of the other men filing into the room, Talion's tall, powerful body was still fit, and his muscles were evident even beneath the material of his uniform. Mercedes noted that apart from herself there were no women among this gathering of the tip of the top brass.

She promised herself that she would review the rolls and see if she could find any senior woman officer who could be promoted to a command position. There had to be some qualified woman who was commanding a ship who could be included. Mercedes had a queasy moment where she wondered if this was diversity for its own sake and if it might endanger soldiers. *No*, she decided, *everyone has to buy into this fight, or we're doomed. I can't be a unicorn.*

Another random thought flashed past. The bows needed to stop. They were military officers engaged in a life-and-death struggle. Her royal status should be beside the point. *But will I be any good as a military leader? Maybe figurehead is all I can do?* She gave her head a shake, trying to dislodge the questioning voice, and watched as several of the men blanched. *Watch it. They're sure as hell watching you and trying to read meaning into everything.*

Mercedes took her chair. The men remained standing rigidly behind theirs. She nodded to indicate they should be seated. A few of the chairs squeaked as they were swung out, and a couple creaked as they took the weight of their occupants. Mercedes made a mental note to inform the engineer to have his techs inspect the chairs to make sure they were securely bolted and ready to withstand combat, for combat would surely come.

"So, let me tell you where we are at," Mercedes said. "*Exploradors* have been outfitted with spectrographic equipment and sensitive radio telescopes to search for traces of the rare elements used by our foes. The scouts have been ordered to retreat into Fold should they come in contact with the enemy. We need their readings more than we need …" Mercedes paused, looking for a tactful way to say it, only to have Talion give voice to her initial thought.

"Dead heroes?" Talion suggested.

"Exactly. They have been sent beyond the edges of League space. As one of my professors pointed out, space is big, so this may take some time."

"Do we have it? Time, I mean, Majesty?" It was Captain Baron Kyle Golden, who commanded the *acorazado Minerva*. The dreadnought was seventy years old and had been hurriedly upgraded and put back in service. Which made Golden's rather sharp tone understandable. Not that Mercedes's flagship was much better. It was forty years old. *We got complacent,* she thought.

"Probably not, but since we haven't figured out how to stop time or wind it backwards it will have to suffice. Moving on. Round the clock shifts are mandated at all shipyards. As new ships come online, the older ships will be pulled back to provide planetary security. All graduating high school seniors, unless they will be studying STEM subjects or medicine, are being denied college entrance and will be immediately conscripted."

"I trust *all* does not literally mean *all.*" It was Admiral Lord Mustafa Lewis. Another of the alumni from the *Nuestra Señora.*

Mercedes blinked several times as she tried to parse both the words and the tone. Her TapPad dinged. Gelb had just sent her a message. *He has twin daughters graduating The*

High Ground this spring. She gave a slight nod to indicate she had understood.

"Yes, all. Graduates from The High Ground will be immediately placed aboard ships, and *intitulado* children at eighteen will be drafted into the various services." Lewis nodded, though he looked neither mollified nor comforted.

A glance down at her pad brought Mercedes back to the agenda. "R&D is continuing to research the capabilities of the alien weapons and is looking to develop countermeasures. Unfortunately, we're not there yet, so we are retrofitting ships with extra chaff and decoy countermeasures. You will be notified of your ship's time in the rotation for this retrofit."

Flag Captain Abioye Mbadinuju, who was Talion's flag captain, spoke up. "Have our xenobiologists or linguists learned anything that might aid us? Talking is also a tool it might be useful to utilize."

"Unfortunately, we have very limited samples of their language and, of course, none of us have actually seen a living or dead xenomorph. It will be the task of our battle groups to rectify that," Mercedes said.

"Preferably dead," someone at the table murmured. It was unspoken, but agreement with the sentiment filled the room with the taint of violence.

"Ma'am." It was Gelb. "I was reviewing the search patterns and noticed that we haven't sent ships into Sector 470. The fact that we've lost a number of ships in that sector might be an indication that it holds the home world of our present foe."

Time seemed to dilate as Mercedes considered and rejected various responses. *Sector 470, the place where ships went to die. The place where the crown sent men who needed to die. Could Gelb be right, and the ship killers were there? But she'd already lost over half of one fleet. Nothing had ever returned from that sector. She couldn't risk what remained.*

Fortunately, Gelb realized he had stepped in it, and he rescued her. "Pardon me, ma'am, I've spoken about classified matters."

"Yes, Flag Captain, you are correct. We cannot discuss the matter in this location." She stood and they all leaped to their feet. "Your formal orders have been dispatched. Let's go get these sons of bitches." She concluded with the motto of the *Orden de la Estrella*. "May we touch the stars with glory." The bass rumble of the men echoed her.

✦ ✦ ✦

ONLY THREE HOURS remained until the *Swiftsure* was scheduled to disembark. And a third of the supplies had still to be loaded. The ordinance had come aboard first, which meant they were waiting on the things that kept body and soul together and men fighting.

Tracy had been acidly pointing this out to his supply officer, Procurement Chief Jake Chang, and he concluded by saying, "The crew can't eat guns, missiles, and ammo, Chief."

Chang chewed on his Tiponi stim stick and glared. "So maybe the captain should have told Lieutenant Commander Condé Washington and Lieutenant Commander Cabellero Cassutt that the captain preferred to have the victuals and soap and spare parts bumped to the front of the line. Sir."

Tracy realized he was busted. He hadn't been paying attention to the details. He sighed, ran a hand across his chin, and noted he needed to shave. One couldn't have the captain of a League military vessel, especially one who was an *intitulado*, looking unkempt. He sat down and motioned to another chair in his office.

"You're right. So, what do you need, Chief? More loaders, more people?"

"Both. But there's a big mother of a destroyer getting supplied and they've sucked up all the available stevedores."

Cocking a thumb in the general direction of the space station where they were docked, Tracy said, "There's a shitload of Isanjo and Hajin out there."

"They're not cleared to load military vessels, sir." Chang's tone had become decidedly more respectful, and he was no longer obviously forcing himself to add the honorific.

"Well, that's some bullshit." Tracy stood, grabbed his cap, and headed out the door. He looked back. Chang was frowning in confusion. "Well, come on." The Chief scrambled out of the chair. As Tracy left the office, his two-man security detail fell into step behind them.

They took the elevator down to the supply deck where the giant umbilical kept them tethered to the station. There, Chang's *hombres* were driving loaders stacked with pallets up the gangplank and into the ship.

The material of the tether flexed and swayed slightly beneath Tracy's boots. The detail stayed doggedly with them. They hit the more solid footing of the station itself and Tracy rounded on his security.

"*Ay Dios mio!* We're docked at an O-Trell station in orbit

around the planet that houses fleet headquarters. What the hell do you think is going to happen to me? Shoo! Go do something useful."

"Yeah, go help my boys," Chang added.

The *fusileros* exchanged puzzled glances, then smiled, nodded, saluted, and went over to where a sweating, harried *hombre* was directing the efforts.

"So, what? We going all press-gang on the BEMs?" Chang asked.

A bit startled by the historic allusion, Tracy shot a glance at the shorter man. "I thought I'd ask for volunteers first."

"Yeah, good luck with that. Everybody's got their own fish to fry," Chang mumbled around his now limp stim stick. "Hey, where are we going?"

"Janitorial."

"There are just BEM"—Chang coughed and corrected himself—"aliens there."

Tracy didn't respond, just continued dodging stressed and rushing soldiers. Occasionally one of the lower-ranked officers or an *hombre* would notice his captain's bars and offer a salute which Tracy would answer, but most were intent on their own pressing issues. The docking area smelled of lubricant, fuel, rifle propellant from the nearby gun range, and the pungent reek of male sweat. As they approached the dock maintenance office, the sweat took on different tones: some sweeter, some more acrid. Chang was giving him sideways glances. Tracy ignored the office where a fat human sat behind the desk staring at his TapPad. Instead, he headed to the locker room where Hajin and Isanjo workers were changing out of their coveralls having finished their shift.

"Halana nuri toddara," he said in Vestic, which was the most common of the Hajin languages, and added in Nilou, the dominant Isanjo language, *"Chuk rill keke."* Locker doors sighed shut and alien eyes swiveled to face them.

"Your accent's terrible, Captain," said a tall Hajin whose mane had been roached into a mohawk. He had added electric orange and neon blue stripes to the natural tan and white.

"But a human who knows our languages," said a silver coated Isanjo. "Don't be a dick." That was addressed to the tall Hajin.

"Don't give me more credit than I deserve," Tracy said. "What you just heard and my ability to ask for directions to the head and order a beer is pretty much the extent of my knowledge."

"Still, you tried," said another Hajin. "Counts for something."

"So, what do you need?" the mohawk Hajin demanded. "I know when I'm getting the old soft soap."

"I know you've just finished your shifts, but I need manpower to help load the last of our supplies. We're supposed to untether in three hours, and I've got bullets but no bread. I'll pay."

"How much?"

Another Hajin punched him on the arm. "Again, with the dick thing, Yaggi. They're going to be protecting us, too. Let's get them out there so they can."

"So far they've had a pretty shitty success rate," Yaggi muttered.

The dismissive remark sent dull red washing up Chang's

neck and into his broad face. “You goddamn pony. We’re out there dying and you’re probably hoping these bastards take us out.”

He lunged forward. Tracy clotheslined him and Chang went staggering back, coughing with his hand pressed to his throat. “I do not tolerate racist slurs from any member of my crew.” He turned back to the pugnacious young Hajin. “And I also don’t appreciate your lack of gratitude for our service. So, are you going to take my money and help, or see how well your jackassery will spend at your local watering hole?”

The aliens went into a huddle. Tracy waited, fingering the credit spike in his pocket. They broke and returned to him. “Okay, we’ll help.”

“Great. Chief Chang will assign you. We’ll settle up when you’re done.”

Nobody, alien or human, looked all that happy with him as he left. “Blessed are the fools in the middle for they shall be despised by all sides,” Tracy murmured.

A few hours later Commander Marquis Valada-Viers entered Tracy’s office. After saluting he said, “All the supplies have been loaded, sir. We’ll make our schedule launch.”

“Good. Wait, what about the added workers? I promised to pay them.”

“I discussed the matter with Chief Chang. I think it sets a bad precedent if captains are required to pay personally for what are clearly ship-related expenses. We took the money out of our restocking funds.”

“I see.” Tracy tossed aside his stylus and stood. “And you didn’t see fit to discuss this decision with me first?”

Valada-Viers looked nonplussed. “Sir, I was simply trying to—"

"Keep the *intitulado* from making what you perceived to be a faux pas?"

Valada-Viers snapped to stiff attention. "No, sir … well, perhaps a bit, sir, but I was more concerned about the reputation of O-Trell. The idea that the corps lacks funds could turn into speculation regarding the financial well-being of not just the service, but the government as well."

Tracy's indignation faded. Partly from Valada-Viers honesty and mostly because the nobleman was right when it came to the necessity to quash rumors. When Tracy nodded in slow agreement, his XO relaxed slightly from his ramrod brace.

"Very well. You were right, but in the future please discuss issues that bear directly on my decisions with me before you act on my behalf."

"Very good, sir."

"I don't want you to feel like I'm breathing down your neck, Tony, but I also don't want you going around me or trying to manage me. Are we clear?"

"Very, sir."

"Shall we go to the bridge?"

"Yes, sir."

5

CAN'T ANYONE BE TRUSTED?

THE SAN PEDRO *cosmódromo* had a number of bars for their kind. Before the war started, the station was the private market for spacecraft as well as a place where fast, cheap, but competent repairs could be made on civilian ships. Since Isanjo specialized in just that kind of work, there were more Isanjo bars than watering holes for Hajin, Tiponi, and Sidone, but since the arrival of a new alien threat, the alien citizens of the League had found themselves consolidating into a handful of locations and many of the establishments catering to aliens had been shuttered. Thus far the BEMs weren't hearing a lot of overtly racist remarks or receiving threats from their human overlords, but they got looks … lots and lots of nervous, suspicious, and outright hostile looks. In fact, Ernie had stopped joining them for afternoon libations, saying he was tired of being called a BEM Beau when he was seen in their company.

That had Jahan staring into her beer as if the foam could be used for divination. Could they trust the only human member of their crew, or should they replace him? And if they did might Ernie try a little payback? Report them to the *Seguridad Imperial*? Their innocence or lack thereof wouldn't matter once the imperial security forces started looking at them, and truth be told they weren't all that innocent.

They traded with Hidden Worlds, they traded in contraband birth control, their former captain was a disgraced O-Trell officer who had lived under an alias and had boinked the now empress, then heir to the throne, of the Solar League. The public story was that Mercedes had been rescued by Captain Randall and taken straight to the arms of her loving husband. The truth was she had lingered in Tracy's company for several weeks. A close examination of the ship might reveal that inconvenient fact. Jahan was pretty sure they had only avoided a closer look because of the news of the royal heir, and then the attempted coup that had led to the death of Mercedes's father. Thus far they had escaped notice. Better to keep it that way with a profile so low they might as well be underground.

Tracy's final order before reporting for duty had been that the *Selkie* stop making its shadow run to the Hidden Worlds and keep their noses clean. Jahan had followed that order, but after the horrendous events on Kronos she wasn't sure she could continue to obey that particular command. The people on the Hidden Worlds deserved to know about what was happening in the wider galaxy. Some worlds had purchased the Foldstream technology that allowed them to eavesdrop on the League's news feeds, but many had not, and those worlds needed to be on their guard should any strange ships arrive. She took another long pull on her beer and wiped the foam off her upper lip.

"So how much surplus have we got?" she asked Jax, who like most Tiponi was a whiz at math and not only kept the books, he also helped pick the cargo to maximize profit.

Her casual tone didn't fool him, and his fronds stiffened and stuck out in all directions. "I'm not going to like this, am I?" he asked.

Before Jahan could answer, Dalea spoke up. "Maybe we should check on the ship," she said, and she gave them both a gimlet-eyed glare out of her wide-set eyes.

"Good idea," Kielli said and downed his shot of tequila. A flicker of resentment ran through Jahan. Wasn't she captain? But in fairness, they were right, so she shrugged, chugged down the rest of her beer, and they trooped out.

Ernie looked surprised when they returned. He had his feet up on the table in the galley and was watching a streaming *telenovela* on his TapPad. "I thought you were having dinner on the station," he said as they deposited their takeout containers on the table.

"Decided it was too cold—"

"Or too hot," Dalea said, interrupting Jahan.

"We brought you barbecue," Kielli said as he handed over the container to Ernie.

"Thanks." He opened the top, took a deep sniff, and picked up one of the ribs. It dripped sauce across the table on its way to his mouth. "So, is this a powwow?"

"Yes," Jahan said.

At the same time, Kielli asked plaintively, "What's a powwow?"

"Odd human word for a conference," Jax answered.

"So, what's up, Cap?" Ernie asked Jahan.

"We're going to resume the shadow runs to Hidden Worlds."

Dalea and Jax looked like they'd swallowed a giant bug. Jax's fronds were waving up and down like a mad conductor. Dalea's large brown eyes were rimmed with white. Kielli looked confused and Ernie had that attentive look humans got when they sensed something was up. Their hairless faces could hide almost nothing. Even the ones who affected facial hair were easily read by the tightening of skin around their eyes, and by the way their lips pressed together, and jaws and necks tightened.

"Then perhaps it would be prudent to terminate Señor Gantz's employment," Jax fluted.

"And maybe you should just fuck the hell right off," Ernie said, glaring at the Tiponi Flute.

"Before we brought you aboard, we traded with a lot of Hidden Worlds," Jahan said.

Ernie blew his cheeks out then released the air in a loud puff. "Christ on a tricycle. A disgraced O-Trell officer running under an alias, trading illegal drugs, not reporting renegade human worlds. Is there any illegal thing you sons a bitches haven't done?"

"We don't steal," Dalea said primly.

Jax made a clicking noise. "Well, that's not exactly accurate. There were the blank credit spikes."

"They were stolen for us," Jahan objected.

"Oh, that makes it all better," Ernie said and gave a bit of a hysterical laugh.

"And why are you such a pedant?" Dalea demanded of Jax.

"I like to be honest and accurate," the Flute replied.

"Ah, sweet Jesus, you're killing me," Ernie gasped, and

dropped his face into his hands.

"Well, we've never killed anybody." Jahan huffed a bit, stung by the human's reaction.

"You're clearly sweet little angels. So, tell me about why we're going to break the law by contacting Hidden Worlds and, worse, failing to report them to the League?"

"Because a lot of them probably don't know about the attacks. Ships show up, they're going to think it's the League and find out too late that it's not. That it's something a whole lot worse," Jahan said.

"My concern is that if you rattle them this way, they'll open fire on anything that shows up. League ships, black marketeers," Dalea said.

"We have to give them some warning," Kielli cried. "If we don't, we're just as guilty as the aliens!"

Jahan patted her young relative on the shoulder. "I'm going to have to speak to your mother about allowing you to carry on like this." Kielli glared at her, and she said firmly, "I know you're young, but don't be so overly dramatic."

"Yes, there is a big difference between us committing a sin of omission and creatures who are blowing up cities," Jax said.

"In the end we'll remember not the words of our enemies but the silence of our friends," Kielli shot back. It sounded like a quote, but Jahan couldn't place it.

"So, what's the issue?" Ernie said. "It seems like you've already made up your mind, so what's the point of this palaver?"

"We're going to need a cover if we go dark while we warn the worlds. The League is used to us carrying goods for them.

We can't just disappear without arousing suspicion," Jahan said.

Ernie sighed and ran a hand across his face. The rasp of skin on stubble was loud in the room. "You're gonna get my ass thrown in jail, aren't you?"

"Our asses would be right next door," Jax countered.

"Nah, they'll execute you BEMs. So, tell me why I should go along with this?"

"Because those worlds are human worlds. Your people," Dalea suggested.

Ernie shrugged. "Don't know 'em. Why should I care about 'em?"

Jahan glanced around the table at the appalled faces. Jax's eyes were whirling and his fronds quivering, a sure sign of agitation. She hid her smile. "You'll go because you love the *Selkie* more than us. Also, you'd love the chance to poke the League in the eye and prove you're smarter than *el pollino.*" She deliberately used the derogatory term idiot or donkey for the League's civilian constabulary. "While you might not know the Hidden Worlders, you do know us, and I think you like us just a little bit."

Ernie tipped his hand back and forth in that universal gesture of *not so sure*, but he took away part of the sting by saying, "Yeah, you're almost people."

"And finally, I know you ran with the *cosarios* and there are still arrest warrants out for any of you pirates."

The human stiffened, then burst out laughing. "Okay. We got our fingers so tangled in each other's short hairs we got no choice but to stick together."

"Eeew," said Kielli.

Ernie continued, "So how about this. I put out the word that we need a tachyon infuser."

"Yeah, good luck finding *that* since they're almost never found on the open market." There was the derision of arrogant youth in Kielli's voice, driven by the sting of his aunt's reprimand.

"And that's the point, child," Dalea said softly. "Then when we drop out of sight people will think we had an engine problem—"

"And even better, we don't have to squander money buying a part we don't actually need," Jax added. "Well done, Ernie."

Jahan slapped her hands on the tabletop and stood. "Okay, let's go warn some good people about some bad aliens."

"Guess that means we get to be the good aliens," Dalea said. "That'll be a nice change."

"Only in the context of the Hidden World humans. According to the League humans, this course of action makes us very bad aliens," Jax said.

"Remember what I just said about being a pedantic asshole," the ship's doctor huffed as they left the galley.

Jahan laughed and realized it sounded very hollow. *Please God, don't let this be a mistake.*

✦ ✦ ✦

"BLESS ME, FATHER, for I have sinned. It's been … well, I don't actually want to tell you how long it's been," Tracy said. There was a bubble of laughter from the other side of the screen.

"Would it offend you if I said I'm not surprised?" Father Ken answered.

The air in the ship's small chapel was redolent with the musky scent of frankincense. What was missing was the faint odor of candle wax and soot. Tracy had an aversion to any open flame on a spaceship, and Father Ken had been fine with his request that they use electric candles.

"You know me too well."

"Actually, Tracy, I don't. When we were serving together on the *Triunfo* you didn't socialize with the other junior officers much, and you were always singing for the captain and senior officers. Then you were transferred away."

"You were there for me during the court-martial."

"Again, not exactly fun times and you probably weren't at your shining best."

Tracy laughed and leaned back against the wood of the confessional. "True that, but to be honest, I don't know if I have a shining best. Sometimes I think I'm kind of an asshole."

"Why is that?"

"Okay, is this confession or therapy?" Tracy asked.

The priest chuckled again. "Is there a difference?" He paused, then asked, "So what do you do for fun?"

"Uh …" Tracy's mind seemed to have become a wiped Etch A Sketch. "Umm … I like to read."

"Okay, not exactly a social activity," Ken said.

Tracy remembered after dinner evenings on the *Selkie* with him and his crew taking turns reading aloud books from their various cultures. "It can be."

"I think there's a story there. I'll get it out of you later. Do you play chess?"

"Yes. I'd beat you," Tracy said and chuckled.

"Oh ho, a challenge. Accepted, Captain."

"I'm going to resume fencing now that I have people around who actually know how to fence."

"Do you sing any longer? You had a beautiful voice."

"Not regularly, and I sure as hell can't do it now. I need their respect. And Father, these are desperate times."

"Yes, and you can't buckle under the strain, Tracy." They sat in silence for a long moment.

The priest was a shadowy figure through the latticework. Tracy leaned forward and laced his fingers through the filigreed wood. "Ken, would it be all right if I tell you I'm scared?"

"What better place? And I don't think you're alone in that." There was again a long silence. There was the whisper of material as the priest shifted. "So, tell me those sins."

Tracy sifted through the myriad of sins. Some of which he didn't consider to be sins venal or otherwise. Many of which he wasn't going to mention. He certainly wasn't going to mention the Hidden Worlds. He trusted Ken, but only so far, and he had a feeling the seal of the confessional might find itself a bit wobbly if he mentioned something that profoundly illegal. He prevaricated. "I traded in contraband items."

"How contraband and how harmful?"

"Very, and I suppose the harm depends on your point of view," Tracy hedged.

"What's your view?"

"That I don't see anything wrong with birth control."

"Ah." There was another long silence from the other side of the confessional. "I've read some interesting articles that argue that only when women had control over their biology could they truly be equal."

"Do you think they're equal now?" Tracy asked.

"I think they're … cherished."

"Which implies not equal."

"You have a young woman officer. Do you think she's competent?" Ken asked.

"I don't know. Any more than I know if the male lieutenants are competent. We'll find out. Three of my crew aboard the trading vessel were females. Granted, they weren't human women, but they were very competent. One of them was my first officer. And a woman leads the League. Do you think she's competent, Father?"

"I guess we'll find out," the priest responded. "But back to you. Anything else?"

The mention of Mercedes brought him up against it. Once again, he opted for evasion. "I had an affair with a married woman." In the shadows, a pair of dark eyes seemed to form. Tracy closed his own eyes and willed them away.

"Did you love her?"

"Always and forever. With all my heart."

"Then where is the sin, my son?"

"That I would kill her husband if I had the chance!" It burst out of him like poison from a diseased wound.

"But you haven't."

Tracy gave a bitter chuckle. "No, I doubt I could get to him."

"Tracy, you must put this aside." Ken's voice had lost its gentle humor. He was now as serious as the grave and his voice was just as cold. "Or it will destroy you."

✦ ✦ ✦

MERCEDES LOOKED OVER the list of ship assignments. As soon as ships came off the assembly line, they were being assigned to one of the two fleets, with the bulk of the new builds going to the decimated Blue. She did some quick calculations and realized that at this pace she would have the Blue back to full strength in eighteen months. Assuming that none of the shipyards were hit and that the stamina of the workers didn't flag, and she didn't lose too many more of the ships currently on active duty. As her eye slid down the list of ships being assigned to her fleet, a name leaped out at her. *Belmanor, Thracius. Captain.* Commanding the fire lance frigate *Swiftsure.* An image seemed to impose itself over the lines of print, floating in the air in front of her. A darkened room, moonlight through shutters throwing silver lines on the polished wood floor, the soft swaying of the bed as the treehouse danced with the wind. A man's hands stroking her flanks, his lips and tongue caressing her nipples, her fingers tangled in his tousled hair. Heat rushed into her groin and she squeezed her thighs together.

Mercedes threw herself back in her chair, recoiling from the memory. She drew in a deep breath and stared at the name. Inevitably, they would come in contact with each other: staff meetings, officers' dinners, and, most importantly, tactical and strategic planning sessions. How could they possibly interact and not be discovered? They had been intimate. She had hidden from him that he was the father of her child. She quickly offered a brief prayer of thanks that at least so far Cyprian looked more like her then his actual father.

She continued to dither. Tracy had graduated second in their class at The High Ground. His intellect would be invaluable to her. The battered Blue fleet desperately needed the state-of-the-art frigate and Tracy's brilliance.

No, it was impossible; neither of them were very good actors. She abruptly reached out and shifted the *Swiftsure* out of the Blue and into the Gold. It was the right thing to do. Tracy had served with Talion. They would be a good team.

Excuses, all excuses. You know it's because you *can't be trusted.*

6

SO MANY BASTARDS

FLEET SPACE TRAFFIC control had sent over the coordinates. Tracy stood on the bridge, his eyes flicking between the play of his navigator's hands across the console, the computer holos, and the figures flashing across the computer holograms suspended above. The guidance system telemetry control computer currently held sway over the *Swiftsure,* moving at a speed no human navigator could match, but Tracy still liked to have a human as a backstop. After a few minutes, he accepted that everything was proceeding with smooth efficiency and the muscles in his shoulders relaxed. He leaned down and tapped the control panel on the arm of his chair. The front screen shifted from a telemetry graphic to an actual view of the fleet into which they were currently inserting themselves.

Three large dreadnoughts formed a three-dimensional cone. Orbiting the giant ships were seventeen *destructores*, thirty *cruseros*, and ten frigates, but the *Swiftsure* was the only *lanza de fuego fragata*. Tracy didn't know if that made him secretly proud or nervous as hell. The tiny *exploradors* were hard to spot among the effluvia from the subspace drives of their larger brethren that formed glittering lines and etched a complex web of crystal and silver against the dark of space.

Tracy seated himself and called up the combat mission support officer. Lieutenant Flintoff's bell-like voice responded, and Tracy remembered he had assigned her to operations so she could get a sense on what kept a fleet flying. "Lieutenant, please make a note of all Gold ships present, command structure, and cross-reference with necessary combat resources."

"Yes, sir." She broke the connection.

"Any reason for that, sir?" Valada-Viers asked.

"More information is better than not enough, XO."

Valada-Viers leaned down and said quietly, "And the way those sons of bitches are burning through us, we might find ourselves responsible for more than just this ship, eh, Captain?"

"Like I said, let's know who we're fighting alongside," Tracy replied in an undertone.

"Hail from the flagship, sir," the comm officer called.

"Accept."

The Scoop function on his chair went green and a holograph of Jasper Talion sprang to life in front of him. "Belmanor. You amazing bastard. You look good for a man who was dead," Talion said.

Taking his cue from the jocular greeting, Tracy followed suit. "And you look like a bastard who enjoys that chair more than humping a rifle."

Talion gave that sharp barking laugh that had always sounded more predatory than humorous. "Roger that. Does explain why all you shipboard types had such big asses though. Dinner. Tonight. Nineteen hundred. Aboard the *Blenheim.*"

"Yes, sir." The connection broke and Talion vanished.

"I take it you're acquainted, sir," Valada-Viers said.

"We attended The High Ground together."

"So, what's the word on him?"

Tracy thought about a long-ago soccer game, an opponent's broken leg, Talion's ejection from the game, and their team's eventual victory because of that injury. "He's very … determined."

"Which could be said of all of us, sir." The XO sounded exasperated.

Tracy sighed and elaborated. "Let's just say he'll do anything to win."

"Probably not a bad trait in our present situation," Valada-Viers replied.

Perhaps, Tracy thought. *But how many of us is he likely to sacrifice in the process?*

✦ ✦ ✦

OURANOS'S OTHER MAJOR population center was Almaty on the planet's fourth and smallest continent. Hissilek owed its location to the fabulous beaches and ease of access to the ocean for shipping. Almaty was in the mountains, which made it an ideal location for building civil defense shelters. Boho, wearing a hard hat and a belted safari jacket, walked with the foreman at this fifth site. The noise was deafening as earthmovers ground past shoving the dirt being excavated by the huge drills that were gnawing into the sides of the cliffs.

There was the occasional blast of explosive as granite was pulverized.

Walking with him and slipping a bit in their handmade loafers and oxfords were the head of the Disaster Relief Department, a grizzled older man, Dillion Jukke, who had been the head of procurement for O-Trell before his retirement, Lord Ian Rogers, head of the *Seguridad Imperial* known as SEGU, and Anselmo, who was busily taking notes on his TapPad. Anselmo occasionally dropped back to instruct the palace photographer which shots of the Consort he wanted for the press release.

"So, when we're done," the foreman was bellowing in Boho's ear, "we'll be able to house five hundred thousand people."

"When can we start moving in supplies?" Boho asked. His throat felt raw from the dust and all the shouting.

"Three months, my lord."

"And when will the site be ready to receive people?"

"Ten months, my lord. Eight if we go to round-the-clock shifts," the man replied. He rightly interpreted Boho's expression, and his head seemed to sink down between his shoulders.

The DRD administrator stepped in. "We don't need sanitation facilities for cases of water, MREs, and nonperishable medicines, sir. There's a lot more involved when you're housing people."

"And the mayor of Almaty has been deeply engaged on this, my lord," Ian said. "Frankly, they're farther along than we are in Hissilek." Was there an implied criticism in the intelligence chief's words? Boho wasn't sure.

Boho glanced over at Anselmo. "Make a note. I want a meeting on disaster preparedness for Hissilek as soon as we're back. I suspect the unions are being difficult." He turned to Ian. "Find out who's tossing sand in the gears and let's deal with them."

"Very good, sir," the head of the intelligence service said, but there was something in his look that had the skin between Boho's shoulders tingling.

They moved on, with the foreman droning on about tons of debris moved. They had to pretend to admire a few more metal behemoths, and then they were joined by the civil engineer, which only added to Boho's frustration. The man was even more boring than the foreman as he discussed blast radius calculations based on the Kronos attack and the necessary depth and reinforcement necessary to protect the humans who would eventually take shelter in these man-made caves. Boho decided he had had enough and metaphorically speaking, he tossed the DRD administrator under the treads of one of the earthmovers.

"This is all fascinating, *señores*, but I think administrator Jukke will be of far more use to you. He has a far greater understanding than me. Jukke, you can call for a shuttle when you're ready to return to the capital." And with that, he made his escape.

Back on the shuttle, Boho's Isanjo batBEM, Ivoga, immediately recognized his master's most pressing need and rushed to prepare him a gin and tonic. Within minutes the rest of the men were sipping cocktails of their choice. All except the sanctimonious prig, Rogers, who would accept only a tonic water and lime. As the shuttle boosted for the suborbital flight that would soon have them back in Hissilek, the conversation turned to lighter topics: gossip over the latest FFH marital affair, the screaming catfight that had erupted between two female vid stars at the latest awards ceremony. Rogers suddenly broke in, his words falling like a boulder in the midst of a cheerfully bubbling stream.

"Who gets to take shelter? How will the selection be made? And how much warning will there actually be so our people can reach shelter?" Boho opened his mouth to respond, only to have the head of SEGU go rushing on. "Or is this just a way to lull the citizenry into believing they are being protected and shovel money to companies owned by members of our class?"

"Good God, sir! You insult the Consort," Anselmo yelped as he came out of his seat.

"Do I?" Rogers turned a gimlet gaze on Boho. "Have I offended you … sir?"

Boho rather distantly noticed that the knuckles of his hand gripping the highball glass had gone white. He gulped down the drink and set it with ever so much care down on the table. "You know you have. And if we were younger and I was less tired, I'd be asking for my blade or, more likely, a horsewhip. Of course, it's a goddamn scam! But it keeps the *intitulados* calm, and shovels money into the pockets of the FFH and keeps *them* calm, and as for who gets picked? You know the answer to that. Our people and a few prominent commoners to keep the peasants with pitchforks from rushing the shuttles or the cave entrances until we're all safely tucked away."

"You really are a disgrace, Cullen, you know that?" Rogers gritted.

"No, I'm a pragmatist."

"That's money we should be spending on ships! On training and equipping our soldiers. Caring for refugees! This is disgraceful! Dishonorable!"

"*Dios mio!* Rogers, you are such a fucking plaster saint! We're at war. Honor has no place in this. Or conscience, or ethics. Right now, we're just animals fighting to survive. Just be glad you're one of the people who gets to stay alive. Or maybe you'd like me to take your family off the list to prove how moral and upright you are?"

"You're a bastard, Cullen." Rogers forced the words from between stiff lips.

"Yeah. I am. But I get the job done."

✦ ✦ ✦

THE DINING ROOM aboard the *Blenheim* was an elegant space that reflected Talion's martial nature. In place of mirrors, paintings, and tapestries, the walls were decorated with swords and pistols arrayed in creative designs, and the battle flag of the Gold dominated the far end of the room. Tracy checked at the entrance, startled by the sight of not one but three women, and one of them wore a captain's bars. Truthfully, a person would have to have been marooned on a distant planet not to recognize the captain. For years, gossip columns had been filled with stories about most of the royal princesses, and several years ago Tracy himself had seen this one riding in a carriage on her way to her sister's coronation. Captain Princess Beatrisa Arango had her hair shaved to a soft fuzz, and the tight-fitting slacks revealed muscular legs. She seemed completely at ease. Because of the constant press, Tracy knew that Beatrisa was forty-one, and there were whispered rumors in the tabloid press about her "unnatural" proclivities.

While the presence of royalty was a bit nerve-wracking, the inclusion of several XOs, among them the other two women, reassured Tracy that it had been all right to bring Valada-Viers along to the dinner. The aforementioned officer gave a low whistle and said quietly, "We are in exalted company, sir."

"We are indeed." Tracy spotted Talion over by the steel-and-glass cellarette, which sported not only storage for wine and liquor, but racks for stemware. "Best go pay our respects to the admiral of the fleet."

They wove their way through the crowd. Talion spotted Tracy and held up his glass in salute. Tracy stopped, braced, and gave a more formal salute. Talion switched his glass into his left hand and returned a proper salute. "By God, Belmanor, it's good to see you."

"You as well, sir. Honored to be serving with you."

"Where the devil did you get to after that mess?" Talion asked. Fortunately, Tracy was spared the necessity of answering because Talion went rushing on. "Did you keep up with the fencing? I know old Exeteur took you in hand when we were aboard the *Triunfo*, and I need a partner with whom I can cross blades."

"I did, indeed, sir, and I wager I could give you a run for your money now," Tracy replied.

"Oh ho, a challenge. Accepted. Let's have our aides find a

time before the necessity of war consumes us all."

"May I present my XO, Commander Marquis Valada-Viers."

Valada-Viers stepped forward and he and Talion shook hands. "Honored, sir."

"Everybody's so honored. I hope it stays that way and I do better with the Gold than poor old Pulkkinen did with the Blue. He royally cocked that up."

Tracy tensed at the words. Davin Pulkkinen had been one of the few members of the FFH who had befriended Tracy, and to hear Davin's sacrifice dismissed so cavalierly spurred his far too-ready temper.

"It's worth remembering that when Pulkkinen lost his arm during our first year at the High Ground he could have gotten out of serving, but instead he chose to stay." Tracy managed to refrain from adding that Talion had done his required five years and gone back to his life as the pampered heir to a planetary system while Davin had stayed in the service. "And he did pay for that cock up with his life," Tracy concluded.

There was a long silence. Valada-Viers looked like he wanted the floor to open and swallow him. As for Tracy and Talion, their eyes were locked. Tracy counted his heartbeats and wondered if he'd just ended his career again. Then Talion gave his head a rueful shake and Tracy relaxed.

"Glad to see you're still the same stiff-necked son of a bitch that you were back in the day." He leaned in close and whispered, "And I need somebody in this crowd who won't kiss my ass but give me honest advice." He straightened and said in a normal tone of voice, "Go get a drink before dinner."

Tracy and Valada-Viers obeyed. Tracy would have loved a shot of bourbon. He had never been good at these sorts of events, and years away from the FFH had left him very much out of practice, but wisdom prevailed, and he settled on a flute of champagne. Valada-Viers had joined a group of younger men who had clearly been his classmates. Tracy watched the princess and wished he had the status (and the nerve) to approach her. He longed to know how Mercedes was doing, but of course that was a question he dared not ask. He finally forced himself to join a group who were discussing the alien's tactics and not too long after, a bell chimed, drawing them to the table.

It was very much an above and below the salt affair. The commanders were all seated at the foot of the table. The captains closer to Talion, who sat at the head. There seemed to be a pecking order even among the captains. The commanders of the large capital ships were closest to Talion and the captains of smaller vessels farther down the table. Tracy wasn't surprised by his position next to the lower-ranking people. He was an *intitulado*. The captain directly across from him commanded a troop transport. The chair next to him was spun out. Tracy glanced up to see his dinner companion and was surprised to see royalty. He had assumed that Talion would bend protocol for a royal sister, but instead Beatrisa was seated with the other captains who commanded *exploradors*. It actually spoke well of Talion, Tracy decided. Or perhaps the princess herself.

She turned to face him and held out her hand. "Captain Beatrisa Arango," she said. He noted that she left off her title.

"Captain Thracius Belmanor," he replied. She had a surprisingly strong handshake for a woman.

"You have the *Swiftsure*," she said.

"Yes," he said, surprised.

"I'm so fucking jealous." Tracy was startled by the profanity. It was not common to hear such crude language from a lady of the FFH. Beatrisa seemed to be telepathic because she gave him an ironic glance. "Yeah, I'm nobody's vision of the FFH ideal."

"I meant no offense, Highness."

"None taken unless you keep calling me Highness. Then I'm going to be pissed."

"All right, Captain."

"Beatrisa."

Tracy held up an admonishing finger. "Now that is a bridge too far."

Beatrisa gave a theatrical sigh. "Oh, all right, Captain." She glanced around and then smiled, a surprisingly impish expression. "I see we're forming the squishy middle. I'm too exalted, despite my recent promotion, to be at the absolute bottom of the table, and while you've got the sexiest ship in the fleet you don't have enough …" She paused, cocked her head to the side, and searched for a word.

"Exalt?" Tracy suggested.

She laughed. "Yes, exactly. Not nearly enough exalt to be near the head of the table."

"Well, you always want the middle to hold," Tracy said. "So perhaps we're in the right place."

"I like you," Beatrisa said bluntly.

"Why, thank you."

The soup course was placed before them, and Tracy waited until they had both had a few mouthfuls before he asked, "So, if I may inquire, how many of the royal family are on active duty?"

Beatrisa blew across a spoonful of soup, sipped it, and then answered. "Well, obviously *la Emperatriz* is commanding the Blue. Then you've got me, Carisa has just returned to active duty and been assigned to the Gold. Big sister wants me to keep an eye on our baby sister," she laughed.

"She's not here tonight?" Tracy asked.

"No, she's a Captain Lieutenant and there's nobody here under the rank of commander."

"Princess doesn't trump commander?"

"Not if the princess is smart. No sense getting people's backs up," Beatrisa said prosaically. "Then there are a niece and three nephews also serving. The rest of the rug rats are too young, though if this war goes on long enough another niece will be joining us."

"Let us pray that doesn't happen," Tracy said and crossed himself.

Beatrisa quickly followed suit. "Amen." She sighed. "I suppose older generations always fight in the hope the younger ones won't have to. Pity it never works out that way."

"We had a pretty good run. Two hundred years without a major war," Tracy said.

"True. Rather wish it could have lasted another two hundred. I hate it that all of this is falling on Merce—" She broke off and corrected herself. "On La Em—" Beatrisa broke off again. "Oh, to hell with it. On my sister."

As do I, Tracy thought.

Their soup bowls were removed, and the mains were delivered. Tracy had gone with the vegetarian choice. Unfortunately, Beatrisa had the lamb and dumplings, and Tracy gave her plate a brief longing look. "I gather from your demeanor this wasn't an ethical stance," Beatrisa said, gesturing at his plate.

"No. Health. It's been more than a few years since I followed the O-Trell physical regimen." He patted his slight paunch.

"I admit I love training even though it's rather stupid if you're not a *fusilero*. I mean, it's not like we're going to punch the fucking aliens in the mouth," Beatrisa said.

"Believe me, I'd like to after Kronos," Tracy said.

"Fucking A. So, are you married, Captain?" Beatrisa asked with an abrupt change of subject.

"No." He had hoped his expression was appropriately neutral but once again his inability to keep a poker face betrayed him.

"Ah, I sense a tragic story. Let us pick some neutral topic. Have you read Gladstone's latest novel?"

And with that they moved to safer ground. They were down to dessert, which Tracy resolutely pushed aside, when his ScoopRing began tapping his finger in a particular rhythm that meant trouble. He stood, wiped his lips, and gave Beatrisa a slight bow. "If you will excuse me, ma'am."

The head was just off the Captain's Mess. Once the door closed, Tracy glanced under stall doors to be sure he was alone. He then keyed his ring. The image of Jahan sprang up in front of him. "I believe I told you specifically not to do what you're doing and not to be where you are," he said while Jahan gaped at him.

+ + +

"WELL, FUCK ME! You're spying on us?" Jahan yelped at the image of Tracy floating in the middle of the bridge.

"Yes. Now get the hell out of there or I will take the ship. I'm not going to ask twice because I've got to end this before somebody decides to intercept this call."

"You're a right sneaky bastard, you are," Jahan complained.

"Yep, a bastard who has a fifty-three percent interest in the ship. Don't do this again." The connection was broken, and Tracy's image vanished.

Kielli, from his position at navigation, looked over at her. "Are we going to do as we're told?"

Jahan studied the distant sun that provided the only light to this system buried deep in a cosmic cloud. It was one of the major reasons the Hidden World had managed to go undetected by the League for several centuries. Freehold was probably the most advanced of the Hidden Worlds where the *Selkie* had plied her trade, and Jahan really liked their trading partners. Still, she had been given a direct order from her friend, former captain, and major owner of the ship. She decided to opt for discretion.

"Yeah, we are." Jahan headed for the access ladder. "Now I just have to figure out where he's hidden the trackers," she muttered to herself. She swung onto the ladder only to have her ring signal a call. Tracy appeared again. "And don't go looking for my bugs. I'll know if you remove them." And he was gone again only to return a second later. "And Jahan, do give me a little credit. And trust me."

Jahan returned to the bridge and gave the order to set a course back to League space, all the while wondering about Tracy's cryptic final remark.

7

PROMISES MADE

"I THOUGHT I might find you still up," her mother said softly from the doorway.

Mercedes looked up from her TapPad, pushed back an errant lock of hair, and gave Maribel a tired smile. "We've got to find a way to protect our planets and we can't afford to build enough ships to garrison every world. And even if the treasury could afford it, we're looking at years before we'd have sufficient numbers."

"Well, I can't provide more money or more ships, but I have got hot cocoa and cinnamon toast," Maribel said, and looked at Mercedes expectantly.

The lights in the home office of Maribel's current husband, Lord Hector Braganza, were sufficiently low that it was unlikely Maribel could see Mercedes's expression of confusion. Was cocoa and toast supposed to be a thing? If so, it was as thing that Mercedes didn't understand. "Uh, thank you."

Maribel stared down at the cup and plate and her shoulders slumped. "Of course, I never did this for you, did I? You were so little when … when …"

"Father divorced you?"

"Yes, that."

Maribel came into the room and set the cup and plate down on the desk. She took the chair on the other side of the desk. Her hair was down, flowing across the shoulders and back of the lace peignoir she wore. The riotous curls were now more silver than black.

Mercedes leaned back in the chair and stretched until her back popped. "Is this something you did for my half-brothers?" She picked up the toast and took a bite. It was thick with powdered sugar and cinnamon and the melted butter suffused the bread. "Mmm, good," Mercedes said, and managed to blow a film of sugar across the desk as she tried to talk around the mouthful. "Oh, fuck," she muttered.

Maribel laughed. "Hector won't mind. He constantly spills things on the desk. And yes, it was the universal cure for skinned knees and broken hearts from lost games and lost girls." She fidgeted with the sash of her robe for a few seconds. "Two of them are in your fleet."

"I'm sorry; I didn't know. I should have looked. I'll do my best to see them safe."

"I know you will." Her mother reached out and snagged the handle of the mug, took a sip of the cocoa. Mercedes noted that her nails were cut very short and unpolished. It was a change. The other times she had seen her mother, her nails had been long and beautifully polished. Her mother caught her look.

"I've been volunteering at the supply depot packing med kits for the ground troops. Three of the boys are *fusileros*. Our youngest is doing civil defense here on Yggdrasil. Working side by side with Hector."

"I wish I knew them better," Mercedes said. She set aside the toast, having lost her appetite.

"It's all right. It's not like you don't have an entire government and military to manage. And your own more immediate family." There was again a long pause. "What are you doing to keep Cyprian safe?"

"Everything I can."

"But he's still on Ouranos," her mother said, and it sounded accusatory.

"I have to. How would it look if I moved my own child to safety and not other families' children? Besides, tell me where any place is safe?" Maribel looked stricken. Mercedes gave her head a shake and rapped her knuckles on the TapPad. "That's what I'm wrestling with. Looking for a way to make at least a few planets safe."

"You'll think of something."

"No, I'm doing this, so I don't feel guilty for stopping to visit you. I'm not a strategist. The fleet would be better served if they put me in an *infierno* and let me fight. That, I'm good at. This …" She tossed her TapPad onto the desk and waved at it. "They're all looking to me. The soldiers, the citizens, the BEMs, everybody. It's like a constant weight on me. Sometimes I feel like I can't breathe …" Her voice had risen, and she panted, trying to draw air into her lungs.

Maribel jumped up and ran to her. Enfolded her in an embrace. Mercedes began to cry at the smell of her mother's favorite perfume. It was the same scent Maribel had been wearing on that long ago day when she had said farewell to a four-year-old Mercedes.

"Oh, my darling, my darling," her mother murmured

because there was nothing else she could offer.

✦ ✦ ✦

IT WAS CYPRIAN'S first trip through Fold space, and Boho was gratified to see that his son handled the transition from normal space into the eerie not-our-universe with ease. It wasn't recommended that children under the age of three travel in Fold, but Cypri was about to celebrate his fourth birthday, so Boho decided to take the risk. He also thought it would do both mother and child good if they got to see each other. He also wouldn't mind a conjugal visit. He had been very good over the past two months about not visiting one of his paramours. When several noble ladies had queried him, he'd fobbed them off with the argument that everyone must make sacrifices in war. All of them save one had taken it well, and the one shrieking harpy had been handled by Anselmo, who arranged for her husband's lightly illegal business dealings to become public, which required them to relocate to the family's country estate on Belán and pushed Boho's name out of the gossip columns.

It was ironic, he reflected, *that if he went to a brothel, it would cause far less comment than his seduction of FFH wives.* He stood just behind his son while Cyprian peered out in fascination at the twisting grey tendrils of Fold space and the flashing sparks of passing Foldstream messages. Boho's wandering thoughts continued. Truth was, he didn't particularly care for the atmosphere in whorehouses. Even those that catered to the FFH by hiring the most beautiful girls, serving the finest champagne, and decorating in the best of taste had the feel of rot behind the gilding. What Boho really liked was taking his pleasure with a noble wife in the spousal bed. So maybe what really excited and aroused him wasn't the sex, but the knowledge of his dominance over the cuckolded husband.

He reached down and gently ruffled his son's tawny brown hair and reflected on how fast time passed. Before he knew it, Cypri would be sixteen and ready for his introduction to the art of love. Boho decided he would select the girl himself. It was, after all, a father's duty to see that his son was properly instructed so his first sexual encounter would be a good one.

"You must really be horny," he muttered to himself. "Because you're getting way ahead of yourself."

Right now, the biggest issue was Cypri's birthday party. Boho had instructed Anselmo to round up some garrison children on Hellfire to attend the party. Otherwise, the only guest would be Cipriana's only surviving child. As was his wont, Hayden McKenzie stood off to the side watching the father and son rather than the grey tendrils beyond the port. He was fourteen, and Boho brightened at the thought that he could stand in loco parentis to the boy. In two years, he would need a father's guidance in the art of seduction.

"Papa, are those fairies?" Cypri asked, pulling Boho's attention back from thoughts of brothels and sex. The little boy pointed at the flashes of colored light of the messages streaking through the grey haze. Boho noticed that the baby chubbiness was starting to retreat.

"No, those are messages people are sending to each other."

"Like the ones we send to Mama?"

"Exactly."

"Can we hear them?"

"No."

"Can I go outside?"

"No."

"I'll wear a spacesuit."

"Not even then. Fold space isn't like real space. You'd get lost." He leaned down and hugged the boy tight. "And I can't ever lose you."

Cypri yawned and Boho picked him up. His son wrapped his arms around Boho's neck, and for an instant he felt like his heart was being crushed, so powerful was the emotion. "Time for bed."

"We see mommy tomorrow?"

"Yes, and the day after that is your birthday party. How old are you going to be?"

Cypri held up four fingers.

Their *Servicio Protector Imperial* agents fell in behind the trio as they returned to the cabin. Boho handed Cypri off to his nurse.

Elizabeth crooned, "Little poppet is almost asleep." She gently pinched his cheek. "Can you wake up enough to have dinner, Your Highness?" Cyprian gave a drowsy nod. "What do you want?"

"Mac and cheese," he lisped out.

Boho shook his head. "That seems to be all he eats. And crackers."

"He'll outgrow it, sir. They all do."

"I'll check in before I turn in," Boho said.

"Very good, sir."

Boho looked down at Hayden. "Would you like to eat dinner with me?"

The boy looked startled, then shook his head. "I have homework, sir. I promised Father Dimitri I wouldn't fall behind on this trip. Elizabeth can get something for me."

"All right but remember there's more to life than schoolwork."

"I want to be ready for The High Ground," Hayden said, and there was a fierce light in his eyes.

"We're going to handle this before you ever have to fight."

"Pardon me if I'm being rude, but I hope not, sir."

The door slid shut on the boy's grim expression. Boho gave his head a shake and gestured to the guards. Two of the SPI agents took up their positions by the door. The other two fell in behind Boho as he headed for the dining room aboard the imperial yacht. He'd had to rely on fleet headquarters to keep track of Mercedes and the Blue. They had been at Yggdrasil, where her mother and stepfather ruled, but now the fleet was apparently back at Hellfire. Boho wasn't sorry. If an attack should come, being at the heavily fortified command center instead of the less well-guarded civilian planet would be much safer. It might also be a prime target.

That contrary thought stole Boho's appetite. He barely touched the four courses the chef had prepared and, at the end, realized he had barely tasted what he had eaten. He waved away the cheese tray and settled for the staff refilling his wine glass. He then waved them all away, too. Twisting the stem of the wine glass between his fingers, he watched the ruby liquid wash across the sides of the glass and tried to analyze his melancholy. The sharp edges of terror that had gripped him after the attack on Kronos had subsided, but he found he was far more comfortable aboard a ship than on a planet's surface. It was hard to find a ship in the vastness of space, which was why he had decided not to travel in a convoy. A single small, if luxurious, ship could more easily be overlooked. So, was he really bringing Cypri so he could see his mother and they could celebrate the boy's birthday together, or was it just a way to ease that sense of being trapped when he was on Ouranos? Not only on the capital world but living in the damn palace. It had to be ground zero for their enemies. Perhaps he and Cyprian should just stay aboard ship. Keep moving. Stay safe.

✦ ✦ ✦

TRACY SHIFTED, TRYING to find a way to ease his numb butt and aching bladder as the meeting wore on. They were in the big conference room aboard the *Blenheim*, and there were so many holographic images of research officers and supply officers and tactical officers on other ships and distant worlds, that many of the figures looked like they were standing in the laps of those who were physically present.

Talion stood before a projected map of the Milky Way with the league worlds, ship positions, and shipping corridors labeled and illuminated in various colors. Tracy tried to stay focused, but they were coming up on five hours without a bathroom break. The coffee tureen had been emptied, filled, and emptied again, and judging from the shifts and expressions, others were feeling as desperate as himself.

He found his mind wandering back to the *Selkie.* Wondering where they were. What they were doing. He wished he had a Jax aboard the *Swiftsure*. Tracy had known that being a captain involved a lot of clerical work, but when he'd been aboard the *Selkie*, Jax's brilliance with figures and mind for detail had relieved him of much of that tedium. Then he always knew it was done right the first time. Now, Tracy often found errors on the part of his staff. He knew a lot of it was due to fatigue—no one on a ship ever got enough rest—but it was adding to his burdens and cutting into *his* rest. At least he was good at math.

His wandering thoughts had reduced the ongoing presentations to dull baritone drones in the background when a familiar voice brought him out of his stupor. Admiral Marqués Ernesto Chapman-Owiti was speaking, and his words were searing.

"Basically, most of this discussion amounts to us fiddling while the League burns around us. We need solid intel. We need an alien ship to study. We need captives to interrogate. To understand them, we must learn their language, discover what they worship, their goals and fears. We're fighting blind here and more ships, more guns, and more bombs aren't the solution. They certainly haven't been so far."

Chapman-Owiti was the senior research scientist at the foremost R&D lab on Hellfire, so no one caviled at his tone or his words. He and Tracy had been classmates at The High Ground, and Ernesto had taken the top honors at the school, beating out Tracy by a significant amount. He was a stone-cold genius and all the men and women assembled knew it.

"So, *get me something*," he concluded, and broke the connection. His image flickered and vanished.

The silence seemed tangible. Talion cleared his throat. "All right, then. You've heard the man. Go get him something." He stood and they all followed suit. "Your orders have been sent to your TapPads." And indeed, the room was filled with chimes and buzzes as the pads indicated the incoming messages. "Don't disappoint me." Talion strode out and the assembled captains exchanged glances.

"Why do I get the feeling that what he was really saying was *come home carrying your shield or on it*?" Beatrisa said as she fell into step with Tracy.

Tracy looked down at the Princess. "You wouldn't be wrong." Picking his words with care, Tracy added, "Jasper is a man who doesn't like to lose."

"Great," a bandy-legged man whose shock of red hair set a contrast with his dark skin murmured to them. The man had been seated farther up the table from Tracy at the welcoming banquet, and Tracy couldn't remember his name, but did remember the ship he commanded, a destroyer called the *Desafiante*. "I just hope some of these baby captains don't take risks thinking that dead heroes are just as good as living failures."

Tracy laughed. "Yes, at least a failure has a chance to turn things around." *Look at me,* he thought.

The man gave a huff of agreement and hitched up his trousers. "Well, best get to it. Luck to you, Captains."

"And to you."

Just before he and Beatrisa parted at the shuttle bays, the princess held up her TapPad. "Like Christmas morning wondering what's in the big shiny box and hoping it's not something *practical.*"

"I'm just hoping it's not a lump of coal," Tracy said.

"Oh, I think it's that for all of us. These bastards are tough."

And winning, Tracy thought, but he didn't say that. He just nodded and went to the bay that held his shuttle waiting to ferry him back to the *Swiftsure.* As they pulled away from the bulk of the dreadnaught, Tracy gazed out the window at the other shuttles scattering like fluff being expelled from the seed head of a dandelion.

He opened his TapPad, then realized that as anxious as he was to discover the task Talion had selected for him and his crew, a more immediate need had to be met. The shuttle didn't have a gravity generator, so Tracy released his restraints and kicked off, sending himself flying to the head. Switching on the fan, he pulled down the tube and funnel, inserted his dick, and sighed in relief as suction and his own desperate need drained his bladder. Sanitary wipes were utilized, and he returned to his couch to strap back in.

He entered his security code and read the orders. Two *exploradors* were being assigned to him—the *Chenault* and the *Wasp.* Which meant he had a small squadron. Tracy rather wished he had something with a bit more firepower, but perhaps speed was the best way they could serve. They could cover the sector to which they had been assigned with alacrity and see what they could find. To whomever located the home world of their foes would go the honor. Also, probably a swift death if only a handful of League ships turned up in orbit around the enemy's home world, so perhaps that was one honor he could do without. Tracy mused that he wished again that the crown's press office would come up with a final name for these bastards. They had tried several—the Crux, since their first attack had been in the Crux spiral arm of the galaxy, *El Forajido*, the Sentinels, but nothing had stuck. Since they had never managed to talk to one of the aliens, the humans had no idea what they called themselves, so right now the press was still reduced to using *the enemy* or *our foes*.

He brought up the crew manifests for the two smaller ships and discovered that the *Wasp* was under the command of Captain Princess Beatrisa de Arango. *That* he had not expected. He leaned his head against the headrest and gave a low whistle. At almost the same time, his ScoopRing chimed with an incoming message. A message that was heavily encrypted. His stomach seemed to have taken up residence in his boots, but reading this message would have to wait until he was back in his office. The next seventy minutes as they made their way back to the *Swiftsure* seemed endless, but finally he was exchanging salutes with his crew and hurrying to his office. Once inside, he set the privacy dampers and keyed the message. There was no image. Just text.

I can't think of anyone better. So, I put my sister in your hands. Take care of her. Mercedes.

His eyes were prickling; he wouldn't call them tears. Tracy reached out and gently laid a forefinger on the Lucite cube that held his Sidone weaving. "I'll keep her safe, Mer. I swear it."

8

BRAVE FRONTS

THE FRENZIED HUGS had left her with a bit of neck ache. Cyprian was in her arms, his legs locked around her waist, his arms around her neck, and his cheek pressed against hers. "Whoof, you're getting heavy, my little man," Mercedes whispered in his ear. "Can Mommy put you down now?"

He nodded, gave her another kiss on the cheek, and allowed her to slide him down. At that point Boho advanced on her with that sassy, crooked grin and leaned in to kiss her. Mercedes wanted to punch him hard in the face, but she accepted the kiss and kept smiling since the entire bridge crew was shamelessly watching. Mercedes promised herself the reckoning would come just as soon as they were alone. Hayden stood off to the side, a silent shadow. She turned to him and decided against the hug she had been about to bestow on the boy. He seemed far too aloof. Instead, she laid a hand briefly on his shoulder. "Hayden, I'm so happy to see you."

He gave a perfect court bow. "And I also, Your Majesty."

Cyprian had begun tugging urgently on the hem of her jacket. "Mommy come home now?" he asked.

“Not yet, sweetie.” His face screwed up and his cheeks reddened.

Elizabeth swept forward and gathered him in her arms. “He’s tired, Majesty.”

“Perhaps we should withdraw and allow the crew to get back to work,” Boho said.

It felt like a usurpation of her power and authority, but Mercedes had to wonder if her reaction, or perhaps overreaction, was due to him leaving Hissilek with their son and taking him on a deep space flight when they had no clear intelligence on the whereabouts of their foes. Still, he shouldn’t have given her orders on the bridge of her own flagship. She gave a tense nod.

Gelb stepped forward. “Admiral, I’ll make my quarters available for the crown prince and his nanny.”

“Thank you, Marcus, that is most thoughtful of you. I believe we have a spare bunk in the lieutenants’ berth for Hayden,” Mercedes said before Boho could speak.

“I’ll see to it, ma’am. Lieutenant Salim, please show Señor …” He hesitated and glanced at the boy.

“McKenzie,” Hayden said quietly.

Gelb shot Mercedes a startled look. She gave a minute nod. “Mr. McKenzie to his quarters.”

Mercedes then led the way to the lift, followed by Boho, Cyprian, Elizabeth, Boho’s batBEM Ivoga, the young lieutenant, and Hayden. As they rode the elevator toward the personnel deck, Cyprian kept up a stream of artless prattle about how his stomach went all bouncy when they went into Fold and how he saw puppies running in the clouds outside the window.

"Sweetheart, there are no puppies in Fold space," Mercedes said.

He gave her a disgusted look. "I *know*, Mama. They *looked* like puppies. The cloud stuff."

"Oh, I understand now. You'll have to show me."

"When we go home?" Cypri asked hopefully.

Mercedes didn't like to lie to her child, so she temporized. "Sometime," she said. Cyprian was a bright child. He understood, and his expression clouded once more.

Elizabeth laid a hand on his shoulder. "Now, now, Highness, is that any way to treat your momma when she hasn't seen you in ever so long?"

The little boy swallowed a sob and rubbed a sleeve across his nose and eyes. "But it's my birthday … almost."

"And we'll have a very nice party," Mercedes soothed. The elevator slid to a gentle stop and the doors opened. The corridor on the officers' level stretched before them, filled mostly with batBEMs all rushing to accomplish various tasks for their officers and a few officers returning from shift. Salim led Hayden off to the right while Mercedes and her family and retainers went to the left. "But right now," she continued, "you need to wash your face and hands, and then we'll all have a nice dinner."

"Mac and cheese?" Cypri said hopefully.

"I'm sure that can be arranged."

As they approached Gelb's quarters, his Hajin batBEM emerged carrying his master's holdall and a garment bag. He stopped and bowed Elizabeth and Cyprian into the room. Mercedes continued down the hallway toward her quarters. Boho easily kept pace with her fast walk. The silence felt like steel knives. Once inside, Mercedes curtly ordered her batBEM, Venia, out of the cabin. The Hajin clattered out as if a firecracker had been placed beneath her tail. Mercedes rounded on Boho.

"Oh, so we're going to have one of *those* talks," Boho said. He turned to Ivoga. "You'd best shove off, too." The Isanjo bowed and left.

"What in the *hell* were you thinking?"

"I thought I sensed icy disapproval. I brought you your child so he can celebrate his fourth birthday with you, and maybe he'll stop crying himself to sleep every damn night," he shot back.

The accusation hit and hurt. Probably because it was true, and she knew it. Mercedes wanted to wilt under the condemnation, but she stiffened her back and responded. "Oh, don't even! Don't you dare try to guilt me this way. I'm doing what I must to protect him. To protect every mother's child."

"By leaving us vulnerable on a prime target?" Boho shouted. "That's some twisted view of maternal love!" He began pacing. His great height and long legs carried him back and forth across the sitting area in only three strides. "It's only a matter of time until Ouranos is hit. You *know* that."

Icy claws seemed to close on her chest. "I know," she forced past suddenly stiff lips. "Don't you think it tortures me with worry every single moment of every single day? But if you leave, then panic begins, and that can destroy us from within. We must be united to win."

"We have to have a damn plan to win!" Boho snapped.

"God, don't you think I'm trying? Every strategist in O-Trell is running simulations looking for something to give us the edge. And where would you be safe? In the middle of a fleet that will sooner or later be in combat? On one of the other cardinal worlds? We can't predict who'll be hit next."

"Aboard the imperial yacht. Staying in Fold most of the time," Boho gritted.

"That's not healthy for a child."

"Being dead also isn't healthy," Boho shot back.

It was all too much. She didn't mean to, didn't want to, but the tears came anyway. Mercedes sank down on the edge of her bunk. "I'm so tired. And I'm so afraid." There was a flicker of emotion across Boho's face that she couldn't quite identify. "I can't sleep worrying about Cypri. And I don't want to die." The words emerged as a wail. "I want to watch him grow up, marry, have children of his own. I want to be there for it all, and I don't think I will be. They're going to win." Her face was drenched, nose running as she sobbed, then Boho was there pressing his handkerchief into her flailing hand. She gulped, wiped her streaming eyes, and blew her nose. His hand was on her shoulder, warm and heavy. She opened her arms, and he enfolded her in an embrace. She rested her wet cheek against his chest, listening to the slow beat of his heart.

"I'm sorry," she whispered.

"I'm here, love. Hang onto me. I won't let you go."

✦ ✦ ✦

IT WAS A nervous tic, but Tracy found himself checking the

coffee urn for the fourth time. It was just as full as it had been the previous three times. Both cream and milk were available in elegant silver pitchers, sugar cubes in a silver bowl complete with tongs, a selection of teas in a polished wood case, a self-heating kettle with water. There were cups and saucers rather than mugs, neatly folded linen napkins, small china plates and forks and spoons laid out. His Hajin batBEM, Kallapus, entered carrying a tray of small cakes prepared by the ship's cook. Unlike most of his kind, his mane and tail were a solid glittering white, and as the mane climbed over the top of his long head it fell into his eyes, giving him a rakish look.

"I trust everything is to your liking, sir?" the alien asked as he deposited the tray on the sideboard.

"Yes, excellently done. How did you get …" Tracy gestured at the china and silver.

"I took the liberty of putting in an order just before the supply convoy departed from Dragonfly. Chief Chang authorized the charge." Kallapus had a deep baritone voice and long sweeping lashes that he lowered to cover his dark eyes rimmed in deep blue. Tracy had the feeling he was a lady-killer among his own kind. He had a brief embarrassed moment where he wondered if any human women ever found a Hajin male arousing.

"Uh … very good. But tell the Chief to get me the bill and I'll reimburse the ship for the cost."

"Yes, sir." The batBEM bowed and left.

Tracy paced. Took the chair at the head of the conference table. Stood up and paced again. Started to pour himself a coffee, hesitated. Should he be standing when they arrived or seated with a cup? Would that be seen as disrespectful? He decided it would and returned the cup and saucer to its place on the table. He had just returned to his selected seat when the doors slid open and the two *explorador* captains, their XOs, and Valada-Viers entered. Tracy's hand twitched at his side, but he forced himself to wait for their salutes before he returned the salutation. It was hard not to acknowledge royalty.

"Please, help yourselves." Tracy gestured to the table. The next few minutes were taken up with people preparing cups, selecting among the various types of cake. The room was filled with low murmurs of conversation. *"Pardon me. May I have the sugar? No, I take milk."*

Tracy noted that the princess took tea with milk and three cakes. Her XO, an older grizzled man named Sokolov went with black coffee. Tracy approved. Valada-Viers drank tea straight and eschewed the cakes. The captain of the second *explorador*, the *Audacious*, had that shoulders back, chin up bearing that allowed a member of the FFH to always seem to be looking down their nose at lesser beings. Tracy assumed it was something that was taught in their exclusive private schools. After the shock of realizing he had the princess in his small squadron and had been tasked with protecting her, Tracy had rather neglected looking into the other captain, but he had corrected that oversight that very morning.

Captain Vizcondé Enrique Petek was the eldest son of Yves Petek, the Duque de Telqual. Yves had been one of Tracy's classmates at The High Ground, but had washed out at the end of the first year and had gratefully returned to his life as a noble heir. Apparently the old duque had been gathered to his ancestors and Yves had taken the title. This young man was obviously his heir. *Another one I have to keep safe,* Tracy thought. Enrique had an aggressively receding hairline and an equally aggressive outthrust chin which made his face seem out of balance. Unlike his father, who had run to fat, Enrique was tall and rawboned. He also exuded FFH arrogance.

His XO was younger, maybe mid to late twenties, and was a surprisingly small man with dark gold hair, which was rare among League citizens, skin that was significantly paler than even Tracy's coloring, and warm brown eyes. He doctored his coffee with a large dollop of cream and five sugar cubes and had taken a cake. Ryszard Oort was from Reichart's World and, judging from his lack of a title, had been a scholarship student to The High Ground. Given Oort's coloring, it was pretty clear he was descended from some of the original settlers of the Hidden World and wasn't a League carpetbagger. That made it a bit better.

Reichart's World was a fraught topic for Tracy. After the formerly Hidden World had been discovered and assimilated, Tracy's grandfather had entered the lottery and won a factory. They had then been cheated out of it by the FFH and had been forced to return to Ouranos burdened with debt. Tracy gave his head a small shake. Even after forty years, any thought, much less mention, of Reichart's World gave him a visceral reaction.

Once they had all settled at the table, Tracy brought up a star map that had their particular sector highlighted, but also showed the rest of League space. "So, I've been correlating the sightings of alien vessels. They've been avoiding the major worlds, but there is a pattern of fast flybys of some of the lesser planets."

"Scouting for the next target?" Valada-Viers asked.

"That's what I surmise," Tracy answered.

Beatrisa turned her ScoopRing so it created a laser pointer and indicated a planetary system. "There's been significant activity around Wasua and that's on the edge of our sector," she said.

Tracy was pleased at her quickness. "Yes."

"You're not proposing that we try to garrison Wasua?" Petek said. The derision was barely disguised.

"No, but I intend to make them think we're being sent to do just that."

"Pardon me, Captain, but they're never going to fall for it. Not with only one frigate and two *exploradors*." Oort's cheeks were a bright red. He clearly knew what he had just said would have sent a lot of captains into a rage. Tracy liked the fact it hadn't dissuaded the young officer.

"You're quite right, Lieutenant Commander. Which is why we're going to provide them with a destroyer." Five puzzled frowns were directed at him.

"And just how are we going to do that?" the princess royal asked.

"By going first to Cuandru."

✦ ✦ ✦

THEY HAD MANAGED to find four children, ages eleven, six, four, and two, in addition to Hayden to attend Cyprian's birthday party. The eleven-year-old was clearly only there because her parents had insisted because they wanted to rub elbows with royalty, but apart from eye rolls the girl had been well behaved while her parents tried desperately to engage Boho or Mercedes in conversation. They were well-to-do commoners who owned a string of modestly priced restaurants on Hellfire that catered to the military. Two sets of parents were military personnel assigned to the Hellfire base, and the final couple were elderly people, the grandparents of the six-year-old.

Whatever her failing as a mother might be, Cipriana had instilled in her son excellent manners. Hayden was even now managing to coax a grudging smile out of the eleven-year-old.

Boho had been afraid that the limited numbers would bring on an explosion from his son. There had been over a hundred children at Cyprian's third birthday party, but the presence of his mother seemed to have mollified the toddler. There was a large stack of gaily wrapped presents in one corner of the Captain's Mess. The majordomos at various noble houses had noticed the presence of the royal family at Hellfire, put that together with the date, and arranged to have gifts purchased from local stores and delivered to the flagship. Cyprian had gotten his wish from his cousin's party, and there was a yellow cake with chocolate icing. Four tall and elaborately shaped candles stood like alien sentries in the swirls and curves of the *Happy Birthday Prince Cyprian* that adorned the top of the cake. Given the size of the cake, it was likely a number of officers, at least, would get a piece.

Cyprian was busy rocking back and forth on a beautifully

made glowing-white rocking horse with a mane and tail of real horsehair. The boy already displayed his mother's love of horses, and Boho had a real pony waiting back at the palace on Ouranos. The two-year-old was, so far, patiently waiting his turn for a ride while Elizabeth made sure there were no eruptions of childish fury. Mercedes was over talking with the parents of the children. Boho joined her in time to hear her say, "I'm fine with him receiving and opening the gifts from your children, but I don't want him opening all these other gifts."

A few confused glances were exchanged. Boho found himself equally puzzled by his wife's statement, but the elderly woman nodded sagely. "Very wise, Your Majesty. Too many gifts when they aren't tethered to anything beyond his status isn't healthy for any child."

"That's my concern," Mercedes said, bestowing a smile on the woman. "I don't want him to grow into a spoiled and entitled little man."

"So how do you propose that we dispose of this mountain of gifts without causing heartbreak?" Boho asked.

"I, too, will be interested to see how you handle that, Majesty," the father of the eleven-year-old said. He glanced over at his daughter. "Our Maggie is a tad bit spoiled."

Mercedes didn't answer, but instead went off to join the children. The man looked like he wanted to sink through the floor as he realized he had been rather encroaching. After another thirty minutes of light chatter, Mercedes went to where Cypri was instructing the six-year-old on the proper way to hold the reins on the rocking horse. His brow was furrowed in concentration as he helped the other boy position his hands. "I've never seen a real horse," the boy said shyly.

"We have lots and lots. You have to come and see them. Can Madjimoyo"—he stumbled a bit over the long name but made a credible effort—"come visit, Momma?" Cypri asked.

"If his mommy and daddy say it's okay," Mercedes answered.

"They will. I'm the prince," Cyprian said, then looked worried at his mother's frown.

"No, Cypri. That's up to his parents. Not you. Now it's time for cake and for you to open your presents." He brightened at that and went scampering to the table.

Boho lifted him up so he could stand on the chair while Elizabeth lit the candles. They all sang happy birthday. "Now make a wish," Mercedes whispered.

She stood on his left to steady him while Boho spotted him on the right. Cypri squeezed his eyes tightly shut and blew hard. The candles went out. Then after five seconds they turned into sparklers that sent multicolored and sweet-smelling sparks flying toward the ceiling. Everyone laughed and clapped, and the children shrieked. Even the eleven-year-old lost her bored look. Cake and ice cream were served. Cypri's face was soon smeared with icing, and he had a dribble of ice cream on his chin. The hands that eagerly tore wrapping paper off his gifts were equally sticky.

His tongue stuck out the corner of his mouth as he focused on opening the seven presents that were from his guests and his parents and his nurse. Boho reached out and brushed a hand across his dark amber curls, and again had the feeling his heart was in a vise. As each gift emerged from its gayly wrapped cocoon there were oohs and aahs. Mercedes only had to prod Cypri once to say thank you. Once he was done, his eyes slid toward the stack of presents in the corner.

Mercedes lifted him out of the chair, took his hand, and led him over to the gifts. She knelt down so they were eye to eye. "Cypri, now that you've opened your presents, you're going to get to do something even more fun that will make lots of boys and girls as happy as you are right now. And this is something that only a prince like you can do." She gestured at the stack of presents behind them. "You and Daddy are going to give presents to boys and girls who are sick and hurt and you're going to make them feel better and not be sad. Won't that be wonderful?" Cypri had been frowning, but at Mercedes's cheerful tone and bright smile, he, too, began to smile and nod.

The older woman stepped in next to Boho and said softly, "Perfectly done. The obligations of a ruler are presented as a treat. You are very fortunate, your grace."

"Yes, yes, I am."

He joined his wife and child and kissed them both. He then helped Mercedes to her feet, and taking each of them in a hand, he led Cyprian back to his toys and new friends. He and Mercedes stepped aside. "So, what do you want me to do?"

"Go to New Hope. Let him take gifts to the children in hospital there."

"I won't allow him to see anything truly horrible," Boho warned.

"Yes, of course, that's fine, but so many of these children lost their entire families on Kronos. We need to try to help."

9

LAYING PLANS

"OKAY, I THOUGHT you were crazy before. Now I *know* you're crazy," Jahan said. Tracy gave her a hurt look.

He was the only human in the midst of Isanjo, her extended family to be precise. Great-Grandfather Pelan was hunched in his armchair. His granddaughter, Jahan's mother Foss, was tenderly smoothing his ragged fur. Babies crawled on the floor of the tree house and older children tested out their climbing skills on the dangling vines and the thin branches this high in the great tree. When the winter came and the vines shriveled, ropes would replace them. Teenagers kept an eye on the younger kits. All the adults were gathered around Tracy as he sat uncomfortably on a chair designed for far narrower posteriors. She noticed that he had lost weight in the intervening months since he had left the *Selkie*.

They were in the family grove situated south and east of Shuushuram, the capital city of Cuandru. Not the best neighborhood but comfortably solid with good neighbors, shops, and decent public schools. It was a long way from the area north of the city that catered mostly to their human overlords. Here, there were no lifts, just ropes and handholds. The only reason Tracy had been able to reach the family room was because of the lift they had rigged for Pelan, who was now too old to climb.

Her husband touched the base of her neck like the caress of a feather. "Just hear him out." Tageri had always had the power to calm her worst impulses. Jahan sighed and nodded.

Tracy set aside the cup of tea he had been offered. "We've got to have intel. I think I have a way to get it, but I need master builders. I need Isanjo."

"In what capacity?" It was Jahan's brother and Kielli's father. Dulac was an orbital steelworker who rotated up to the shipyards every ten days. Though now with the push to build ships at an ever-faster pace, the construction crews worked twenty straight days. There had been accidents and deaths because of the intense schedule, and Jahan worried for her brother's safety. "Here we're subcontractors. Aboard your League ships, we're servants. Or are you going to make us *hombres* in O-Trell?"

"I can't do that, but I'll see you get paid and paid well, and you'd be helping the war effort."

"Yeah, fuck your war!" It was Jahan's youngest sister, Lenna, who also worked on the platforms. Three of the kits on babysitting duty were hers. Fatherless now because her husband had been a batBEM aboard one of the ships destroyed when the Blue had been defeated. Tracy jerked back at the intensity of Lenna's rage. "I lost my Avvam to your damn war. Why should we do *shit* for you?"

"Because war comes to all, whether you want to be involved or not." Jahan knew that Tracy had a quick temper, but he was holding it in check though it was clearly an effort for him to do so. "Look, I understand this is a hard ask." He got a faraway look then shook off the reverie. "I've come a long way from that cocky young lieutenant who did his first tour in O-Trell. I've seen firsthand how our government has treated you. As a result of some of those lessons, I ended up aboard a trading vessel with a mostly alien crew. And they taught me a lot. If I can change my attitudes, maybe this government can, too, and the best way to work toward that is for us to all be united in this fight."

Jahan was touched but could see the words hadn't swayed a number of her relatives. "He's being modest. He ended up cashiered and disgraced because he defended a bunch of half-alien, half-human kids from the humans who wanted to kill them. He shot his own kind to protect ours, and when the government tried to cover it up—"

"Did cover it up," Tracy interrupted. "Otherwise, you wouldn't have to be telling them about it. *Which I wish you wouldn't.*"

He was blushing and looked uncomfortable. Jahan turned a severe look on him. "You … hush. I'm singing your praises."

"And embarrassing me."

"Tough! And if you want our help, then … *hush*!" She turned back to her sister. "I spent almost fifteen years working alongside Tracy. We all owned shares in the ship. We shared in the profits. When he was recalled to duty, he turned the ship over to me. Yeah, he would occasionally say something that was casually bigoted. He's a product of his culture, but when he was called on it, he owned up to his biases—probably wouldn't hurt for us to do the same—and he sure as hell didn't act on them. The other thing I know is that if Tracy's got a plan, it's probably a damn good one. So, I think we should listen and probably help."

Old Pelan gave a dusty chuckle. "You sure have gone from thinking he's crazy to signing up in a light-speed second."

Jahan opened her mouth to object, then snapped it closed. "Okay … yes … Look, you've all seen the pictures from Kronos, and I was fucking there! Do you want to see our mother trees burning? Our world reduced to rubble?" Horrified silence gripped the room as they contemplated that image.

A discreet cough brought their attention back to Tracy. "For better or worse, we humans have the only military. And I understand that we disarmed all the civilized races, and that's on us, but right now we're the only game in town, and you need protection, and we need help."

"And what do your admirals and generals think about this plan of yours?" It was Foss, Jahan's mother, who had turned away from the brazier where she had been grilling the family dinner.

Tracy's expression was a study in indecision. "Oh, shit," Jahan said. "You're going rogue."

His mouth worked for a moment, and then he said, "Okay, I admit I won't be telling the high command what we're going to try until we either succeed or fail. And if we fail, I give you my word that I'll take the fall. None of this will come back on you."

"How can you possibly guarantee that?" Tageri asked.

"He's got friends in high places," Jahan said, and slid a

sideways glance at Tracy.

"Wouldn't that mean they'd be more likely to protect him and burn us?" Lenna challenged.

Tracy gave a snort of laughter. "Trust me, they wouldn't."

"I'm more worried you're going to get my daughter and great-nephew killed," Foss said. "I'm assuming the *Selkie* is a part of your plan?"

"Yes—"

Jahan interrupted. "Oh, Mama, like we couldn't get killed running supplies for the League." She turned to Tracy. "So, what would we be doing?"

"Running supplies."

✦ ✦ ✦

THE CABIN FELT like a yawning cavern. Mercedes's breaths seemed loud, but it was actually just the air filtration system. She sank down on the edge of her bunk and laid a hand on one of the pillows. A short dark hair was all that remained of Boho's presence. She hadn't yet allowed Venia to pack away the air mattress where Cypri had slept on the floor next to their bed. The presence of her little boy had curtailed romance, but she couldn't stand having him in a different cabin. She and Boho had had one frantic coupling while he was off with Hayden. The years they had spent together had given them a comfortable familiarity. She certainly didn't see stars when they made love, but at least he had become somewhat more attentive to her desires. She ran a hand across her lower lip, remembering the touch of another man's embrace. Soft kisses that gave way to gentle bites—

Mercedes leaped to her feet and pushed aside the memories and the sudden wash of heat through her pelvis. "You would think after four years you could put him out of your mind," she said aloud to the room. She bent and gathered up the blanket from Cypri's bed. With a clunk, the handheld game that had been one of his birthday presents fell out of the folds. "Oh, dear." She hoped the discovery of the missing gift would not bring on a storm of tears. She knew Elizabeth would know how to handle it. She just hoped Boho stayed patient. Of course, the trip to New Hope and the hospital visits might distract Cypri from noticing the missing game.

She keyed it on, curious to see what game her son had been playing. It was a maze game where a player had to pilot a ship through an entire series of obstacles to land the ship. She played for a few minutes until an incautious finger twitch sent her ship into the path of an asteroid and it exploded in a spectacular display. She found herself remembering the maze of asteroids the corsairs had constructed around their base. It had done them little good against the assembled might of the League's star ships.

But what if the maze wasn't formed with big rocks?

She sank back down onto the bunk, fingers closed tightly on the game. She didn't want to look like a fool in front of her assembled command staff. A private call to Ernesto was in order. She could count on him to give her a blunt assessment of her idea without consideration of her rank or her feelings.

As she headed for the door another small voice whispered, *you know who else would do that ...*

Go away, she ordered, and she wasn't sure if it was meant

for the voice or the ghost that she was unable to exorcise.

✦ ✦ ✦

"WHERE ARE WE supposed to put them all, sir?" Lieutenant Flintoff was scrupulously polite, but Tracy could see her confusion when the orbital elevator began disgorging Isanjo, all of them carrying rucksacks, and all of them headed for the small squadron in their three adjoining berths. In the end, he had ninety-three volunteers, not counting Jahan and Kielli who were going to be staying with the *Selkie* and would rendezvous with them in the asteroid belt in the Wasua system. Tracy and his officers were all standing in the outer ring of the main station that gave direct access into the umbilicals. "I mean, every available bunk has been assigned to our own *hombres* and *fusileros*." As she talked, Flintoff's confusion was morphing into quiet panic.

Tracy gave her an encouraging smile. "They're Isanjo. They have sleeping hammocks that they can secure from the ceilings in the launch bays and down in the cargo hold. And don't worry, I've instructed Chang to expand our food supplies. We'll be taking sixty-three." He looked first at the captain princess and then at the vizcondé. "That will leave only fifteen for each of you to accommodate."

Petek's chin jutted out. "With respect, sir, I must protest this. To expect my men to share quarters with these squirrels … it's not to be borne and I will not tolerate it!"

As had so often happened in his life, Tracy's body and quick temper reacted before his mind caught up. Almost before he knew it had happened, he had Petek by the throat, had propelled him across the corridor and slammed him into the far wall. Petek was wheezing, his fingers clawing at Tracy's hand. Tracy loosened his grip slightly.

Now that he was well and truly in the situation there was nothing for it but to go with it.

"Really?" Tracy growled. "You won't tolerate it? Well, I say you *shall, sir*."

Petek was matching him glare for glare. They were so close that Petek's breath puffed against Tracy's face. It was an errant, distant thought in the moment, but Tracy noted his bad breath. "You have laid hands on me, sir. I demand satisfaction!" The challenge would have been more impressive if it hadn't emerged as a throttled squeak.

"*Ay Dios mio*, not this crap again. I wish to hell the academy hadn't promoted this stupid custom. No, I am not going to duel with you. You, sir, are insubordinate. You have questioned a direct order from your commanding officer and have undermined good order and discipline. Now, would you like to try this again? What do you say, *Captain*?"

"*Vete al diablo!*" Petek spat.

"Wrong answer." A crowd was gathering: a number of officers from all three ships and some of the *hombres* returning from shore leave. Tracy spotted young Oort. "Lieutenant Commander, get over here."

"Sir!" He arrived quivering like a racing greyhound.

"How would you like to be a captain?"

The boy's Adam's apple bobbed up and down. "Uh … uh …"

"I'll take that as a yes." Tracy waved over Beatrisa. "As the other senior captain present, please record that Lieutenant Commander Oort has received a field promotion to captain and assign a security detail to escort Captain Petek to the brig."

"Yes, sir. Do you wish him confined aboard the *Swiftsure*, or the military brig here?" the princess asked.

"I don't want to take the time to deliver him to Hellfire. Lock him up here. I'll be drafting my letter of reprimand and my request for a special court-martial."

Valada-Viers gave a snap of his fingers and two *fusileros* came clattering over. "You heard the captain," the XO said.

As the soldiers escorted Petek away, he yelled back over his shoulder. "You shall be hearing from my father!"

Tracy rubbed at his chin. "Is this the moment where I should tell you that I went to school with your dad and that we were friends?" Petek gaped at him. "Yes, I believe that it is." Tracy made a shooing gesture to send the threesome on their way.

Valada-Viers leaned in and said softly, "Are you sure this is wise, sir?"

"Oh, I'm pretty sure that it's not, but I had a hell of a time getting the Isanjo to volunteer, and I need them a hell of a lot more than I need a bigoted aristocratic prick, no offense," he added belatedly to his XO." He gave Beatrisa a sideways glance. "And how do *you* feel about Isanjo aboard your ship?"

"I'm fine with it, though I'm curious as to what you're planning," she said.

"I'd like to second that, sir," Valada-Viers said.

"In good time. Now help Flintoff get the Isanjo settled. She looks on the ragged edge of hysterics."

Valada-Viers gave him a quick grin. "Right away, sir."

Beatrisa planted her fists on her hips and looked up at him. "My sister said you were not at all in the usual mold. She was right."

"You checked up on me?"

She gave him a quick smile. "Of course. I've been in the service since I graduated from The High Ground. I know how many nincompoops there are wearing an officer's brass. Now I'd best go get my Isanjo settled." She snapped off a salute and headed down the umbilical toward her ship.

Tracy beckoned to Oort to join him. "I apologize for springing this on you. Can you handle it, or do we hold here while I ask fleet headquarters for a replacement?"

There was a wild light in the younger man's eyes and two hectic red spots high on his cheeks. "I can do it, sir. And I … I can't thank you enough for this opportunity. I won't let you down! I swear it! And if there is any service I can—"

Tracy patted the air. "*Cálmese joven*, you don't have to offer your firstborn. You're a scholarship student, so I know you're smart, and I'd rather have you than some thoroughbred patrician spraying his decaying family tree."

"Kiss me, Kate!" Ryszard blurted out.

"A man who knows his Cole Porter." Tracy clapped a hand briefly on the young man's shoulder. "You've managed to impress me even more."

Oort gave him a shy glance. "My family brought a collection of Broadway musicals with them from Earth. I grew up listening to them."

"Do you sing?"

"Not a note. In fact, people beg me not to." He gave a

theatrical sigh. "I'm a grave disappointment to my family."

Tracy clapped him on the shoulder. "We'll try to make them proud in other ways."

"Yes, sir!" A textbook salute and the light of hero worship in the brown eyes. Tracy gave a mental sigh and prayed like hell that nothing he did would dim that light. Oort rushed off to see to his Isanjo.

A few minutes later Flintoff returned. She was looking very worried. Tracy was forcibly reminded of a kitten or baby bunny faced with something terrifying. "Yes, Lieutenant?"

"Sir, this may be presumptuous, sir, but my foster mother has a lot of sway with people—"

Tracy held up an admonishing hand to stop the tumbling words. "Thank you, but that won't be necessary, Lieutenant. Consider this to be an object lesson. The sacred first rule of Officer Career Advancement is this: misery is directly proportional to the amount of embarrassment you bring upon your Commanding Officer. Also, shit rolls downhill. Learn it well. You are dismissed, Lieutenant."

"Yes, sir!"

What he saw in the girl's blue eyes was a match to what he'd seen in Oort's. Tracy prayed harder.

✦ ✦ ✦

BOHO LINGERED IN the door to the sunroom/playroom where the sick and injured children had gathered. Cyprian was darting from child to child, presents clutched in his chubby hands. His eyes were sparkling with excitement. *Yes, my son is a far better person than I and will grow up into a far better man. I would never willing have given away my presents when I was his age.*

Boho's smile deepened and he shook his head. Mercedes had been so right to make this suggestion. He stepped back, leaving Cyprian with his nanny, new friends, doctors, nurses, and guards, and went to meet the hospital administrators who would no doubt scream for more supplies and more money. He couldn't disagree, but he wanted something in return.

One doctor stood out in the knot of men waiting to take him on a tour of the various hospitals. Unlike the others, he didn't have the look of an administrator. His white coat was rumpled; one pocket sagged from the weight of a medical scanner. He also had an old-style stethoscope hung around his neck. His shock of white hair set a stark contrast with his dark skin, and he leaned on a cane with a silver dragon with ruby eyes for the grip. He was also almost as tall as Boho. Introductions and bows were exchanged. The older doctor with the cane didn't bow. He thrust out his hand. Anselmo stepped forward, prepared to remonstrate with the man, but Boho waved him back. He was more intrigued than piqued, so he accepted the proffered hand.

"Well, shall we begin?" Boho said. He noted as they moved through the wards and rode shuttles to nearby medical centers that Engelberg kept studying him with frowning intensity. As they were walking down a long hall on their way to inspect a trauma center, Boho fell into step with Engelberg. "It seems you have something to say to me."

"I'd like to if we could ever get past this dog and pony show. Do you really give a shit about seeing another operating theater, or would you like to hear an actual report?"

The chief administrator, a man who rejoiced in the plebeian name of Smith, overheard and, jowls quivering, came rushing back. "Ah, Highness, I'm afraid Michael is our resident curmudgeon. I hope you will—"

"Actually, I think Doctor Engelberg makes a valid point. Why don't we retire someplace where I can sample your coffee? I'm told hospital coffee is notoriously bad. I'd like to see if it can dislodge O-Trell coffee as the absolute worst." There were polite and awkward chuckles, and they made their way to a cafeteria.

There were a handful of tired nurses and doctors, and a few tables occupied by sad and worried people, no doubt family members of patients currently undergoing care. Anselmo smoothly moved them all out, and Boho and the seven physicians settled at a table. Boho sent his security detail for beverages and food. Then folding his hands in front of him as he sat at the head of the table he ordered, "Talk to me."

They did. There were requests for troop transport ships to be designated to carry patients back to New Hope. There was the expected request for seventy million Reals to expand the wards and operating theaters. A request that doctors be brought in from other planets to bolster the exhausted staffs at the various hospitals.

Engelberg interrupted. "Here's one thing that could help right now. Take any promising women in the nursing programs and move them over to medical school for training as doctors. We need manpower, so why not make it woman power?"

The chief administrator gave an indulgent and also embarrassed chuckle. "Doctor Engelberg has a new young wife to whom he is very partial. It might color his opinions."

"My wife may be called a nurse, but she's a fucking brilliant researcher. How many more women are being underutilized because of custom? And it seems like in a crisis this custom can go hang."

Smith's smile was becoming more of a grimace. "Well, Michael, what good is it to win the war if we lose ourselves?"

"Not being dead?" Engelberg snapped back.

Boho decided it was time to insert himself. "Well, as a man married to a woman who is certainly a break from custom, I think your suggestion has merit and should be investigated." He gestured to Anselmo, who made a note on his TapPad. "Now, however, I have a few *requests* that would go a long way toward getting you what you need. I want more doctors working here on New Hope, and those recently graduated from your superior medical schools, to start lining up at the recruitment stations I'm about to establish here in the temperate zone. Nurses as well. We're building ships at a furious pace. We need medical personnel aboard those ships." Glances were exchanged around the table, then nods of acquiescence.

"Excellent. Next, we're calling up pretty much anybody able-bodied enough to get through basic training and pull a trigger. Which means we're going to have more women serving. Primarily in support positions, but they will be rubbing shoulders with actively serving troops. What we don't need are a lot of them getting knocked up, so we're bringing a bill to the floor of parliament that will lift the ban on contraceptives for active military personnel. Which means we're going to need a stable and legal supply of drugs. We don't want to be relying on the black-market trade in the stuff. You have a number of pharmaceutical companies here on New Hope. We need to get a few manufacturing birth control. So, if any of you might possibly have a lead on where samples can be obtained, the crown would be grateful." Boho had thought that might raise some objections, but no one demurred. It seemed doctors were more liberal than the average citizen when it came to women's health.

"I need older physicians, maybe even retired doctors, to volunteer to train first responders on various League worlds. Some of the newer colonies aren't as well organized." Glances were exchanged and then nods of agreement went around the table. Boho stood up. "Good, then we're agreed. I'll get you your money. You get me my bodies. And now, I have to get back to my son." He drained the last of his coffee. "And by the way, your coffee is gourmet quality compared to O-Trell's."

He headed for the door with Anselmo at his side and the detail walking just behind. Engelberg limped to catch up. "So, this is what you do. Convince people to do things they don't want to do and make them feel like it's their idea?" the doctor said.

"Pretty much," Boho replied. *Women, too,* he mentally added.

They met up with Elizabeth, Cyprian, and Hayden in the lobby of the hospital. His son had fallen asleep, and Elizabeth was holding him. His head was on her shoulder and his arms wound around her neck. His soft brown curls brushed at his cheek, and something seemed to squeeze his heart. Boho stepped forward and took Cypri out of her arms. The child murmured an inarticulate objection but had soon gripped his father's neck. Boho kissed the top of his head.

"Where to now, sir?" Anselmo asked.

"Back to Ouranos. I'm betting the parliament needs a reminder of just who is in charge."

Anselmo grinned at him. "Excellent, sir. I do love cowing politicians."

✦ ✦ ✦

THE FUCKING, FAWNING press made it virtually impossible for Tracy to avoid seeing images and vids of the royal family. He didn't mind so much when it was just Mercedes, but when it was Mercedes and her son, resentment settled like a stone in the center of his chest. And when it was the crown prince and Cullen … resentment flared into rage.

Mercedes had left his arms, his bed, gone back to her husband, fucked him, and borne a child. Tracy had briefly suspected—*hoped*—the prince might be his, but Dalea had shot that down by simply asking, *"Wouldn't Mercedes have told you?"* He had to believe she would, which meant that once again she had placed the League above her own happiness, *their* happiness.

Apparently, their love meant nothing when weighed against the needs of empire.

Right now, the news feeds were filled with gushing stories about the little prince delivering gifts to sick and injured children on New Hope, and try as he might, Tracy couldn't avoid seeing Boho with that infernal pride-filled smirk, his hand resting lightly on the four-year-old's shoulder. Tracy didn't see much of Boho in the child; he looked far more like his mother.

Sadness replaced rage. Would he ever have a family of his own? Tracy mentally answered the question. *No.* It would be grossly unfair to any woman. His heart belonged to one woman and one woman only. It always would.

He forced himself to return to work. Work buried pain, forced aside the loneliness, unhappiness, and longing that always lurked in his hidden heart. And work was the one way he could aid his love; by helping her win this war.

10

TRAPS & TRIBULATIONS

"YOU ARE EITHER a fucking genius or crazier than a male Hajin in rutting season," Beatrisa said as they stood on the scarred surface of an asteroid and watched the frenzied activity around another longer, wider rock. *Infierno* fighters were being used to ferry large composite panels out of the *Selkie* and over to the asteroid where torches and suit jets flared in the darkness as spacesuited Isanjo maneuvered them into position and welded them together. This far out, the star that anchored the Wasua system was a distant pinpoint of light.

Tracy glanced over at her. Behind the faceplate of her helmet, her smile was evident. "I think that's a compliment. I'm going to take it as a compliment, so, thank you," Tracy said.

Suit jets flared as Oort boosted over to join them. He landed on one foot on an upraised section of rock and started to topple. In the almost nonexistent gravity, he began to float away. Tracy caught him by one windmilling arm and pulled him back onto the surface of the asteroid. He gave a salute. "The heaters, lights, and oxygen tanks have been set and tethered, sir."

"Excellent."

Another suited figure came flying to them. It was Jahan, using her tail as a rudder as she simply used inertia and a powerful leap to send her over. A memory resurfaced of another time when Jahan had come flying at him. A time when he lived under an assumed name, they had traded and smuggled, and life had been generally simpler and far less had been riding on Tracy's decisions. She didn't salute.

"We should have one half completed at the end of shift," the alien said. "It'll take three more shifts to finish and rig up the final touches. To really sell it, though, we should have a few bodies floating around the wreck."

"You gonna volunteer?" Tracy asked.

"Uh … No."

The princess looked thoughtful. "Not a terrible idea. We've got spare suits."

"Scans would reveal they were empty," Tracy demurred. "Just like they would have revealed a shell ship, which is why I wanted it built around an asteroid so it would read as having mass."

"If there is one thing, we Isanjo have, it's a whole lot of meat in our stores. We could stuff some of the suits with that. Would even read as animal matter if their scans are that sensitive."

"Okay," Tracy said. "Oort, get your people on that."

"Yes, sir." The young man sound giddy with glee. He boosted away.

"Just try not to barbecue our supplies when the shooting does start," Jahan said.

"Precooked for the celebratory banquet," Tracy said.

"Just as long as it isn't for a wake," Jahan said rather acidly.

"Hey, the Captain Princess says I'm a genius." He cocked an amused glance at Beatrisa.

"Or a rutting Hajin," Beatrisa reminded him.

"I am being overwhelmed with estrogen, and I'm outnumbered now," Tracy complained. "I'll remove myself so you can carry on insulting me behind my back."

"Oh, I'll do it in front of you, too," Jahan said with a laugh.

"I know you would. Carry on, ladies."

Tracy kicked off the surface of the asteroid, then fired his suit jets to send him toward the *Swiftsure*. From this vantage he could again admire the sleek lines of his beautiful ship. The bay doors were open for the *infiernos*. The ship's artificial gravity tugged him to the floor and his magnetic boots clicked onto the composite panels. He made his way to the personnel airlock and entered the ship proper. Kallapus was waiting to help him out of his suit and help him shrug back into his jacket. As he lifted his arm, Tracy got a whiff from his armpit. He wrinkled his nose. "Maybe a shower first, Kal."

"Very good, sir. One does tend to perspire in a suit."

"I would rephrase that as sweat like a pig," Tracy said.

They went to his cabin and Tracy took the three-minute shower that was standard for all O-Trell crew. As captain, he could have taken longer, but didn't think it was fair. Once dressed, he instructed Kallapus to bring a sandwich and coffee to his office.

Tracy settled behind his desk and ran his figures again.

The weight distribution did line up with an *Orden de la Estrella destructor*. His command staff, together with the top officers of the *exploradors*, had worked to calculate the amount of heat that would need to be generated to approximate the surviving crew. Now, he just had to get a scrambled message to Hellfire and Star Command to disregard the emergency beacon and distress call from the bogus ship. He would like to hope that the high command would have enough sense to realize that the ship wasn't actually in the registry, but he knew enough about the military to assume that FUBAR would occur if one was not careful.

The biggest worry was that the heat bleed from the frigate and the two smaller craft would show up and not be subsumed in what would seem to be the heat being given off by the damaged destroyer. He also knew that what he was going to ask of his small squadron was going to leave some number of his people dead. It wasn't enough to simply blow the shit out of the enemy ship. They needed to board and seize the ship and capture at least one living prisoner. Which reminded him that he needed to discuss the tactics Lieutenant Commander Lord Condé D'Shane Washington was going to employ. The two *exploradors* had only a small contingent of *fusileros*, but they would have to be folded into Washington's troops. They probably needed to start drilling together right away.

He reached for his radio and realized that he was stiff and that several hours had passed. Before he could stretch to ease his back, the voice of young Flintoff came over the intercom. "Sir, there is a priority encrypted message coming in from Hellfire." She sounded nervous, and with good reason;

priority messages from fleet command rarely held good news.

"Put it through," Tracy said, his tone level and calm while mentally he was saying, *don't fuck this up for us, don't give me an order I have to obey, don't fuck this up for us.*

The message arrived on his TapPad and Tracy ran it through decryption. It was the elderly admiral who was primarily in charge of supply and logistics. The holographic image resolved out of the chaos of encryption. The man's silver-grey spade beard and mustache set a strong contrast with his dark skin. "Captain Belmanor, the enemy has struck Ouranos; there are reports of heavy casualties. You are ordered to return to the capital for blockade assignment. Eringin, out."

The image faded. Cold and oily dread roiled through his gut. He pictured his father's apartment building in flames, the tailor shop reduced to rubble, his father dead in those ruins. His hand jerked toward his ScoopRing to send an urgent message—*Are you all right? Are you safe?—Dear God, let him be safe.* He froze before he keyed the ring. If he sent a message, it would prove he had received the admiral's transmission. They would then have no choice but to abandon their plan with the decoy almost completed. To do what? Guard the barn after the horses were well and truly gone? They were three ships, and the *exploradors* were hardly useful for planetary defense.

Oort wouldn't know about the order, but Beatrisa was another matter. The admiral might not have messaged her directly, but it was likely that she would hear the news from Mercedes. Tracy called up to the bridge. "Please contact

Captain Princess Arango for me."

"Aye, sir," Flintoff replied.

A few moments later, Beatrisa's holograph sprang to life in the center of his desk. "What's your pleasure, Captain?" she asked.

"Could you please join me aboard the *Swiftsure*?"

"Yes, sir. Is there a problem?"

Tracy didn't answer, just broke the connection.

Almost thirty minutes later, she entered his office. After snapping off a perfect salute, she said without preamble, "You were rude. Since I've never known you be rude, I have to assume you've heard about Ouranos, and the top brass has our tits and nuts in a wringer." She had kept her usual slightly bored and always sarcastic tone, but Tracy saw through the facade. Grief lay like a shadow in her eyes.

"Is your family safe?" he asked gently.

"Don't know yet. Mercedes contacted me. She's rushing to the capital. She sort of has to. The prince and the consort are safe. They managed to reach the bunkers just ahead of the bombardment. She's not sure about several of our sisters."

"I'm sorry. It's inadequate, I know, but ..." He made a vague gesture.

"You got people on Ouranos?"

"My father. He has a shop in Hissilek."

"Hissilek was hit pretty bad."

"Then maybe he doesn't have a shop anymore, and you obviously have a better source of information than I."

Beatrisa gave him a speculative look. "But I expect *you* have our orders."

Tracy pulled in a deep breath. "I do ... and I intend to

ignore them." The words rolled out as if they had weight. The silence that followed was equally heavy.

Beatrisa ran a hand across her shorn head, gave a soundless whistle, walked in a small circle, and finally looked at him. "May I know your reasoning, sir?"

"We have a chance to actually do something useful. The capture of an enemy ship would be of enormous help—"

"*If.* If we capture a ship."

"True, we have to hope the distress signal finds a target and that it draws them in. But I still feel it will be of more use than going back now, which would serve no useful purpose beyond handholding the justifiably terrified civilian populace. We're three ships. We won't do much to help prevent the next attack."

She studied him in silence for what felt like an eternity. Then Beatrisa said, "Terrible how that message was so garbled when it arrived, wasn't it, sir?"

"Yes. Yes, it was," Tracy said.

"I'll make a note of that in my log."

"Very good, Captain." He rubbed at his forehead. "Now, we just have to hope we catch a really big fish."

"That would go a long way to keeping us out of a court-martial," Beatrisa said.

"Well, if it should happen, just stick with me, Captain, I'm an expert at them."

"That is *not* comforting," she said.

✦ ✦ ✦

FIREFIGHTERS WERE BATTLING blazes across Hissilek. Most of

the fires were from the bombardment, but several had been started when League fighters had managed to down some of the enemy's fighters. Those ships had self-destructed, burning with fierce fire that consumed all but the barest remains of the ship and left nothing of the occupants. The toll on any surrounding buildings had been equally bad. With the amount of smoke and debris in the air, Mercedes was very grateful for her particulate respirator face mask. She noticed shell-shocked survivors picking through the ruins, many with just cheap cloth masks and a few with dampened scarves across their faces. She made a mental note to have O-Trell get particulate respirators into the first responders' kits, though right now they needed to arrange to have them distributed to people in Ouranos's hard-hit cities.

Glass was crunching beneath the soles of her boots. Around her, Mercedes could hear the whine of engines as cranes worked to shift debris and the ululating wail of ambulance flitters rushing to pick up the injured as they were freed from the wreckage. It was the cries of pain and grief, and the desperate words of encouragement from the first responders, that were the hardest to endure.

Three frightened dogs, one with most of his fur burned away, ran past her. A cat perched on a twisted girder arched its back and hissed at her. It wore a pretty collar dotted with pink crystal, which had a bell attached with a name etched into the silver—*Princess*. Mercedes wondered if the little girl who had owned the cat was somewhere nearby buried beneath the rubble.

She had heard from Boho that he and Cypri and Hayden were fine, along with Estella, Delia, and Izzara and their various offspring. They had made it to the bunkers buried beneath the northern hills before the enemy ships began their bombardment. Dulcinea had gone back into the city to try and help evacuate the schools and bring other children to the bunkers. No one had heard from her for almost eighteen hours, and Mercedes feared the worst. She had given a standing order to the rescue crews checking area schools to report if Dulcinea were found.

Lord Ian Rogers walked at her side. At times, his hand moved as if to touch her arm or shoulder and was quickly pulled back. Ian had been the head of her security detail. Now he was the director of the League's intelligence service, *Seguridad Imperial*, but usually referred to by the shorthand SEGU. She also had seven *fusileros* from the *San Francisco de Asis* serving as her security detail.

Once again, the alien attackers had vanished back into Fold before an effective counterattack could be marshaled. The fact they were willing to risk destruction by jumping into Fold this deep in a star's planetary system showed a disregard for their own lives and supported the idea that they had ships to burn. Mercedes wished she had that level of surplus. Each ship they lost was a tragedy. She wondered what it said about her that she was more concerned over the loss of the ships than the men and women that crewed them. The truth was it took longer to build a replacement ship than it did to find more people to be thrown into war's maw.

There was a supply center on a corner handing out bottles of water and MREs to the exhausted, shell-shocked people. A child with a soot-streaked face sat on a curb gnawing on one of the protein bars. Tears ran down his face as he stared dully at a point just a few inches from his face. Mercedes crossed to him.

"*Hola, pequeño.*" She knelt down in front of him, and he stared at her with empty eyes. "Do you know where your *mamacita* and papa are?" He shook his head. "Do you live near here?" He half turned and pointed at a pile of rubble where a multistory apartment building had once stood. All seventeen stories had come down, plunging into the basement and undoubtably killing the people who had managed to shelter there.

"I was riding my tricycle," he whispered.

And thus you lived, Mercedes thought. "Okay." Her throat hurt as she forced out the word. "You wait here. I'll get you some water."

She stood and hurried over to the first responders. There was a murmur through the crowd, and people began to curtsy and bow. Mercedes held up her hands. "Thank you, but none of this is necessary. Right now, we are all united, all equal, all one. Let's not waste time on trivialities." There were cheers from a number of people.

A limping Hajin had been walking by as she spoke. Keeping his eyes focused on the glass strewn pavement, he muttered, "Yeah, well, some are more equal than others."

Two of her security detail leaped forward, fists clenched. "No!" Mercedes's snapped command froze them in place even as the Hajin shrank back. While the physical reaction showed fear, the expression in the large eyes was defiant. "You're not wrong," she said. "But right now, those bombs aren't discriminating." She raised her voice to encompass the entire crowd. "And I want you to know that I will fight to defend *every* citizen of the League, whether human, Isanjo, Hajin, Tiponi, or Sidone. Upon that you can depend." She turned to the workers. "I need a bottle of water, please." A shy young woman handed it to her. "Thank you."

Before she could return to the shell-shocked child, the crowd began to gather close, as if her very presence would protect them. She shook hands with some of the men and hugged some of the women. Eventually, she made it back to the boy. She twisted off the cap and handed him the bottle. While he gulped down the water, she turned to one of her guards. "Please take him to the nearest refugee center."

"Majesty, I shouldn't leave—"

"Right now, I'm less concerned about an assassination attempt than I am about the welfare of my people." She eyed the other six members of her detail. "In fact, all of you get busy helping with the relief efforts. I'm quite certain that Lord Rogers is capable of defending me." She laid a hand lightly on the pistol she wore. "As am I."

They bowed and went off to be assigned. She and Ian continued walking down the rubble-strewn street. She stopped at a few more supply centers, handed out water and MREs, chatted with people and bestowed hugs. They were almost all pathetically grateful, and she felt like an utter fraud. She was their empress, and she had failed to keep them safe.

11

LOSSES

THE SUN WAS starting to set when she spotted a hunched figure digging at bricks and plaster with his bare hands. A partly burned sign lay in the street. *lmanor & Son*. The first few letters had been burned away, but she knew what they had been. *Belmanor*. Had it been by accident or had her wandering journey had a purpose all along? The old man hunched on the rubble was Alexander Belmanor, Tracy's father. She ran across the street and knelt down beside him.

"Alexander."

"Whu … whut?"

His speech was still slurred by his downturned mouth, legacy of a stroke years ago. A stroke brought on by Tracy's court-martial. A court-martial Mercedes had approved in an effort to hush up a massacre. The government had succeeded in hiding the truth, but it had resulted in an entire alien race simply vanishing from known space. To this day, no one knew where the Cara'ot had gone.

Sometimes Mercedes wished it had been the Cara'ot returning to take vengeance. She knew they could beat the Cara'ot. They had done it before. She wasn't so sure about this new lot. Perhaps humanity had met their match.

The old man was peering at her, then recognition dawned. "Majesty." He scrambled to his feet and executed an impeccable court bow, which was incongruous in the setting. Flickering flames lit the side of the old man's face.

"Alexander, what are you doing?"

"My shop was here. My staff had come in early to open. We had so many orders for tuxedoes for the Christmas holiday." Tears filled his eyes. "I hadn't felt well, so I stayed in bed an extra hour. I should have been here," he cried.

"And then you'd be dead, too." She laid a hand on his shoulder. "Come. You can't stay out here. It's getting dark and looks likely to rain. Come."

"Majesty, I could not—"

"I insist. Tracy will want to know you are safe. Have you contacted him?" He shook his head. "Well, we must see to that." Alexander gave one final devastated look at the burned out and collapsed building. He then went to pick up the partly burned sign.

"Majesty, is this wise?" Ian whispered. "To single out this one man when so many are in need?"

"Señor Belmanor made my wedding gown, Ian."

"Ah, of course. Yes, I understand."

Her ScoopRing tapped her finger in the rhythm that told her it was Boho. She keyed it on. His image appeared, seeming to stand upon the collapsed building. "Where the hell are you?"

"Touring the capital."

"Your son is scared half to death. You need to get out to the bunker. *Now.*"

Her patience snapped. All the death and destruction

turned to rage against the only target that was readily available. "So are thousands of other children who don't have the luxury of living parents and a nearly impenetrable bunker in which to hide. He needs to learn his duty, and I need to be allowed to do mine without you constantly hectoring and undermining me." She broke the connection and stood panting as she wrestled her anger into submission.

Ian stood politely off to one side; his gaze averted. "I'm sorry you had to hear that," Mercedes said quietly.

"Hear what, Majesty?"

"Oh, Ian, do you know that you are practically perfect?"

A sun seemed to ignite on his face, and he took several quick steps toward her, hand once more outstretched. "Oh, Mercedes, if only I could ease your—" He broke off at her dismayed expression and the quick backward step she had taken. "Ah, forgive me, Majesty. I forgot myself."

"Let it go, Ian, we have no time for personal theatrics right now." She glanced over at Alexander Belmanor, who seemingly was unaware of the drama that had just taken place. Memories and emotions tore through her, and she drew in a shaky breath. "And … and while I value you deeply, Ian, I do not … cannot … love you."

"I understand," he said through stiff lips.

No, you really don't, she thought.

The exchange with Boho had made her realize that bringing Alexander Belmanor anywhere near her husband was not wise. While Boho might not know the father well, he certainly knew the son, and they had shared a poisonous past. And she didn't want anything to bring memories of Thracius Belmanor to the forefront. Not when Cyprian was anywhere nearby.

"Let's get Señor Belmanor to a refugee center. And we'd best go see what, if anything, remains of the palace."

The answer was not much. The main building was heavily damaged. The small palace that had been Mercedes and Boho's home until her father's death was standing, but one outer wall had collapsed. Mercifully, the stables had been untouched and the Hajin and Isanjo grooms had released all the horses and had driven them out onto the chaparral and away from the attack. Three of the horses were lame, and one of the carriage horses had broken its leg, and when they arrived the Master of the Horse had been putting the suffering creature out of its misery. Why this, in the face of all the death and injury she had seen, left her throat tight and her eyes stinging Mercedes could not fathom.

They picked their way through the ruins while medics searched for survivors among the twisted bodies. Here and there some odd item had been spared, a vase, a tapestry, a single bookcase. The entrance to the basements had been blocked by falling debris. Mercedes and Ian joined with the rescue crews to pull away fallen beams, stones, and marble to free the handful of people who had managed to reach safety in time. They crept out, and Mercedes was once more delivering hugs and murmured words of encouragement. There were plaintive questions: *is Jessica all right? My husband? My daughter?* None of which she could answer, and during this her ScoopRing signaled her. It was the head of Home Defense.

Mercedes stepped aside to take the call. "Majesty, we have found Princess Dulcinea." She didn't need to ask

Dulcinea's condition. The man's tone and expression told all.

"Thank you, please send me the location," she said, and she was relieved that her voice didn't break. "I'll come at once."

"I had taken the liberty of checking on the condition of several other of your sisters, Majesty. By God's mercy, the convent where one of your sisters resides was spared. Unfortunately, the prison where Princess Julieta was incarcerated was bombed. While some prisoners escaped, your sister was not among them."

"Her condition?"

"She's not expected to live, ma'am."

"I see. Thank you, my lord."

✦ ✦ ✦

THE HOURS THAT followed Admiral Eringin's message had been hellish. Tracy had tried to contact his father, but all non-essential Foldstream communication had been shut down. He tried to push away the gnawing dread by touring the decoy as the Isanjo placed the final finishing touches on their Trojan ship. He returned to the *Swiftsure* tired and sick with worry for his father and the staff of the tailor shop. He had waved off Kallapus when the batBEM had inquired what he'd like for dinner. Tracy was staring unseeing at a report from Valada-Viers when the chime on his cabin door sounded.

"Come."

The Hajin entered carrying a tray with a rare steak, reconstituted vegetables, and a glass of red wine.

"I told you I'm not hungry," Tracy snapped. The alien ignored him and instead carried the tray to the small fold-down table and snapped open the napkin. "Excuse me, but are you deaf or ignorant?" Tracy growled.

"Jahan contacted me," Kallapus said. "Told me that you liked protein after a protracted spacewalk. And that you liked it bloody."

Tracy wrestled with the feeling of being handled, not sure if he liked it or not. Kallapus seemed to sense the direction of his thoughts. "Word has begun to trickle through the convoy about the attack on Ouranos. We are aware that you have family there, and since we're all counting on you to keep us from getting killed, sir, we are naturally concerned for your welfare."

Realizing that he had been churlish and not eating wasn't going to do one damn thing to change what might have happened to his father, Tracy acquiesced, reminding himself it cost nothing to be courteous.

"Thank you, I appreciate your thoughtfulness." He waved his dismissal, and Kallapus bowed his way out.

He was down to the final sip of wine when the lieutenant on the first watch called from the bridge. "Incoming message for you, sir." Lopamaua had the physique of his Samoan ancestors. Towering at six feet five inches and as broad as a stone plinth, he was an imposing figure. One expected a rolling bass from that body and instead there came a rather high piping tenor.

"Send it through." Tracy moved to his desk. A few moments later his father's voice came over the speaker. It was an old man's voice, thin and quavering.

"Tracy."

"Dad," Tracy said at the same time.

"They say I can only talk for two minutes."

"They don't want the enemy to pinpoint us," Tracy explained.

"Oh. Okay. Maybe I better not—"

"No, Dad. Stay on the line. How are you?"

"All right. But Bajit and Selcuk and Caleb are dead." Tears thickened his father's voice, and Tracy's own throat tightened when he considered the old Hajin who had been with his father since Tracy had been a little boy. "I had asked them to come in early and now they're dead. I killed them, Tracy. I did it."

"No, Dad. Those fuckers killed them. Where are you now?"

"At a shelter. The apartment building was damaged and … and … the shop. The shop is gone. I'm not sure how I'll manage."

"Don't worry, Dad. Like I told you when I came home, I've got money. You didn't have to work any longer."

"I wish I had listened. If I had retired, closed the shop, Bajit and the two youngsters would still be alive."

"No, Dad, and I didn't mean it that way, you mustn't think like that." There was a warning chime. "Wait. No, don't cut us off," he called to the faceless monitoring SEGU agents. "Dad, I love you." But he was talking to silence.

For a long time, he just sat at the desk remembering the years and weeks and days he had sat sewing next to Bajit before his scholarship had taken him to The High Ground and on to a very different life than the one into which he had been born. Bajit, with his soft lisp, seated behind a sewing machine. Bajit assuring Tracy of his father's love after Alexander had humiliated him in front of the man who was now Mercedes's husband. Later, Tracy had understood that his father had been manipulating him, forcing him to accept The High Ground scholarship. It had been an act of ultimate sacrifice. Bajit had known that. Tracy, stupid, angry, and eighteen, hadn't understood, but the gentle alien had.

He remembered Alexander and Bajit in long conversations about whether to follow the latest quirk in men's fashion or stick with the classic suits they had been tailoring. Occasionally, they had even played Go or chess together. Yes, Bajit had worked for his father, but that had been a partnership and a friendship. Was that where Tracy had learned, despite the bigotry of his society, to accept and work with aliens? Was the fact he had blended together humans and aliens in the war effort due to a simple tailor and his alien helper?

Tracy whispered a prayer for the lost lives, crossed himself, and hailed his XO. "Anthony, send the order. It's time we gave these sons of bitches a thrashing."

"Yes, *sir!*"

✦ ✦ ✦

DULCINEA'S BODY WAS in a classroom at one of the local elementary schools in a middle-class neighborhood. She was face down on the slate floor and bullet holes riddled her back. She had been shielding a young boy, but the powerful rounds from a strafing fighter had passed through the roof of the building as if it had been meringue, through Dulcinea's body, and through the little boy she had been trying to protect. They lay in death's embrace.

Mercedes had to step over the bodies of other little boys to reach her half-sister. She had seen the bodies of people subjected to violent death, but the images of six-year-olds with half their faces blown away, tiny bodies cut almost in half by a hail of metal, nearly broke her. She swayed, fought back the faintness, and sank to her knees at Dulcinea's side. She pulled the body of her sister into her arms. Ian stood in the shattered doorway and waved away the rescue workers, allowing Mercedes privacy.

"Why?" she whispered into her sister's ear. "Why did you leave? Why couldn't you stay where it was safe?"

And why did you leave and try to help when my husband didn't? That wicked, ugly thought added to the anger she was feeling. The twins had always been the sweetest and kindest of the nine princesses. They had also been inseparable even to the point of marrying brothers so they wouldn't be separated. She could not imagine how Delia was going to handle this loss of her other self. And to prove the universe was fundamentally unfair, Tanis, the most toxic of all the girls, survived. It also established that God had a very unpleasant sense of irony. She kissed Dulcinea on the forehead and laid her back down.

When she stood, rage had replaced horror and grief. "They will pay."

She next ordered Ian to take her to the hospital where Julieta lay dying. As the armored flitter made its way across the burning city, she called Estella and asked her to meet her there. The three of them were the first born and full sisters. Julieta had been the youngest. The fairy princess. But she had gambled everything by following her husband into treason and lost. He had paid for that on the gallows. Julieta had been sentenced to twenty years. *Well, at least she's been spared that,* Mercedes thought. She would die having only served four. Mercedes knew this trip to the hospital was an act of cowardice. Instead of going to the bunker and informing Delia that her twin was dead and telling an eight-year-old that her mother wasn't coming back, she would go sit with a woman who would be unaware of her presence. Mercedes began to shake. Partly from anxiety of the coming conversations, but also wondering how Cyprian would handle such news. Was it right for her to be aboard a warship? But after the attack on Ouranos, it was clear that no place was safe …

"We trade with Hidden Worlds."

Tracy explaining why he and the crew of the *Selkie* didn't want a lot of scrutiny, since some of their cargo came from worlds unknown to the League. Places off the beaten path …

Mercedes grasped at the thought and followed it to its ultimate conclusion. It did seem that this enemy force was singularly focused on the League. Which made sense, since they were a far bigger threat than a few scattered planets. *But those planets might be a place to protect the League's children.* She would order SEGU and military intelligence to start a search for the *Selkie.*

Which would terrify the crew and perhaps cause them to vanish.

Did Tracy have a way to communicate with his former shipmates? Maybe. Probably. *Or is this just an excuse to talk with him?* Thus far she had been good, avoided hearing his voice or seeing his image. She had just sent terse messages. But a request this big might require something more. She realized she was nervously spinning her wedding ring around and around her finger. Over four years since they had parted on Cuandru. Years spent imagining Tracy's touch during the more and more infrequent times when she and Boho had sex. She assumed Boho was seeking release elsewhere. She didn't care, as long as there were no more bastards, and since Cyprian's birth there hadn't been. Boho was clearly aware that he needed to protect Cyprian's sole claim to the throne. *No bastards,* she thought, and surpassed the urge to laugh hysterically.

The flitter banked sharply, bringing her back to the moment. They were coming in for a landing. Medical staff were waiting to rush her to her sister's room, and the doctor gave her a terse briefing as they walked down the halls. Only one decision was left to be made. Mercedes hadn't seen Julieta since her conviction. The intervening years of incarceration and prison fare had thickened the once slim body, not to mention seven pregnancies. Grey streaked the dark brown hair. Julieta was on a ventilator and tubes snaked from her arms. Her head looked misshapen where the right side of her skull had been crushed. She was floating in gel to try and ease the pain of the burns that covered much of her body. *Oh, little sister, where have you gone?* Mercedes throat ached so much she could scarcely swallow. The anger and betrayal were gone, replaced with weary grief. Ian pulled over a chair and Mercedes sat at Julieta's side waiting for Estella to arrive.

Her sister glided through the door, threw aside her coat,

and rushed to Mercedes's side. Estella had always been the most beautiful of the trio, and that beauty had not faded, only matured into the elegant woman who now hugged her tight.

"Is there any hope?" Estella asked softly.

Mercedes shook her head. "No. They didn't even bother to relieve the pressure on her brain. All that remains is for us to tell them when to ..." Mercedes waved at the machinery that was keeping Julieta's body in a facsimile of life.

Ian once again unobtrusively brought up a chair and placed it next to Mercedes. He then slipped out of the room.

"And Dulcinea?" Estella asked. Mercedes just shook her head. "I'll take Penelope," referring to Dulcinea's daughter, "unless Delia wishes to foster the girl."

"I'm sure Delia will take her."

"Does she know?"

"No. Neither of them knows. I thought we'd handle the easier task first," Mercedes said.

They sat in silence contemplating the motionless form of their sister. "Has she had a priest?"

"Yes. Not that she could confess."

"What about you? Have you forgiven her?" Estella asked.

"I don't know. She helped put me in Mihalis's hands. He was going to kill me and my unborn child. How do you forgive that kind of betrayal?"

"I think you have to try, Mer. You don't want to die with that burden on your soul."

A shiver went through her. *I have so many.*

12

SCHEMES & MORE SCHEMES

"MERCED ... MAJESTY," Tracy stuttered, trying to turn the use of her given name into a more appropriate salutation. His incoherence was understandable; it's disconcerting when the holographic image of your lover, your ruler, and your commanding officer appears in the center of your office. The message was so heavily encrypted that periodically static like red lightning ran through and distorted her image. He leaped to his feet, braced, and saluted.

"Tracy." It was a mournful cry.

So, it was going to be a different kind of conversation. He relaxed and eagerly devoured her features, blurred though they might be. She looked tired and her eyes seemed sunken. She was too thin, her lush curves reduced to sharp angles.

"Thank you for allowing my dad to call."

"Of course."

"What's this about? What's wrong?" he asked.

"I need to get in touch with Jahan and the *Selkie*, but SpaceCom has lost track of them. We traced them to the San Pedro *Cosmódromo* but then we lost track of them, and—"

"Actually, they're with me."

"What? Why?" A frown marred that high forehead. "Are

you using your squadron to *trade*?" Fury edged the words. "I can't imagine Beatrisa—"

"No, no." He patted the air, trying to ease her down. "They're helping me with a … a … project. They brought supplies."

"What project?"

"How about if I ask for forgiveness rather than permission?" he temporized.

She pressed a hand to her forehead. "Oh, God, you've got a scheme."

"Sounds like you do, too," he countered.

"You're not going to tell me, are you?"

"Nope. Better you have deniability in case it all goes pear-shaped. Then you can burn me like…" He broke off abruptly.

"Like I did before?" she said. He couldn't really read her expression in the flickering hologram.

"I wasn't going to say it. It would have been a cheap shot."

"Maybe you're finally getting past collecting grievances, Tracy."

"I can be taught. Now, what did you need?"

"I need to talk with Jahan and you. How soon can she join you?"

"Forty minutes. She can fly the *Talon* over."

"God, do you still have that ancient crate?" Mercedes said with a smile that seemed forced.

"Hey, it saved your royal ass," Tracy replied, and he also tried to smile.

"Granted. Get her over to this secured channel. I'll call back in forty-five."

"Yes, ma'am."

✦ ✦ ✦

HE LOOKED GOOD. Slimmer than when they had been together. There was more grey in his dishwater blond hair, but there was more grey in her hair, too. He also had the febrile look she remembered from school. Whatever he was up to, it had him wound tighter than a piano wire. She wearily levered herself out of the chair that had been set up in the secured compartment where classified information could be safely exchanged. She opened the door and stepped out into the bunker. It smelled of cooking food and a mass of humanity that hadn't had access to showers and changes of clothing. This particular bunker might have been reserved for the FFH and various critical government officials, but noble birth didn't mean a person didn't sweat.

Cyprian spotted her and ran to her. "Mama!" The way he hugged her, one would have thought she had been away from him for months rather than a few minutes. If Tracy and Jahan agreed, there was no way she would see her child again until this was over. She could not risk revealing the location of the Hidden World to their enemy. She clutched him even tighter, breathing in the smell of little boy and peanut butter, and blinked hard to hold back tears. *Please God, let them agree to help.* Perhaps she should step aside. Let Boho take command. Go with her son. Be a mother, not an empress.

... People shall have true peace at all time by our judgment.

The words of her coronation oath came back to haunt

her. She had sworn to protect them. All of them. Not just her child. Her sister's actions rose up and shamed her. Dulcinea had left her only daughter and gone to the aid of other women's children. How could she do less?

I have to part from you, but how will I bear not seeing you?

She rained kisses on her little boy and didn't let him go until it was time to call back.

✦ ✦ ✦

"AND WHOSE KIDS get to go? Just yours? Only the kids of the FFH? Only human kids? What's the rule here, Majesty?"

Jahan hadn't meant for it to come out quite so snidely, and frankly angry, but it had, and the words couldn't be recalled. The holograph of the tall human woman in her immaculate uniform was an imposing figure even with all the static. Jahan tried to superimpose the image of Mercedes dressed in a pair of Luis's pants and a stained tee shirt over the reality. It helped to quell the fear … a little. Tracy's glare was like a knife cutting at her. Since when had he gotten so respectful? As if he and the then *Infanta* hadn't been boinking madly the entire time she'd been aboard the *Selkie*. She decided she may as well go for the sheep rather than the lamb.

"Look, I've got kits, even a few grandkits. I don't want them burning in the trees of Cuandru. And there are Hajin fawns, and those fires will do a number on Tiponi shoots and Sidone frylings. So, I repeat—*whose kids get saved*?"

Mercedes had been looking shattered and guilty, but she

drew herself up and gave Jahan a haughty look. "We're talking millions here. How many Hidden Worlds have you got up your sleeves?" Her dark eyes flicked to Tracy.

He finally joined in. "A few. Some of them aren't all that lush, but livable. And one of them is really hidden. But we can't just start showing up with ships full of kids. We need to at least ask."

"And we find the ships to carry them," Jahan broke in. "We don't use League ships."

"Well, of course, we wouldn't use military vessels. Too much chance—"

"I mean any legit ships," Jahan interrupted. "We go to the people like us. The people living in the cracks, sliding by under the radar."

"In other words, criminals," Mercedes snapped back. Tracy closed his eyes as if pained.

Jahan gave a sharp laugh and nudged him hard with her elbow. "Relax, Tracy. The lady and I are just laying out the ground rules. You boys are so sensitive." Mercedes gave a faint laugh and Tracy looked annoyed.

"All right. I agree to your terms, but there better be a lot of these illegitimate ships out there."

"Oh, Princess, you have no idea," Jahan said.

"That's Empress to you, Jahan."

"Yes, ma'am."

The connection was broken. Tracy whirled on her. "*Princess? Princess?* Really? *Dios mio*, Jahan, she's the goddamn Empress of the Solar League!"

Jahan shrugged. "Yeah, and we knew her when. And you *really* knew her." She drew back her lips in a grin that revealed her fangs.

"And she still went back to that asshole husband and even bore him a son," Tracy said. "You know this is all about just getting her kid out of harm's way."

"Yeah, so … what? You want the kid to die?" Jahan asked.

"No, of course not … I just … I don't know." He ran an agitated hand through his hair. "I want the universe to be different," he said. "I was good. I'd come to terms with it. We hadn't communicated or spoken in four years, and now I'm hearing from her all the damn time and … and it's killing me."

"So, let's save her son. For her sake. And for the sake of my kits and my brother's kits, and all the others."

He closed his eyes, sighed, and nodded. "How soon can you be ready to leave?"

"Pretty much immediately. All the supplies are off-loaded. The decoy's done."

"Do you want to take back the Isanjo workers?" Tracy asked.

"First, I'm not sure I can fit all of them and their tools aboard the *Selkie*. And second, wouldn't you like to have them to assist with the boarding action?" she asked.

"How did you …?"

She shrugged. "How else are you going to get a prisoner or three? Nobody's as good at spacewalking as my people. And we know how to fight."

Tracy paced behind his desk. Lit a Tiponi stem stick. Took a puff. Put it out. Gave her an embarrassed look from beneath his long lashes. "There's no polite way to ask this, so

I'll just say it. How can we be sure that … that …"

"That the evil BEMs won't shoot you all in the back the minute we have the chance?" She was struggling to control her fury.

"You know I don't think that, but some of troops are going to … wonder."

"Tell them this. Yeah, we're a subject people, and, yeah, some of us hate you humans. But right now, there's a Big Bad out there that doesn't care who they kill. And you're our only chance to beat them so for now we're all on the same side."

She could see he was considering it. He had picked up the Lucite cube that held a small Sidone weaving and was turning it around and around in his hand. After several long minutes had passed, he shook his head.

"Look, I appreciate the offer, but I don't think I can. It adds another variable to an already unpredictable situation. The Isanjo stay on the ships." She stared at him until he was forced to drop his eyes.

Another awkward silence ensued. Finally, she broke it. "Well, okay, then. I better get going." She leaped up onto the desk so that she and Tracy could be eye to eye. She allowed her long tail to lightly brush his cheek. "I know you're going to be a macho asshole and lead this boarding party. Try not to get killed, okay? Or at least tell me you have a will ready and that the crew and I get the *Selkie*."

He smiled at her and rested a hand briefly on her shoulder. "I'll answer those statements in order. Yes. I'll try. And yes—though you have me rethinking my bequests right now."

She hopped down and headed for the door. "I'll let you

know what the Freeholders say. Then I'll hit Al-Nefud and feel them out."

"What about the other three?" Tracy asked.

"I'll get to them after I see how it plays with the folks we know really well."

"Good luck."

"You're the one who's going to need it," she said and left.

✦ ✦ ✦

"FOR FUCK'S SAKE, Mercedes! You're proposing to send my son, our only child, *the heir to the throne*, to some planet we've never heard of into the hands of people we don't know and probably can't trust."

Boho had to stop and pant. Anger was making it hard for him to breath. They were in a series of small rooms that had been carved into the rock and set aside for the use of the royals. In contrast with the rest of the bunker, which contained cots, chemical toilets, community showers, and a shared kitchen, it was opulently decorated with some of the more precious and antique furnishings from the palace. Boho was proud of that decision. Otherwise, centuries of history would be so much cinder now. Other sections of the bunker rooms held the stained-glass windows from the cathedral and art from the museums.

"He's not your son ... I mean, he's more than just our child," she hurriedly added. "He's a symbol to all the people of the League. Cyprian belongs to them as much as he is ours. We don't just rule, Boho, we serve. And he won't be going alone. We'll be evacuating children from all around the

League. Assuming the people on these Hidden Worlds agree. And while I can't speak to the honesty of the people on these worlds, the people who can make contact *are* people that I trust."

"And just who are these people that you trust so much?" He stalked over to the small bar and splashed whisky into a glass.

"People I met when I was traveling on that trading vessel."

"And you're not going to tell me who they are," he gritted. He threw back the drink. It burned on the way down and did little to ease the tension in his chest.

"No, because you'd send Anselmo to dig into every aspect of their lives, and since they're not all that trusting of the authorities, it would ruin everything."

"If you do this, I'm going with him," Boho said.

"No, you're not."

That left him gaping at her. "What? No! I won't do whatever bullshit task you make up for me! I'm—"

"I'm giving you a squadron."

The glass started to slip from his hand. He clutched at it. "Really?"

"Yes. I need you. Anselmo and Rafe can handle procurement and recruitment from here."

"In which fleet?" Boho asked.

"Mine." She took his hands in hers, looked down, and then glanced up at him from beneath her lashes. "It would help me … knowing you're close. And you can be brilliant when you pay attention. I'm not; I'm a plodder, and right now we need brilliance."

The knot in his chest dissolved. He hugged her to him. "I won't let you down," he whispered into her curls. They stood in the embrace for a long time. He then held her at arm's length. "Who have you got for brilliance in the Gold? And don't say Talion. The man's a fighter and brave as they come. He'll stand toe-to-toe with the enemy and slug it out, but he's a blunt instrument."

"I've got a few captains who command squadrons. But we can discuss all that later. Right now, we need to see to the relief efforts. Our people need us." She tucked his arm through hers and began guiding him to the door. "And we won't have an answer for many weeks, depending on the location of these planets. We can hold our little boy close until then."

13

GIVE 'EM HELL

THEY HAD BEEN on alert and on low power for seventeen days, and Tracy knew that he would soon be hearing from fleet headquarters. They would be expecting his squadron to arrive at Ouranos in two days, and when they didn't all hell was going to break loose.

The patience of his crew had also been exhausted. They had been enduring cold meals and low temperatures in the ship. They had also been subsisting mostly on protein bars since the actual meat had been stuffed into suits and set to float around the fake destroyer.

The crews of the two small scout ships had it easier; they got to take turns pretending to be the advance sentry for the crippled destroyer, so they could turn up the heat and serve hot food during those rotations. His people aboard the frigate didn't have that luxury. They had to remain in a cocoon of asteroids that provided their cover. They had been continuously beaming the distress signal nonstop, but so far no one had taken the bait. Tracy knew he couldn't keep this up indefinitely, or he would have a crew unable and perhaps unwilling to fight. The breaths of his bridge crew formed pale white banners on the frigid command deck. He decided he would give it three more days and then assume he'd gambled and lost.

He had just begun to stand up when a signal came in from the *Wasp*. Ostensibly, it was being beamed to the destroyer. It was Beatrisa herself and not her communications officer. "They're coming."

"How many?" Tracy asked.

"Praise God, only one … so far." She broke the connection.

Tracy raked his crew with a glance. The depressed looks and frowns were gone, replaced with excitement and worry. "Let's do this." Valada-Viers stepped off the elevator. Tracy clapped him on the shoulder. "The bridge is yours, Commander. Give 'em Hell."

"I urge you to reconsider. Let me lead the assault," his XO said.

"We've discussed this. If this fails, you have a better chance of surviving if I'm not around to muck things up during the board of inquiry. Your status also offers more protection to the crews. Now remember, pull the bastards in as close as you can before you detonate."

"Yes, sir. And … good luck, sir."

Rather than wait for the elevator to take him down the seven levels, Tracy gripped the sides of the access ladder and slid down to the lowest level, which housed the launch bay. As he ran to the armor locker, he radioed Beatrisa. The communication crews from all three ships had labored for many hours to construct a relay that would make it appear that the scout vessel on patrol was radioing the decoy destroyer and not the ships hidden among the rocks.

"Report."

"Weapons are hot, sir. They are still thirty-two minutes from effective range."

"You have your orders."

"Yes, sir. Our tactics are clear."

Her voice in his ear vanished. Tracy hoped their exchange had been sufficiently oblique that should the enemy actually understand League Spanish, they wouldn't understand the significance. Tracy ripped open his locker and pulled out his combat armor. Kallapus was suddenly at his side stripping off his jacket and assisting him into the armor. Just before he dogged down the helmet the Hajin said, "Kick their asses, sir!"

Tracy bumped fists with him since the batBEM lacked a radio and couldn't hear him with the helmet sealed. All around him *fusileros* were finishing final weapons checks and heading to the shuttles. *Infierno* pilots were closing their canopies. They were now producing a lot of heat. Tracy just hoped that the heaters they had installed in the decoy and the engines of the *Wasp* were sufficient to hide the presence of the other two ships. He took his place in the shuttle alongside Commander Condé Washington. The commander of the *fusileros* had a smile more predatory than amused, and his teeth were bared, setting a contrast against his dark skin.

"Let's go bag some bad guys, Captain."

"You should be on the other shuttle," Tracy said.

"Commander Valada-Viers said to stay close and watch your behind."

"You're my officers, not my damn nannies."

"Take it up with Anthony. I'm just a simple soldier following his orders."

"You're both assholes are what you are," Tracy said.

"That, too," Washington agreed with a grin.

Tracy tapped his wrist piece, and his heads-up display sprang to life. From here he could monitor not only the view from his bridge, but from the bridges of the *Wasp* and the *Audacious* and the cameras on the decoy. His eyes flicked from image to image. He watched tensely as the *Wasp* boosted for the supposed safety of the destroyer. Closing fast was the alien ship. The protrusions and angles of the ship weren't normal to human eyes. In fact, they repelled the eye as if space itself was twisting. Yes, he had seen the images from all the other encounters, but perhaps it was the fact he would soon be clamping his boots on the skin of the alien vessel and that the survival of the men and woman under his command depended on how fast they could neutralize the ship that made the thing even more terrifying.

The enemy ship had fired those dangerously destructive missiles. ETA ten minutes. The *Wasp* responded with chaff and intercept drones. Beatrisa ordered defensive maneuvers. Tracy switched to the cameras on the decoy. Upped the magnification until he could see both ships. Sharks and minnows leaped to mind. *Dear God, I have a princess of the royal family facing off against a ship seven times the size of her own. I must be out of my mind.* Cassutt, on the weapons deck, remotely triggered the lasers they had placed on the decoy ship. They were out of range of the advancing ship, but it made a nice light show and again helped sell the illusion that this was an actual ship.

Minute after agonizing minute crept past. Chaff and

decoys began to detonate the incoming missiles. The *Wasp* was buffeted. One got through, and debris flew off the small ship in that balletic movement that weightlessness created. Another flick of the eye and Tracy brought up the damage report. Bad but not crippling. Beatrisa was retreating while still throwing everything she could at the incoming ship.

Please, bad guys, don't hold out of range and pound on our Trojan Horse, Tracy prayed, while at the same time he was trying to mentally communicate to Valada-Viers *not yet, not yet, let them get closer.*

Beatrisa barked an order, and on one of the small displays Tracy saw the *Wasp* fire grapples into a small, tumbling rock of perhaps a kilometer in diameter. The *Wasp* ducked beneath the captured rock and then released the grappling hooks. The inertia of the ship and the blast from the clamps blowing loose sent the rock into the path of the larger ship. While everything is moving relatively quickly in space, space is big, so the enemy ship had plenty of time to react. But they were going to be forced to either demolish the rock or get out of the way, and either decision meant they would not be shooting at the *Wasp* or the decoy, and if they moved it would take them much closer to the fake ship.

Please move, please move, please move. And for once, magical thinking worked. The big ship altered its trajectory to avoid the nuisance that had been thrown in its way.

Tracy felt sweat trickling through his sideburns as he looked from the actual view to the display that gave him hard data rather than the questionable evidence of his eyes. Valada-Viers on the bridge had the same information, and what it told was that the enemy spaceship was now well within the blast radius. A harsh warning signal was blasted over the radio, and the *Wasp* fired all engines and ran for the cover of a large asteroid. Almost immediately after sending the warning, Valada-Viers detonated the massive number of explosives that had been drilled into the surface of the asteroid. The rock and the false ship blew spectacularly apart, and one-quarter of that highly accelerated ejecta smashed into the alien ship. Tracy had come up with the idea when he thought back on the trap that the citizens of a Hidden World had laid for an imperial squadron. A trap that destroyed that squadron. The result was just as devastating here.

Atmosphere jetted from breaches in the hull, forming white plumes as air turned to ice. Actual bodies joined the meat-stuffed suits that Tracy's squadron had seeded near the supposed wreck. The big ship was rocked onto its side by the force of the explosion. One of the engines began to burn before it was snuffed out when blast doors must have closed. *Well, we've established they breath something with at least twenty percent oxygen in the mix,* Tracy thought.

Then he gave the order. "Squadron, let's take them down."

The bay doors opened, and, with a lurch, his shuttle launched, flanked by the screamingly fast *infiernos.*

Moments later the *Swiftsure* herself rose out of hiding, a shadow against the stars. The *Audacious* went in the opposite direction, seeking to come up from beneath the wounded enemy ship. Both ships were going to have to navigate the debris from the demolished asteroid, but their shields and armor should be sufficient to blunt the worst of the rubble. The *Wasp* was returning to join in the fight. The *fusilero* contingents from the two *exploradors* had now launched. All three ships were focusing their fire on the engines as they sought to disable rather than destroy.

Tracy opened a channel to the squad and platoon leaders. "I suggest we use the holes the asteroid made for us for access."

"They'll be ready for that, sir. There'll be strong resistance there." It was the voice of the *fusilero* commander from the *Audacious*. There was a squeak in the voice. He sounded very young.

"Were you under the impression that there wasn't going to be fighting, Captain Lieutenant?" Tracy inquired dryly.

"Um … ah … no, sir."

It was time to deass the slow, vulnerable shuttles and finish closing with the wounded ship via their armor's maneuvering jets. Tracy nodded to Washington, who gave the order to deploy. Their shuttle pilot opened the doors to the vacuum. The ship was bucking as the alien ship began to target the advancing vessels. As Tracy had hoped, the aliens were training most of their fire on the frigate and the scout ships, but some was coming their way. Tracy's magnetic boots reluctantly released from the floor of the shuttle when he gave a hard kick, and then he was flying free. His breaths were loud inside the confines of his helmet. He winced as he saw the *Swiftsure* take a particularly hard hit from a missile and watched plating drifting away. He forced himself to dial down the volume from the bridges of the three ships. It was now in the hands of the princess, young Oort, and Valada-Viers. Tracy needed to concentrate on the troops.

It would have been nice if the advancing troops could be

mistaken for fragments of the asteroid, but the flare of their jump jets made them stand out like Roman candles against the dark of space. The advantage they had was that most ships of war carried weapons designed to hit larger targets, as in other ships. Trying to hit the suited figures rushing them would have been like hitting an ant with a cannon while blindfolded. The shuttles had no such advantage, and there was a brilliant flare as the slugs from the rail gun mounted on the top of the enemy ship hit one of the retreating shuttles and tore it apart. Tracy cringed. Assuming they came out of this alive, he was going to have to justify the requisition for its replacement. In a distant part of his brain, he wondered what it said about him that he was more concerned about replacing a shuttle than the two men who had flown her, but the sad truth of war was that people were far more easily replaced than equipment.

"Can somebody take out that rail gun?" he yelled on an open channel.

"Relax, Tracy, we've got this," said a new and very familiar voice. The incongruity threw him so much that for an instant Tracy couldn't respond. *Jahan? But she was supposed to be light-years away.*

✦ ✦ ✦

"JAHAN? GODDAMN IT! What the fuck are you doing here? What are any of you doing here?" He was yelling. Jahan dialed down the volume to spare her ears. Humans never seemed to remember that Isanjo had very acute hearing.

All around her were Isanjo in their distinctive five appendage suits that were built to accommodate their prehensile tails and allow them to be utilized. Eight of them, four to a tool, were hauling large laser cutters as they boosted toward the listing spaceship. She had been surprised at the response when she'd slipped off the *Selkie* before the ship's departure and approached the workers about helping. She had made it clear this was purely on a volunteer basis, yet forty-three had stepped forward. Unlike the humans, they were having no trouble negotiating the debris field. There was a reason most of the shipbuilders doing the grunt work were Isanjo. Space was just like flying through their trees but without gravity to get in the way.

She responded to Tracy. "We figured you could use the help."

"I didn't authorize this! In fact, I told you specifically *not* to do this!" Tracy yelled.

"Yeah, well, that wouldn't stop my sister … she doesn't listen to anybody," called Dulac.

The big sister in her hadn't wanted him to volunteer, but he had been the foreman overseeing the building of the decoy and was respected by the other workers. When he stepped forward, that had garnered far more support than she had expected. To quell her own fears, she quipped sweetly, "And that goes double for you, baby brother." Jahan blew him a raspberry.

"Cut the chatter and get it done," Tracy growled. "I'll deal with you later, Jahan," he added on a private radio channel.

"Says the guy who was always going on about forgiveness rather than permission," she muttered.

"I heard that!"

"I meant you to." She broke the connection.

They had successfully negotiated the bits of rock and pieces of fake ship, but now alien fighters joined the mix. Unlike the human soldiers, the Isanjo had used inertia to carry them toward the target and were only occasionally using their maneuvering jets. The humans looked like Roman candles. Jahan whispered a prayer and crossed herself. She didn't have a lot of truck with religion, but this seemed like a good time to hedge her bets.

They reached the surface of the spaceship. The recoil of the rail gun jarred up through the soles of her boots and seemed to shake her bones. She looked around and did a fast count. They had begun with forty-three. Forty workers were still with them. She made a silent promise that their bodies would be recovered. She leaped to Dulac's side to help clamp the cutter to the ship's hull, but her focus kept slipping away as she tried to spot Tracy. Her brother tapped her helmet. "We got this, Sis. Go find your human. Besides, I'm better at this than you are."

"Like hell, but we'll debate that at another time." She kicked loose. "Thanks," she called, and went in search of Tracy.

\+ + +

A SWARM OF small craft had erupted from several launch bays on the crippled spaceship and were wreaking havoc among the *fusileros*. The *infiernos* raced in to protect them, but not before acceleration rounds from the fighters tore through a number of Tracy's soldiers. Air and blood boiled from the suits and the bodies and formed a frozen nimbus of white and red around the bodies. Tracy found a piece of rock going roughly in the same direction as himself and used it for cover. He watched the range finder on his display counting down the meters to the enemy ship and prayed.

Three minutes later his boots clicked onto the surface of the ship. Off to his left, he could see the flare of cutters as the Isanjo worked to tear apart the rail gun. All around him *fusileros* in his platoon dropped onto the ship. Washington motioned, and they moved across the surface toward one of the holes in the hull. "Kid wasn't wrong about the welcoming committee," Washington warned. "So be ready."

"Also, might want to remember that these fuckers destroy their ships rather than get captured, so you might want to do it … uh … fast." The voice of Beatrisa.

"The princess ain't wrong," a sergeant grunted. They began to double-time toward the opening.

"Just about got the rail gun fucked up." It was Dulac. "If someone will give us a scan of a high-power use area, we can try to cut directly into the bridge," the alien offered.

"I know we've got to take the bridge, but we've also got to take at least one of them alive," Tracy said. "Exposing them to vacuum is probably not the best plan."

"You gotta assume they follow the same protocols as us and wear suits when they enter combat." It was the young captain lieutenant leading the *fusileros* from the *Wasp*.

"If there is one thing I have learned from the military, it's to *assume nothing*," Tracy said.

"Uh … yes, sir. Sorry, sir."

They had reached the opening and using their maneuvering jets the platoon dove down the side of the ship and through the ragged opening. Tracy allowed the young men to take point. There was a jumble of radio cross talk. *Heavy fire. On your left! Shit! Got him!*

He made the jump, but before his boots found purchase in the interior of the spaceship a heavy and accustomed weight hit his back. It was Jahan clinging to his shoulders, her helmeted head next to his. She fired her maneuvering jets to help him adjust for the sudden added weight and inertial push. He gave her a sideways look.

"Delivering our report. Mission accomplished, sir."

"What? Your radio stopped working?"

"I've got to keep you breathing," Jahan said.

"Doesn't that sort of thwart your cunning plan to inherit the *Selkie*?"

"Damn! I knew there was something I missed."

14

DIOS, YOU ARE UGLY

HIS BOOTS HIT the flooring with a hard jar that had his teeth snapping together. He clutched his rifle tighter. Suited figures were tumbling in the weightlessness, and flares from the acceleration rounds lit the dim space. The human blood formed scarlet bubbles. The alien corpses were leaching blood that was a dark purple color. Details from his exobiology class returned. The red color indicated hemoglobin, which was based on iron, to carry oxygen. He was forcefully reminded that he was seriously out of practice for this kind of action when Jahan frantically snatched the pistol out of his thigh holster and fired three shots into the body of an attacking figure, hitting it multiple times in the chest. Tracy hoped there was something vulnerable in that particular spot, but apparently there was because the alien stopped moving, the force of the rounds sending the body floating away.

She slapped his helmet with the butt of the pistol. "Head in the game, please!"

"Thanks." Tracy panted as fear slowly released its grip on his chest. The bodies in their pressure suits had four limbs and wore helmets indicating a head, but with only an eye slit so their features were obscured. The suits echoed the same disturbing angles as the ship.

Now that he had a moment to study the bodies, Tracy's initial impression was that their foes followed the exobiologists' theories that aliens would have symmetrical bodies, some sort of protection for the brain, and manipulative digits. Those theories had certainly been borne out by the aliens they had discovered after humans left Earth, and this bunch underscored the belief that certain evolutionary norms were going to apply across the universe.

With the resistance neutralized, his remaining troops were forming up around Washington. The commander used hand signals and a few short commands to send them advancing deeper into the wounded ship. Tracy grunted and panted as long unused muscles tried to remember how to maneuver in battle armor so he could keep up with the leapfrogging marines.

"If they're going to try to blow the ship that will happen in engineering. Get some demolition experts down there," he panted to Washington.

"Yes, sir. Wish we had an engineer."

Tracy turned his head to look at Jahan just as she raised her hand. "I don't have a fancy degree, but I know engines."

"Go," Tracy ordered, and he ordered six of the troops to accompany her.

She held an upthrust finger in front of his face. "Remember. Do. Not. Get. Killed," she warned.

The commander of the *fusileros* from the *Audacious* broke in on the radio. "Sir, the squirrels have cut us an opening. And they came in with us, sir." He sounded faintly aggrieved by that. "We seem to be above you three decks on the starboard side."

Valada-Viers came in on a priority channel. "Sir, they're pounding the shit out of the scouts. I've got to pull them back or lose them. Whatever you're going to do, you better do it fast."

Tracy switched channels back to the Isanjo foreman. "Dulac, you build ships. Now that you're inside, where do you think they've stashed the bridge?"

"Just a sec." There were some sounds he couldn't identify then the alien came back on the comm channel. "I cut into the wall. Based on the amount of wiring and conduits and their direction, my best guess is on the lowest level."

"Interesting. Well, okay." Tracy turned to Washington. "Let's find the stairs."

✦ ✦ ✦

JAHAN USED HER magnetic boots to run along the side of the corridor walls and even on the ceiling to avoid being jostled by the big men in their battle armor. It was also safer because the ship's artificial gravity was failing. At moments they were weightless, then briefly heavier than normal. It seemed their foes came from a higher-gravity world than the League races. The light was also dimmer than what she was accustomed to and had a faint orange-red tinge. She couldn't tell if that was due to emergency lighting or if this was the normal illumination for these creatures.

They did not advance unopposed, though the resistance seemed to be confused and disorganized. Jahan could understand why. They had assumed they were going to destroy a vulnerable foe and instead found themselves shredded. They had to have lost a significant number of their crew in the initial explosion, and now they had humans rampaging through their ship. Jahan reflected that that should be enough to loosen the bowels in *any* species. Especially given that the humans had been getting pounded and this was their first chance to bring a little up close and personal payback.

Dulac was giving her a whispered running commentary in pidgin Nilou. Neither one of them had paid much attention to learning their native language when they were in school. It had seemed pointless given the ubiquitousness of Spanish and English. "Head toward the stern. Makes sense to put the engine room with easy access to the engines."

"So why bridge in basement?" Jahan asked.

"Closer to fighters?" Dulac suggested.

"Shuttles for escape?" Jahan added.

"Jesús maldito Cristo!" He broke into Spanish, and she could hear the breathless terror in his voice.

"What? Are you okay?" she cried.

"Yeah, that one was a little too close."

"Please stay safe."

"Trying. Please don't let them blow this thing up with us inside."

"Trying," she shot back.

They had reached a massive door. One of the *fusileros* ran a scan. "Lotta power behind those doors," he said.

"I bet there's a lotta guns, too," said another, his voice spiraling up, and Jahan realized he had to be very young.

"Any chance we can get one of those cutters down here?" the sergeant asked her.

"Not quickly enough."

"How about I set a charge and we blow the thing? Follow the blast in guns blazing," the demolitions officer offered.

Jahan had been studying the walls and ceiling. Using the magnets, she climbed up the wall, sounding the panels with her fist as she went. She hit one that gave a hollow ring near the top. "How about you do that, and we use an access panel to go in from the top?" Jahan suggested.

"We aren't going to fit through there," the sergeant objected.

"But I will. Give me a grenade or something. I'll drop it on them when you're ready to blow open the door."

"How do you even know you can get to the engine room?" the demolition officer asked.

"Because there has to be ventilation and cooling into the engine room. Those rooms run hot. They may be aliens, but physics is physics all over the galaxy."

"Okay. Do it." The sergeant tossed her a grenade. "The captain wants prisoners, so this is a stun grenade." He tossed up another grenade. "If that doesn't work, toss in this one and blow them to hell."

"Got it." Jahan opened the panel and wriggled inside.

"And be sure to close your eyes and cut audio after you drop the first one, so you don't get flattened by it, too."

"Right. Important safety tip, thanks."

She slid into the ventilation duct and wriggled forward, feeling like she was making a tremendous amount of noise. On the other hand, there was a lot of noise from weapons fire, missiles hitting, shattered pieces of asteroid banging on the hull. It was likely her advance would be ignored … she hoped.

She reached the grating in the ceiling of the engine room and peered down. Seven figures. None of them were in spacesuits, though suit lockers were open, indicating they had thought about it. Instead, they were all huddled at a control panel while one of the creatures was on its back on the floor working with wiring. They were tall, close to eight feet, Jahan guessed, and wore formfitting uniforms with long flaring vests that had pockets and loops to hold tools and weapons. The uniforms also had cutouts to accommodate the bony protrusions at the multiple joints on their arms. There were more blade-like protrusions at their knees and heels, and the faces were long and skull-like with grinding mandibles and multiple eyes. It was as if birds and spiders had decided to fuck and have mutant babies.

"*Dios*, you are *ugly*," she whispered to herself.

"In place," she whispered into her throat mike, and studied the room. It was a round space with controls lining the walls and a pulsing light from a glass-covered opening in the center of the floor. Oddly, the guts of the engine seemed to be beneath the engine room rather than behind it.

"In seven," the platoon leader whispered back.

She watched the chronometer in the arm of her suit. With five seconds remaining, she used the laser cutter embedded in her suit glove to cut an opening. The jagged faces craned up at her. "Surprise!" She pulled the pin and dropped the grenade, then muted her helmet and scrabbled away from the opening as a flash lit the room. She turned back on her audio to hear the yelled commands from the human soldiers. "Kick away his rifle! Look out! On your left!" There was the snap and rattle of gunfire. Then the sergeant radioed her.

"All clear. Come in and start defusing this thing."

Jahan kicked out the grating and dropped to the floor. One of the human solders was dead. All seven of the aliens were down—dead or unconscious. She dragged the one who had been working on a panel out by his ankles and studied the notation on the panels. It was inexplicable, but as she had said, physics was physics and Fold engines, no matter which species designed them, had certain things in common. Also, the open panel gave her a hint where to start. It seemed the aliens had been making repairs to something when she had rudely interrupted them. What also became clear was that the self-destruct mechanism was not jury-rigged. Her best guess was that the command could be keyed from the engine room, but it was probably also linked to the bridge. She got on the radio.

"Tracy, you better haul ass to the bridge. The self-destruct is built into the system, and I'm betting they can detonate from there. It looks like it took some damage, but they may have been able to repair it."

"Working on it," came the panting reply. "Can you disrupt the signal?"

"I can try."

"Try very hard."

✦ ✦ ✦

DULAC WAS WITH him as they ran down a corridor. With the fluctuating gravity, it was safer to keep their magnetic boots firmly against the ship's floor, sides, or ceiling. In space, the concept of up and down was more of a suggestion, so Tracy made it a point to check in all directions lest there be an ambush. Personally, he wished the gravity would fail completely. They could have moved faster in free fall. Periodically the Isanjo would stop, cut out a section of wall and inspect the wiring and piping inside. "Next crossing corridor we go left and then down."

"You're sure?" The look the alien gave him was all the answer he needed.

"Can he cut the wiring to try and keep the signal from being sent?" Washington asked.

"There might be a fail-safe that causes an automatic detonation if tampering is detected," Tracy panted.

Dulac nodded. "What the captain said."

They hit the corner, and everyone froze while the lead *fusileros* took a quick glance around then signaled all clear. A few hundred yards down the corridor they found a ramp leading down. Quite different from human ships that used access ladders and lifts. The only other time he had seen this particular design was on the derelict Cara'ot ship they had discovered years ago.

Washington jerked up his arm and made a fist. They came to a halt. "I'd have a welcoming committee at the bottom."

"Roll some grenades down there?" It was part question, part suggestion.

"Sounds good." The two *fusileros* who carried grenade

launchers moved forward and sent five of them down into the darkness at the foot of the ramp. The League soldiers got a flurry of gunfire in return. Tracy pressed himself against a wall as one round found its target but was mercifully stopped by his battle armor. It still felt like he'd been kicked in the side by a mule. The grenades detonated and the gunfire stopped. They advanced by leapfrogging. Once again Tracy was kept to the rear.

There were bodies at the base of the ramp leaking purple blood through rents in their suits. A couple were still feebly moving. "Put 'em out of their misery?" someone in the platoon suggested and gave a hoarse laugh.

"We don't kill the wounded," Tracy snapped, then added sweetly, "Not unless you'd like them to return the favor?"

"Sorry, *Capitan*."

Dulac had gone loping ahead. He returned. "Got some heavy blast doors ahead. Looks like we found the bridge."

They regrouped and advanced to the doors. They were impressive. "Cutters?" Tracy asked.

Dulac studied the doors, tapped at the material with a forefinger. "Take a couple of hours."

"We've got a couple of minutes," Washington warned.

"Can we blow them?" Tracy asked his *fusilero* commander.

"It would take a shitload of explosive."

Tracy stared at the implacable doors, felt the seconds ticking away, measuring how long they all had to live. He turned to the Isanjo construction worker. "We need to do something that will force them to open the doors."

"Yeah, something corrosive or explosive," Washington

said with enthusiasm. He turned to the alien. “Can you do that?”

“With what?” Dulac yelped. “Ships try not to have shit in them that when mixed turns toxic or goes boom!”

Tracy was tapping nervously at the side of his helmet. Jahan’s voice came over Tracy’s radio. She had been eavesdropping. “You’ll be pleased to know that they’ve been pinging their big fucking bomb for the past twenty seconds. I did manage to interrupt the signal, but eventually they’ll find a work-around that I can’t counter in time.”

He pushed down the panic that shortened his breaths and had his thoughts scrambling like a rat in a trap. *Think. Think.*

Then it came to him. “Electricity,” he said. “Create a feedback loop that will electrify the floor, walls, everything.”

“Which will also knock the shit out of their electronics,” Dulac said. He gave Tracy an admiring look. “Yeah, *that* I can do.”

“I’ll help. Used to know a bit about this.”

The hand laser made quick work of the wall, and the Isanjo set to work cutting and splicing wires. Then he held two sparking wires, one in each hand, and gave Tracy a look. “Here goes nothing … or something.” He twisted them together and electricity went arcing and crawling along the inside of the wall racing in both directions. The ship shuddered and keeled even more onto its side. Tracy reoriented himself to what was now down and motioned to his troops to take up positions on all sides of the door. He could feel sweat crawling down his cheeks and chest while he stared at the door until his eyes began to water.

"Shit, hope I didn't short out the door, too," Dulac muttered.

"There'll be a manual override," Tracy muttered back.

"Oh, good. I'd hate to have cocked this up."

Then the doors shrieked in their tracks and opened. Through the now open doorway, Tracy could see a few figures dancing as if they had St. Vitus as the electricity coursed through their bodies. Several others were using the boosters on their suits to stay off the now deadly floor and walls. Tracy found himself staring into the faceplate of the alien who had forced open the door. The creature fired his jets and slammed into Tracy, driving them both across the corridor and into the far wall. The knife-like extrusions on the suit were pressing against Tracy's and a warning popped up that suit integrity was compromised. Tracy tried to bring up the rifle so he could at least bash the alien. His arm was knocked aside, and he felt the jar up into his shoulder. One thing was now abundantly clear—the creatures were much stronger than a human. Part of the platoon was dealing with the aliens on the bridge as Dulac cut the current into the room. Washington and another *fusilero* had noticed Tracy's predicament and were swinging around to help, but the aliens who had avoided electrocution were now joining the chaotic hand-to-hand fight. For the moment, Tracy was on his own.

Over his opponent's shoulder, Tracy saw Dulac holding sparking wires in each hand and frantically waving them while giving head jerks. Tracy got the message but wasn't sure how he was going to do what the Isanjo wanted. Then the artificial gravity once again failed, and he saw his chance.

Gathering all his strength, Tracy managed to push the alien back enough that he could plant his boot in the alien's midriff and give a hard shove. The alien went floating away from him. Dulac came up behind him and thrust the wires against the creature's back. Electricity arced through the suit and the alien quit moving. Tracy set his suit to auto-repair, and then went to join the fight only to find the younger men had managed to neutralize the aliens. But not without cost. There was red blood mingling with the floating drops of purple blood, and three suits showed no vital signs.

"Bridge," Tracy panted. "Disarm." A stitch in his side had him bending over in pain. This was definitely a young man's game, and he decided he maybe wouldn't do this again.

A few moments later Washington gave him a thumbs-up.

Messages were coming in from the other teams that the resistance had been neutralized. A final count revealed they had seven prisoners.

It was over. The ship was theirs.

15

BACKBITING & BROWNNOSING

"WELL ... THEY are certainly ..." The ever-elegant Valada-Viers gave up looking for a word and merely shrugged.

"Butt-ugly?" Cassutt suggested.

"Terrifying?" Lieutenant Flintoff volunteered, and she gave a shiver. Her deep blue eyes were shadowed with horror as she studied the seven creatures in the *Swiftsure*'s brig. Just to be sure the aliens couldn't get up to any mischief, they were all in separate cells.

A test of the atmosphere in the enemy ship revealed that though the air inside the human ship would seem thin, they would be able to breath the standard atmosphere mix. Four of the seven had remained unconscious once they were brought to the *Swiftsure*, but three of them regained consciousness and looked ready to resume the fight.

Fearing that their suits might contain concealed weapons or explosives, Tracy had ordered the brig flooded with sleeping gas so they could be stripped of their suits. It turned out that the blade-like extrusions on the suits weren't just for effect. The bodies of the aliens had the same bony protrusions at their arm and leg joints. Their skin was hardened plates of mottled purple and grey, and they had elongated heads and small mouths filled with needlelike teeth. Slung beneath their jaws were mandibles that looked like they could rip through bone. There were no exterior ears, just holes in the side of the long skulls, and three eyes in a triangle formation that were set into their skulls. There were eight long fingers on each hand, and they could be stiffened to serve as knives, as one of the *fusileros* had discovered when one of the aliens had briefly become conscious before being pounded in the head with rifle butts until it succumbed. The human soldier had been rushed to the med bay and was expected to survive.

While they were unconscious, Afumba had entered and drawn blood, taken skin samples and swabs from inside the mouths, and raced back to the medical center to begin running tests. Techs had managed to lift messages off the bridge consoles, and the guttural sounds with an underlying whine had the effect of nails on a blackboard or chewing on tinfoil. Tracy could not imagine anyone singing in such a language. His final conclusion: they were the most dangerous-looking creatures Tracy had ever seen and just as disturbing as their ships.

"Well, now that we've seen them, perhaps we can stop calling them the enemy," Valada-Viers said.

"Or motherfuckers," Washington muttered.

"*Hijos de puta*," was Cassutt's offering.

"Bastards," a guard muttered.

Then Flintoff said softly, "*Necrófagos.*"

"I think they're more devils than ghouls," Cassutt said thoughtfully.

"And I'm sure they think we're also devils." They all turned at the quiet comment. Father Ken walked past them and studied the creatures in their cells.

"So, you're saying we shouldn't have fought?" Washington's tone was belligerent.

"No, they did attack us first, and we're entitled to defend ourselves—"

"Nice of you to acknowledge that, Padre," Cassutt sneered.

"*But* we should make an effort to understand what drove them to do this. Communication can lead to understanding and understanding to peace."

"I admire your belief in the intrinsic good of all God's creatures, Father," Tracy said. "But I'm not sure I share your optimism. A species who would rather die than surrender isn't likely to be open to a discussion."

Ken reached up and patted him on the upper arm. "One must have faith, my son." The warm brown eyes swept across all of them. For Ken, it was a stern look. "I understand you are angry but let us not become what we resist. Treat these creatures with the same kindness and care you would want our prisoners to receive were the situation reversed."

And with that he left.

Feeling chastised by their spiritual advisor, the gaggle began to break up. Valada-Viers fell into step with Tracy. "What are your plans, Captain?"

"Get a skeleton crew and the Isanjo on the alien ship and send it and the prisoners back to Hellfire with the *exploradors* as escorts. Get them repaired at headquarters."

"And the *Swiftsure*?"

"We'll head back to Wasua." The Exec gave that little cough which Tracy now knew meant strong disagreement. "I take it you have an opinion?"

"With respect, sir, it might be wise for you, as squadron commander, to report first to the fleet admiral who is your immediate superior rather than let him find out after the fact of our activities and the capture of an enemy ship. Otherwise, the admiral might feel you were … er …"

"Hogging the glory?" Tracy suggested.

"Exactly so, sir."

"So, what you're saying is I have to give Talion first crack at taking all the credit?" There was a hot knot of resentment in the center of his chest, and Tracy swallowed hard, struggling to control his notoriously short temper.

"That is perhaps more forthright than I would have been, sir, but … yes."

"So, we leave Wasua unprotected."

"Somehow it doesn't strike me as a likely target for our … for the *necrófagos*. My guess is that this ship was scouting for a likely planetary target, heard the distress call, and her captain decided to … er … grab a bit of glory."

"A warning to us all, Commander," Tracy said dryly.

+ + +

ONE OF THE bright boys from CentCom was demonstrating the complex pattern they had designed for deploying the mines and the equally complex navigational program that had been written to enable the League ships to advance and engage the enemy once they had been (one hoped) softened up by said minefield. Mercedes hoped that her affect—a frown between her brows, fingers pressed against her lips—would convince everyone that she was completely engrossed. In truth, she was thinking about Cyprian. She and Boho had spent two weeks on Ouranos helping coordinate recovery efforts, but the war called, and they had to leave. They had left their weeping, screaming child in the care of her full sister Estella.

She really had been the only choice. Delia was coping with the death of her twin and taking Dulcinea's daughter into her household, and Mercedes and Izzara had never been particularly close. Estella had always been Mercedes's confidant and fierce supporter. She was also a loving mother, but Mercedes could not shake the memory of that little tear-streaked face and the hands reaching desperately for her as they turned to leave.

The young tactician paused for breath, and one of the older admirals spoke up. "Forgive me, Majesty, but a number of us in CentCom are quite concerned over this redirection of funds, materials, and manpower from shipbuilding to construction of these devices. We strongly feel this is a poor use of resources in a time of crisis."

Apslund possessed the looks that the media would want in a military figure. Square-jawed, silver-haired, with piercing dark eyes and a still fit body. It was also clear that he was the spokesman for several other men who were nodding in agreement. Among them Eringin, who oversaw procurements.

They were ensconced with the top brass of O-Trell in an underground bunker on Hellfire. The recirculated air brought in a faint whiff of *calabacitas* from the lunch that had been served in the canteen. It almost overcame the scent from the stim sticks being smoked in the room.

Mercedes gestured to the young tactician to wait and addressed Apslund. "Because, Admiral, they have now devastated two of our planets. Our first obligation is to defend our citizens and their families and homes. We can't ring a planet with warships, and, frankly, up to now we haven't displayed a marked ability to win against these creatures in a stand-up fight. In order to stop them, we've got to weaken them *before* they reach the planet, and then allow our ships to engage."

"I understand your concern for your subjects, Majesty, such sentiments do you credit, and while civilian casualties are always regrettable, our sole focus must be on defeating the enemy."

Mercedes stiffened. She had not missed the use of the word *sentiment* in Apslund's statement and understood what he was trying to convey to the other men in the meeting. *How typical of a woman. Soft, weak, and unable to make the hard choices.* She looked briefly over at Boho, who lowered one eyelid in a slow wink and made a slight throat-cutting gesture.

"Why, thank you, Admiral," Mercedes said sweetly. Then as he began to relax, she said in a tone of ice and steel, "How condescending of you." She risked another glance to her husband. Boho was sipping his coffee. His legs were stretched out in front of him, and he was leaning back with the air of man prepared to enjoy a show. "But it might behoove you to recall that *I* am the Empress and Supreme Commander of our armed forces, and this is not a discussion. This is my will, and it shall be done."

"Yes, your Majesty. My apologies if my words were misunderstood. I meant no offense," Apslund said, and he looked like this particular set of words was about to choke him.

Mercedes turned back to the young officer who looked like he was trying to become invisible. "Please continue with your briefing, Commander."

After a nervous throat clearing, he resumed. "Each mine is linked to a quantum computer that will constantly adjust their trajectories, but in a random manner determined by the computer. The use of the computer will prevent any unfortunate collisions between the mines and enable us to move them aside to allow for League supply and merchant ships to pass."

"This sounds quite complicated," another officer said.

The young commander gave him a smile. "Rather. It's the most complex bit of programming we've ever done." Which seemed to delight him.

While this exchange was happening, Eringin, the admiral in charge of supply and logistics, leaned over to Apslund and murmured, "Mihalis would never have agreed to something this stupid."

"That's the fucking truth."

Unfortunately for them, their words landed in one of those conversational lulls that Boho's mother liked to call *waiting for Gabriel's trumpet* moments. The words carried with the stunning clarity of a large boulder falling into a lake, and an appalled silence fell across the room. Mercedes slowly turned her head to look at her security detail. "Sergeant, take Admiral Apslund and Vice Admiral Eringin into custody while SCID investigates questions of sedition. If evidence is found, a court-martial will be convened."

"You can't do this," Apslund sputtered.

"Did you already forget that whole Empress, Supreme Commander thing?" Boho asked. "It means that she can, and she did. Get them out of here." They were hauled, protesting, from the room.

It bothered Mercedes that Boho had taken it upon himself to issue the order for their removal, but she let it go. There was again silence, then one of the young aides-de-camp said brightly, "Hey, two vacancies in the top ranks. More opportunity for promotion?" He looked suddenly appalled and absurdly young, and he literally clapped a hand to his mouth. Everyone looked nervously to Mercedes, who chuckled and nodded.

"To bloody war or a sickly season," Mercedes said as she smiled at him. "It was an old toast in the wet Navy back on Earth," she explained at his look of evident confusion.

"Or to talking trash about our Empress," the young aide added, and gazed at her with adoration.

Please God, don't let me get him killed, Mercedes prayed.

✦ ✦ ✦

THERE HAD BEEN weird glances from the human officers when Jahan and Dulac were found to be in the conference room aboard the *Swiftsure*, but Tracy's offhanded attitude toward the presence of two aliens seemed to quell any further reaction. In addition to the two Isanjo, Tracy had summoned the top officers from all three ships. Jahan had itched to perch on the back of Tracy's chair like she used to do in the old days aboard the *Selkie*, but she knew that really *was* a bridge too far. His officers undoubtably thought he was strange enough without adding to the impression.

The big doctor from the frigate, Afumba, was giving the final tally of dead and injured. Jahan liked him. He had treated the wounded Isanjo just as he did the humans, in fact bumping the aliens whose injuries were more severe in front of humans whose injuries were less critical. The news wasn't great, but it could also have been a lot worse.

Tracy had ordered the uninjured Isanjo to work on repairs to the two *exploradors* which had taken the brunt of the damage.

"So, we have the prize," the princess said. Jahan studied her curiously, looking for similarities to the sister she did know and finding a few in the set of her eyes and line of her jaw. "Now how the hell do we get it back to Hellfire?"

"I wouldn't want to try and tow a ship that big in Fold," Lal said, and Dulac nodded in agreement, which earned him a sideways glance from the engineering chief of the frigate.

Tracy set aside his TapPad and turned to Jahan and her brother. "Can you fix it up enough so it can survive translation in and out of Fold?"

They exchanged a long glance. "Yeah, think so," Dulac said.

"I need you to know so," Tracy responded.

"Give us a little more time to study it," Jahan said.

"Time is the one thing we haven't got," Tracy said. "At

some point what passes for fleet command for these bastards is going to notice they've lost a ship and send someone to investigate. And I'm assuming they'll come in force, so I'd like us all not to be here when they do arrive."

"And what about finishing the repairs on our ships?" the young captain of the *Audacious* asked.

"If they aren't critical, leave them for later," Tracy ordered.

"You actually think you can fly an alien craft?" Valada-Viers asked Jahan.

She shrugged. "Physics is physics all over the universe."

"And there are only certain ways machines can work," Lal said in a surprising show of support. "Together we can figure this out."

Tracy tugged at his lower lip and frowned off into space. It was a gesture and an expression Jahan had seen for many years back when she thought his name was Oliver. He looked up and pinned her with a glance. "Jahan, Dulac, I'm going to put your people aboard the prize along with a skeleton O-Trell crew. It's imperative that we get this ship back safely to the Gold." Tracy nodded at the princess. "Captain Arango, is your exec ready to take a command of the alien vessel?"

"He is. Sokolov was slated for command but took retirement when his wife fell ill. He was out for a few years, but he's forgotten nothing."

"Okay, let him know and get him over to the ship. We'll pull a few people from the *Swiftsure* to fill out his complement. You all know what you have to do. Dismissed." He gave a small gesture to Jahan to hang back.

"What's up?" she asked after the door closed behind the

gaggle.

"You going to catch up with the *Selkie*?" Tracy asked.

"Yeah, I'll radio them just before we leave. Have them meet me at Hellfire."

"Good. I need you to get on that other task as soon as possible."

"I know. We will."

Before she got to the door he called softly, "And Jahan, thank you. You saved my life."

The sincerity and affection in his voice embarrassed her. She turned back and held up two fingers. "Twice." She gave him a grin.

He sighed and rolled his eyes as he tried to hide a smile. "Yeah, okay, twice." Then he startled the hell out her by crossing to her and giving her a hug. "Be safe. All of you."

She didn't say the same to him. She was wise enough to know that in his case that wasn't possible. She just punched him on the arm and left.

+ + +

"SO LET ME get this straight. You left your post—"

Tracy was braced at parade rest, hands tightly clasped behind his back, chin up, eyes staring at the wall over Talion's head. His summons to the big dreadnaught flagship had been curt and immediate. "My instructions were to patrol, sir," Tracy said.

"With the *exploradors,* not turn our newest and most high-tech frigate into a scout vessel."

"I believe the *Swiftsure* ably displayed her ability as a

fighting vessel, sir."

Beyond the large port in the flagship's main conference room, Tracy could see the battered alien vessel. Occasionally there would be a flare from a welder as the Isanjo he had recruited worked on making repairs to protect the integrity of the enemy ship.

"You spent O-Trell funds—"

"Actually, I mostly spent my own."

"Stop interrupting me!"

"Yes, sir. Sorry, sir."

"You brought uncleared and unvetted aliens aboard military vessels." Tracy started to open his mouth then clamped his jaw shut. "You embarked on an unauthorized military operation that could have resulted in the loss of your squadron and the death of your crews."

"Yes, but it didn't." Both Tracy and Talion reacted to the new voice. Tracy glanced back over his shoulder to see Beatrisa. She snapped off a perfect salute to Talion, then walked up and stood shoulder to shoulder with Tracy. "If I may, sir."

Talion's eyes had narrowed, and he was frowning, making the white scars that crisscrossed one side of his dark face all the more pronounced. He eventually nodded his assent. "I was so struck by your encouragement to your officers to show initiative and the way you set an example of just that sort of behavior," Beatrisa said.

Tracy wondered what the hell she was going on about, and judging from Talion's expression he felt the same, but a man rarely discourages praise flowing in their direction, so Talion merely nodded for her to continue.

"I distinctly remember your forceful order to *go and get us something* when Admiral Marqués Chapman-Owiti told us what we had to have in order to win. Without your encouragement, I doubt Captain Belmanor would have gone to such lengths. In many ways, this victory is *entirely* due to *your* decisive leadership, sir."

The smile that followed her words had more in common with a snarl than a smile. "All right, Captain Princess. I don't mind being stroked, but don't slather me with chocolate sauce and whipped cream while you're doing it."

"Wouldn't dream of it, sir."

Talion moved to a chair and sat down. He didn't invite them to join him. "We need to get that ship and the prisoners to Hellfire."

"That was my original plan," Tracy said.

"And I should send you back to Wasua," Talion added.

"Also, part of the plan," Tracy said.

Talion's fingers drummed on the conference table, and he frowned down at the toes of his polished boots. He looked up at Tracy. "Be that as it may, Captain, you didn't get prior authorization for this operation. I'm your commanding officer. I deserved to be informed. I should have you up on charges."

"Because punishing initiative is always such a good idea. Might explain why we keep losing," Tracy snapped.

Talion came out of his chair, anger etched in every line of his body. Beatrisa shot Tracy an exasperated look and stepped between him and the admiral.

"Sir, you can't control talk, particularly not from the aliens. It would be bound to leak that you punished the commander who brought us our first decisive win, and you would only end up looking petty."

Don't goad him, don't goad him, Tracy mentally begged. Beatrisa hadn't gone to school with Talion the way Tracy had, so she didn't know that just beneath the skin of an FFH noble dwelled a psychopathic monster.

She seemed to sense some of that, for she lowered her eyes and took a step back. "Or that's how people who are unfamiliar with your leadership abilities might view it, sir," she added.

Talion didn't look convinced, but he finally nodded. "All right, but you need to take your ship back to Wasua."

"Yes, sir," Tracy said. He saluted and turned to leave.

"You'll just have to order him to return, Admiral," Beatrisa said.

"Oh? And why is that?"

"Captain Belmanor led the assault on the *necrófagos* ship—"

"The what?"

"The alien ship. We got tired of saying enemy all the time so we … um …" Beatrisa stammered.

"Took it upon yourselves to name them, too. I see. But do go on, Captain Princess." Talion's voice was a purr.

"As I was saying, the captain developed the plan and led the attack." It was an exaggeration, but Tracy didn't demur. It might take him awhile, but he eventually figured out when to shut up. "He is very familiar with the *necró*—" Beatrisa broke off and corrected herself. "The aliens' tactics and strategy. Military intelligence is going to want to personally debrief him."

It was a good argument because it also had the benefit of being true. Talion stared at them for a long time. "Fine. Go." They saluted, but before they could leave Talion added, "But not you, Captain Princess. You and the other *explorador* will be assigned to another squadron since we aren't certain when Captain Belmanor will be returning to us."

They nodded and left the conference room. "Whew," Beatrisa said once they were well down the corridor heading for the shuttle bay. "Is he always like this?"

"No. Something is eating him," Tracy replied. "It was an honor serving with you, Captain Princess," he said formally.

"Oh, please. The honor was mine, and I have a feeling we'll be doing it again. I know Mercedes asked you to babysit me."

"You do? How …?"

"No offense, but there were plenty of other captains with much fancier titles and better birth, but instead she assigned me to serve under a scholarship student who had once been cashiered. I could only assume she had extraordinary faith in your abilities. So, she'll probably make sure I end up back with you in short order." She held out her hand and they shook. "*Vaya con Dios*, Captain."

"Same to you, Princess."

16

ROCKING THE BOAT

BOHO STUDIED HER from beneath his lashes as he opened a bottle of wine. They were now back in her cabin on the flagship waiting for their late lunch to be delivered from the galley. He could tell from how she was slumped in the chair that she was beyond exhausted, and indeed the meeting had been interminable and capped off with two senior officers on their way to being cashiered.

His ScoopRing pinged, indicating that it was almost time for their daily call to Cyprian. Coordinating the time differences across light-years was challenging, but it was important they stayed in contact. Over the intervening weeks, the communications officers on their respective ships had worked out a system that when the empress and consort called the capital, both their holograms would be present. Sitting at the table while Cyprian ate his dinner, with him while he had his bath, got tucked into bed, and they could even read him stories until he fell asleep. The holographs weren't the same as a warm hug, but at least their child could see them and knew they loved him. Once he was evacuated to these Hidden Worlds that wouldn't be possible. Contemplating it still made his stomach ache.

Mercedes finally looked up. Her face seemed drawn and the rich, warm color of her skin seemed to have an underlying tinge of grey. "I wonder how many other officers are secretly regretting that Mihalis and Musa failed in their coup." She threw her tap pad aside. "God, I need a victory. Fuck, I shouldn't say that. The last time I chased that goal it caused a disaster."

The cork came out with a satisfying pop, and Boho filled two glasses and carried one over to her. "No, the operation against the corsairs went splendidly."

She accepted the glass. "Thank you. But then I got greedy. Thought I could bring another Hidden World into the fold. All I did was make a lot of people dead." She gulped down some wine. "What if I'm doing that again?"

"You're not. This defensive shield idea is brilliant." She just shook her head and drained her glass in one long gulp.

Boho handed her his, and took the empty and returned to the cellaret to refill it. She was staring blindly down into the depths of the glass when he joined her on the couch. He lightly touched her between the brows. "You're still frowning."

She set aside the glass, stood, and started to pace. "The problem is that I have no idea where to place the mines. We don't yet have enough to cover every League world. I'll look a fool if I garrison Wasua and then they hit Dullahan or Melatin or God knows where. We need to show this will work. Hell, *I* need to know if it will work or if I've diverted resources on a fantasy. And if I'm wrong, people will die because I wasn't good enough, smart enough, strong enough!"

The rasp of tears in her voice rattled him. In all the years of their marriage, Boho had rarely seen her cry. He took her in his arms. "You are good and smart and strong. Never doubt that. I love you and I believe in you."

She kept her face buried against his shoulder for a few minutes. The material of his shirt dampened from her tears. She then threw back her head, took a deep breath, and yanked the pins out of her hair. The curls foamed around her face, and he saw the girl he had known since childhood. "So where should I deploy?"

Boho picked up his glass and swirled it slowly, watching the ruby liquid wash across the sides of the glass. He thought about every attack starting with the assault on the *Estrella* Avanzada that had launched this war. Followed by the destruction of the Blue when the fleet tried to stop the aliens advance deeper into League space. Then Kronos and now Ouranos. He turned the information, looking at it from multiple angles. Was there a pattern? If he were invading the League, what would be his strategy? No, it was more than that. What would be his message to the people he was trying to conquer? The answer arrived with a force that staggered him, and he ended up spilling wine across his trousers.

"Earth. They'll go to Earth next," he said as he frantically brushed at the damp spot on his trouser leg.

"What? Earth? It's a … a rubbish heap," Mercedes said. "Why would they—"

He gripped her shoulders. "Think about it. They hit the star base first just to test our defenses and send us a notice that they were coming. Next, they take out one of our fleets, thus establishing our military isn't up to the job. Then

Kronos, the seat of our major stock exchange, and the engine of our economy goes down. Then Ouranos with particular focus on Hissilek and the palace. They're sending a message to our citizens that they can depend on nothing. They are attacking our institutions to create a sense of hopelessness. So, what's left that they can demonstrate that the government is impotent and useless?"

Understanding dawned. "Oh, my God. Rome … the Pope, the Vatican are there."

"And what a message that sends. Even your God can't protect you," Boho said. "Also, the original home of human-kind."

She impulsively grabbed him and kissed him hard. "You are a genius."

"Where are you going?" he called.

"To order the mines deployed to Earth."

"Are you taking the fleet?"

"No, if we put the fleet there it will alert them that we anticipated the attack. And we have to find out if this will work with only the usual contingent of ships to guard a planet."

"Then I better get back to my ship."

"I think we can get away with one flagship, but not two, so I'm going to transfer my flag to the *Potente*." It took a moment, but he placed the ship. It was a frigate, well-armed and well-captained. Mercedes continued. "But let's keep that quiet. If these creatures are running surveillance on us let them think I'm still aboard the *San Francisco de Asis*."

"How much of a force do you want?"

"What do you think?" Mercedes asked.

He ran a finger across his mustache and pondered. "If this works, it'll be a mop-up operation, so frigates and fighters rather than destroyers."

"A destroyer can carry more *infiernos*," Mercedes pointed out.

"We'll have my flagship, and if we cut down on shuttles, we can pack more *infiernos* onto the frigates. It's not like we need shuttles to land troops."

"We might need them to pick up escape pods. We're going to lose ships. It's inevitable," Mercedes cautioned.

"We're going to be in close Earth orbit. They can send up shuttles from the planet to pick up survivors," Boho said.

"All right. You see to the arrangements. I'll tell Gelb that he's in command during my absence. And inform the high command. I hope nobody argues about *this*; I don't want to arrest any more admirals." She started to leave, then whirled and grabbed him in a frenzied hug. "I won't be able to do this again until it's all over."

He kissed her. "Then you should wait until we've had lunch." He gave her a suggestive smile. "And maybe a bit of dessert before you leave?"

She slipped into his arms, and he began dropping quick, soft kisses on her lips. "I think we can spare the time. But don't tell the troops, they might be shocked," Mercedes said.

"Because they're all virgins, or they don't think old people and royals make love?"

Mercedes chuckled. "There might be some virgins among them. They do seem to be getting younger and younger."

"Well, then let's misbehave."

✦ ✦ ✦

THE HARD RESIN flooring and polished composite walls created an acoustical nightmare, especially with so many O-Trell *hombres* and officers rushing through the halls of the main building of the *Ministerio de Guerra*. Add to that the footfalls of the Hajin batBEMs, and Tracy's headache was increasing exponentially.

The Ministry of War was housed in a massive octagonal building that had as many floors below the surface of Hellfire as there were above. Central command and the joint chiefs of every fighting service in the League were housed inside, and literally thousands of people worked at the ministry, both military and civilian. Naturally, most people didn't bother with the full title, just calling it the Octagon or the Octo for short.

And clearly no one had given acoustics a single thought when they designed the building. At least the Isanjo wore soft shoes with split toes so they could us their prehensile feet. The *Swiftsure* had arrived in the early morning hours of Hellfire's day cycle after a nearly two-week journey, and there had been a few tense moments as they waited for the *necrófago* ship.

It should have translated out of Fold only moments after the frigate. Instead, long minutes had crept past while sweat trickled in Tracy's sideburns and an increasing weight seemed to settle on his chest. Finally, the wounded vessel had materialized out of the darkness, and they had begun the day's long journey to the inner planets. During that period the *Selkie* had rendezvoused with them and picked up Jahan. Presumably they were now on their way to Freehold.

Talion had radioed ahead and warned fleet headquarters that they would be arriving so the sudden appearance of an enemy vessel didn't result in loose bowels and pounding hearts on Hellfire, and now they were here. Technicians were already climbing all over the captured ship. The prisoners had been transferred to holding cells on the planet, and physicians and exobiologists were already poking and prodding.

Tracy had been summoned to a meeting with the top brass and Admiral Marqués Ernesto Chapman-Owiti to discuss … his thought stuttered to a stop, he actually had no idea what the meeting was about. He assumed it was just in the nature of military organizations to have meetings. He also had the matter of the surviving Isanjo to settle. He somehow had to get them back to Cuandru, and he had a feeling O-Trell wasn't going to help with that. Maybe some of them would choose to find work on Hellfire and he wouldn't have to buy passage for all of them? He could hope.

His thoughts were interrupted by a youthful voice calling out joyfully, "Oliver! I mean … Tracy!" His eyes picked out a familiar figure among the crowd.

"Luis!" he yelled, equally delighted.

The younger man ran to him and threw his arms exuberantly around Tracy and pounded him on the back. "*Mierda! Eres tú, mi hombre.*" Luis then remembered himself, became aware of the stares from the passing people. He stepped back, braced, and saluted.

Tracy returned the salute then held Luis at arm's length

and looked him up and down. He hadn't seen Luis Baca for well over a year since Luis had been recalled to active duty. A return to the regimen of a serving soldier had broadened his shoulders and narrowed his waist. The once luxuriant black hair had been cut to a more appropriate length. Tracy studied the insignia on Luis's sleeve and collar. He flicked at the ensign's ribbons. "What's this?"

Luis shrugged. "Applied for officer candidate school. And can you believe it? They took me."

"Of course, they did! They're lucky to have you."

"You never gave me this many compliments when I was aboard the *Selkie*," Luis mock complained.

"I didn't want your head to get any more swollen, *hijo*." He buffeted Luis on the shoulder. "Look, I've got to go to a meeting. Are you free later? Ping me your contact info and let me buy you a drink later."

"Not sure you'll get away from the big brass that easily, but if you do, yeah, I'd love to see you."

"How do you know—"

"It's all over headquarters that you captured a *necrófago* ship ..." Tracy couldn't help but smirk a bit that the name Flintoff had bestowed upon the aliens was already spreading through O-Trell. "And brought back prisoners." He laid a fingertip on Tracy's *Distinguido Servicio Cruzar* medal, one of the highest military honors bestowed by the League. "They'll probably give you another one of these."

"Great. This one is already almost too heavy to bear," Tracy said wryly.

"Don't knock it, *Capitan*. You've given us hope when we had almost lost it." Luis stepped back and saluted again.

"*Adios, hasta más tarde.*"

Tracy resumed his hunt for the conference room and finally located it. After being cleared by the steely-eyed security he was allowed to enter. Thankfully he wasn't the last to arrive. The chairs reserved for the top brass were still empty. Ernesto was flipping through messages on his ScoopRing, the images flashing past. Tracy wondered how he absorbed anything he was seeing. Hearing his footfalls, the head of the science division turned his head, and the light caught the single gold earring he was still wearing. He smiled in delight and jumped to his feet, clasping Tracy by the forearms.

"Tracy, *mi amigo*, so good to see you. It has been too long."

"It has been a long, strange journey, Ernesto." Tracy noted that the disdainful expressions on the other officers' faces were quickly being replaced with ones of interest and excitement since he clearly had the favor of the admiral. *People are such sheep,* he thought, and tried not to be bitter.

"I have so many questions, but we must wait for the high command," Chapman-Owiti said.

"As if you don't qualify, *Admiral*," Tracy teased.

"Come on, we eggheads never get the same respect as you warrior types. But seriously, what the hell were you doing leading a boarding party at your age?"

"Ouch!" Tracy held up his hands in defeat and laughed. "All right, enough throwing barbs." Tracy sobered. "I know this will take some time, but you'll keep me informed of what you learn, yes?" Tracy asked.

"Absolutely."

Tracy hesitated, then asked, "Will the Empress be—"

"No, she and the Consort are"—he hesitated, then temporized—"are on a need-to-know mission." Dread coiled in Tracy's gut, and Ernesto easily read his reaction and the question trembling on his lips. The other man leaned in and softly repeated, "Need-to-know."

Further conversation ended when three elderly men who oversaw the ground forces, wet foot navy, and O-Trell arrived along with their support staff. As the head of R&D, Ernesto took his place at the head of the table with them. Then began a grueling nine hours where Tracy gave a detailed report about recruiting the Isanjo, (that did not go over particularly well and he felt like his high collar was tightening around his throat), the construction of the decoy, and how it was rigged to bestow maximum damage on the *necrófago* ship. When he got to his report on the actual assault, the atmosphere became friendlier.

"The individual who disarmed the self-destruct mechanism should be recommended for commendation," one of the senior captains offered when Tracy got to that point in his report.

For a long moment he stood staring at the man, then his eyes flicked nervously to the four admirals who had remained relatively silent as the hours passed. His mind ratcheted through the troops who had accompanied Jahan to the engine room. All of them *fusileros*. Not an engineer among them. If he lied, it would be quickly revealed. If he told the truth … Jahan's large eyes seemed to float in the air before him.

"Captain?" his examiner prodded.

"It was actually an Isanjo, Jahan Sirani." The looks on the faces ranged from shock to disgust to disbelief. It almost made Tracy wish he had lied.

"Good God, Belmanor, you had an alien present during this highly dangerous mission? Are you mad?"

Tracy felt a flush of anger rising in his cheeks. "Actually *aliens*. Plural. And we were damn lucky they and she were there. We took losses getting to that ship. Among them were some of the engineers I had on the assault."

"You didn't hold them back until the ship was secured?" another man asked. Disdain dripped off of every word.

"Given how quickly the enemy destroy their own ships, we didn't believe we had that luxury, sir. And the surviving engineer was way the hell on the other side of the ship. And it was … is a big damn ship. He could never have reached the engine room in time, and Jahan's … Sirani's small size allowed her to ambush the *necrófagos*." He was talking too much and without proper deference. He knew it, but it was hard not to defend himself and his friend.

"Why are we even discussing this?" Ernesto interjected. "We have a captured ship. We have prisoners. And by the way, Captain Belmanor is right about that. It was only due to the surprise nature of the attack he succeeded in securing the ship at all."

"We are discussing it because a possibly dangerous precedent has been set," said Admiral Izawa, who oversaw O-Trell and reported directly to Mercedes. He turned back to Tracy. "Did you actually *arm* these BEMs?"

"Well, they had a couple of big-ass lasers that they used to dismantle the alien's rail gun, and they may have decided to pick up weapons from the fallen *fusileros* and dead aliens, which I would contend was a smarter choice than getting *shot*. So, I guess technically, no, I didn't arm them, but if I'd known they were going to help, I probably would have."

Ernesto gave him a surreptitious *calm down* hand wave out of sight of the big brass. "Sir, we need more such precedents, not fewer," the R&D admiral said. "We are in a situation not dissimilar to our ancestors when they first ventured out into the wider galaxy and discovered they were not alone. Old methods and hoary traditions will not save us. We need new ideas and new outlooks. New ways of looking at problems."

"What are you proposing, Chapman-Owiti? That we recruit BEMs?"

Tracy braced and brought his heels together with a sharp click. "Admiral, I can assure you that right now the Isanjo think of themselves as citizens of the League first and as BEMs second. In fact, I think it's a pretty safe bet that *all* the alien races are under no illusion that the *necrófagos* would spare their worlds. In this, we are all allies."

"Do the two of you think we should arm BEMs?" the admiral repeated.

He and Ernesto exchanged a long look. Tracy tried to communicate with only a look that *this one is on you, hermano. You're the admiral.*

A slender hand went to his ear and Ernesto fidgeted with his earring for a moment. Then drawing in a deep breath, Ernesto said, "I think it's something we should examine. Especially if the situation continues to deteriorate."

+ + +

"IT'S VERY … blue," her husband said as the elegant Rothchild shuttle began its orbital descent toward the planet below.

"Yes, lots more water and a good deal less landmass than we used to have," Henrick Rothchild said. The heir to the Rothchild fortune and titular head of Earth was a good-looking man in his early thirties. The unusual and quite rare blue eyes were striking against his dark skin.

Mercedes had decided to accept his invitation to visit the planet since she was going to need to pay a courtesy visit to the Vatican anyway. The process of laying out the intricate web of mines was tedious and really didn't require any input from her. Boho, as consort, had also been included in the invitation, and Mercedes thought it best to bring him since boredom was not something Boho endured with any degree of equanimity, and when Boho was bored bad things happened.

Unlike every other League world, Earth had been under the rule of one noble family for generations. Probably because Earth was depleted of valuable resources and the remaining population struggled to undo the damage caused by climate change, famine, and water wars. There was not much glory or profit to be gleaned on Earth. Since the Rothchilds were willing to govern despite these drawbacks, they had been granted permanent governorship of the planet.

Before the Fold drive had been invented there were Lunar, Martian, asteroid, and Jovian colonies, but those had quickly been abandoned as humans sought less harsh environs. Now, only planetary scientists lived in the abandoned colonies and inveterate misanthropes mined the asteroids.

In short, the home solar system was a sad backwater, and no major FFH family wanted to foot the bills or lead the efforts for its rehabilitation even with significant financial help from the League. Financial help that was going to have to be severely curtailed in this immediate crisis.

That was not a conversation Mercedes looked forward to having with Henrick Rothchild, so she turned her attention back to the port. Off to the left was the Moon for whom so many songs and poems had been written. Personally, Mercedes had found the small planetoid underwhelming when compared to Ouranos's three moons and the dramatic flare of the nebula that dominated the night sky of the capital world.

Mercedes turned away from the cratered surface and back to the planet. Between the massive population die-offs centuries before and the scramble by the survivors to leave behind the blighted planet, the population of Earth had been reduced from a high of over nine billion at the time of the exodus to slightly over a billion people. Cities had sprung up on the new coastlines that had been formed due to sea level rise. The lights from those cities glittered on the nightside of the planet. Mercedes keyed her ScoopRing and brought up an image of Earth taken from the first permanent orbiting space station back in the late nineteen eighties. She compared that image with the landmasses she was now seeing. The peninsula that had once been Florida was a tiny nub on the southern edge of the North American continent. The isthmus that had once linked Mexico to South America was gone. As the planet rolled beneath them, she was able to see where large sections of south Asia and Australia had vanished. The very small polar ice caps helped explain the encroaching water. Henrick leaned over her shoulder and laid a manicured finger on first the south pole and then the north pole.

"They are improving. Since my great-grandfather's time we've managed to drop median temperatures by three degrees. We're rolling back desertification in the North American southwest and Africa. Australia is going to be harder. Fortunately, the remaining population is passionate about the effort and are willing to make the necessary sacrifices."

"Which are?" Boho asked.

"An almost completely vegetarian diet augmented with some seafood as the oceans begin to recover." Boho made a face and Henrick laughed. "Oh, don't worry, my lord. We do have a few meat animals we raise for guests. We rely primarily on solar and fusion energy. As the native Americans used to say, we try to *tread lightly*."

"Why?" Mercedes asked. He cocked his head questioningly. "Why go through such draconian efforts when there are far more hospitable worlds with abundant resources waiting?"

"Jerusalem, Rome, Mecca, Varanasi, Bodh Gaya."

"All religious sites."

"Yes, Majesty." He shared his smile with both Boho and Mercedes. "And as I understand it, that is why you think the aliens will attack here next."

"Yes," Boho said.

Rothchild went on. "There are also wonders here… those that survived, and we want to preserve them. These are things that remind us of who we are as a species. We arose in these primal seas, crawled ashore, survived an asteroid, and learned to stand upright on the plains of Africa. Like any child, we recognize our mother." He had a nice smile and Mercedes was aware that he wore a light, clean cologne. "And doesn't everybody at some point want to come home? We're trying to make sure home is still here."

"You're a romantic," Mercedes said as he left her side and crossed to the bar to fill flutes with champagne.

"Kind word. Usually people say I'm fanciful, sentimental, nostalgic, or just a damn fool." She accepted the glass with a nod of thanks and took a sip. It was delicious, and he smiled at her reaction. "Yes, it is good. The best grapes are now grown in Siberia."

"So, is your foolishness genetic or a learned behavior? Your family has been at this for several generations," Boho asked.

"Who knows? Bit of both?" He turned his gaze to the port and gazed down at the planet now swelling before them as they made their approach. Mercedes was struck by the light in his eyes. "I just love the old girl. I'll never leave her."

Mercedes smiled at him. "Definitely a romantic. And I think you will succeed, Barón."

"Where will we be staying?" Boho asked.

"One of our estates in Italy. Easier for you to visit the Vatican from there."

The shuttle began to ride some chop and Rothchild took their glasses and strapped into his couch. "You've never been to Earth, Majesty?"

"No."

"If you have the time, ma'am, I would love to show some of the wonders—the Grand Canyon, Victoria Falls." Boho sniffed. "My lord?" Rothchild said politely.

"Holes in the ground and waterfalls. Every world has those."

"We also have the Taj Mahal and the Blue Mosque, the Guggenheim in Bilbao, the Shard in London."

"That would be more interesting," Boho said. "I'm afraid I'm not a man for natural wonders. I'll take a city and all it offers any day." He then bestowed that million-watt smile that had made women into lovers and men into confederates. It had the expected effect on Rothchild.

Mercedes gave a mental sigh and wondered how soon Boho would have the young man guiding him to all the best brothels? She hurried into speech. "I think it sounds delightful, Barón. Though our time is limited." She turned a stern look on Boho. "Once the mines are set, we must return to our ships and see if we guessed correctly."

17

BREAKING THROUGH THE DARKNESS

THEY BROKE THROUGH the darkness of the stellar cloud and the Freehold system lay before them. The single blazing star was like a pearl in the center of an oyster's shell. Around it orbited seven planets. The one they were approaching was the fourth world out and it showed a mix of blue oceans, green and brown continents, large polar ice caps, and was stippled with cloud cover. From this distance, they could see the bifurcation of the night and day sides of the planet. On the nightside, a net of lights glittered on the northern continent as if a massive colony of fireflies had taken up residence. Jahan had sent a hail toward the planet identifying themselves some three hours before. Now that they were in range to have a real-time conversation, the crew had gathered on the bridge.

"Hey, *Selkie*, welcome back. Long time no see. What you got for us?" It was the cheerful voice of Shaniqua Parris, who was the chief economic advisor to the government. Jahan figured Shaniqua had the best chance to get the message to the top people.

"Just news, but scary news. Also, a request from the

League."

"You told them about us?" Shaniqua didn't sound so cheery now.

"Of course not! And it's not exactly news that there are Hidden Worlds. Look, the Empress knows that we have been known to visit such places … upon occasion, and she wanted us to bring you a message. Just take it to your president and we'll take back the answer."

"Oh, no, no, no. Get your asses down here and we'll all go together."

"Oh, no, no, no," Jahan mimicked. "I'm not landing my ship and risk getting grounded when you've clearly got your panties in a twist. I'll come down—"

"I'll come, too," Jax interrupted. "I'm better at explaining things," the Flute added. Kielli snorted as he struggled to suppress a laugh and Jahan glared at him.

"Okay, we'll come down in the *Talon*. Tell us where you want us to land," Jahan said and broke the connection.

"Damn, I really wanted to pick up another package of that muscle relaxant they sell," Ernie said. "And that sore muscle rub."

"I take it that is a hint?" Jax asked.

"Yep," the human answered.

"We could use more frozen lemon juice, and that living lettuce and watercress they sell," Dalea said. "Oh, and more antibiotics."

Jahan turned and glared at her nephew. "Anything you want to add to the shopping list?"

"Nah … no, wait, I like those BattleTech books … the ones by Victor Milán," Kielli said.

"Fine. Give me a consolidated list and if we're not in jail after all this we'll go shopping."

"If you're not in jail maybe we can actually set down," Ernie said.

Jahan held up a warning finger. "Do not push it." She sighed. "How we went from independent traders—"

"And smugglers," Kielli interrupted.

"To agents of the Solar League, I do not know."

"We work with Thracius Ransom Belmanor and he is a chaos magnet," Jax replied dryly.

✦ ✦ ✦

THE ALIENS HAD dropped out of Fold close to Earth orbit but well away from the Moon and had hit the floating minefield, which resulted in them immediately losing two of their seven ships. The remaining five were currently trying to negotiate the ring of death surrounding Earth, but without the key to the random algorithm they weren't having a lot of luck.

One tried to back out of the killing field and looked like they might succeed. Another tried to enter Fold but based on the coruscating nimbus of light around the ship and the strange way space flexed, Mercedes suspected they had come to grief. She wondered if they might have pulled a mine through with them and what effect that might have in the weird not-space of the Fold.

Three down, four to go, she thought.

All around her, the frigate's bridge crew were reporting tactical information. Once they had returned to their ships after the visit to Earth, Mercedes had considered taking command of Boho's dreadnaught, but decided against it. He knew his officers and had their trust, and it was better not to interfere with command structure on the eve of battle. Especially when they were really going to need the dreadnaught's firepower. She just hoped that her presence on the frigate wouldn't be equally disruptive. What she really wanted was to fly an *infierno*, but that was never going to happen, and she just had to resign herself to that reality.

And that's when Mercedes private Foldstream channel overrode her privacy setting, and she suddenly had the holographic image of Ernesto Chapman-Owiti standing in front of her on the frigate's bridge. Other images overlaid his so his body seemed to be crawling with numbers and trajectory lines. It was clear from his expression that he had registered the fact she was wearing combat armor.

"Ernesto, this is *really* not a good time," Mercedes gritted, reflecting that it was the understatement of the century. She also resolved to remember to turn off the emergency override program on her ring when she was *about to enter combat.* "An alien attack squadron just dropped out of Fold and is in the process of getting chewed up by the minefield. I'll try to bring you back a prize," she said, knowing that would make her chief of R&D very happy.

"Don't bother," was the surprising reply. "Our old classmate, Belmanor, captured one of their destroyers. I've got crews crawling all over it right now. I was going to give you a report, but it's clear what you're up to so it can wait." His image flickered and vanished as he cut the connection.

"No, wait! Shit!" Mercedes frantically brought him back. "Belmanor? He captured a ship?"

"Yes. Prisoners, too."

"Oh. My. God."

"Quite. So don't worry about sparing these *pendejos.* Blow them to hell and back and then back again if possible." His image once again vanished.

Mercedes sent a general message to the other captains in the squadron telling them not to worry about prizes or prisoners. She wasn't surprised when Boho responded with a private message.

"What the hell, Mercedes? We need—"

"We've got one already and prisoners."

"What? How? Who?"

Oh, God, he's going to hate this. I need this distraction into psychodrama right now like I need ten years on my life.

For an instant she dithered. Reminding him of Tracy might becloud his thinking. It might also mean nothing to him; it had been almost forty years since their disagreements. On the other hand, Mercedes also wanted her husband to have as few reminders of Tracy as was humanly possible.

"Ernesto didn't give me any details. Time enough for that later. Right now, we have other, more pressing, matters to attend to. It does make our task significantly easier, so let's get to it."

She broke the connection and turned to frigate's captain. "Missiles are ready, Captain?"

"Yes, Admiral. On your order."

She gave the general order and the ship lurched slightly as missiles were launched in progressive waves. Her heads-up display showed the other League ships also firing their complements of missiles. The weapons' tiny brains had all been carefully programmed to negotiate the minefield, but with so many mines already detonated and debris from the damaged ships littering space they were going to lose some of the missiles to inadvertent contact with debris.

The ones that did survive were going to take thirty-seven minutes to reach their targets. Mercedes remembered her weapons professor at The High Ground telling the class that the hardest part of space combat was the waiting. Because, as another professor had once pointed out—space is big.

Data was flowing to her screen, updating every few seconds. Keeping track of the mass of information centered her and also helped pass the time.

Despite the losses and damage, the remaining enemy vessels did succeed in firing a barrage of missiles at the defending League ships. Some of the enemy missiles were hitting mines, but Mercedes knew some would get through and strike her ships. There had been a frantic effort to harden the hulls of O-Trell ships against the enemy ordinance, but despite all these efforts, people were going to die. Hopefully more of them would be on the other side.

The orders crafted in consultation with her top officers were to hold position until their missiles hit, then engage any remaining enemy on an individual basis. Her captains had the key to the maze, though now they would have to also negotiate the debris field. They also needed to move before the enemy's computers managed to crack the randomization code that controlled the mines.

Because of the surprise of the mines, the O-Trell missiles had a four-minute jump on their opponents, a lifetime in space combat. Mercedes's focus shifted between the incoming missiles and how long it would take to fire maneuvering rockets so her ship could reposition and take the hit on its least vulnerable point. Scans revealed the League missiles had reached their targets.

Mercedes closed the helmet on her battle armor and gave the order. "Engage maneuvering rockets." The frigate heeled like a rearing horse.

"Enemy has launched fighters," one of the people at tactical reported.

"Launch *infiernos,*" Mercedes ordered. The fighters were highly maneuverable, and had the key to the maze, but human error was always possible. She hoped they wouldn't lose any of their own to their own mines.

Then the enemy missiles hit. The frigate jerked and rocked, klaxons sounded, and damage reports began flowing in. She evaluated quickly. It wasn't too bad. She didn't worry about casualty reports. She would learn that distressing tally later when it couldn't distract her with emotion she couldn't afford.

She checked the locations and damage reports from the other ships in the squadron. One of the frigates had taken a bad hit and was bleeding air and fire. She ordered them to pull back, and it began limping away. Enemy fighters leaped after it like ravening wolves. She ordered some of the *infiernos* to assist and hoped it would be enough. Turning back to the remaining enemy capital ships, she saw that only three of them were still fighting. As she watched, one heavily damaged craft came apart from a massive explosion within its hull.

She saw Boho's ship, the *Vencedor,* moving in on the ship

that was tumbling with no sign of control and watched as he hammered it with rail gun and missiles until it, too, vanished in a fiery cloud. Two of her frigates and a destroyer were engaging the ship that had retreated beyond reach of the mines, which left only one damaged ship to be engaged. She waited, counting her heartbeats, but Boho's ship didn't begin maneuvers to close with the massive enemy ship.

She was torn between cursing and making excuses. They needed to divide their forces between the damaged enemy destroyer and the lightly damaged enemy flagship. All around her were flares of fire as the small fighters chased each other in sweeping moves like a wheeling flock of birds or school of fish. She sent two frigates to engage the destroyer and ordered the destroyer in her small squadron to join her frigate and close with the enemy dreadnaught. Their advance was of necessity quite slow as they negotiated the remaining mines.

An updated readout told her that the enemy flagship was clearing the mines between it and its beleaguered partner by sweeping the area with lasers. She cursed herself for not thinking of that herself. There was no reason to preserve what remained of the mine maze. It had served its purpose. She ordered the destruction of the mines separating her from her prey, and the big main engines began to rumble as their speed increased.

With most of the mines detonated, she ordered another missile barrage, and ordered the rail gun to begin pounding the enemy flagship. It reciprocated, and the frigate rocked as missiles and lead slugs pounded the hull and, in some places, broke through.

Minutes felt like hours, but it also felt like she didn't have time to absorb and evaluate the torrent of data she was receiving in her heads-up display. The much smaller frigate could not withstand much more. Then finally a telemetry reading gave her hope. The *Vencedor* was finally closing. The firepower from the flagship brought things to a final conclusion. Once again, the enemy ship self-destructed. The two frigates had handled the other ship, battering it into composite pieces. The remaining enemy fighters destroyed themselves when they saw the destruction of the large ships that could have carried them to safety.

The battle for Earth was over and the home world had not taken a single blow.

Mercedes stood and her knees buckled. The frigate captain leaped to her side and caught her by the elbow. "You need to rest, Majesty."

"Soon. After I've gone to sick bay." He nodded in understanding, stepped back, braced, and saluted her. Everyone else on the bridge followed suit. As she walked to the elevator someone called, "To Her Royal Majesty, hip hip hooray." Others picked up the cheer.

She escaped into the elevator, and once the doors closed, she pulled off her helmet, rested her sweat-slick forehead against the wall, and fought back the nausea that threatened to overwhelm her. She should have been elated. Instead, she just felt drained.

✦ ✦ ✦

"YOU'RE ASKING US to take a big risk here," the president of

Freehold said. Alison Newberry had the look of an affectionate grandmother: plump, white-haired, with laugh lines around her mouth. Until you looked in her eyes and saw the steel there.

Jahan found herself inwardly cursing Tracy and Mercedes, and the fucking *necrófagos*, for putting her in this situation. It was *their* fault she was talking to a fucking *president.* As soon as she and Jax had landed in the *Talon*, they had been whisked off to the Residence, which was what the Freeholders called the big building that housed the president's private quarters and also a large number of executive government offices. She then realized that being intimidated was really stupid. Not that long ago she had told off an empress. What was a mere president? The office easily accommodated the four humans and two aliens who were present. In addition to Jahan and Jax and the president, there was the Residence chief of staff, a tall and slim man of Asian descent, Horace Shu, Senator Walter Fineman, and the government's chief economic advisor Shaniqua Parris.

"I know, ma'am, and I wish that you and our empress could discuss this over a cup of tea—"

"Or something stronger," Fineman muttered. He was a tech genius turned politician and had been a trading partner with the *Selkie* for years.

Jahan went on, "But both my immediate boss and *his* boss are busy fighting aliens and trying to save the League."

"And they want us to protect their children," Newberry said.

"As any of us would," Shaniqua said. She was an elegant woman with elaborate and beautiful cornrows decorated with red beads that set a counterpoint to her ebony skin.

"You talking to any of the other Hidden Worlds?" Fineman asked.

"We'll be talking to all of them," Jahan answered. "We don't expect you guys to carry the whole load."

The humans exchanged long glances. "And you guarantee that no official League ships will be used in the evacuation," the chief of staff said.

"We made that point abundantly clear to the Empress," Jax said.

There was again another long pause and more looks exchanged. Fineman ran a hand through his curly grey hair. "Could be worse, Madam President, they could be asking us to join in the fight."

"And what makes you think that won't happen?" Shu muttered darkly.

Jahan shrugged. "It might come to that if things don't get better, but if there's one thing all of us alien races learned, it's that you humans know how to fight. I expect you'll find a way to kick the shit out of this new bunch of aliens, too."

Newberry gave her a sympathetic look. "It must be hard."

"Eh, it's been centuries. You get used to a thing."

"I do have demands," the president said.

"Okay," Jahan said cautiously.

At the same time Jax said, "To be expected."

"I want a negotiated treaty signed off on by not only the Empress, but your parliament as well, that there will be no attempt to incorporate Freehold into the League."

"Your Highness … I mean, your presidentness …"

The chief of staff leaned in. "She's referred to as Madam

President or ma'am."

"Oh, okay. Well, as I was going to say … ma'am, I'm not a diplomat. I'm a star rat, a spacer. I don't know anything about negotiating treaties—"

"Don't worry; I'm going to send diplomats with you."

"And how can you be sure they will not be taken instantly into custody once they make themselves known?" Jax asked.

"No treaty, no kids."

Jax's fronds all shivered, a rattling, shushing sound that was the Tiponi version of laughter. "A persuasive argument," he admitted.

"So, we have a deal?" Newberry asked.

Jahan threw up her hands. "Yeah, sure, okay. It's not like we haven't transported some of your spies before."

"Just think how much nicer that this time it will be happening out in the open," Shu said, and for the first time he cracked a smile.

Newberry sighed and pinched the bridge of her nose. "Okay. So, if your empress is willing, we're going to be doing the whole *bring us your tired, your poor, your huddled masses—*"

"Huh?" Jahan said.

"Old Earth saying, used to be etched on a big statue." Newberry waved it away. "Never mind. I need to inform Congress. They'll argue and dither and piddle around for a while, but we'll bring them around. Meanwhile, I'll bring in the commander of SpaceCom to work out the details with you. Call signals and so forth for these ships that are going to be arriving. But now I need to get back to the other issues setting fire to my inbox, and Horace here has to pick our negotiators."

"If I might make a suggestion," Jax said. Newberry waved her assent. "I would have Shaniqua as one of your negotiators. She's excellent at it, and she looks a lot more like the majority of League citizens than many of you do."

"So, they're not only racist against aliens, but against other humans, too," Shu said.

"No, most of their distinctions are based more on class than on race—are you FFH or a mere *señor*," Jax said. "However, after hundreds of years of interbreeding most people in the League are darker-skinned. Someone with the President's coloring would be taken for a recent transplant from an assimilated Hidden World and thus have less status."

"Thank you, that's good to know," Newberry said, and she stood. They all followed suit. "It was nice meeting you, Jahan. Travel safe."

"Thank you, ma'am, nice meeting you, too."

The door to the office closed behind them. The staff in the outer office were well trained; they kept working, but there were a few curious looks.

"So, we're stuck here for a while," Jahan said.

"We'll get you on your way as quickly as possible," Shu said. "But things don't move fast in a democracy."

"Okay, guess that means we can bring down the *Selkie*, and our crewmates can do their own damn shopping."

18

POWER GAMES

WITHIN HOURS OF the victory the news blackout had been lifted. Boho had hoped to craft the press release with Anselmo, but the delirious joy of the Earth's citizens had required that he and Mercedes return to the planet for the celebration. Cheering crowds had lined the streets, flinging flowers as the Empress and her Consort rode past. The banquet at the Rothchild estate had even been attended by the Pope himself.

When they had returned to the shuttle, Boho had held Mercedes close, nuzzling her hair and whispering that she should return with him to the *Vencedor* rather than the frigate. She had given him a faint smile, but demurred, saying she still had duties aboard the ship that had borne her flag, and she did not wish to insult the officers and crew who had fought so valiantly for her. It had struck him that she had seemed tense and uneasy.

Now he knew why.

Boho sat at his desk staring at the news feeds, grinding anger filling his gut as their heroic defense of the mother world was very much the second story to the news that Captain Thracius Belmanor and his small squadron had captured an enemy destroyer and brought back not only the ship but prisoners to Fleet Command on Hellfire. Boho put a fist through the hologram and managed to send his coffee cup flying off the desk to shatter on the composite floor of his office aboard the flagship.

He pinged Anselmo back on Ouranos and didn't bother with any niceties once the younger man's image appeared. "How the hell did you fuck up the messaging on this so comprehensively?"

"Um, well, it was a little hard to be heard over the Admiral of Gold touting his brilliance in putting Belmanor in charge of a squadron and Princess Beatrisa giving interviews about her commander's creativity and brilliance."

"The Empress and I saved the home world!"

"Yeah, and that was awesome, sir, but the truth is the vast majority of our citizens think Earth is a backwater at best and, er … a shithole at worst."

"I am aware of that, but it is also the world where we rose to sentience and from which we emerged to conquer the goddamn galaxy," Boho gritted through clenched teeth.

Dear Christ, I sound like Rothchild, Boho thought.

"I'm aware of all that, sir, but ships blowing up because they hit a bunch of mines followed by a ship-to-ship battle against already damaged foes doesn't have the … ah … panache that the other story had." Boho remained silent. "I take it you haven't read any of the news stories," Anselmo murmured.

"Give me the short version."

"Decoy, heroic boarding action led by Captain Belmanor himself and assisted by Isanjo workers."

"Fucking glory hound," Boho burst out. He remembered how Belmanor had done the same decades ago when radicals had taken control of the High Ground and threatened Mercedes. Boho had the difficult task of coordinating the student's efforts against the terrorists while Belmanor had hared off to play the hero.

"And that's certainly how some … uh, a number of people are viewing it."

"But not, I take it, a majority?"

Anselmo hesitated. "No, sir. A lot more people think it's rather … awesome."

"Well, for fuck's sake, do what you can to get the Empress as the top-trending story and not this *intitulado*."

"Yes, sir." The image of his factotum vanished, and Boho sat drumming his fingers on the surface of his desk. His batBEM slipped in, eyed the broken china, and quietly began to clean up the shards and spilled coffee.

"Trouble, sir?"

"Just an irritant, Ivoga."

"Very good, sir."

Boho studied the Isanjo. "So, have you heard about the actions of some of your fellows?"

"Yes, sir."

"And?"

"I think it's not wise to draw that much attention to oneself, sir."

"You're a cautious one, aren't you?" Boho said.

"Yes, sir. I think I can better serve you by remaining relatively … invisible."

"Good. Let's keep it that way." Ivoga inclined his head

and slipped out with the remains of the cup.

Boho left the office and made his way to his quarters. Ivoga had collected some of the bouquets that had been strewn before them, and printed out articles from the Earth news sites and a few of the cards left by grateful citizens. Boho stared at the riotous display and felt sick. It all tasted of ashes now.

Using their private channel, he put in a call to Mercedes. Despite the late hour, she was still at her desk and had multiple screens up filled with reports. At the sight of his expression, she minimized the screens and folded her hands primly in front of her. "So, you know," she said simply.

He appreciated that she didn't pretend not to understand the reason for his call. "Did you know? About …" He couldn't bring himself to say the man's name. "About the captured ship?"

"Yes, Ernesto let me know. Just before we engaged the enemy."

"Then we need to go to Hellfire," Boho said.

"I'm sorry, but we can't. Not yet. First, my ship is waiting for me at Ouranos and, more importantly, an emissary from one of the Hidden Worlds is going to meet us in Hissilek to negotiate the terms of the evacuation."

"So, contact both the *San Francisco de Asis* and these renegades and send them to Hellfire."

"I can't. These … renegades, as you call them, are in Fold right now. And besides, I'm not sure I want them getting a good look at fleet headquarters."

"So, you don't trust them?"

"I don't trust them that much," she corrected.

"But you would give them our son?"

"Only if this meeting goes well, which is another reason why I'm not willing to make any change at this late date." Her expression tightened and her eyes slid away from his image. "There's something else you should know. And please don't get mad." A hollow replaced his stomach and Boho braced for what was about to come. "Given what he's accomplished I really don't have a choice." She took a deep breath and rushed out the words. "I'm promoting Belmanor to vice admiral and giving him the new fleet, I'm forming comprised of these newly built ships coming off the line and a few ships from both the Blue and the Gold."

The thought of the man holding the same rank as himself had the hollow replaced by a burning coal in the pit of his stomach. Boho forced himself to keep his tone flat and even. "There are worthy officers of the FFH who will not take kindly to this."

"I know. But right now, we need the *intitulados* supporting the war effort. Having one of their own recognized and honored will help with recruitment and we desperately need bodies. Especially once we locate the aliens' home world."

"So, you're contemplating an invasion. Wouldn't it be easier to stand off and pound the planet back to primordial ooze?"

Her face was drawn with anguish. "I don't think I want to be remembered for killing an entire species."

"Believe me, *our* species won't care after what they've done to us."

"But I will, and that's not a burden I wish to have on my soul when I face judgement, Boho."

The look she gave him begged for comfort, but he couldn't offer any. He felt cheated, forgotten, and disrespected. "I suppose you'll do as you wish. So, I guess we had best get home and meet this mysterious emissary and see our little boy before we have to lose him for the duration of this hellborn war."

✦ ✦ ✦

SHANIQUA HAD INSISTED that Jahan be present for the meeting. *First a president, now the Empress … again*, Jahan thought as she nervously entered the drawing room of a fucking *palace*. Granted it wasn't *the* palace. That one had been bombed to rubble, but even this small palace seemed overwhelmingly opulent to Jahan. Even Mercedes seemed a distant and august figure dressed as she was in a cerise gown with a small diadem of gold and rubies, and Jahan found herself intimidated despite her best efforts to remain blasé. At least she knew the Empress, though it would probably be impolitic to mention that with her husband present.

Jahan had met Beauregard Honorius Sinclair Cullen, Knight of the Shells, Shareholder General of the Grand Cartel, the 20th Duque de Argento y Pepco and now the Prince Consort before, and she prayed God he wouldn't remember. It was when he had stolen the contents of an abandoned Cara'ot ship from the *Selkie* crew, and that encounter had revealed that their captain wasn't whom they had thought. At the time she had thought Cullen's intimidating size was due to the spacesuit, but now that she saw him in the flesh, she realized he really was a very big man. A bigger man than Tracy in every way: taller, broader, and far more handsome as humans judged such things. And judging by his thunderous expression he wasn't all that keen on her or the emissary from Freehold.

Jahan sank into a curtsey, though it seemed gauche to do it dressed in her coveralls and snuck a glance at Mercedes from beneath her lashes as she did so. Truthfully, in these surroundings Jahan couldn't see the woman she had known aboard the *Selkie*. If Mercedes had been haunted by events nearly five years ago, she looked positively hagridden now. She was terribly thin, there was added grey in the long curls and new wrinkles around her eyes, and fear lurked deep in those dark brown eyes. Jahan felt sorry for her. No single individual should have to carry the safety of literally trillions of souls both human and alien on her shoulders.

While Jahan showed obeisance, Shaniqua merely nodded. Once Mercedes indicated for her to rise Jahan made the introduction. "Your Majesty, Your Highness"—she nodded to Cullen—"may I present Shaniqua Parris, chief economic advisor to the President of Freehold."

Shaniqua approached Mercedes with her hand outstretched. "It is considered impolite to touch royalty, *señorita* Shaniqua," Cullen said.

"First, I'm not anybody's little miss, and second, my first name is for my friends. I'm Ms. Parris, and sugar—you don't mind if I call you sugar, do you?—it's my party, so my rules," Shaniqua said.

Cullen seemed to get even larger, and Jahan had to fight the urge to extend her claws. Mercedes laid a hand on her husband's arm and gave Shaniqua a cold glance. "Why don't we all take a breath and start again. Ms. …" She struggled a bit with the unfamiliar title. "Ms. Parris, we are grateful that you are willing to aid us, but the benefit in this relationship isn't flowing in just one direction. It's my navy and my troops that are fighting this alien threat. The fact they haven't reached your planet probably has more to do with luck than any action on your part. So, what say we all agree each side has something of value to offer the other."

Shaniqua smiled. "That sounds fair."

"So, can we now can we get down to making arrangements?"

"Once we have a solid understanding and a binding treaty approved by your congress or parliament or whatever it is you have, stating that the Solar League will never move against Freehold or any other Hidden World that aids in the evacuation of League children."

"Absurd," Cullen snorted. "And surely you can see the wisdom in joining forces with the League. Separate you are helpless against these kinds of threats."

Mercedes again laid a hand lightly on his arm. "I think that *señ*"—she broke off and corrected herself—"Ms. Parris is referring to our practice of annexing Hidden Worlds."

"I think it's more your practice of stealing children that would piss us off," the woman responded. "Which is rather rich considering you're asking our help to shelter yours. So, what's it to be? Binding treaty or do I get back on board the *Selkie* and head home?"

"How do you know so much about our policy toward Hidden Worlds?" Boho asked.

"We've been trading with you. Well, not with *you*, but

with the people you don't notice. Your alien citizens and a few select humans that the aliens have vouched for. They've told us all about your policies and practices."

"Our policies have created a star-spanning empire. It works," Mercedes said.

"Except that one time when it didn't," Jahan blurted, and wanted to throttle herself with her own tail. Mercedes looked both guilty and furious. The consort's brows snapped together in a frown, and he gave Jahan a calculating look. Shaniqua looked confused. "Sorry. Don't mind me." Jahan skittered away and tried to blend in with the furniture. The consort's eyes remained fixed on her.

Shaniqua was shaking her head in disagreement. "No, it doesn't. You gobble up anything you can because your system isn't sustainable. You must be smart enough to know that hereditary titles and a top-heavy aristocracy burdening the folks farther down in the food chain don't make for a vibrant society or economy."

"Such smug belief in your superiority," Cullen said.

Shaniqua shot him a glance. "Yeah, I guess that's true. Guess we'll find out who's right." She turned back to Mercedes. "Look, Your Majesty, we can stand here arguing the relative merits of our political systems, or we can start moving your kids to safety. Your call."

"How do you know you can trust us?" Mercedes asked. "What's to stop me from reneging after this war has ended?"

Parris glanced back at Jahan. "My associates have vouched for you. Said you're a person of honor." She paused for a moment, then added, "Also, we'll have your kids, and you won't know where they are."

Cullen had been back to staring at Jahan but that brought his attention snapping back to Shaniqua. "And what's to stop us from arresting you and this BEM right now, seizing the ship. We'd get the coordinates out of you and then we don't need your fucking treaty." His hands were clenched at his sides and anger turned the angles of his handsome face into an ugly mask of rage.

Shaniqua was unimpressed. "Because we've got ships, too. You want to fight us, or you want to fight the aliens who are killing you?"

"Keep in mind you humans are the meanest fuckers we've ever run across," Jahan said. "You'd do a lot of damage to each other and then the only group that wins are these *necrófagos*. Can't you all just agree that you have each other's tails in a wringer and get on with this?"

"Fine," Mercedes snapped.

"Okay, then," Shaniqua said. "Shall we get to drafting?" They moved to the conference table.

"I'm just going to go and let the other ships know this may be happening and get my ship ready to lift …" Nobody acknowledged her, so Jahan shrugged and left the elegant drawing room.

Only to be brought up short in the hallway by a viselike grip on the back of her neck. Jahan fought the urge to unsheathe her claws. It was the consort, and he forced her across the hall and pushed her face against the wall.

"You were the ship. The one at Kusatsu-Shirane, weren't you? The one that found the empress."

"Umm … maybe."

"I want to talk to your captain."

"You are, sir." She was jerked around to face him, his hand at her throat.

"Bullshit. I want to talk to this Randall fellow."

"He's gone. I think he might even be dead. Had a bad heart. Sold out his share in the ship to the rest of the crew. Very sad …" She was babbling and forced herself to shut up. She could feel her heart hammering in her chest and her lungs seemed incapable of pulling in air. His hand on her throat also wasn't helping.

He was staring at her with an all too calculating expression. "Strange that you wouldn't know if he were alive or dead. Man, you served with for … how long?" Jahan didn't answer. "Tell you what, I'll find out for you."

"That's … so nice. Thank you." They stood in silence for what felt like a couple of years. Finally, Jahan said meekly, "May I go now, sir? I … we really do need to get the ship ready."

He released her and stepped back. As she scampered away, she wondered how quickly Jax could get a death certificate prepared for the late lamented Oliver Randall.

+ + +

"YOU DIDN'T GIVE me the *Swiftsure*," Captain Princess Beatrisa said accusingly after she finished her salute, which was so textbook perfect that Tracy knew it was meant as an insubordinate insult.

"No," Tracy said shortly as he pushed aside the virtual screens that hung over the much larger and more impressive desk that he now occupied. The screens coruscated with colors and numbers as if objecting to his sharp dismissal.

"You gave it to Valada-Viers."

"Yes."

"May I ask why, Vice Admiral?"

Despite the polite wording Tracy was not fooled. She was clearly furious. It was unworthy of him, but he was rather looking forward to her reaction to his next statement. "Because I'm making you my flag captain."

Unfortunately, Beatrisa was in full cry and rode right over his words. "Has my performance been substandard? I held the line against ..." Finally, the moment he had been eager to enjoy arrived. "I ... what did you say?"

"I'm making you my flag captain," Tracy repeated. The princess goggled at him. Tracy looked over to where his batBEM was busy setting out a tea tray. "I think the Captain Princess might require something a bit stronger, Kallapus."

The Hajin bowed. "Very good, sir. Wine, port, or whisky, Highness?"

"Whisky," Beatrisa said. "May I sit down?"

"Please." Tracy gestured at the chair, and she dropped into as if her legs no longer had the power to support her.

Once they both held crystal highball glasses, Tracy motioned to Kallapus to leave. "Why?" Beatrisa said faintly. "Why the hell would you pick *me*? This is a *buque insignia,* an *acorazado.* The only thing I've ever commanded was a fucking *explorador*. This thing is ten times its size. This should have gone to Valada-Viers after his promotion."

"He's not ready. He's been a fine XO, but he needs a smaller command to get his feet wet. Also, he's very familiar with the *Swiftsure*. It's the right place for him."

"And you think the bridge of a dreadnaught is the right place for *me*? You cannot be serious."

"I am, and if you'll stop huffing at me, I'll tell you why." He cocked an eyebrow at her, daring her to talk. She confined herself to taking a big gulp of scotch. "First, you're cool under pressure. You understand tactics and strategy. You run a tight ship. You're already a captain so you know what's required, and you're ready for a larger command, and … I need your… exalt," he said, reminding her of their very first conversation.

"My exalt? How the hell does that apply in this situation?"

"This is a new and understrength fleet. I'm an *intitulado* who has been promoted to admiral over the heads of a fuckload of FFH nobility, but whom *nobody*—meaning your sister—has seen fit to reward with a title. I need *you* to make *me* seem respectable so the noble captains who have to take my orders and just *reek* of exalt will take me seriously."

"So, I'm just a royal figurehead. And I never took you for a title hound."

"For fuck's sake, were you not listening at all? All those compliments and the only thing you grab onto is this?"

"Yeah, because it was shitty, and I expect it was the real reason."

"It is *a* reason, and you know what else is shitty? Getting promoted, given the responsibility, and not getting a title commensurate with that promotion, which clearly signals what the crown thinks of me." He was panting a bit when he finished, and his face felt hot.

He was suddenly eighteen, walking into the gym at The

High Ground past the armor that had belonged to Vice Admiral Øystein Nash, who had also been a scholarship student but had won his title at a famous battle during the Expansion wars. Tracy had pretended that none of the FFH bullshit mattered to him but knew that in his secret heart he had dreamed of winning high honors. Later he had longed for a title so that he might be considered a worthy match for Mercedes. It was a foolish hope then. Now it was sheer idiocy, and he hated that it still had the power to hurt him.

"You do understand there's a reason she didn't ennoble you, right?" Beatrisa pulled him from his resentment. He looked at her in confusion. "We desperately need ordinary people, citizens, to volunteer. You're a symbol. One of their own who has risen to a high position. If you're made a condé or a marquis or a duque then you're just another FFH asshole. Didn't you wonder why there was a press officer assigned to the *Sutābureză*? They're here to cover *you*."

Tracy stared at her. His mouth had gone dry. "A press officer? I didn't know …"

"Well, now you do."

Tracy leaned back and took a long pull of his drink. Let the smokey liquor swirl in his mouth and trace fire down his throat. The knot in his chest began to loosen and he chuckled. Beatrisa gave him an inquiring look.

"So, we both have to be a dog and pony show to our various strata of society while at the same time fighting a war for the very survival of our civilization. Yeah, no pressure."

Beatrisa threw back her head and laughed. "Piece of cake … and speaking of cake. I believe I saw your batBEM arranging some on that tray." She paused. "So, may Flag

Captain Princess Arango help herself?"

"Flag Captain Princess Arango may." They stood and Tracy held out his hand. They shook. "Welcome to the Green and welcome aboard."

19

SEX MAKES YOU STUPID

I MUST NOT *cry! I must not cry!*

Mercedes repeated the mantra over and over to herself as she walked toward the *Selkie.* Cyprian was walking between his parents clinging desperately to their hands. Mercedes was struck by how much he had grown in the ten months since his birthday party.

Hayden paced somberly behind them, walking at Elizabeth's side. Security formed a phalanx around them. The other children who would be aboard the *Selkie* and their parents were kept back several hundred meters to give the royal family privacy.

The *Selkie* had landed on a section of the Hissilek spaceport that had been hastily repaired. To either side were other trading vessels with lines of parents and children heading toward them. The air was filled with the wails of children and crying mothers. And indeed, it was mostly women relinquishing their children. Their husbands had gone to war.

And soon these wives might be joining them, Mercedes thought.

The crews of the trading vessels stood guard around their ships. They had made it clear they wanted no imperial security or military personnel to approach. They didn't trust the government not to try and place trackers on their ships and had in fact demanded they be allowed to disable their transponders during these trips. They weren't wrong to be suspicious. That suggestion had in fact been raised by SEGU and shot down quickly and firmly by Mercedes.

"We have been warned in no uncertain terms that if we try that the deal is off," she had told Ian Rogers. "Our children are the issue here. Besides which, I signed a treaty with one of the worlds and a number of others have demanded reciprocation, and if we violate a treaty we will be seen as faithless and without honor. So, no." Fortunately it was Ian, who was devoted to her, rather than the former head of SEGU. Old Kemel DeLonge would have had no compunction about ignoring her commands.

Cyprian's grip on her hand got tighter, and she feared he was about to make a scene. She leaned over and kissed the top of his head and whispered, "I'm so proud of you. You're so brave and that helps the other children." Her voice quavered a bit on the final words.

He looked up at her and said, "Don't cry, Mommy. Haydy 'splained it all. We watch out for all of them," he stated with no small amount of pride.

Mercedes and Boho exchanged delighted and desperate glances. "That's absolutely right," Boho said, his voice deeper and the tone huskier than normal. "You do look out for all of them." He smiled down at his son. "You're their leader. Their Prince."

"Like you, Daddy."

"Yes." And this time Boho did have to turn his face aside

and give a surreptitious wipe of his eyes. In that moment Mercedes found herself loving him more than she had in years.

They reached the foot of the gangway. Jahan and Dalea were waiting. Dalea bobbed a curtsy. Mercedes extended her hand and lightly touched the tips of Dalea's six fingers. "How do you do?"

"Honored, Your Majesty," the Hajin murmured.

Her eyes were demurely lowered and not by a tremor of an eyelash did she reveal that they had ever met before. Not so Jahan. The Isanjo was standing with a frozen expression, staring at Cyprian. Mercedes cleared her throat. Jahan dropped into an awkward curtsy. She was blinking rapidly as if her eyes had become semaphores. Mercedes again cleared her throat and it seemed to return Jahan to her surroundings.

The Isanjo took a step forward and dropped down so her eyes were on the same level with Cyprian's. She didn't have far to go; the little boy was quite tall for his age.

"Hi," Jahan said. "You must be Prince Cyprian. I'm Jahan and this is Dalea. Over there is my nephew Kielli and that's Ernie." She waved toward the grizzled human and the other Isanjo who were hanging back. They both looked terrified at the presence of royalty in their cargo hold. "Our other crew member is aboard. You'll meet him in a minute. And you guys"—her fang-revealing smile included Hayden as well—"won't be alone. We're taking a lot of other boys and girls. This is going to be fun."

Mercedes wondered why Jahan was babbling. It was unlike her. Hayden and Elizabeth were properly introduced, the boys' holdalls passed over to the older human. Elizabeth carried not only her own clothes, but a case filled with Cyprian's favorite toys. Mercedes stood hesitating, her free hand rubbing Cyprian's back, ruffling his hair.

Dalea said gently, "Majesty, we do need to get all these other children aboard."

"Yes, of course." *Don't cry! Don't cry!* She knelt down in front of her little boy while Boho had Cyprian pressed tightly against his thigh. "Okay, love bug. You be good. Do what Elizabeth and the ship crew tell you. It won't be for long. Mommy and Daddy will bring you home soon and the people you'll stay with are very nice."

She kissed Cyprian's cheeks and eyes and tasted the salt. The reality was beginning to set in, and Cyprian started to lose control. The little boy whispered, "I'm scared, Mommy! I want to stay with you and Daddy!" Sobs shook his small frame.

Mercedes began to make soothing sounds, but Boho turned his son around to face him. "But you can't. We all have our jobs to do, and I know you won't disappoint me. You won't, will you?"

Boho's stern tone shocked Cyprian and his sobs subsided. "No, Daddy," he whispered.

Hayden stepped forward. "I'll be your aide de camp, Cypri. You tell me what to do and I'll carry out your orders, Your Highness." He came to attention and gave the child a very credible salute. He had turned fifteen in the intervening months and the man he would become was starting to emerge. Cyprian looked intrigued at that idea and the waterworks ended.

Mercedes gave Cypri one last kiss, then stood and embraced Hayden. "We'll be all right," the boy whispered to her.

She gave a tight nod and hugged him tighter for a moment. She and Boho stepped back, and they watched the trio follow Dalea into the ship. "Don't worry, ma'am," Jahan said. "We'll take good care of them and so will Freehold."

"They better or—" Boho began.

Mercedes laid a hand on his arm. "No threats. We've had enough killing. *Ve con Dios*, Jahan."

"And you, Majesty."

Boho put an arm around her shoulders, and they walked away. It was only once they were back in the privacy of the imperial flitter that she allowed her tears to come.

✦ ✦ ✦

"JESUS FUCKING CHRIST on a bicycle!" Jahan hissed to Dalea. "If that kid isn't Tracy's, I'm a Sidone." Dalea, her back to Jahan, kept rearranging her medical supplies. "Answer me, damn it!"

"Well, you're not a Sidone," the Hajin smirked.

Jahan sank down onto one of the bunks in the small med bay. "Oh crap, this is not good."

"In what way?"

"If I can see it when he's this little, before too long it's going to be clear to anybody with eyes that the consort did not sire that boy."

"We know Tracy very well," Dalea said placidly. "And humans are very good at seeing what they expect to see. And how likely is it that they will all be in proximity of each other? For all his gifts, Tracy is still an *intitulado*, and there must be thousands of ships and ship captains."

"I've got a newsflash for you, he's now a vice admiral after that stunt we pulled with the *necrófago* ship."

That brought the Hajin around to face her. Now she looked worried. "Oh, I didn't know that. How would you know that?"

Jahan shrugged. "I keep an eye on the Stars and Galaxy website," she said referring to the military's news feed. "It lists deaths and promotions. I check both."

Dalea sat down next to Jahan and put an arm around her shoulders. "You're worried about him."

"Both of them, Tracy and Luis. At least Luis is no longer an *hombre*. Being an officer has to come with some perks, right?"

"Don't see how. If a ship gets blown to pieces, you're going to die whether you're an officer or an *hombre*."

"You are *not* helping."

"And worrying about all of this isn't going to help them either," Dalea said. "Let's focus on what we can do. Protect the future by ferrying these children to safety and carry medical supplies to try and save the wounded."

Jahan leaned her head briefly against her friend's shoulder. "Thank you. But it did feel good to shoot those fuckers."

"I've only killed once, and it's not an experience I'm eager to repeat, so I'll pass on that, but you be as bloodthirsty as you want."

"Faint hope of that. The humans will never arm us," Jahan said while she pondered just who in the hell the gentle Hajin might have killed.

"Well, to be fair, we did kill a lot of them," Dalea said.

"And they killed more of us … and won."

"And now we have two humans in positions of authority who seem to actually like us, trust us, and have some understanding of our issues. That's got to be a good thing and count for something."

Jahan slid off the bunk and ran a hand down the length of her tail to smooth the fur. "You are an incurably optimist pony."

"No. I just know that there is an inexorable pattern to history. And that change does come."

"Yeah, just not very fast and it also sometimes needs a shove."

"What makes you think no one is shoving?" Dalea asked quietly.

The quiet question stopped Jahan before she reached the door. She looked back, but Dalea's expression was bland and unreadable. "What aren't you telling me?"

"Oh, many things. About the husband I abandoned, and what happened at that hospital years ago, and why I never wanted children, and—"

"Okay, fine, keep your secrets."

"For now. Someday …" She shook her head. "No matter. You'd best check on our passengers and try to keep Jax from shedding every frond he's got."

Jahan laughed. "Yeah, I just hope one of these rug rats doesn't try to climb him."

✦ ✦ ✦

"HE'S STILL *HERE?"* Mercedes's voice. *"I thought the Green*

would have deployed by now! I expected to be briefed just by you. I don't really need to hear from him."

Tracy froze just before the corner in the *Ministerio de Guerra*. He and his fleet were still stuck in orbit around the planet because one of the new ships rushed off the assembly line had proved to have a crack in a starboard engine. Dulac had seemed to take it as a personal insult that a newly commissioned ship had such a problem, and he and several other Isanjo had remained behind to help with repairs.

Tracy was chafing at the delay, but it did give him time to evaluate the officers who commanded those ships and to have the Isanjo who had remained at Hellfire inspect them all. The captains' reactions to that order told him a lot about the men he would lead and helped him flag the ones he wanted to replace. Unfortunately, that was easier said than done. He had new ships that needed new crews, and competent people were thin upon the ground. Trying to fill out the complement of crew he needed for the new *exploradors, fragatas, cruseros,* and *destructores* now under his command was proving to be challenging.

As for the ships that he had inherited from the Blue and the Gold, a depressing pattern was starting to emerge. They all had an alarming number of infractions indicating lazy, brutal, or incompetent officers which inevitably led to lazy, sullen, and incompetent crews. The last ship that Tracy had served on before he was cashiered had been just such a ship. He knew very well all the things that could go wrong in peacetime on such a vessel. With them at war, there was the potential for disaster, and not only for that ship, but for the other ships in the fleet.

The melancholy truth was that Tracy hadn't so much inherited these ships as they had been shoved off on him. He expected something like this from Talion, but he hadn't thought Mercedes would be this petty. Then he looked over her command structure and had his answer. Her vice admiral was Cullen. Apparently, the years had not blunted Cullen's animus toward him.

Then in the midst of that clerical headache, he had received a summons to the planet so he could brief a delegation of politicians out from Ouranos on his after-action report about the capture of the enemy ship. He had monitored the arrival of a small squadron of ships of the Blue and had been surprised when it included Mercedes's flagship. He assumed she had merely been serving as escort to the politicos, which included the prime minister, and would soon be moving on, but judging by what he was overhearing that was not to be the case.

"I'm sorry, ma'am, I thought you would want to hear from Belmanor directly. I apologize for my error. I should have checked with you first. Also, they discovered a construction failure in one of the new ships. Delayed them getting underway." There was a pause. *"Again, my apologies …"* Chapman-Owiti's voice trailed away.

"I don't want him here. I can't see him. I just can't."

That hurt. Like a spear of ice entering his heart. Tracy pressed his back against the wall. Prayed the direction they were traveling would not bring them around this particular corner to find him lurking … spying. That's what they would think, though he hadn't meant to. It was hearing her voice that had frozen him in place. Not broken and filled with static. Her voice filled with a warmth like deep bells and warm chocolate. Saying such hurtful words.

"I'll contact him and have him return to his ship." Ernesto gave that dry little cough Tracy remembered from school. It had indicated concern if not outright disapproval. Apparently, Mercedes also remembered, for she said, *"I take it you're not convinced that's the proper course of action."*

"Majesty, he's become the biggest star in O-Trell. What you did at Earth was a tactical and strategic triumph, but what Belmanor pulled off was … was …"

"Theatrical?" Tracy frowned at that.

Ernesto murmured quietly, *"I was going to say inspirational."* There was a long silence, then he resumed. *"Look, Mer, we've been taking a beating. People, more to the point our troops, were starting to think we were outclassed as well as outgunned. That we humans had met our match. He put the spine back in those kids who until this past year had almost never faced actual battle. You need him to be a legend and you need to be seen embracing him."*

That pulled a faint sound from Tracy. He clamped his jaw shut and tried not to remember.

"What more can I do? I made him a vice admiral and gave him a fleet even though it infuriated both Talion and my husband."

"When you're interviewed, mention him and the capture of the ship."

"So, I downplay my own victory?"

"You're expected to win. You're the Empress."

"Why did you have to remind me? All right. We had better get to that meeting." Tracy was about to move when she

added. *"What's he like ... now?"*

"Not much different than when we were in school. Intemperate, tactless, disrespectful to the point of insubordination ... and bloody brilliant."

"Doesn't sound like he's changed at all." She paused. *"But how does he look?"*

"It's been nearly thirty years, Majesty. He looks like all of us do ... older."

✦ ✦ ✦

IT SHOULDN'T HAVE happened, but the fates seemed to be determined to well and truly scramble her life. Ernesto had gone into the shielded conference room followed by the gaggle of politicians out from Hissilek, including Rohan Danilo Marcus Aubrey, Condé de Vargas and current prime minister of the League. Mercedes had paused for a sip of water from a fountain near the restrooms just as Tracy had emerged from the men's room. There was high color in his cheeks and a few drops of water clung to his sideburns, and the lock of hair that flopped onto his forehead was also wet. It seemed he had doused his face with water.

He froze.

She froze.

Then he glared at her, and things were suddenly back to normal. With a curt gesture she ordered her security away. "But Majesty ..." one agent began.

"I am perfectly safe with Admiral Belmanor and I wish to *congratulate him*," she forced between clenched teeth. "For his extraordinary service to the cause of the war and the crown. Wait for me in the conference room."

"But—"

"We are in the middle of the Octagon. What the hell do you think could happen to me?" That did it and they withdrew.

They stared at each other for another long moment as Mercedes's gaze devoured his face and form. The dueling scar that pulled up his left eyebrow giving it a sardonic quirk was still very evident. He was thinner and the years had etched more lines around his eyes and grey streaked his hair. She noticed he was still wearing the bangs that the barber on Cuandru had given him during their magical interlude. The memories of gasping breaths and sweat-slick bodies broke her control. Mercedes grabbed him by the lapels of his coat and shoved him backwards into the ladies' room. There were still so few women in O-Trell, much less in the officer class, that it was likely they would not be disturbed. Just to be sure she took a quick glance beneath the stall doors and then pushed a trash can in front of the door. It wouldn't stop anyone from entering, but it would serve as a warning.

"Okay, what have I done now?" she demanded. His eyes were scanning her face and she realized she was shaking.

"You didn't want to see me." His voice was low, filled with anger, but she sensed that just below the surface was unimaginable pain. She knew because it had underlain her words, too.

"No. Because … because …" It had been almost six years. Years filled with longing, the memory of warm embraces and the fire of passion. "Oh, fuck it!" she raged, and grabbing him by the front of his dress jacket she pulled him into a rough kiss.

Time melted away. His lips softened beneath hers. One hand tangled in the hair at the back of her head. His other hand was at the small of her back pulling her ever closer. His tongue demanded entry and she eagerly complied. He pulled back and rained kisses across her face and eyes, nibbled at her earlobes.

In a groaning whisper he said, “Mercedes, Mercedes, my love. Oh, God, how I’ve missed you.”

She found herself crying, unable to analyze the tangle of emotions that had summoned the tears. “I, too. I think about you … more than I should.”

He pulled back and gave her a wry smile. “Well, you’re doing better than me. I *never* stop thinking of you.”

“Even when you’re heroically boarding an enemy vessel,” she teased.

He chuckled. “Well, okay, maybe not then. Oh, my love.” He pulled her head against his chest, though she had to hunch a bit to do so. He only had a couple of inches on her. “How are you holding up under all … this?” he asked gently.

“I don’t know. I’m afraid if I ever stopped to think about all of it … I’d just fall to pieces,” she confessed.

“No, you won’t. You’re the strongest person I know,” Tracy replied. “I studied your defensive mine strategy. That was brilliant.”

“Full confession, I got the idea from a child’s toy.” She felt him stiffen a bit and hurried on. “But it quite pales in comparison with your derring-do.” She paused. “Did you overhear all of it? Everything I said to Ernesto?”

“Uh-huh.”

She hugged him fiercely. "And … this … is … why … I … didn't … want … to … see … you." She punctuated each word with a kiss on every part of his face. "I knew my self-control would vanish."

"You have no idea how many times I've dreamed of holding you," he murmured against her curls.

"Oh, believe me, love, I expect I do." For a long moment she just stood in the circle of his arms listening to his heartbeats, feeling the puff of his breath across her hair, feeling the warmth rolling off his body. Her body ached for him, responding to the pressure of his erection even blunted by the material of their uniforms. She looked around wildly—the floor, sinks, there were showers. She began to unhook his belt. His hands shot down and grabbed hers.

"No, love, we can't. God knows I want to, but we can't. They'll be looking for you soon."

"You're right. We'll find a way. Do you trust your bat-BEM? I can have Venia reach out to him."

"Maybe. I don't know. Wait, let's use Jahan's brother instead. Dulac is still here. Helping with repairs. I'll get you his information."

She stared into that beloved face then leaned in slowly and pressed her lips on his. Their kiss was long, slow, deep, and passionate. A shriek of metal on tile had her leaping back, her heel slipping as she began to fall. Tracy instinctively reached out to catch her, but he was distracted by a fist smashing against his jaw. Mercedes hit the floor hard, landing on her tailbone, which sent pain shooting through the top of her head. Sick horror filled Mercedes's stomach as she looked up into Boho's rage-filled face.

20

PATHS NOT TAKEN

BLOOD WAS COURSING down the bastard's chin from a cut lip and a large bruise was already blooming on the side of his jaw. The fact that his blood was staining Boho's wedding ring only fanned his rage. Adding injury to the insult, the *intitulado*'s teeth had scored a cut across his own knuckles. Boho's fist lashed out again only this time it was stopped by a sharp block from Belmanor. With a roar, he rushed Belmanor knowing he had four inches and probably sixty pounds on his rival. His charge pushed the other man's back into the metal edge of a sink and Belmanor gave a cry of pain. Elation joined the rage. He would have the bastard begging soon enough. But Belmanor wasn't done yet. He slammed his hands on either side of Boho's head, hitting the tender cartilage of his ears, and brought up his knee searching for Boho's groin. Boho canted his body, so the blow landed on his thigh instead.

Mercedes, struggling to her feet, was shouting. "STOP IT! STOP IT! BOTH OF YOU STOP IT!"

He could not clear the image of his wife in another man's arms. In *this* man's arms. A pounding was behind his eyes, his lungs felt starved for air, and his sight had narrowed to a tunnel with only Belmanor at the end. He drew back his fist, ready to pound Belmanor's face into pulp, only to be hit by a blast of cold water that soaked them both. Gasping, Boho turned to see Mercedes wielding the handheld sprayer head from the shower.

"*Dios*, stop acting like rutting bucks! How do you think it looks to have two of my top admirals brawling?"

Belmanor's expression was frozen, agonized. "I submit to your jurisdiction, your grace. The fault is entirely mine. I forced—"

"Oh, for the love of God!" Mercedes yelled. She threw the hose and the sprayer back into the shower where it flopped like a fish gasping for life on a cold, hard beach. Water drenched the sides of the shower. It periodically spun to send water spraying across their boots. She stalked over, forced herself between them, and gave them both a hard shove. She turned first to the *intitulado*. "You are *not* going to play the noble martyr." Then it was Boho's turn. Mercedes punched him in the chest. "*I* am the one who kissed *him*. So, vent your rage on *me*. Punch *me* if that's the only way you know how to assuage your anger."

"Majesty—" Belmanor began.

"Not one word. Not *one* out of you. Get out! Find dry clothes and for *el amor de Dios* try not to be seen." The *intitulado* braced, saluted, then bowed, and left trailing water.

It was deadly quiet apart from the hysterical hissing from the sprayer. "You would betray me with that filth?" Boho demanded. The throbbing anger in the words seemed to scrape across his throat.

Mercedes moved to the shower and turned off the water. "Oh, that's *rich* coming from you. How many *putas* did you visit while we were on Earth? How many wives and tradesman's daughters have you fucked over the thirty years of our marriage? How many wives and daughters in our own set have you seduced?" She stood, chest heaving as she tried to quiet her breathing. The anger was replaced by sadness. "I cared for him."

"*Jesucristo*, it's been decades."

She stared down at the floor and said softly, "Sometimes you can't help but wonder about the path not taken."

"Well, I hope you've satisfied yourself. I never told you this. I didn't want to hurt you, but he's a criminal. After he was thrown out of O-Trell, he became a smuggler. I caught him looting a ship."

"Once again, Boho, pots and kettles. You were selling promotions to pay for your profligacy. And do tell me about this ship he was looting. Did he use force to capture it? Is he a *corsario*? Is that what you're alleging?" He started to open his mouth, but she rushed on. "Oh, wait, his ship is not armed."

"How would you know a detail like that?" Boho demanded.

For an instant panic like summer lightning flickered across her face. "I … I made inquiries before I had him returned to duty. And we should be glad I did … return him to duty, I mean." She waved a hand as if shooing gnats. "Anyway, what does of any of this matter? I had a youthful crush. I kissed him. You didn't like it. And now it's over and done with. Meanwhile, we have citizens dying and cities being destroyed. I really think our subjects would prefer to have us focused on that rather than on our personal issues."

"I thought we were past having issues," he said.

"Yes. We have only duty now." Her expression was bleak, and she seemed to be looking at something far beyond the confines of the bathroom. "Perhaps that's all we ever had." She paused at the door. "Get a dry uniform and join us. I need to get to the briefing."

The door swung closed behind her.

We have only duty. Perhaps that's all we ever had. The words haunted him. *Was that why she had married him? Of course, it was.* It had always felt like there was some distant core of her that he had never been able to reach, to touch, to understand. Had it been Belmanor lurking there all along? Holding that secret part of her heart? *I will fight you,* Boho said to his absent foe. *And this time I won't settle for just first blood.* Hasta la muerta, bastardo.

✦ ✦ ✦

BOHO SLIPPED INTO the conference room, and Mercedes watched him register that she had left no chair available for him to sit next to her. Instead, he was relegated to the foot of the table, and his displeasure was reflected on his face. Mercedes didn't care. She was angry with him, but also furious with herself for her lack of control, so some of her avoidance was born from guilt. What she had done was stupid, and she had very nearly made a mistake from which there would have been no recovery when she mentioned that Tracy's trading ship had no guns.

Mercifully, when she returned to Boho, he had been too overjoyed at the news of her pregnancy to ask many questions. Then close on the heels of her return had come the coup attempt and the messy aftermath, so he hadn't bothered to investigate Captain Oliver Randall and the crew and ship who had rescued her after the debacle at Kusatsu-Shirane. If he had, he would eventually have discovered that Randall was in fact Tracy and that she had spent a significant amount of time with him.

Now her anger and embarrassment might have endangered that secret. Actually, what might have endangered it was her own behavior. But when she had seen Tracy after such a long absence, her body had yearned for him, and her mind had lost any ability to process risk. She had just wanted to feel him pressed against her, his mouth on hers … Even thinking about it had heat running through her body and a heavy ache deep in her groin.

She had lost the thread of the conversation and forced herself to once again pay attention. Rohan had obviously asked Ernesto about the prisoners, since the R&D chief was saying, "Right now we are working to form a rapport and begin to build trust. Because the aliens' appearance is so disturbing to humans, it hasn't been easy finding interrogators who can overcome their revulsion."

"Have you considered using some of our alien citizens?" Mercedes asked. "A Tiponi or a Sidone might not find the *necrófagos* as alarming as we do."

The young lieutenant who was keeping notes on the meeting looked up in surprise and his fingers froze over the keyboard. He wasn't the only one reacting to her suggestion.

"Intriguing idea, Majesty," Ernesto said and gave her that blazing smile.

"Do you know if the Isanjo have the same aversion as we do?" Boho asked, forcing himself into the conversation. Everyone exchanged glances and shrugged, not knowing the answer.

"They are certainly closer to us in both biology and outlook than either the Sidone or the Flutes," Ernesto said.

"We've got a passel of them running around Hellfire looking for work or a way home," said Admiral Lord Fenris DeGroot.

The rotation had brought the head of the wet foot navy into the position of chairman of the joint chiefs, and he was a good deal younger than the heads of the other services. Because his branch of the service wasn't given a lot of attention, Mercedes did not know him well. He was also a fourth son from a provincial FFH family that lacked both money and prestige. He had been notably quiet thus far, but now he spoke up.

"I mean, radical thought here. We could actually ask one of them. We've also got Flutes working at the Octo and maybe we could scare up a spider or two, show them the bastards, and see what they think."

"For better or worse, the precedent has already been set of utilizing aliens in a more overt way," Boho said.

Rohan shifted his bulk in his chair and said, "Let me offer a word of caution. The more we involve our alien subjects in the war effort, the more they will feel entitled to fuller participation in our politics after this war is over. They're going to want full suffrage and there are more of them than there are of us."

"I think there is a vast difference between including some aliens in the effort to interrogate our prisoners and having them integrated into the armed forces," Mercedes said.

Rohan interrupted. "I second the consort's statement. Belmanor already did that."

Ernesto stepped in. "My understanding is that the Isanjo took it upon themselves to join in the fight. It was not on Captain … Admiral Belmanor's order.

"Shocking, something he's *not* getting credit for," Boho said tightly.

Ernesto gave Boho a long, expressionless look from beneath his lashes. "Well, to be fair, he did think to utilize the particular abilities of the Isanjo and put them aboard his ships."

"BEM lover," someone in the room muttered, but Mercedes couldn't pinpoint who it was.

Rohan brought his hand down on the top of the table, the sharp rap silencing the murmurs running through the room. "For now, let us table this particular discussion and get back to our immediate alien problem."

"Fortunately, the Empress and the Consort have proved we now have a way to protect our worlds and hurt the bastards, so we don't need aliens," the head of the *fusileros* offered.

"That advantage will only last until one of them manages to escape or get off a message," Mercedes cautioned. "The mines will only be effective for so long."

"Nonetheless, we need to ramp up production and get the maze deployed around all our worlds," DeGroot ordered.

"We need time," Ernesto said. "If they buy me time that will be an enormous help. If we can turn one of these creatures, gain their trust and get them to talk, we can take the fight to their worlds."

"You think they have something similar to our league?" Mercedes asked.

"I think to mount this level of attack they would have to have available the resources of numerous systems," one of the tactical officers said.

"Well, that's depressing," Boho muttered. Gallows laughter whispered through the assembled men as they nodded in agreement.

✦ ✦ ✦

"KIDS CRYING. KIDS puking. Kids pooping. Kids falling down and then crying. Kids fighting and then crying. I thought I was done with all that once my kits got past fifteen. Well, okay, eighteen. Well, actually, they still fight. Whatever. It was fine on the first run, we had the Emp—We had a nanny with us, and another passenger who could help, but on this latest run it was just me and my crew, and we can't fly the ship and care for a gaggle of screaming, puking, pooping, fighting kids."

"Take a breath, Jahan, and have a drink." Lisbet Montego held out a glass of saki.

They were in Lisbet's office at the Sweet Retreat, one of the three joy houses on the San Pedro *cosmódromo*. Lisbet had once been Tracy's lover until life had thrown the Empress into his arms. She was an attractive woman in her mid-fifties with deep chocolate skin, and any grey in her hair was covered by the striped colors she affected in imitation of a Hajin's mane. Jahan trusted her not to go blabbing to the authorities about their runs with shiploads of kids to Hidden Worlds. For one thing, the *Selkie* provided Lisbet and her girls with illicit birth control medication, so Lisbet steered clear of the *polícia. And it wasn't like Lisbet knew the actual coordinates of the planets,* Jahan thought. Besides which, the parents loading their kids onto trading ships knew they were being taken to Hidden Worlds. She was being paranoid. Which was probably just fine given the fact Jahan and her crew lived just a little bit to the side of the law.

The office was utilitarian, as opposed to the faux luxury of the main salon where the girls met their customers and the bedrooms where they serviced them. Lisbet was a businesswoman and a professional, and Jahan felt she was a kindred spirit despite the fact they were different species.

Jahan gratefully grabbed the glass and took a large swallow. It was the chilled type and tasted of plum and ice. "Oh, that's good. But I think I need something a *lot* stronger," Jahan said and rested her aching head in one hand.

"What you need is help," Lisbet said.

"That, too. I could probably get some of my people and maybe even Hajin—"

"No." Jahan's fur lifted and her back arched a bit at the single word. Especially delivered as it had been with such force.

"Excuse me?"

"Have you never wondered why we humans don't use aliens to care for childcare?"

"Alien cooties? But seriously, I can see why you wouldn't have a Sidone. Scare the poop right out of a kid if one of those spiders were handing them a bottle. But we're fluffy and Hajin look sweet with those long faces and big eyes and …" Lisbet was laughing. "What?"

"You never struck me as the type to go running on like this."

"I'm stressed, okay? I've had like no sleep for days and the exchequer is taking their own sweet time about paying us for our services, so I'm running on credit with the fuel depot, and we're way off the point. Why, Lisbet," she asked in that singsong tone of false inquiry, "don't you let us raise your children?" Then she added rather waspishly, "We do everything else for you." Jahan paused and took another swallow of saki.

"We can't. Not when they're little. Young children bond with and identify with the people they are around. We need that to be humans, not you BEMs."

They stared at each other across the top of Lisbet's desk. "Of course," Jahan said slowly. "Because you want them to be able to kill us should the need arise."

The human woman flinched. "Well, there is that." Jahan respected her for not demurring to her bleak assessment. "But I think there's a bigger reason. Those children might grow up and start to question the status quo."

"Can't have that," Jahan said and tossed off the last of her drink. She then handed over the medicine she had brought from Freehold. "Here's your birth control. Shouldn't be a problem keeping you stocked up on them. I'm going to be making a lot of runs to our suppliers."

"Thank you, but it isn't as urgent now that contraceptives are being issued to O-Trell. I can always manage to buy a supply off a less than honest supply quartermaster. But you never let me make my suggestion." Jahan looked confused and Lisbet laughed. "About getting help."

"Okay." She sat back down.

"Use us. *La dama de corte.*" Jahan noted Lisbet didn't use the cruder words for the oldest profession—*meca* or *puta*—instead using courtesan. "There are always children in a joy house, and we all take part in the child rearing. And you should go to the Church," she added.

"Beg pardon?"

"To the *Celestial Novias de Cristo.* Those nuns not only teach children they bear them for the priests."

Jahan jumped to her feet. "Lisbet, you are a fucking genius. I'm sure the League can come up with some money to compensate you."

"I think most of us will consider it our contribution to the war effort."

"Yeah, but if we empty out all the joy houses the soldiers aren't going to be real happy, and that might end up hindering the war effort," Jahan joked.

"I'm sure we can leave enough *fille de joie* behind that our boys won't suffer." A smile grew, crinkling the edges of Lisbet's eyes. She shook her head, setting the beads and tiny bells that were woven into her braids to clash and ring. "That is going to be a sight."

Lisbet filled their glasses again and they raised them in a toast. "To the madonnas and the whores, may they suffer the little children," Jahan said. They drained their glasses in a single gulp, flipped them over, and slammed them onto the desk.

✦ ✦ ✦

"WE'RE BEGINNING TO figure out techniques to fight the *necrófagos*, but even when we don't lose ships, we lose people when those ships are damaged," Mercedes was saying to Commandant Baron Tarek El-Ghazzawy in his office at The High Ground.

"War is a greedy god who requires constant sacrifice," Tarek replied.

"Is that a quote?" Mercedes asked.

"Only if you consider me quotable," Tarek said with a smile that quickly faded. He sighed. "It does seem that the graduating officers get younger and the volunteers and draftees from among the populace get older. This goes on much longer and we'll find ourselves running out of males of an appropriate age."

"So, we'll draft the women."

"God, will it come to that?" El-Ghazzawy asked.

Mercedes shrugged. "Who the hell knows?"

While she was talking, Tarek's assistant tapped discreetly on the door, entered, and said quietly, "Ma'am, sir, Admiral Lady Delecroix-McKenzie is demanding entrance and she's being rather … er … emphatic in her demand."

"Ah, threatened to cut off your balls, did she, Glenn?" El-Ghazzawy asked, and the aide ran a finger around his high collar and nodded. "Give us five and then send her in."

After the door closed, Mercedes asked, "Is she ready?"

"Physically, intellectually, absolutely. Mentally and emotionally …" Tarek's voice trailed away, and he just shook his head.

"What does that mean? Is she a danger to the League?"

"No. Only to herself. We train soldiers to kill. We don't want them to live only for that," Tarek answered.

The door opened and Cipriana entered. El-Ghazzawy politely exited with a murmured, "I'll give you both time to catch up."

Mercedes studied her friend. The human eye showed as little expression as the high-tech implant that had been placed in Cipriana's empty right eye socket. The artificial eye restored her sight and had a few added improvements such as high resolution and extreme distance focus. It could have been made to look real, but just as Davin had refused to have his artificial arm and hand covered in skin, so, too, had Cipri refused a normal eye. That, combined with the burn scars that covered one side of her face and the uncompromising expression, made her seem less than human.

"I wanted you to know that you don't have to worry. Hayden is with Cyprian on a Hidden World. They're both safe and away from the fighting," Mercedes said.

"Good. That's what I wanted. Now am I getting assigned to a ship or not?" Cipriana said.

Mercedes sighed and rubbed at her eyes, gritty from exhaustion. It seemed that all her relationships right now were fraught. She and Boho had returned to their respective ships without addressing the elephant looming between them, and the Blue had gone first to Dullahan to check on mine production, and from there they had returned to

Ouranos to pick up the latest crop of graduates from The High Ground. Hence her presence at the academy this day.

Mercedes pulled herself back to the moment and stared at this stranger who had replaced the friend she had known since childhood. Cipriana had been one of her ladies-in-waiting and her companion when she entered the military academy all those long years ago, and now she was glaring at her. Mercedes had hoped that the months Cipriana had spent at The High Ground would have lessened the icy rage. It hadn't.

"You know if I do that, I have to demote you," Mercedes said. "When I made you an admiral you were commanding a station and it was to give you a larger pension when you retired. The situation has changed."

"I don't care if you make me a fucking *hombre*! Just let me fight."

"All right." Mercedes unrolled a keyboard and began typing. "Effective immediately you have been reduced in rank to commander. I'm going to assign you to the Green. They're understaffed and undermanned, so there should be plenty for you to do."

"You're hoping Belmanor will keep me out of trouble," Cipri accused.

"That, too." Mercedes looked up into her friend's rigid face.

"Am I dismissed, *Emperatriz*?"

It hurt. Mercedes pushed back the vexation. "You are. You'll find your orders on your ring in the next hour."

Cipriana executed a sharp salute, turned on her heel, and left. Tarek re-entered and gave her an inquiring lift of an eyebrow. Mercedes sighed and ran her hands through her hair. "She's gone to find death," she said.

"I expect she'll take a number of the enemy with her before she does," he replied.

"That is not comforting, Tarek."

He shrugged. "It's hard to dissuade someone who has decided there is nothing left to live for."

"She has a son!"

"Who she thinks she failed. A mother who didn't protect her children."

"And she thinks death will wash away the guilt," Mercedes mused.

"Exactly."

"I wish I had hugged her before she left," Mercedes said softly.

21

THE SECRETS WE HIDE

"GOOD GOD, LIEUTENANT, you have to stop trying to outguess the computer. It is faster than you are and based on your performance a good deal smarter than you as well."

Luis's shoulders hunched and the tendons in his neck tensed. It was visible now that he was a serving officer in O-Trell. When he had worked for Tracy aboard the *Selkie*, he had reveled in his luxurious black curls that almost brushed his shoulders.

"Yes, sir. Sorry, sir." It was respectful … just barely.

"Lieutenant, I think running some laps might be beneficial for you. Report to Chief Babcock. Lieutenant Vaughn, you're up," Tracy said to the young woman lieutenant.

He heard her gulp from across the bridge. She left her position at the lidar and thermal scanning station and moved to the navigators' chair. Tracy noticed that the long ponytail she had been wearing when she first came aboard was gone, and she was emulating Beatrisa with her shaved head, leaving only peach fuzz adorning her skull. She and Luis exchanged parade ground perfect salutes. Luis headed for the access ladder rather than the elevator. The rap of his bootheels were very loud on the composite floor of the bridge of the *Sutābureză*.

The Green was running combat drills designed by Tracy, the princess, and the weapons officer, with the goal of increasing the difficulty with each test. There were so many new faces aboard the giant flagship, but Tracy had brought over some of his officers from the *Swiftsure* so he had the comfort of a few familiar faces and people whose abilities he could trust. Cassutt was one of them, as was the physician, Afumba. Valada-Viers wasn't happy about losing Cassutt, but then decided to take it as a challenge and see if he could develop a weapons officer who could surpass Cassutt. Tracy was happy to engage in the competition. Anything that made his understrength fleet better was fine by him, however it might be achieved. He also made the drills into full war games, so the captains and crews were in competition with each other. Simulations just couldn't match having an actual opponent.

The drills also served another purpose. They laid bare the inadequacies of the hand-me-down ships and captains, and enabled Tracy to justifiably scramble the command structure aboard those ships in an effort to improve not only performance, but good order as well. He also knew that his ruthless culling of the officers was making him enemies, but he'd take enemies over death for himself or the thousands of men and women who were now under his command. There were going to be casualties, he knew that, but he wanted to reduce them as much as possible. He watched the top of Luis's head disappear down the access shaft and gave a mental sigh.

I asked for you, he sent mentally to the young man. *Now*

it's my job to keep you safe. Someday you'll understand that. Maybe. I hope.

Three hours later they had completed the elaborate maneuver and only had one mishap, when a *crusero* swung too close to a dummy mine and in an effort not to brush against it they had hard fired their port engines, which had sent them slamming into the *explorador* that was supposed to be using them to mask their presence so they could make a run on the enemy ship. Fortunately, the damage to the scout ship was minor and the injuries consisted of a broken arm and a concussion. They could put in at San Pedro for repairs and give his stressed, overworked, and probably resentful crews a brief shore leave.

He stood, straightened his back until the vertebrae popped, and gave his shoulders a roll to try and loosen the knot of tension that had settled in his neck. "The bridge is yours, Captain," he said to Beatrisa and he went to the elevator. He considered the ladder, then decided he was too stiff for the long climb.

He wished he could go to the gym for a workout, but a mountain of paperwork was waiting on the screens in his office. And the accident between the two ships had just made the list that much longer. Being an admiral was not aligning with the fantasies he'd woven back when he was a student at The High Ground, Tracy reflected as he entered his office. The three holo screens over his desk seemed to wink and mock him as more notes sprang to life.

Tracy knew it wasn't just combat readiness that had him driving his fleet and himself this hard. It was an effort to forget the frenzied kisses he and Mercedes had exchanged.

Also, to forget how stupid it had been on both their parts. He wondered how Mercedes had explained it to Cullen. He hadn't received a formal challenge to duel, so he had to conclude Mercedes had mollified Cullen in some way. It had galled him to offer himself up to Cullen for discipline, but protecting Mercedes was more important than his own feelings. Still, he desperately wished he could deliver a beatdown to the arrogant asshole, and it would be pleasant to do it with the weapons of Cullen's class.

The chime on his door sounded, and he touched the enter key. It was Beatrisa. "Some new problem?" he asked.

"Yes. You."

"I beg your pardon, Captain." He didn't make it a question. It was a challenge and a warning. He suddenly realized he had used his FFH accent, and then a part of him wondered when he had become an entitled asshole.

Beatrisa took a chair without asking. She was also clearly rocking her entitlement, too. "So, exactly what is this Baca kid to you? Bastard son? Boyfriend?"

He gaped at her for a moment, then gave a wild shake of his head. "No, no, no, no. None of those. Why would you think—"

"Because you're so fucking hard on him. Since you were trying so hard not to show favoritism by busting his balls, I figured he had to be more to you than just some random young lieutenant."

"No … yes … well, maybe." He paused and tried to untangle his thoughts. "I'm trying to keep him safe."

"Shouldn't that apply to … oh … all of us?"

"Yes, of course, but Luis was one of my crew when I ran

the trading vessel. Good kid. I encouraged him to go OCS when he got called up. I feel responsible for him."

"Well, at the rate you're going you are going to wreck him. He's going to second-guess himself and freeze at a critical moment. And *I'll* probably be the one who gets their ass shot off," she added in an aggrieved tone. She stood and glared down at him. "So, knock it the hell off."

A bubble of laughter formed in his chest and Tracy's outrage evaporated. "Is this sort of ass-kicking listed among the duties of a flag captain?"

"Damned if I know," Beatrisa said.

"Well, if it isn't, it should be." He held out his hand. "Thank you, Captain. Never hesitate to tell me when I'm out of line. God knows my first officer aboard the *Selkie* never did."

"That little Isanjo," Beatrisa said.

"Yes, Jahan."

"I wish I had had the opportunity to get to know her better."

"You two would have gotten along. You're a lot alike," Tracy said.

Beatrisa cocked her head and gave him a contemplative look. "You say these odd things and never seem to realize how odd they really are. You realize most of my set would consider being compared to a BEM an unpardonable insult."

"And you? How are you taking it?" Tracy asked.

She pondered his question for a moment. "It makes me uncomfortable," she finally admitted. "And the fact it does probably means I need to spend some time thinking about this." She gave him a wry look. "Thank you, Admiral, for returning the kick in the ass."

"We're a good ass-kicking team, Highness."

"Oh, please. Call me Bee. At least in private."

✦ ✦ ✦

"IT MUST BE serious if you had me leave the capital and meet you all the way out here," Anselmo said as he picked up items from Boho's desk, set them down again. He paced to the credenza and began picking up and inspecting the liquor bottles. Drew his fingers along the edge of the bar as if testing for dust, impossible aboard a spaceship. His coiled manic energy was infectious, and Boho found himself nervously tapping his fingers on his desk. The low rumble of the flagship's engines was like a beating heart.

"It is. I want—"

"Even on a liner it's no picnic. Half the cabins are carrying freight or wounded, being taken to New Hope." Anselmo spun to face him and held out a bottle. "Drink?"

The interruption shattered Boho's focus as if it were glass. "What? Yes … no."

"Do you mind if I …?" The younger man jerked a thumb at the racked glasses.

"No. Go ahead. I want—"

Anselmo interrupted again. "I think a lot of the companies are going to go under unless we get this wrapped—"

Boho slammed his hands onto his desk and shot out of his chair. "Goddamn it! Stop talking and *listen*."

Anselmo froze, his drink halfway to his lips. "Uh … okay."

"I want someone killed."

Anselmo slowly set down his glass. Rubbed at his fingertips. Laced and unlaced his fingers. Ran a hand through his hair and finally thrust his hands into his pockets. "Well. You definitely have my attention now." He picked up his glass again and tossed off its contents. "And thus fortified I'm ready to hear the identity of this unfortunate individual."

"Thracius Belmanor."

"Oh … uh …" He filled his glass again. "May I sit down?" Boho nodded. "Isn't he an admiral?"

"Yes."

"Big hero."

"Some would argue that."

"But not you, I take it?"

"He's a jumped-up little nobody. Lowborn scum with an insolent attitude toward his betters. I wouldn't be surprised to discover that other people, better people, came up with this plan to capture the enemy ship."

Anselmo rolled his glass between his palms and gazed intently at the amber liquor like a man gazing into a scrying bowl. "Sir, we've been together a long time. You raised me up out of the obscurity of being a sixth son and changed my life. You know I'm loyal and have done whatever you asked—set up a honey trap for a politician, blackmail a journalist, pay off a mistress—hell, I even suggested a few and I've done them all and never questioned. But now we're talking murder, so we've got to be straight with each other. What's actually behind this?"

The image of Mercedes in the arms of that man brought Boho to his feet. He paced away and back again. Boho hesitated, drew in a deep breath. How could he possibly reveal the events that had brought him to this deadly point? He would be seen as the man who couldn't hold his wife. But rage burned through his veins and the image could not be banished and he wondered how he would ever sleep or function again with this gnawing at him.

"This must stay absolutely confidential."

Anselmo grinned at him. "Like every other unsavory thing I've ever done for you."

"I … I think there might be something between him and …" It cost him to say it. "The Empress."

That got Anselmo's attention. His mouth literally dropped open. "Um … that's not what I expected. Do you have reason to believe that?"

"Just the fact I caught them kissing."

"Uh … oh." Anselmo carefully set aside his glass and rose to his feet. "Well, that does cast things in a different light. On the other hand, has the Empress ever given you any cause to doubt her faithfulness? It's obvious to anyone with eyes that both Rogers and Jaakon have been in love with her for decades, but there never been a whisper that the Empress ever acted on that."

What his chief of staff was saying was demonstrably true. It injected a sliver of doubt into Boho's certainty, and he frowned. Anselmo continued. "Both of those men are of our class, handsome, articulate, devoted, so why would she respond to an *intitulado*?"

"She said she had a crush on him. Mused about paths not taken."

"Your grace, sir … Boho, we're all under unbelievable

stress. None more than your lady. So, she did something foolish. The fact she's been absolutely faithful to you through three decades has to count for something. Look, I'll take care of this man, but let's not rush into this. For one thing, if something happened to him so close on the heels of the Empress's … er … ah, indiscretion, she might become suspicious. Also, war is our friend. He might get killed anyway."

"I want to do it." Before Anselmo quickly looked away, Boho read in the younger man's expression just what he was thinking—*but it won't* be *you.* Boho hurriedly added, "I want him to know it was me," Boho growled.

"Okay, then I'll work on that, but let's take this slow. For now, I'll dig into his background, see what I can find."

"I know he was running a trading vessel. I caught him looting an abandoned Cara'ot ship."

"So maybe he was smuggling. Did you get the name of his ship?"

"Dammit, no. I didn't think to. Also, I couldn't draw attention to the fact that *I* was trading in contraband, too." Boho went and prepared himself a drink.

"What do you remember about the encounter?" Anselmo had unlimbered his tap pad and was taking notes.

"He had aliens with him, a spider and an Isanjo. Didn't get a very good look at them. They were all in spacesuits. And they all pretty much look alike. Oh, there was a human kid, too."

"Whoa!" Surprise rolled off the word.

"What? What did you find?"

"According to this, Thracius Ransom Belmanor died

twenty-two years ago." They stared at each other for a long moment. Boho could hear his heart beating. He swallowed past a sudden obstruction in his throat. Anselmo went blithely on. "So how did the Empress know he was alive and able to be returned to active service?"

Boho slammed his hand onto the surface of the pad. "Stop! Stop now. I need to think … about all this."

"So, I take it we're tabling the killing thing?"

"For now."

"Let me know when you want me to resume looking."

"Yes. Fine. All right. You can go."

"Leave the office? Or return to Ouranos?"

"Dear God, when did you become so obtuse? The office. At least for now. I'll be in touch." Anselmo left. Boho drained the last of his drink and sat down. Weariness and sadness dragged at his bones. He desperately wanted to know, while also fearing what he might learn. He covered his face with his hands and sat for a very long time.

✦ ✦ ✦

DESPITE THE POPULARITY of Sidone weavings in the wider League the spaceport in the capital city of Paranzal was sparsely populated. Not surprising, considering that most humans found the Sidone disturbing and did not enjoy a journey to Melatin, the home world of the spiders. Since the *Selkie* only had one human aboard, Jahan had volunteered her crew to shuttle spiderlings to Al-Nefud. Unlike most human colonies, Al-Nefud had been founded as an Islamic colony, and Islam venerated spiders because supposedly a spider had saved the prophet by spinning a web over the mouth of the cave in which he was hidden. Also, Sidone weavings did not normally depict actual objects, but were abstract, which made them extremely popular with the people of Al-Nefud. They were happy to take Sidone children.

As Jahan hit the controls to lower the ramp, Ernie gave a shiver and announced, "I'll be in the engine room. Gonna stay there until we drop off the bugs."

"What about meals?" Dalea asked. "It's ten days to Al-Nefud.

"I got protein bars and booze."

Kielli wrinkled his nose. "You gonna just poop in a corner?"

Ernie glared at him. "No, I'll slip out as necessary. Hopefully when these critters are asleep."

He vanished, and Jahan turned to greet the delegation from the Spiderling Welfare Office. Two females and a significantly smaller male Sidone made their way up the ramp, the claws on their combined twenty-four legs clicking like castanets. Behind them was a wave of dark bodies, tiny spiderlings, surrounded by mothers carrying holdalls in several claws while other appendages wrapped around their broods. In the distance Jahan could see part of the city, pillared buildings carved out of the soaring rock cliffs.

Dalea voiced what Jahan was thinking. "I thought there'd be more."

The male Sidone replied, "The caves in which our ancestors lived are still available to us. Many families felt they could ride out any attack there."

"But be assured we are grateful to the people of Al-Nefud for taking our spiderlings," one of the females said.

The wave of small Sidone arrived. Dalea and Jax set about getting them settled while mothers murmured instructions and avowals of love in both Spanish and Sid to their anxious children. There was much clicking of beaks, a sign of distress among Sidone.

Jahan rubbed at the fur on the back of her neck as she debated but decided to ask the question. "Look, I know this is probably stupid—I mean, it's a big planet, and it's not like you all know each other—but I used to travel with a Sidone. Graarack. She kind of just upped and disappeared a few years back, and I'd kind of like to know what happened to her. I mean, it's not that common for you folks to crew on ships and so … I thought … I'd just … ask … if any of you had heard of her …"

The threesome exchanged looks with several of their faceted eyes.

"I'm afraid not," the other female said.

"Thanks, I knew it was a long shot. I worry about her. I'd like to know if she's okay."

+ + +

"I'M SO GLAD you're back," Jaakon said. Mercedes hadn't seen him for months, and she was suddenly aware of the grey lacing his tight black curls, the lines around his eyes. He had added reading glasses and was clearly embarrassed to be caught wearing them because he quickly pulled them off and thrust them into a pocket.

"Well, I'm glad somebody is," she said and watched his expression turn from joy to embarrassment. "Oh, hell, Jaakon, that came out all wrong. I didn't mean it the way it sounded. I just meant that there is never a convenient time for me to be away from either the fleet or the capital. I'm discovering it's impossible to be both Star Admiral and Empress." She held out both hands to him. "I am, however, very happy to see you."

With the destruction of the palace and the extreme damage to the parliament building, the work of government was being done out of a downtown skyscraper that had once housed insurance companies, lawyers' offices, and brokerage firms. Instead of elegance it offered industrial competence. The past twenty years had seen a rejection of the more baroque style of earlier architecture and an embrace of a style that was meant to imply efficiency but only came off as cold. After a lifetime spent around marble and cornices, painted ceilings, and chandeliers, it seemed impersonal to Mercedes and rather like a lab or, worse, a maze where rats could be tested since the offices were mere cubicles formed by movable, sound-deadening panels.

The other thing that was startling was the number of women working in those cubicles. She realized she shouldn't be surprised. Someone had to keep the business of empire going, and with most of the men away at war that left only old men or women. There was the usual contingent of BEMs delivering tea or coffee, emptying trash cans, mopping the hard composite floors. The panels worked very well, so it was eerily quiet apart from the rap of her and Jaakon's heels on the floor.

"This way. We've kept an office for you," Jaakon said. "I'm right out front."

She looked at the desk that seemed more like it had been left by accident in front of the wall with its narrow glass-filled slits and an embossed metal door. "You're just out here? In traffic?"

"Oh, it's not too bad." He looked suddenly guilty.

"What?" Mercedes said and dug her elbow into his side.

"Well, at times I do avail myself of your office so people will stop bothering me."

"It's quite all right, Jaakon. It's not like I'm here most of the time."

"I'll get you a coffee," he said.

"Thank you. I'm going to need it."

Mercedes entered and Jaakon closed the door behind her. Arranged on the desk were actual stacks of real paper. Bills out of Parliament to be signed, petitions for redress. She had a list of requests for meetings and interviews that had been sent electronically. She would sit with Jaakon and decide which to accept and which to deny courteously, but that had to wait until she had dealt with the drudgery. She had signed through half of the first stack when Jaakon entered with a china cup and saucer and a sterling silver coffee pot, creamer, and sugar bowl, and a plate of shortbread cookies. There was a dent in the side of the coffee pot, but she recognized the set. It was part of the royal household. He noticed her looking.

"I rescued what I could out of the palace, ma'am."

Her eyes were suddenly burning, and Mercedes spun her chair away so she could look out the window at the workmen and machinery still busy clearing away the rubble. "Good to know some things remain," she said. If her voice was a bit husky perhaps, he would put it down to weariness.

"Yes, Majesty. You. And that's the most important thing." He had slipped away again by the time she turned back. That was probably good. Then he wouldn't see how much his words burdened her.

A few hours later Jaakon returned to roll down the blackout shade on the big windows and turn on a desk lamp. "Would you like me to bring you some dinner, ma'am?"

"Yes, that would be nice. Just some soup, I think."

He hadn't reached the door before a priority signal began flashing on the communications array. Jaakon hurried back to answer. "I have Admiral Chapman-Owiti for Her Majesty, Mercedes—"

"Yes, yes," Mercedes interrupted. "Put him through." Jaakon set up the security protocols as he left, and she nodded her thanks.

"Mercedes how are you?" the holograph of Ernesto inquired.

"Tired. You?"

"Same. But I have some updates on our guests."

"They've told you where they live?"

"Well, unfortunately no, but we have begun to get a sense of their religion and their language. That's what I wanted to talk to you about. It's strange."

Settling back in her chair Mercedes nodded at him to go on. If nothing else, the past months had taught her not to waste time with meaningless verbal niceties and comments designed merely to bring attention back to the speaker.

"I've brought in a number of linguists to help us crack it.

The shape of the *necrófagos* soft palate makes it difficult for humans to duplicate some of the sounds. Sidone seem to come closest with that, but that's neither here nor there. The issue is the language itself. It is so … structured and logical that the linguists think it's a created language."

That had her leaning forward, straining toward his image. "What does that even mean?"

"That it wouldn't have grown holistically as a species evolved and society changed. It's more like Esperanto or some of the languages that were created in fiction or for old-style vid shows from Earth before the Ad Astra diaspora."

"I ask again, what does that mean, Ernesto?"

"Honestly, I'm not sure, Majesty. My passion for my entire life has been exobiology. There is something about this that makes me feel like we're not seeing the whole picture." He paused and frowned down at the toes of his boots. "And that makes me … uneasy."

And now Mercedes was, too.

22

GÖTTERDÄMMERUNG IS NOT A STRATEGY

"I'M FOURTEEN AND a half… actually fifteen and ten months. Boys got to be midshipmen in the British navy when they were fourteen and they were *officers.*" Honesty compelled Hayden to add, "Well, sort of officers."

Jahan stared up at the boy, seeing the man in the set of his jaw and the determination in his dark eyes. She also saw the child. She had faced just such expressions on the faces of her own kits. They were standing on the burn-scarred concrete of the Tesla spaceport. A small holdall was at his feet. He had clearly come prepared. The air was filled with the sound of kids crying, adults soothing, somebody blasting music from a media box, the beeping sound of service vehicles scooting between the ships, carrying cargo, mechanics, foster parents, and crews to the various ships that dotted the field like exotic growths and carrying away either sobbing, sullen, or excited children. She wondered how the hell he had travelled from the house where he and the prince were situated and out to the spaceport. A question that could wait to be answered in the face of her immediate problem.

"Yeah, and that was like a million years ago in ships that

sailed on water. And they weren't at war—"

"They were, too. And they got to fight and die—" Hayden broke off abruptly as he realized that probably wasn't his best argument. He changed tack. "Please, please, Jahan, let me come with you. I can help." The wheedling tone dropped his age to about seven in an instant. He seemed to realize that. His expression hardened and he clenched his hands at his sides. "I have to do *something*. I have to!" His voice throbbed with desperation.

"*Chiquillo*, I can't take you. If something happened to you, how would I ever face your mother … or the Empress, for that matter?"

"My mother doesn't care. And the Empress has bigger things to worry about."

All of which was true, Jahan reflected. She grasped for another straw. "What about the *Infante*? Won't he miss you?"

Hayden frowned and pondered on that for a few minutes. "I don't think so. We're staying with a family who have three kids, and two of them are a lot closer to him in age. They play together all the time. And the third one's a baby, so I've got nobody …" His voice trailed away.

"Ah. I see." She thought about her situation. The addition of the nuns and the joy girls had certainly helped with the kids, but Ernie and Kielli were busting their asses loading supplies for the kids and supplies for the war effort. She eyed the breadth of the boy's shoulders and his height. He might actually be a help. *What am I thinking?* Her expression must have given her away, because the boy stepped in close, hope blooming in his eyes.

"You're thinking about it, aren't you?"

"No," she said firmly.

The ground shook as a ship at the far end of the port lifted off. Hayden was talking, but Jahan couldn't hear a word over the rumble and roar and the fact she had pulled up her ear protectors to dampen the sound. She waved at him to wait. He stood fidgeting, shifting his weight from foot to foot until they heard the sonic boom. She pulled off her headphones and nodded to him.

"You were saying."

"I won't change my mind. If you don't take me, I'll find somebody who will."

"I am not going to let that happen."

"How are you going to stop me? Tell the Keims to keep me locked up? And you can't warn off every captain. They'll be new ships arriving after you leave and you're lifting off in twelve hours."

"Did your homework, didn't you, you little shit?" He grinned at her.

She realized it was one of the first times she had ever seen him smile, and it brought into even sharper focus his incredible beauty. This was a boy who was going to break hearts in a scant year or so. She sighed and smoothed the fur around her eyes. Sooner or later, he would find a captain and a ship who would take him, and that thought filled her with dread. They tried to be selective about who got recruited for the evacuation efforts, but not every one of the smugglers were as honest as the crew of the *Selkie*. She acknowledged the dissonance in her thinking, but there was illegal and then there was *Illegal* and the *Selkie* always tried to stay on the small *i* side of the equation. A child who looked like this would be in danger from human traffickers.

"Please," the boy said.

It was time to admit defeat. She squeezed her eyes shut and sent up a prayer that she wasn't making a terrible mistake. "Okay, but we're going to go and tell the Keims. You're not just going to run away and have everybody frantic with worry." She grabbed him by the wrist and began chivvying him toward the gate.

"Thank you," he breathed.

"You won't be saying that for long. I'm going to work your ass off," she warned.

✦ ✦ ✦

FATHER KEN TOOK a sip of the butternut squash soup and nodded his approval. "You have a good chef."

It was just the two of them in the Captain's Mess. Since the expense of decorating a Captain's Mess fell to the man who commanded the ship, Tracy had been faced with dipping into his savings to trick out the room. So, he went minimalist and had had to suffer through various officers praising his exquisite Zen-like taste. It had taken all his control not to simply and loudly announce *No, I'm just cheap*. He had lined the walls with an ice-blue wallpaper, the chandelier over the clear Lucite table was a series of crystal rods of varying lengths, and the only decorations were three vases in celadon green with Asian-style flower arrangements and a single watercolor painting of a grey and white cat against a stark white background. Tracy knew he should have more dinner parties with his top officers, but it made him tense and upset his stomach when he had to hold court over people who outranked him, at least socially. The priest was a comforting figure who despite his noble birth had renounced it all to serve God. He had also seen Tracy at the lowest point in Tracy's life, so there was no judgement where Ken was concerned.

"The fact I have to even have a chef still seems bizarre to me," Tracy replied. "And I can't take the credit for finding him. I pawned if off on Beatrisa."

"And how did that go over?" Ken asked.

"About as well as you would expect. Fortunately, she immediately delegated it to Lieutenant Flintoff, who dealt with it in her overly dedicated way. Hence the presence of René, who had a string of very successful restaurants on Kronos until alimony payments followed by an alien invasion left him bankrupt. So, he's aboard and he isn't even technically in the service." Tracy shook his head over the absurdity of it all and took a sip of wine.

"I served on a ship when I was first starting out where the captain had a sommelier as well as a personal masseur and a barber," Ken mused, and gave that sweet distant smile. "Barber gave the best hot towel shaves I've ever had."

"Sorry I'm falling down on the ostentatious display front," Tracy said. Kallapus removed their soup bowls, refilled their wine glasses, and went off to the galley to gather up their main course.

"Tracy, it's okay to admit you're suffering from imposter syndrome," Father Ken said.

"I know you're a priest, but sometimes I swear you've

made a deal with the Devil," Tracy complained. "When did you become a mind reader?"

"All I have to do is look at your face," was the reply.

"Yeah, yeah, I know. Open book, don't play poker, heart on my sleeve, et cetera, et cetera and blah, blah blah." Tracy drained his wine.

"So, talk to me."

He sat silent for a long moment trying to figure out how to put into words what was just an inchoate feeling. "It's not so much imposter syndrome as the feeling that I'm being set up to fail. Yes, I'm an admiral. Yes, I have my own fleet, but we have half the number of ships as the Blue and the Gold. I've got babies and burnouts and brand-new ships that have been rushed off the line and old war-horses, so breakdowns on both are likely." He swirled the wine in his glass, watching the way the ruby liquid sheeted across the sides of the goblet. "And I feel like the past is pressing in on me from every side."

"Okay, that's not what I expected. What do you mean?"

Kallapus arrived with the prawns in curry sauce and a large green salad. He then bowed and withdrew from the room. Tracy resumed. "This afternoon I was notified that I'm getting a new commander. A Lady Cipriana Delecroix-McKenzie. We were classmates. Served together on our first tour of duty."

"I'm not seeing the problem."

"I feel like I can't escape the ghosts and the fruitless dreams … well, fantasies, really. They keep coming back to remind me of … of everything I've done, every failure, everything I've lost … everything I can't have," he concluded quietly. The priest remained silent, leaning back in his chair as he rolled the wine glass between his palms. "Take young Flintoff. I knew her mother, well, foster mother."

"Another classmate?" Ken asked.

"Yes. And I managed to get the love of her life killed, which derailed Sumiko's career and left the Empress with only a single woman for support. A certain Lady Cipriana Delecroix. And I failed her, too. Something terrible happened to Cipri on that first cruise and I should have done something. Even if it cost me everything."

"Tracy, you have abundantly proved that you will risk everything to do what is right. I don't think you need to feel any guilt."

"But I do. Over Hugo and Cipriana." It suddenly struck Tracy that he had returned to duty and hadn't made a single effort to determine if Wessen had remained in the service, also been returned to duty, or been killed. He was an admiral now. Maybe he could finally get justice for Cipriana.

"I can see the wheels turning. What are you thinking?"

"That rank does have its privileges."

"I find myself vaguely concerned by that answer," Ken said. "Don't forget it also comes with responsibilities."

"Responsibilities … yes." Tracy met Ken's warm brown eyes. "Here's a question for you. There's a very high-level officer, another classmate, and I've known since school that he's … dangerous. I worry because he has the power of life and death over so many people. Do I say anything? And would anybody listen? Of course, if he turns that psychopathy against the enemy then it's all good, right? Or does my silence already prove my hypocrisy? That I'm rationalizing, justifying keeping quiet."

"A difficult question. Has this man done anything *recently* that you can point to as proof of your concerns?"

"No, damn it."

"Does he outrank you?"

"A bit. One grade above me."

"Titled?"

"Yes." Tracy bit off the word. The fact he had yet to be ennobled rankled no matter how much he tried to tell himself he didn't care.

"Then I fear if you spoke out it would be viewed as nothing more than resentment and jealousy on your part."

"Yeah, you're probably right."

"So, what has brought on all these heart burnings?" the priest asked.

"I'm just sick of being reminded of the past."

"You can't rewrite it, and to forget it would negate all that you've learned from those experiences. And really, it's not all that unusual that you would come into contact with these fellow travelers. You all belonged to a rather elite club. How many people manage to graduate from The High Ground in a given year?"

"Only about a quarter make it through. Or at least that used to be the case."

"There you go. And they are coming back because we are at war."

Tracy gave the priest a rueful smile. "You always have the kindest, most gentle way of telling me to fucking get over myself."

Ken just smiled and patted his lips with his napkin. "Shall

we see what René has planned for dessert? And I look forward to meeting this Lady Cipriana."

✦ ✦ ✦

IT WAS COMING up on six months since Boho had caught Mercedes in Belmanor's arms. He hadn't acted on his first murderous impulse because the damn aliens had, as predicted, figured out the mine maze and altered their tactics. It had at least worked to protect the hospitals on New Hope, and Reichart's World, but after that the *necrófagos* no longer translated out of Fold deep inside a system but instead divided their forces and translated at multiple points at the edges of a system. It required the humans to garrison League systems with massive numbers of ships, and trying to anticipate where an enemy ship might appear had crews sleepless and on edge. At Dullahan, a trigger-happy destroyer crew had shot up a space liner which had just returned to normal space, killing half the passengers and sending much-needed supplies into the void.

There had been pitched space battles as well, and while O-Trell was getting better at countering the alien's tactics, there were still losses of men and ships. Mercifully Boho had missed all of those, primarily because Mercedes had tasked him with overseeing the recruitment efforts and helping assign the new graduates from The High Ground to various ships. He tried to tell himself it was because of his popularity with the people, but he feared that she knew of his cowardice.

They hadn't actually seen each other since that ill-fated day on Hellfire. Mercedes had decreed that they would alternate visits to Ouranos so that at least one royal would always be present at the capital. Boho didn't mind giving patriotic speeches to adoring crowds, but the drudgery of ship assignments bored him, and he left it to his flag captain. Friedman was good at it and seemed to actually enjoy reading over duty rosters.

Boho had been desperate to feel sun on his face and stand on the shore listening to the boom of the waves die into a sighing hiss upon the sand while the smell of salt and seaweed hung heavy in the air. After his security detail had cleared the beach, Boho had ordered them to remain on the dunes above him. He, who had always been so gregarious, wanting companions for his adventures and women for his bed, now found himself craving privacy. Though it was not a comfortable place. Without the clamor and distraction, he had only himself for company, and that was giving him far too much time for reflection and worry: about his son, his marriage, his loneliness.

Thrusting his hands into his pockets, he walked down the beach watching the tiny piping birds play tag with the foaming water as they searched for food. He had spent the first night back at the small palace that had been their home for much of their marriage, but it forcibly reminded him of his son's absence and nights of passion spent with Mercedes, so he had repaired to the Prime Minister's Suite at the Royal Mark.

At some point he assumed they would have to discuss what had occurred between her and Belmanor on Hellfire, but how do you ask your wife of almost thirty years if she actually loved him? Her remarks indicated that she didn't.

That for her this marriage had merely been duty.

And for him? Was it love that had him agree to wed Mercedes or merely ambition? It wasn't like they had ever discussed the matter. There had been no romance. He hadn't even proposed to her himself. Her father and his father had made the deal and their children had acquiesced. Had he ever really loved anyone?

A kaleidoscope of faces tumbled through his memories. Most had no names, just bodies and faces either in repose or in the throes of passion. All but one. One stood out. One had a name. *Paloma Flintoff*. He had believed she loved him. He thought he loved her. And then it had all been proven to be a lie. She was an agent for SEGU using her delicate beauty in service of the crown. Beneath that helpless, adoring, and fragile exterior dwelled a powerful mind and an even stronger will. They had had one final interaction during the attempted coup and then never spoken again.

He sank down to sit on the warm sand. Of course, he had seen her in the intervening years. They were of the same class and moved in the same circles, but he had made certain he kept on the other side of any ballroom from her and made certain never to be seated near her at a dinner party. Why had he done it? Shame? Anger? Distrust? He wasn't sure.

When he saw her dancing with another man there would be a flare of … jealousy … bitterness … a sense of proprietorship … then he would remind himself that the man whose arms might encircle that tiny waist was probably a target of the spy agency. This belief had been buttressed by the fact that she hadn't married even though she was now in her twenties. Most girls of her class were wed immediately out of high school, though some might convince a doting father to allow them to attend university and postpone the inevitable until they were twenty-one. In the *paso doble* of power that engaged every FFH family, girls were mere commodities.

Overhead, seabirds argued with raucous cries and occasionally arrowed into the water to emerge triumphant with a fish skewered on their razor-like beaks. In the distance a few sailboats spread their sails to catch the wind like flowers opening to the sun's touch.

Boho was suddenly seized with a desperate need to speak to Paloma. It was stupid. Of course, it was stupid. What did he hope would come of it? What was he looking for? None of the arguments lessened the desire. He dug his hands into the sand and leaned forward to press his forehead against his knees. His ScoopRing pricked his finger. He took the call on audio only. It was the head of his detail. "Sir, are you unwell? Do you need anything?"

Boho looked back over his shoulder at the men standing guard above him. Picked out the figure of the commander. "No, no, I'm fine, Colonel. Just weighed down with … worries."

"I completely understand, sir. You have lives in your hands." The evident sympathy in the man's voice shamed Boho, because far from worrying about the fate of the League and the safety of her citizens, he was sitting here feeling sorry for himself.

He stood up abruptly and brushed the sand from the seat of his trousers. "Time for us to get back to it, Colonel."

"Very good, sir."

As he climbed up the hill using the tufts of stiff marsh

grass for purchase, he called Anselmo. "I need you to find someone."

"Okay."

"Lady Paloma Flintoff."

"Oh … uh … is that wise?"

"Probably not, but I'm going to do it anyway."

+ + +

IT WAS HARD not to stare. Cipriana had been the avowed beauty of the four women who had been the first to attend The High Ground. Tracy might love Mercedes, but a man would have to be blind not to acknowledge that she was eclipsed by Cipriana. Or she had been. The grotesque burns across the right side of Cipriana's face formed twisted ridges and pulled up the side of her mouth into an angry grimace. Her ear was gone, leaving just a hole in the skull, and the right eye was a prosthetic. There had been no attempt to match the obsidian black of her left eye. The artificial orb was dull grey with a pinprick of glowing red in the center. One could read no expression in that eye, but it wasn't all that different from the left, which was equally flat and cold.

After delivering a parade ground perfect salute, Cipriana gave a humorless smile which made the twisted expression even more disturbing. "Like what you see? Or rather what you're trying *not* to see?"

Tracy came around from behind his desk. "I'm sorry. I didn't realize … I thought you would have …"

"Let them do their medical magic? A little Botox and plastic surgery to smooth it all away? *No!* I wanted *this.*" She gestured down the length of her body. "To match my soul. I wanted all the smug, fat, comfortable people to see what's at stake. To be afraid."

Every sense was screaming a warning to Tracy that this was not someone he wanted on his ship, much less in the fleet. "I think everyone is well aware what's at stake. They've buried husbands and wives and children." He thought there was a slight flinch, but it was gone before he could be sure. "And it's our job to ease those fears and to keep them safe."

"With all due respect, sir, that is not correct. Our job to kill aliens. Preferably *all* of them."

The vitriol was shocking, and the corner of his desk beckoned as a point of support. Tracy sank down onto it. "Let's put rank aside for the moment." He folded his hands in his lap. "Cipri, what's wrong?"

"What's wrong?" It was a harsh cry that seemed to echo off the walls of his office. "Is that a serious question?"

"I'll right, I'll stop trying to be diplomatic. I don't know what it is you think you came out here to do—"

"We have to end it. All of it. Whatever the cost."

"*Götterdämmerung* is not a strategy, and genocide is not a solution."

"Whatever. Just give me my assignment and let me go do my job. I specialized in weaponry when I returned to the academy."

"All right." Tracy returned to his desk, typed in his instructions, and hit send. Her ring flared as his orders arrived. Her face held mad joy as she brought up the text, that curdled into fury. "You're making me a CSAR? I'm a goddamn combat specialist. You can't do this!"

“Can. Did. You will command one of the combat search and rescue teams. Unless you’d prefer to serve out your tour in the brig, Commander?”

“Why are you doing this?” Cipriana demanded. “I have to … I have to … make them …” She didn’t finish. He could guess the final word. *Pay.*

“I need you to remember you’re a human being, Cipri. I think that can best happen if you’re assisting the wounded. You are dismissed, Commander.”

The human eye was glistening with unshed tears. Grief or fury? Tracy couldn’t tell. Her face was frozen, expressionless. She took one step back, saluted, whirled, and left his office. Tracy keyed his intercom.

“Father, we need to talk.”

23

A PERFECT SET OF FOOLS

THE SHOUTS OF children at play and the occasional admonition from an adult supervisor accompanied Boho as he walked past the makeshift playground. It was off to the side of the building now housing war orphans. He found himself comparing the dilapidated swing set, slide, teeter-totter, and monkey bars with the activities that had been available at the last royal birthday party. It shocked him to realize that party for Dulcinea's daughter had been almost three years ago. War compressed time, it seemed.

Eventually these playing children would probably be evacuated, but without parents to advocate for them they were well down that list. Also, the government had made the decision to place some aliens above these lost children in an attempt to try and assure there were no budding fifth columnists behind the lines.

Once inside, he wrinkled his nose at the smells: a mix of diapers, talcum powder, chili, and that indescribable baby and child smell. This orphanage only housed children to age ten. Older orphans were at another facility where more formalized schooling was the focus. *And the intent to grab them into the service the moment they turn eighteen.* A cynical thought, that. Boho pushed it aside. A harried-looking nun was hurrying past. Boho held up a hand.

"Pardon me, Sister, but I'm looking for Lady Paloma Flintoff. I was told she was here."

"Yes, she's upstairs helping get the children ready for bed."

"Thank you." He took the stairs rather than the lift.

As he walked down the hall, he glanced into rooms filled with bunk beds, one that was clearly a playroom with balls, dolls, puzzles, toy flitters and toy spaceships, toy guns. The fifteen or so children were abnormally quiet, several just sat and stared. Others gripped the toys as if they were lifelines. In addition to two nuns, there was a white-coated physician also watching and making notes on his TapPad. One door flew open, and a wet, naked little boy ran out shrieking with laughter. A blob of bubbles on the top of his head made him look like he was wearing a bizarre sugar-loaf hat, and the soap bubbles set a sharp contrast to his rich, dark skin. Paloma, her brown hair tied back with a scarf, came racing out after him. She was wearing a split riding skirt and pale pink blouse which brought out the rosy, brown hue of her skin. She was still breathtakingly beautiful, and Boho froze for an instant.

He then leaped forward and captured the fleeing child. The little boy was a plump, wet, wriggling armful and Boho felt his shirt growing damp as he hugged him close. Some of the bubbles brushed off on his lips and he tasted soap. The little boy gave a gurgling laugh, and Boho was seized by a desperate longing for his own child. He told himself it was just the soap that was making his eyes water. Paloma came up and relieved him of the toddler.

"What are you doing here?" she asked. Her expression was not encouraging.

"I … I came to see you," Boho said awkwardly.

"I see. Well, come on. I have to finish with Robin's bath."

He followed her into the bathroom, where a tub had been placed over the central drain for the room and hoses jury-rigged water from the sinks. She dumped Robin back in the bath and finished rinsing his hair with handfuls of water. She then pulled him out. "Hand me that towel." She indicated it with a jerk of her chin. Boho obeyed, and she quickly wrapped the boy in the rather threadbare linen.

"Not very luxurious," he said with a nod to the towel.

"No. We make do with donations. The tub was salvaged from a bombed-out house. Okay, Robin Red Breast, let's get you in your jammies and then off to bed."

"Read me a story?" the boy suggested.

"Do you think you deserve a story after running away like that?"

"Uh-huh," he said, and he gave her a heart-melting smile.

Paloma looked over at Boho. "Typical male."

He helped her get the kid into his onesie, and they crossed the hall to one of the dorm rooms where she tucked him into a lower bunk. Women volunteers and several nuns were doing the same with other children. It turned out one of the nuns was reading a story, so Boho and Paloma left.

"What are you doing now?" he asked.

"Going home."

"May I buy you dinner?"

"Perhaps you may have noticed we are at war. There is a

curfew. And most restaurants stop serving at sundown."

"Someone will stay open for me," he answered.

She stared up at him. There was a bubble caught in one of her curls. He flicked it away, remembering when those curls would fall across his face and caress his chest as she slid down his body to take his cock in her mouth. He felt the nudge of an erection against his zipper. She noticed.

"You never will change, will you?"

He was grinning like an idiot. A forced grimace even as she insulted him. "Probably not. Men don't, you know. What you see at sixteen is what you get at sixty. But women … you change constantly. We poor males can't keep up. You're a mystery to us." He was babbling and it bewildered him.

From puberty he had had the ability to talk a woman into bed. In fact, he had fucked this woman … No, not fucked, made love to, but on her part, it had been mere duty and he had been the one being manipulated. She had seduced him with her beauty and innocence as part of her work as an agent of SEGU, all to trap him as he had tried to play all sides in the coup d'état. So why in the hell was he even here? Why this need to see her?

Because I want somebody to love me. I want to love someone.

Somehow, she read his sadness and loneliness. Her aloof expression softened. "All right. Let's test your persuasive powers. And perhaps we can get the restaurant to provide me with some carry away for the family. We lost our cook. He enlisted and we've yet to find a replacement."

Boho felt as if someone had just opened champagne in his head. The dirty walls of the hallway seemed to gleam, and his hand was trembling as he pulled her arm through his. It all felt so right. Her next words brought him back to Earth.

"And I'm not going to sleep with you."

"Too old," he said lightly.

"Not honorable."

With that, he realized just how far he had to go to win back her respect. He then realized this wasn't a case of getting anything back. He had never had her respect. The knowledge shamed him.

✦ ✦ ✦

SHE WAS BACK on Hellfire, which was giving rise to all manner of uncomfortable and unpleasant memories. Mercedes's back was stiff with tension, and she felt like two pairs of eyes were boring into the back of her neck. At the head of the table, Ernesto stood, a laser pointer in hand, as the light from the rotating galaxy map threw his features into high relief. The rest of the room at fleet headquarters was in relative darkness. Which was good, because Mercedes really did not want to see the faces or read the expressions of the two men who were currently staring at her.

Because of the sensitivity of what Ernesto had to impart, only the commanders of the three fleets plus the overall commander of the fusileros and the senior admiral who led the wet foot navy were present. Technically, Boho shouldn't have been here since it was Mercedes who commanded the Blue, but after her indiscretion with Tracy she knew she couldn't leave her husband behind. Tracy and Boho had seated themselves with as much distance between them as was physically possible, but Mercedes could scarcely breath because of the tension. She just prayed that neither Talion nor the other two officers would sense it. Mercedes forced her attention back to Ernesto.

"It was biology that gave us the final piece of the puzzle," the scientist was saying. "We were lucky that one of the prisoners died from injuries sustained during his capture, enabling us to do a more detailed analysis of their physiology."

Mercedes repressed a shudder as she pictured the grizzly scene. Biology class had been her least favorite thing at The High Ground. Dissecting those alien cadavers had been horrifying. *More horrifying than killing them?* Mercedes found herself defensively answering … herself. *Those were donated bodies. They died of natural causes.*

Like we didn't massacre our aliens during the Expansion Wars. Like we're going to do to this lot.

Shut up. They started this. You sound like a five-year-old.

That reminder that her son was fast approaching that very birthday snapped her back to the present. *Yes, I would kill them all to keep him safe,* she answered that hectoring part of herself.

I'm sure there's a mother on the necrófago *home world who feels exactly the same.* She clutched at her head, trying to still the furious internal debate.

"Majesty?" Ernesto said, breaking off his talk.

"Nothing. Headache. Do continue."

"The analysis of eye development and how their bodies process vitamins gave us a strong sense of the star that would have given rise to their particular biology. Our best analysis is a K-type star, orange to red and trending more toward orange. This was supported by our study of the ship and spectrum analysis of the lighting used by the aliens. We set about writing a program that would analyze all the alien movements and correlating that with K-type stars that possess planets of sufficient density to match what was normal for the *necrófago* based on analysis of the artificial gravity generator aboard the captured ship."

"All this process is fascinating, but do we have a conclusion yet?" Boho drawled.

"Our best guess is that they are located somewhere in this area of the Scutum-Crux spiral." His virtual pointer circled an area on the galaxy map.

"And how many K-type stars with planets have you located?" Talion asked.

"Well, since there are roughly two hundred billion stars in the Milky Way, our radio telescopes have pinpointed seven thousand three hundred and twenty-three possible planetary systems ..." His voice trailed away at their expressions. "We are aggressively scanning to see if we can pick up radio or Foldstream messages emanating from any particular system, but again it all takes ... time."

Boho surged to his feet. "This is bloody useless. We don't have *time*. We've just been lucky they haven't hit Cuandru, and even with the minefield and a large number of ships posted on guard duty there, they might get through. One lucky shot and our major shipyard is destroyed and then where will we be?"

"We can use unmanned probes fitted out with Fold capability. Send them to the identified stars." It was Tracy speaking, and his contempt for Boho was showing. "They can do a flyby and scan for activity on the planets. Since there won't be crews aboard, they can move at speeds beyond what we can endure in normal space. If they find anything, they pulse out a Foldstream message."

Mercedes hurried into speech. "That could work." She looked to Admiral Ritchie, who commanded the shipyard at Cuandru and who was joining them via Foldstream. "How soon can we start fabricating these probes?"

Ritchie rubbed a hand across his mouth. "We've got one berth that's empty. Ship just came off the line. We can retool it. Take about three days. Of course, we have to have the specs on these probes first."

She looked to Ernesto. He nodded. "We can get that. Give us a few days for the tech boys to do a redesign. They're not currently equipped to move at the speeds I think Admiral Belmanor has in mind."

"Hopefully the design will be ready at about the same time as the berth," Tracy said.

"The team will do their best."

"I suggest that they do better than best," Boho snapped.

"Then I'd *best* get to it," Ritchie said stiffly, and Mercedes noted he left off the *sir*. His image flickered and vanished.

"So, we find this planet," Talion said. "Then what?"

Mercedes waited, then realized everyone was looking to her. "Combine the fleets. Head for their home world."

"They'll yell for help," Boho warned. "And bring back *their* fleets."

"I expect that is Her Majesty's plan," Tracy said. "One final powerful blow to break their backs."

"And what if they break ours, instead?" Boho demanded, rounding on Tracy. "We'd be leaving nothing in reserve."

"I'm sure you would volunteer to command those reserves," Tracy sneered. There was a collective gasp of indrawn breath. Mercedes started to stand, then Tracy went on. "Given your strategic skills, you would no doubt have an excellent plan that would extract us from the situation should we find ourselves in difficulty."

Everyone relaxed but no one was fooled. Tracy had a very faint smile. Boho's brows snapped together in a ferocious frown. Mercedes wanted to kill them both, but mostly Tracy. The only solution was to end the fraught meeting. She stood. The men all followed suit.

"Then we await the results of your research, Admiral," she said to Ernesto. "In the meantime, we have to return to our job of protecting our citizens."

+ + +

THE ODORS EMERGING from an Isanjo restaurant slowed Tracy's steps. He had elected to walk back to the spaceport and his shuttle rather than take a flitter. It gave him time to quiet his raging emotions. At moments like this he wished he had never been promoted past captain. If he was still the commander of the *Swiftsure*, he would not have to be in a room with Mercedes or Cullen. So, he had walked, and now alluring scents had finally brought him to a halt.

Here near the noise and stink of the spaceport were the alien ghettos, so the restaurants catered to that population. Tracy found himself transported back in time, when he and his father would meet every Friday after Tracy finished school and have dinner out. It was never anything fancy, they hadn't the money for that, but it was a treat, a break from the grinding labor that defined their lives and a way for them to just spend time together. Tracy had talked about his classes and his dreams while his father listened and softly smiled. That smile was gone now. The stroke had left Alexander's face frozen on the right side. And his dreams? Surprisingly, Tracy had realized some of them and had just been regretting that achievement.

"Let that be a lesson to you," he murmured aloud. "Maybe getting what you want isn't always all that it's cracked up to be."

Tracy shook off his reverie and considered. While his chef could prepare virtually any human cuisine he had no idea about alien dishes, and Tracy, who had a taste for highly spiced food, had always loved Isanjo cookery. He decided to stop and treat himself.

Inside Tracy found a traditional Isanjo space. There were platforms attached to the walls and an artificial tree was set in the center, again with platforms attached. Living plants, ferns in pots, and climbing ivy were hung about and writhed up the walls. Ropes and braided walkways crisscrossed the ceiling. There were only a handful of tables on the floor with chairs that would be suitable for a human's frame. When he entered, conversations died to nothing. Most had been in Spanish, or English, but he had heard some Isanji being spoken. Seventeen pairs of neotenous eyes were turned toward him and a waiter swarmed down a rope net and dropped to the floor in front of him.

"Chuk rill keke," Tracy said in Nilou, and there was a whispered reaction from the diners and staff. He had picked up some of the language from Jahan. He also knew his pronunciation was abysmal; human mouths and Isanjo muzzles had little in common, and the League's attitude was that it was the responsibility of the aliens to learn the primary human languages, not the other way around which meant no formal training was available. "May I be seated?"

"Of course, my lord," said the waiter bowing to him.

"Just a citizen," Tracy corrected.

"Not with those on your collar and cuffs." The voice quavered a bit. Tracy located the speaker, and judging by the grey of the fur on his face he was quite elderly.

"I've got rank but no title, *demosene*," he replied.

"*Hmmmph*, I'm no grandfather to you with your hairless ass, and you throw around a lot of Nilou, human." The words were sharp but there was humor underlying it all.

"Grandfather, you are being rude," the young female Isanjo who was dining with him muttered.

Tracy grinned at the old Isanjo. "I bet you were bossy as hell to the soldier you served. And sometimes I think the hair up here"—he patted his head—"is trying to migrate down to my ass."

That strange coughing laugh of the Isanjo went around the room. The old alien hopped down from his table and gazed up at Tracy. "You're right. I was a batBEM. Forty years I served. Now they say I'm too old, but my grandbaby is going. Signed up to serve some of these lady soldiers. Hope they can fight."

"As well as your ladies can, *demosene*."

"Good to hear. Enjoy your meal, Admiral."

Tracy was led over to a table and a menu was procured. He ordered one of the strong Isanjo beers and selected the hot pot he had always enjoyed. A bowl of crispy chips was brought and salsa for dipping. He sat enjoying the flavors and the burn. He ordered another beer and his entree arrived. He began to tuck in, mopping up the thick stew with a coarse brown bread, and was surprised when an Isanjo entered and walked up to his table.

"My lord would like to invite you to a dance," the alien said.

Tracy leaned back in his chair and wiped his fingers on his napkin. "Oh, really, and who is your lord?"

"Admiral Prince Cullen."

"Tell him I'd be delighted but I have to pick up my dancing shoes."

"He says he can loan you shoes since you probably lack them."

"You can tell Cullen that it's been thirty years, and I don't need any man's charity."

"Very good, sir."

"And where are we dancing?"

"He thought perhaps it would be best to conduct this gavotte at the Palisade Park near the bandstand. In one hour."

"I'll be there. I'm looking forward to it. Are we the only couple or do I need to bring some additional dancers?"

"My lord says he's merely giving you a lesson."

"Understood." Tracy made a shooing motion. "Go. I'd like to finish my dinner."

✦ ✦ ✦

TWILIGHT WAS CLOSING in and the lights in the park were starting to wink to life. Boho had ordered his security to set up a perimeter but give him privacy for what was about to occur. He now paced in front of the bandstand swinging his rapier. The blade decapitated the tips of the grass, releasing a rich green scent that reminded him of family picnics at the country estate. He had a sudden longing for the place and the past. A caretaker managed the house and the grounds since he didn't have time and his sisters had all married off-world. He exchanged occasional messages with them, did his best to set up their children in lucrative positions, invited the daughters to the palace for balls and parties to try and get them married off, but much of it he delegated to Anselmo. Unlike Mercedes, he didn't have strong feelings for any of them. Mercedes loved her sisters—at least the ones who hadn't betrayed her—and stayed in close contact with them even when separated by light-years. He wondered what his lack of emotional connection said about him.

He was pulled from his brief moment of self-reflection by the sound of someone whistling the latest hit song. Belmanor appeared. He had a sheathed sword cocked jauntily over his shoulder and he didn't look nervous at all. The lights on the bandstand sprang to life and the native flowers rotated and opened their petals to soak in the photons. The light glittered on the inlaid and jeweled hilt of the *intitulado*'s sword. This was no cheap blade from a fencing school; this was a deadly weapon. That was when Boho started to feel the first flutterings of alarm.

"Shall we discuss—" Belmanor said.

"You were kissing my wife. There is nothing to discuss. I am going to kill you."

Belmanor released a gust of air in a startled *whoof.* "Well, all righty then. Look, before you try to kill me, why don't we address the elephant standing between us, but without all the bloodshed—"

"Coward."

"Oh, I wouldn't go there, Cullen; I really wouldn't if I were you. But putting that aside … allow me to confess. Yes, I love your wife. I have loved her since I was eighteen, but the operative words in that statement are *your wife*. She married you even knowing how I felt. She hasn't left you. She gave you a son. So, I don't understand why we're engaging in this nonsensical exercise."

Because I suspect you are the better man? The thought shook Boho, as had Belmanor's speech. He felt off-balance. He had expected bluster or groveling, not this matter-of-fact conversation. "Don't you want to fight me?" Boho touched his left eyebrow. "Try to pay me back for giving you that scar?"

Belmanor looked thoughtful and rubbed at the puckered scar that disappeared into the hair at his temple and pulled his left eyebrow up in a sardonic arch. "Once I did. When I was younger." He pulled the sword off his shoulder, unsheathed it, and inspected the blade. "Got this sword. Learned to fence. For just that reason. But we're damn near fifty, Cullen. Don't you think we'll look like a pair of perfect fools staggering about trying to stab each other?"

Boho rested the point of his sword on the ground and leaned on the hilt. He was confused but also amused. "This is *not* how I pictured this going."

"Same for me. When your batBEM brought your message, I was all full of piss and vinegar and ready to fight. Then when *my* batBEM showed up with my sword, he gave me this look that clearly said, *you daft old bugger*. And then I had to walk over here lugging a sword, and I got more incredulous looks from soldiers and civilians alike—"

"You should have taken a flitter. I did."

"Whatever, point being I absolutely knew what they were thinking. *Stop fucking around and protect us.* So shall we table this until we finish the war?"

Boho considered, then held out his hand. "Truce." Belmanor hesitated, but he eventually took it, and they shook. "But if you touch my wife again, I will just have someone shoot you."

"Fair enough." Belmanor started to leave, then turned back. "You know she would probably be furious with the both of us. Talking as if we have the power to dictate her actions or make choices and decisions for her."

He vanished among the trees, and Boho slowly sat down on the steps of the bandstand. *But what if she were to choose him?*

24

A LONG WAY FROM HELP

IT TOOK SIX months before a probe sent back a positive reading. It hadn't been a quiet time. There had been skirmishes and battles at various League worlds. The *necrófagos* had managed to destroy six domes on Paradise Lost with an initial loss of life of seventy thousand, but thirty thousand more were seriously ill from exposure to the plant toxins on the planet. There had been a work stoppage on Cuandru when Isanjo workers became incensed over a false rumor that only the human residents of the planet were being provided with beacons that would allow them to be evacuated from the planet, in the event of an attack by special O-Trell ships. The governor, Darmali, had overreacted and sent in troops to quell the strike. Thirteen Isanjo had been killed and forty-seven arrested. Mercedes had been forced to come to the planet and personally remove the man, which had led to outrage back in Hissilek as Darmali had connections both financial and marital in parliament.

Fortunately, Mercedes had a secret weapon in the person of Rohan Danilo Marcus Aubrey, Condé de Vargas and current prime minister. Decades of swimming in the political swamp left him knowing where every body was buried and who wanted to gore whose ox. Rohan had recommended a replacement who could make concessions to some of Darmali's more fervent supporters and offer an opportunity to his enemies to wreak a little vengeance.

Mercedes had arranged for the imprisoned aliens to be released and reparations paid to the families of the slain. It also gave her an opportunity to hold a conference call with all the League governors and stress that creating enemies behind their lines by antagonizing their alien subjects was maybe not the best plan and would result in more of the governors losing their positions if it happened again.

And now it was time. She gazed out at a stretch of space around *Nueva Terra* that was filled with ships. The star system was the closest jump-off point to what they hoped was the *necrófagos* home world. It was still a significant distance from League space. They would be in Fold for twenty-three days. A long time for the crews to contemplate and worry about the upcoming battle.

The light from the system's sun glinted on the hulls of the thirty-seven hundred ships enfolding those crews. They represented the assembled might of the Blue, Gold, and Green fleets. Thrusters glowed red as they maneuvered into position for the staggered, but still massive, Fold maneuver they were about to attempt. With this many ships it wasn't possible to arrive too close to the pinpointed planet, so there would be at least a few days before they would be in position to deliver the payback that the *necrófagos* so richly deserved.

Gelb, standing next to the command chair, checked an incoming message on his ScoopRing. He leaned down and said softly, "Majesty, your sisters have arrived, and the admirals are in transit to the flagship."

"Thank you, Captain. How long do I have before the admirals arrive?" Mercedes asked.

"About fifty minutes, ma'am."

"Fifty minutes," she mused. "Such a small amount of time when I haven't seen them in months."

"We end this, and we'll have all the time in the world to spend with our families."

"Not everyone, Captain. There will be casualties." He bowed, acknowledging the truth of her statement.

✦ ✦ ✦

"AH, NEPHILIM, GARDEN spot of the galaxy," Ernie said.

"I am going to assume that is irony," Jax replied.

Everyone except Hayden was gathered on the bridge watching the planet swell in the viewport. The cargo they carried was medical supplies to be stockpiled in case of attack. Their return cargo would be lithium and, she supposed, children, though the port authorities had been a bit vague on that point. The lift door opened and the smell of coffee and cocoa preceded Hayden's entrance. She swore the boy had shot up two inches in the seven months since he had come aboard, and his voice was wavering between baritone and soprano in that adorable way of male human adolescents.

His arrival had had one downside. Being much closer in age to Kielli, the human boy's occasional lapse into teenage fuckery sometimes had Kielli regressing, too, but Jahan mostly let these go. Dalea had told her the boy was far too serious for his age, and it was good to see him starting to occasionally act like a teenager. For the most part, Hayden was a useful and sober member of the crew. That didn't mean Jahan had forgotten he was a child. She had him studying math with Jax, and Dalea took over the literary and biology parts of his education. Ernie had him helping in the engine room. Jahan wasn't sure if she added anything of value to the educational mix. *Maybe it's okay if I'm just the mom figure,* she thought. *Well, that's depressing.* And she was suddenly seized by a desperate longing to feel Tageri's arms around her and to hear him breathing softly next to her while he slept. So far, Cuandru had avoided any attack, which was strange because it was a prime target because of the shipyards. It was also very well guarded, so perhaps that was the reason.

She accepted her cup of tea from Hayden. He looked at the screen and asked, "How long until we dock?" He sounded wistful.

"About twenty-six hours, and we won't be visiting the planet. Just the station," she warned.

"That's okay. It'll be bigger than the ship."

"And have shops," Kielli added. "We can try to find the new Magic Quest," he added, directing the remark to the human boy.

"That would be awesome if they have it."

"You kids and these silly games," Ernie grunted. "We haven't got enough war for you in real life?"

Hayden looked down at the toes of his boots. "In the games we can win," he said softly. A silence fell across the bridge, making the rumble of the engines and the pings from the scanner seem unbelievably loud.

Dalea hurried to the boy's side and put an arm around him. "We're going to win in real life, too. We've got the Empress, and your mother, and our former captain Admiral Belmanor all fighting for us."

He looked up at her. "I hope so."

Jahan hopped up onto the back of the captain's chair and raked them all with a look. "Us standing around up here for hours won't make the ship go any faster. Let's get back to work. Those crates aren't going to shift themselves."

✦ ✦ ✦

MERCEDES RODE THE elevator down to the officer's deck and instructed her security detail to remain in the hallway outside her cabin. The moment she entered she was grabbed from two directions by Carisa and Beatrisa and tightly hugged. They were laughing and Mercedes was chagrined to find herself both crying and laughing. After the last frenzied hug and kiss, she was released, and she stepped back so she could survey her half-sisters. She wasn't surprised by Beatrisa's shorn head, but the fact that Carisa had followed suit had her crying out in protest.

"Oh, Cari, really? Your beautiful hair."

The youngest Arango daughter ran a hand across the dark fuzz and grinned up at Mercedes. "It's all Beatrisa's fault. She set the fashion and now almost every female officer is following suit."

"Having the word fashion in any kind of proximity to me gives me hives," the middle sister huffed.

Mercedes flipped her long braid over her shoulder. In the years since her hair had been cut in an effort to disguise her identity, it had grown once more into a mane that hung almost to the middle of her back. Mercedes pushed aside thoughts and memories of that time and instead said with feigned indignation, "They aren't taking their cue from their empress?"

"Trust me, you'll never go back once you've done the buzz," Carisa said.

"Boho would probably divorce me."

"That would be such a bad thing?" Beatrisa asked, and there was no humor in her voice.

"Hush. We do all right together. I couldn't have gotten through this without him."

Carisa slipped an arm around her waist and pulled her over to the bunk. They sat down on the bed while Beatrisa dropped down to sit cross-legged on the floor in front of them. "How are you holding up? Really," Carisa asked.

"I'm scared to death. We're committing everything to this attack."

"And we're sure this is the *necrófago* home world?" Beatrisa asked.

"Ernesto puts it at eighty-seven percent. And if it's not, we've found another habitable world."

"Which already has inhabitants. It's going to be a little hard to convince them we come in peace when we arrive with an armada," Carisa said.

"Which we fucking don't, Cari," Beatrisa said bluntly. "We'll do to them what we did to the Isanjo and Hajin and—"

"We get your drift, Bea. No need to belabor the point,"

Mercedes said sharply.

"What other choice did we have? They already had a hegemony when we arrived. We were the newcomers. We had to secure our position," Carisa argued.

"Sorry. My admiral's attitudes toward aliens may be rubbing off on me," Beatrisa said.

"What's he like? Belmanor. Can't be easy for an *intitulado* in this situation." Mercedes hoped she sounded casual and merely curious. A commander getting an opinion from a trusted advisor. Nothing more.

"Brilliant. Fair. Hot-tempered. He sometimes pushes people too hard but he's willing to listen to criticism, so I can tell him when he's being a jackass."

Mercedes looked at Carisa. "And Talion?"

"Brilliant. Not fair. Ruthless but we get the job done. If the *necrófagos* didn't blow themselves up when they lose, he'd do it for them. He's not a take prisoners sort of *hombre*."

"You don't like him."

Carisa frowned down at her clasped hands. "I'm afraid of him. Now that I have an *explorador* to command, I'm very aware of those five hundred and sixty lives that I hold in my hands. Talion would sacrifice us all without a moment's hesitation if it would get him the win."

"You could argue that's a good thing," Beatrisa said. "We're soldiers. It's the risk we take."

"I'm just not sure he's willing to make the same sacrifice. He wants to win, maybe at all costs, but he does it with the lives of others. I think we're all disposable to him."

Mercedes gave her a hug. "Well, we'll end this, and he can quietly retire back to Nephilim."

"And you? What will you do when this is all over and we're at peace?" Carisa asked.

"Get back my son. And never let him go again," Mercedes said.

Beatrisa gave a snort. "Yeah, good luck on that *peace* thing. We're going to have the problem of these Hidden Worlds to manage. The politicians are not going to want a change in our policies. The *hidalgos* are all going to be salivating over the chance to become a royal governor."

"We do that, and we'll just be in another war, but this time against fellow humans," Mercedes said. "And I get the feeling some of these places are better prepared to resist us than the worlds we've found so far."

Carisa stroked Mercedes's forehead trying to smooth away the frown. "A problem for another day, Mer."

"Yeah, we have to win the battle in front of us first," Beatrisa said grimly.

✦ ✦ ✦

"YOU'RE MAKING US the tip of the spear," Tracy said slowly after Gelb had finished speaking. He was trying hard not to make it sound accusatory; he had a feeling he had failed. He also knew that Mercedes had noted the exchange of glances between himself and her sister when the tactics had been unveiled.

The three admirals and their flag captains were assembled in the conference room aboard the *San Francisco de Asis*.

Tracy wondered why Mercedes was allowing her flag

captain to handle the final briefing before they entered Fold. Did she think that Talion wouldn't accept the plan if she presented it? He was deeply relieved that Cullen wasn't present, but, really, why would he have been? Yes, his nemesis held the same rank as Tracy—vice admiral—but Cullen commanded a squadron, not a fleet. Though to be fair, Cullen's squadron had damn near as many ships as Tracy's understrength fleet.

All of which made Tracy's next statement mandatory. He cleared his throat and added, "You do know we're the weakest fleet in terms of both numbers and … and …"

"Fighting spirit," Beatrisa offered as Tracy groped to find the right words.

"And that's why you will ascertain any enemy presence, launch missiles and your fighters, and then immediately fall back," Gelb explained. "Once Blue and Gold arrive you will send over all tactical information, and then act as a rear guard, watching for any stragglers or *necrófago* ships returning. Your job is to keep them off our backs while we finish off the main resistance that might be guarding the planet. We anticipate that it won't be significant."

"And why do you *anticipate that*?" Talion's voice rasped out. "They might have as many fleets as us. They might have an entire fleet defending the home world."

"Given their habit of self-destructing, we don't think they have enough ships for more than one fleet," Gelb answered.

"But you don't know."

"No. It's one of our known unknowns."

"How … comforting," Talion drawled.

Gelb looked away uncomfortably. Tracy found himself

regretting that that bit of jargon had ever entered into the military's lexicon. Tracy cleared his throat again and realized that probably made him seem nervous. Honestly, he was damn nervous.

He shook it off and said, "Tabling for the moment how many ships they may or may not have, they're going to have the advantage because they will already be in formation while we'll be translating out of Fold in staggered waves. Ships are going to be out of position and not hit their marks on time. And some might not emerge at all. Granted it's rare, but it does happen, and we have a shitload of ships in this armada."

"Yes, none of this is ideal—" Gelb began, only to be interrupted by Beatrisa.

"Bit of an understatement." Her status as a royal princess allowed her to take that tone, but Tracy wished she hadn't in front of all these men. Her disrespect might have the effect of undermining her sister. "We're jumping into a system blind apart from *one* surveillance drone."

"It was *my* decision not to send any more drones," Mercedes said sharply. "We couldn't risk alerting them that we had located their home system. We have to act quickly and decisively and the only advantage we have is the element of surprise." Mercedes stood, indicating the meeting was over and no more discussion would be allowed. "You all have your orders. We translate in forty hours. Good luck and God speed."

She whirled and left the conference room, Gelb at her heels, as the admirals and captains leaped to their feet and saluted her.

The room cleared quickly until only Tracy and Beatrisa

remained. He stood, but she didn't move. "You okay?" he asked.

"Any of us could die, and the last exchange I'll potentially ever have had with my sister was me being snotty to her. I know she's empress and her dignity must be maintained, but I should have hugged her …" Her head drooped lower. "I wish I had hugged her."

Me too, Tracy thought.

✦ ✦ ✦

"WHAT THEY HELL are Ingram and Bhutti doing here?" Jahan muttered as Kielli feathered the steering jets and allowed the grapples from the Abraxos *Cosmódromo* to lock onto the *Selkie*'s grips and pull them into the docking berth.

"Who are they? And you don't sound happy," Hayden said.

"Swindlers and miscreants," Jax said. "They give honest traders like us a bad name."

"But you're not honest … well, not all the time," the human boy objected. "And I don't mean you're *dishonest* dishonest, like bad guys, but you do trade with Hidden Worlds, and we carry prohibited drugs and stuff."

"The League now has a treaty with the Hidden Worlds so we're all good there, and since the military has approved the use of contraceptives, I think that we more *bend* the law when we provide it to civilians," Jahan said.

"And we never cheat people," Jax huffed. "We deliver what we promise."

"Whether it's legal or not," Hayden said, and he was

grinning. He ducked and laughed as Jax reached out with a long frond and cuffed him on the ear.

"You are becoming quite unbecomingly pert," the Flute huffed.

"And what does that even mean?" Hayden asked looking to Jahan.

"That you're a smartass," Jahan said. Please, the boy smiled again and stepped over to Kielli to watch as the Isanjo shut down the engines. "And I'm very glad to see it," Jahan added quietly to herself.

Jax began running refueling cost numbers. Jahan watched his fronds flicking aside multiple holo screens and wondered how he could absorb anything from the flashing numbers. She rolled her shoulders and felt something in her neck pop. *This getting old is hell. I'm supposed to be home with Tageri, not running around the galaxy in the middle of a war. And I should be raising my own kits, not this human boy. But God knows he needs a mom, so I guess I'll keep filling the role.*

What she said aloud was, "Okay, team, let's get those crates ready to go."

Everyone except the Flute headed for the access ladder. Jahan went sliding all the way down to the cargo bay and found Ernie and Dalea already at work. Dalea was checking off crates against the list. Kielli and Hayden started unhooking the straps from the pallets so they could be off-loaded. They were standing on a top crate, releasing a clip from the wall of the ship, but also messing around, shoulder bumping, pretending to trip each other. The human boy was already inches taller than her nephew, but Kielli was grown and had the bulk to hold his own. She had just opened her mouth to yell *cut it out* when the inevitable happened. One of the top crates had been dislodged by their antics and when the shipping strap released the crate fell to the floor and the boys with it. The crate hit on one corner and burst open, sending its contents in all directions.

"Owww, owww, owww," Kielli wailed and held his ankle.

"Oh, shit, I'm sorry," Hayden was saying. Blood was trailing over his hand from a cut on his wrist. The red was startling against his ebony skin.

Everyone rushed to them. Dalea was clucking as she ran a hand over Kielli's ankle. "You're lucky you're an Isanjo and not wearing a boot that I'd have to pull off," she scolded.

"How bad is it?"

"Just sprained." She stood.

Jahan turned her ire on these youngest members of the crew. "I swear, you two. Now you've made double the work for the rest of us. Both of you get to the med bay."

"I can keep working—"

"And keep bleeding all over my ship? No!"

"It's just a cut," Hayden muttered mulishly. "It's almost stopped—"

"Jahan." It was Dalea.

"What?" Jahan spun to look at the Hajin. The tall alien was holding packets in each hand, frowning at the labels.

"We were told these were supplies for emergency first responders, right?"

"Yeah. So?"

"That's not what's in this carton." Dalea waved a packet at her. "This is childhood vaccines, and this is a vaccine used to prevent reaction to new strains of bacteria. It's given to colonists on newly settled worlds." She dug through more of the spilled contents. "This is flu vaccine, and this—"

"Okay, okay. I'm getting the drift. In other words, none of this stuff is useful for first responders or in a warship's med bay."

"Exactly."

They all exchanged looks. There were soft pings from the hull as the engines cooled down and metal and composite flexed. "So maybe this is a case of graft. Some politician sneaking in something for a local hospital in his district …" It sounded lame even to her own ears.

"Maybe we should take a look inside a few more crates," Ernie said. "We can seal it up so nobody will ever know," he added in response to Jahan's worried expression.

"Okay."

They sent for Jax to come down and help them unlock the key codes that kept the crates sealed. Dalea inspected the contents and shook her head. "These are all the sort of things you would expect if you were setting up a civilian hospital or immunizing colonists against alien toxins."

"They found a new Goldilocks planet," Ernie said.

"And didn't report it," Jahan added grimly. "Even in the middle of this mess that would be big news. I wonder what Ingram and Bhutti were hauling? We need to find out."

"So now we're going to be play at being SEGU?" Jax asked. "I have no idea how to be a spy, and we could get into real trouble if we go snooping about."

"Only if we get caught," Hayden said. "Look, nobody notices kids or aliens. Kielli and I could do it. He can pretend to be my servant." The boy looked over at the Isanjo. "Sorry, but we can't just be friends … even if we are."

"Yeah, ain't that the truth," Kielli said.

"I'm sorry," the human said.

"It's okay. It's just the reality."

"And how are you gonna try to get information?" Ernie objected. You start asking questions—"

"We'll find an arcade or a park. Someplace where kids gather. Someone will talk. They'll have overheard their parents. And I'm going to complain about you. Say you're my grandfather who dragged me aboard this ship and how I don't want to be a merchant."

"When did I get promoted to grandfather?" Ernie groused. "Do I look that old?" He got back a chorus of yeses.

"And it's not like I can be Jahan or Dalea or Jax's kid," Hayden offered in that serious way he had.

Ernie grinned, reached out, grabbed Hayden by the back of the neck, and gave him an affectionate shake. "Son, I'd happily have you as my grandkid. After we off-load all these crates, I'll find a bar and bitch a bit about all the regulations the League puts on me."

"I mean, this may all be nothing," Dalea murmured.

Jahan braced her. "Do you believe that? Honestly?"

The Hajin's big eyes dropped, and she shook her head. "No. It just feels like we're a long way from help if things go pear-shaped, as the captain used to say. I'll go pick up some medical supplies and see what I hear."

Jahan nodded. "Okay, let's get this off-loaded and get paid so we can leave if things are looking questionable."

"And I'm going to stay on the ship with the doors locked

and hope you don't all get arrested," Jax said. "I'm also going to make sure we are fueled up and ready to go in anticipation of those pears arriving."

25

SOMETHING'S ROTTEN IN NEPHILIM

THE NIGHT CYCLE before they were to enter Fold, Tracy instructed René to prepare a banquet, then ordered all the captains from his fleet to join him aboard the *Sutābureză*. He had already briefed them on the plan, and their navigation systems were programmed with the calculations for their formations. The briefings had been tense and silent; the captains just listening, grim-faced.

He had hoped the gourmet dinner would mollify them, but as he scanned the room, he wasn't sure it was working. This would be the final time they would share a meal until they had emerged from Fold, engaged the enemy, and hopefully won and ended the war. *And how many of us will still be alive at the conclusion of the battle?* Tracy wondered.

Now that he commanded a flagship and seven thousand people, Father Ken had been augmented with a protestant chaplain, a rabbi, and an imam. Tracy noted that many of his guests were availing themselves of the opportunity to speak with the holy men. The smaller ships didn't have the luxury of multiple chaplains, and since Catholicism was the state religion, they usually got a priest.

It didn't escape his notice that a lot of drinking was also

occurring. With a lifted eyebrow and a tip of his head, Tracy summoned Kallapus to his side.

"It's about time to start closing down the bar and get dinner on the table," he said quietly.

"Yes, sir."

Tracy gave a start when Valada-Viers said quietly, "So, how do you think it will go?" His former first officer had slipped up to him in that secretive way he had that was reminiscent of hunting panthers. "Especially with that bunch." He jerked his chin toward a clot of older captains who were muttering to each other.

"They've improved. I think we've got them positioned so they can't easily cut and run." Tracy shrugged. "It's the best we can do. We know this plan won't survive contact with the enemy."

"Hell, it won't survive coming out of Fold. There are going to be collisions and ships out of position since we've been ordered to enter Fold in close formation."

"We'll have a few days to get sorted out before we reach the planet."

"Unless we translate into the middle of their waiting fleet."

Tracy snagged a glass of champagne from the tray that Kallapus was carrying through the crowd, lifted the nearly empty flute from Valada-Viers hand, and said, "You're just a cheery bundle of joy, aren't you? Have another drink."

"You're not worried," Valada-Viers challenged.

"Extremely." He drained his own glass and took another. Nodded to the Hajin to move on. "But there's not a damn thing I can do about it tonight."

Valada-Viers gazed into his glass as if the rising bubbles held some guidance for the future. "I've got a family on Belán. We're stripping every ship away from our worlds. Risking everything on this one throw of the dice. What if they take the opportunity to attack our now defenseless planets?"

"Admiral Chapman-Owiti's bright psi-op boys say that won't be the reaction. Based on their interrogations of the captured aliens they are pretty confident that the home world will yell for help and the fleets will return to defend the planet."

"Pretty confident doesn't make *me* at all confident," Valada-Viers sighed.

Tracy clapped him on the shoulder. "Wouldn't you rush home to protect your family?"

"Yeah, which is why I'm worried." He again nodded toward the knot of captains who Tracy had mentally dubbed *the drones*. "What do you think they'll do if they get a message from home in the middle of a battle?"

"Guess we'll find out," Tracy said, but he decided it was worth raising the issue with the other fleet admirals. It might be wise to block all incoming Foldstream messages once they reached the *necrófago* home world.

✦ ✦ ✦

JAHAN SIGNED OFF on the delivery with the clearing agent, and asked about the shipment they were supposed to pick up. What she got back was hedging and an excuse about a breakdown in the line. Her sense that something was very,

very wrong intensified. The agent was looking at her intently, so she shrugged, smiled, and said, "No problem. Gives me time to buy groceries. Any idea where I can do that?"

She was directed to take the station mag train four stops. She thanked the human and pretended to head for the train stop, but instead doubled back to the *Selkie*. She used the refueling line to swarm up to a buttress high overhead and kept watch. The composite was hard against her backside and the area trapped heat and the smells of rocket fuel, cooking, shorting wires, and human BO. Below her, crates formed towers and walls like the remnants of some ancient temple. After some forty minutes she noticed that the same two human men kept coming by and studying the ship. She pinged Ernie and quietly asked, "Anything?"

"Hang on." She heard him grunt and say, "Wife. Gotta take this or I'll never stop hearing about it." Jahan listened to his footfalls. "Okay, I can talk now. What a bunch a cheap, closemouthed bastards," he muttered quietly. "I bought a couple of rounds, and they didn't even reciprocate. Also, nobody's talking to the stranger. I've been gettin' some looks, and a couple of guys looked me over—"

"These guys?" She set her ring to record and turned it toward the men below her who were now strolling casually away.

"Yeah, that's them."

"You better get back. How are you on cold engine starts?"

"Don't love 'em. Lots of shit can go wrong."

"Agreed, but I think we're looking at one."

"Want me to swing by and get the kids?"

"No, I'll do it. You find Dalea."

She started to slide back down the fuel line when she stopped, hands clasped tightly around the pipe. She neither heard nor felt the flow of fuel through the line. "Motherfuckers," she murmured. She reached the floor of the station, ducked into a small opening between a number of crates, and pinged Jax. "Check our fuel status." He didn't waste time asking why. She watched his fronds jiggling as he hurried out of camera range. A few minutes later he came back.

"It's stopped just below the halfway point."

"Okay, I'm going to try and get it started again and then go collect Kielli and Hayden. Keep us locked down tight unless it's one of us. Ernie will be heading back once he gets Dalea."

"Be careful."

Using crates for cover, she slipped over to where the refueling station was located. This particular hub handled eight berths. She could see two men inside drinking coffee and smoking stim sticks. She could see no way to get inside and turn the spigot back on. She checked out one of the lines and felt the flow of fuel beneath her palm. Looked again through the window of the station at the massive control panel and wondered if it could be spoofed. She called Jax again.

"Do you think you might be able to hack the fuel center's computer and make it look like the fuel to berth four is still flowing, but actually turn on our fuel line to berth seven instead?"

"And I presume still have it read as if berth four is refueling, correct?"

"You got it."

"Yes, probably, but I'd need you to actually get on the system and input a code."

"Great, there are two guys in there." She stood thinking. "I need a distraction. Lemme go get the kids."

"We are so fucked," Jax said mournfully.

She used the boys' rings to locate them. It wasn't far to the station's green band. In among the grass, trees, and flowers was a floatboard park, playground equipment for younger kids, and even an old-fashioned carousel. Kielli and Hayden had rented floatboards. Hayden was pretty good for a human, but the Isanjo, even with his sprained ankle, clearly had the advantage with his prehensile feet and tail. Jahan hoped that some of the human kids standing around watching weren't going to try some of the stunts her nephew could pull off. She also wasn't happy he was drawing that much attention to them. Hayden spotted her, and she beckoned him to come. He flew his board next to Kielli and said something.

Within minutes they had turned in their boards and joined her.

"I need you—" she began, only to be interrupted by Hayden.

"They've discovered four systems with habitable worlds."

"One of them has *three* habitable planets. It's crazy; the entire system has twelve planets," Kielli offered.

"And apparently there's a lot of resources," Hayden said.

Jahan was shocked into momentary silence. She found her voice and said, "That's supposed to be reported to the planetary settlement agency."

"Exactly!" Hayden said.

"The baron is putting a big push on settling the worlds," Kielli said.

"That would explain our weird cargo, and why they shut down our refuel."

"What?" her nephew squawked. "They're trying to keep us here?"

"I think so, which is why I need you kid—"

"Not a kid. Twenty-three," Kielli said.

"To me, you are a kid. Anyway, I need a distraction to draw two guys out of the refueling control center."

The two boys looked at each other and grinned. "We can manage that," Kielli said.

"Don't do anything that would get you arrested and most important—don't get hurt! Or hurt worse," Jahan said in her best auntie voice. The kids just rolled their eyes.

✦ ✦ ✦

IT WAS DEEP in the night cycle, but sleep was eluding him. Brandy in hand, Boho paced his quarters. *Twenty-three days in Fold*; that alone was enough to set him on edge and they were only five days into it. But it was what was waiting when they emerged that had him unable to rest—the largest battle of the war. The one for all the marbles. The one where a lot of people were going to die.

What if they didn't win? Would there be enough time to retreat?

What if both he and Mercedes died?

The League would be left rudderless. It was crazy that he was included in the strike force. Of course, Mercedes had to take part. War leader was the primary role of the ruler of the League, but the real business of government was overseeing the various agencies, interacting with parliament, handling issues with various planetary governors. Things at which he excelled. He should have been left in Hissilek to serve as regent until Cyprian came of age should anything… unfortunate occur. Not that he was hoping for that, he thought, as he recalled how devasted he had been when she went missing. She might not be the great love of his life (and hadn't she admitted as much to him about her own feelings?) but he was deeply fond of her.

The point was that this was a reckless plan, and it left the League vulnerable. Boho felt feverish and went into the bathroom and splashed cold water on his face. When he looked up, water dripping from his nose and beading like tears on his cheeks, he met his own green-eyed gaze.

At least be honest with yourself, Beauregard, you're scared shitless. You're a coward.

It's not a sin, he argued back to himself. *And a person can be scared and wise at the same time.*

So, was there a way to avoid the battle? It would require changing the coordinates in the computer. But an overt change would be detected. It needed to be subtle. Everything would have to look normal to the navigators when they came on post. And he couldn't just change it to some League system. That would also be a clue that this wasn't an accident. It would have to send them to an empty sector. Boho was forcibly reminded of sector 470 where ships vanished, and emperors sent inconvenient people to also vanish. Unknown space carried its own risks. They might translate into something worse than the *necrófago* system. Or they might not emerge at all. It did happen, and blindly translating into the uncharted might result in a worse fate than dying in battle.

Boho buried his face in his hands, frozen with indecision.

+ + +

JAHAN HAD ONCE again taken to the heights where she could watch the control center. She debated trying to call Tracy and hope he wasn't in Fold, but frankly at the moment she was more worried about her nephew and Hayden then the fate of the League. She was surprised to see Kielli go limping frantically into the room. His ring was set so she could overhear the conversation.

"Please, sirs, the young man I serve has been hurt. I don't have the strength to lift the—"

Jahan had to admire Kielli's ability to take that obsequious tone of a servant in an FFH household.

"Call the authorities," came a man's voice.

"He is Reginald Austin Talion, third son of Lord Fletcher Talion, grandson of the royal governor. I'm sure my lord's father and grandfather would be grateful—"

Jahan frantically checked her ring, and sure enough Reginald was a grandson of the man who ruled Nephilim. *Maybe it wasn't a bad thing to have a scion of nobility aboard the ship,* she thought.

"Where's the kid?"

"Follow me. It will likely take both of you to extricate him. As you can see, I got hurt trying."

Jahan watched as the threesome left. She then went leaping down from the girder and sprinted into the control room. "Okay, Jax, I'm in and at the computer. What do I do?"

"What type of machine is it?"

"A Calcutech."

"Piece of cake. Look around to see if they left their password—"

"They ran out of here so fast they're still logged in."

"*Dios*, idiots. Makes it easy for us. Enter in this code."

Jax read off the number and letters. Jax was in, and he guided her through switching the fuel flow from berth four to berth seven but spoofing the readings, so it seemed as if nothing had changed. "Got it," she said. "I'm heading back."

"Kids are already here," Jax said.

"How the hell did that happen?"

"Ask them yourself."

She raced back to the *Selkie* and Jax let her in. She found the youngest members of the crew chattering excitedly in the galley and backslapping each other. "What the hell did you do to those guys?"

"Told 'em the young lord was in this storage locker and a crate had fallen on him," Kielli said.

"And when they went in, we yanked off their ScoopRings, shut the door, and we locked them in," Hayden continued. His eyes were sparkling with excitement and mischief.

"Great, theft and false imprisonment. Great. Now we really have to get out of here. Where the hell are Ernie and Dalea?"

As if she had summoned them, they got a frantic call

from Ernie. Again, the bay doors were opened. Jahan, Kielli, and Hayden went sliding down the access ladder to the cargo bay as the Hajin and the human came clattering aboard. The big door was whining shut behind them. They were both out of breath, and Dalea had a black eye forming.

"What happened to you?" Jahan squeaked.

"Bastards at the *farmacia* at the clinic were trying to force her to stay," Ernie panted. He rested his hands on his knees and leaned forward trying to catch his breath.

"When I said I was leaving, one of the men hit me. Ernie grabbed a stool and hit him—"

"Add assault to our list of felonies," Jax said over the intercom.

"There was a box of preloaded syringes near me. Sedatives. I injected the other one as he was attacking Ernie, then took care of the one who was down so Ernie wouldn't have to hit him hard enough to knock him out and risk brain damage."

"Yeah, God forbid we hurt the *pendejos* who were trying to make you an indentured servant," Ernie grunted.

"What's clear is that they need bodies for something. They said they needed more medics," Dalea said.

"They found a bunch of habitable planets," Hayden said.

"They must be trying to make sure the new colonies have people with skills," Kielli said.

"Whether they're willing or not," Jahan added. "How we coming on the refuel?"

"Close," Jax said.

"Close enough that we can get back to Hellfire or Ouranos and warn the League?"

"I'll check," Kielli said, and he bolted for the ladder. The minutes seemed to crawl past. "We're good."

"How do we stop the refuel?" Hayden asked.

"I'm still logged in," Jax said. "I can do it remotely."

"The line will still be clamped to the ship. Shouldn't we release it?" Hayden asked.

"Fuck 'em. Too bad if it rips when we say *adios*," Ernie said. "I better get to the engine room and start prepping that cold start." He hurried away.

"We never got to pick up our shipment," Dalea said as they all crammed into the elevator to head for the bridge.

"I have a feeling those crates were going to weigh just enough to think they were lithium but probably just hold dryer lint," Jahan said. "And you," she said to the Hajin. "Go to the med bay and get some ice on that eye."

"You should let me wrap that ankle," Dalea said to Kielli.

"Once we're safely away," Jahan ordered.

✦ ✦ ✦

SHE WAS ALONE in the dreadnaught's darkened chapel. While she was praying, the door had irised open and an hombre peeked in, spotted the empress, and immediately withdrew.

Mercedes felt bad denying the young man the solace of this holy space, but she needed to be there to call into the silence: *Is this right? Is it a sin to pray for victory knowing what that actually entails? Was a* necrófago *commander somewhere in the galaxy praying to his or her gods seeking the same outcome?*

Mercedes rested her forehead on her folded hands. The

rosary clutched between her fingers was almost cutting into her flesh so tight was her grip. Military leaders for millennia had talked about the loneliness of command; she was feeling it now. She longed for her child, to feel her son's curls tickling at her chin, the solid weight of his body. What would that feel like now? She hadn't seen him in almost a year.

Perhaps she should have had Boho as her flag captain. At least there would be arms to hold her when she returned to her cabin. Someone to whom she could confide her fears, the grief she already felt for the men and women who would inevitably die in the coming battle.

But as she thought about a partner to comfort her, it wasn't green eyes she saw, but dark grey ones. She tried to push away the image of Tracy's face. How could she kneel before God and think of the man with whom she had sinned? She had no right to God's grace or forgiveness.

Blinded by the tears she couldn't contain; Mercedes fled the chapel.

+ + +

THE LIFT STOPPED on the crew deck and Dalea drooped away. Jahan, Kielli, and Hayden continued on to the bridge and stepped off just in time to hear Jax say, "Uh-oh."

"What uh-oh? I hate uh-oh," Jahan demanded.

"I've been monitoring station communications. Apparently, the new shift just arrived to relieve the other men and have reacted to the fact they are missing. They have alerted station security."

Jahan slammed a hand down on the intercom. "Ernie, we

need to go … like now."

"Not for seven more minutes. I can't change physics, Jahan."

Jahan checked the small clock in her sleeve, watched as one minute and forty seconds slowly slipped past. Jax gave a shiver, setting all his fronds to rustling. "We don't have six minutes and twenty seconds. They have just locked down the station. The docking clamps will no longer release on our signal."

They all exchanged looks. Kielli gave a fang-baring smile. "No worries. There are mechanical overrides. I'll go out and manually release the clamps." Jahan's heart felt like it was being crushed, but she forced herself to nod in agreement.

"No." The single word brought them all around to look at the young human. "I should do it."

"Do you have any idea how to—" Kielli began.

"No, but you can walk me through it."

"I can't let—" Jahan began.

"You must. We can't use Ernie. He has to start the engines, and whoever does this is going to get caught, and you're all aliens."

Jahan stared at him, wondering if this was nascent bigotry finally showing itself. Dalea, a cool pack on her eye, came off the lift and onto the bridge. The one eye that was visible darted from person to person reading the tension in the room. The human boy also seemed to realize something had changed, and he looked chagrined as he figured it out. "I didn't mean it *that* way. I meant that I'm a kid. I'm human. I'm FFH. *And* my grandfather is the Duque de Nico-Hathaway. He might not have liked my dad and thought

Mom married beneath her, but he's really proud and he will raise a fuss if anything happens to me."

More looks were exchanged. "Hayden is correct in his analysis," Jax said in his precise way.

"No! He is a child. We are not going to leave him in the hands of people who—"

"If we don't, none of us leave," Jahan said, interrupting Dalea.

"Ah, shit," was Kielli's observation. He hobbled over and grabbed Hayden around the neck and hugged him hard. "You take care and screw you for getting the big adventure and getting to be the hero."

Ernie's voice came over the intercom. "Engine sequence is beginning. Are we going or are we gonna tear off the front of the ship?"

Jahan nodded at Hayden, who ran for the ladder and began to slide down. She followed. They couldn't risk opening the bay doors so he could use the pressurized umbilical, so he was going to have to go out an airlock on the crew deck. Hayden scrambled into a spacesuit, dogged the helmet, and gave her a nod. She hugged him hard.

"We'll be back for you. I promise." And she sealed the inner door. The outer door opened on the dark of space. He gave one last wave and fired his maneuvering jets. With luck, he would have the manual release keyed before station security realized what was happening. She ran back to the ladder and scampered up to the bridge while watching the time tick past.

Kielli was murmuring instructions into the radio. "No, not the lever on the left. It's the smaller one below the flange."

"I'm feathering the engines, but I can't keep doing this too much longer," Ernie's voice said over the intercom.

Kielli was staring intently at the controls. Jahan's breaths and her heartbeat seemed to be all she could hear. Finally, Kielli gave a shout. "Docking clamps released."

"Do we go?" Ernie asked.

"No, give him time to get to safety. Hayden, are you in the station?" she radioed.

"Not yet, almost. You should go." Kielli's hand was poised over the panel. He stared at her desperately. The ship was vibrating as the engines came to full power.

"We gotta go!" Ernie yelled over the radio.

"I'm good," Hayden called.

Kielli brought down his hand, firing the front maneuvering rockets, and the *Selkie* ripped loose from the station, leaving the fuel line twisting in the vacuum. The radio exploded with station command screaming at them. "Trade ship *Selkie*! You are in violation and have damaged imperial property. You will shut down engines—"

Jahan killed the audio. "Shut you down, assholes," she muttered.

"They're going to have the military down on us," Jax warned.

"Fortunately, they are looking for threats *arriving*. Not leaving," Jahan snapped back. "We just have to translate before we hit the surveillance patrols."

"We're going to Fold this deep in the system?" Dalea asked faintly.

"Yep."

"We're all gonna die," Kielli said.

"We're all going to die if we don't," was Jahan's response.

"If we should survive, we are going to take a bath on this financially," Jax said. "No payment for the cargo delivered. No cargo to sell."

"Hey, look on the bright side," Ernie said. "We didn't have to pay for the fuel, being as how we stole it."

"So where are we going … again assuming we survive?" Kielli asked.

Jahan pondered for a moment. "Hellfire. They can get word to the Empress that something is rotten in Nephilim."

"Okay." Kielli turned back to his board and set the coordinates. "Translating to Fold in ten … nine … eight …"

There was nothing left to do but pray, and Jahan indulged in a few as the seconds counted down.

26

ROLLING THE DICE

"THANK YOU FOR bringing us this information. We'll make inquiries."

Jahan stared up into the bland face of the young officer manning the front desk at the Octagon. It was an enormous space with a high vaulted ceiling of grey glass. The floor was black marble, so the rap of bootheels as military personal hurried in and out was deafening. The chime from ScoopRings and the men and the occasional woman muttering in answer to those calls added to the cacophony. She glanced around at the rest of the crew, who gave her nods of encouragement.

"No offense, sir," she said in her most ingratiating voice. "But we do feel this information is urgent and if we could maybe talk to—"

"I'll pass along your concerns. Now if you will please move aside." He waved them away like a man shooing gnats.

Jahan extended a bit of claw, grabbed the front of the desk, and hung on. "Please, sir, I really think—"

"Do you want me to call security?" The young man wasn't looking so blandly genial any longer. His expression showed both anger and contempt. Jahan stepped back, ready to admit defeat, when Ernie stepped in front of her.

"Look, sonny, I was doing my service before you were even a glint in your daddy's eye, so believe me when I say this is fucking serious, and you passing it up to some lieutenant JG who'll pass it to some lieutenant who'll pass it to some captain lieutenant ain't gonna cut it. This is serious shit, and the grownups need to talk. So, get on that comm and get somebody down here who has more brass and more brains."

"Security!" the ensign bawled.

✦ ✦ ✦

BEYOND THE VIEWPORT, the Fold dimension writhed and roiled, the grey tendrils looking like matted grey hair, as if a galaxy-sized witch were tossing her dirty locks. A message flared onto Tracy's faceplate—*heart rate and breathing elevated*. He blinked to banish the message. He didn't need his battle armor reminding him he was tense as hell. During the twenty-three days they had been in Fold, he had spent time on the observation deck watching Fold messages flash through the grey void. Messages sent by the League showed up as lances of prismatic color. What they assumed to be messages between *necrófago* ships, and their home world were obsidian black spears piercing the Fold. Similar technology but with obvious differences. Perhaps the research division would learn something once they were done subduing the aliens. *You make it sound so easy*, he told himself.

He checked the chronometer; they were twenty seconds from translation back into normal space. For this maneuver

Tracy had taken the command chair from Beatrisa. Weapons were hot, missiles and rail gun primed. They were of no use in Fold. Weapon fire just vanished into the vapor. But if they emerged to find ships waiting, he would be ready.

They had been the first ships to enter Fold from the staging area, but Tracy's flagship had been the last ship of his fleet to enter. Not because he was afraid to be the first out once they reached the *necrófago* home system, but because he had worried that some of his less reliable captains might not enter at all. And to be sure they had set the coordinates of the system in their systems; Tracy had let them know that his cyber weapons expert had hacked their ships' controls and he was watching to make sure "no errors were made."

Beatrisa was on his left, and she reached down and briefly squeezed his shoulder as the count reached ten seconds. The grip of her armored hand was both comforting and painful, augmented as it was by the power gimbals. On his right was one of Ernesto's bright boys, a linguistic expert who had helped analyze the *necrófago* language and had done a crash course to learn it. He was ready to monitor all communications so the Green could be warned of impending enemy action.

"Translation to normal space in three, two, one," Luis, who was at navigation, intoned.

✦ ✦ ✦

"WELL. THAT COULD have gone better," Jax said as security abandoned them on the street that ran in front of headquarters. Flitters passed by overhead and the sun seemed to strike sparks from the pedestrian walkway.

"So, what do we do now?" Kielli asked mournfully.

"I'm going to call the Empress," she announced.

"Can we maybe not use our private line to the ruler of the League while we're standing on the fucking street?" Jax said, his fronds shaking in agitation.

"Good point. Back to the ship."

They splurged on a flitter, though it took a while to find one that would carry three aliens and a human. Once aboard the *Selkie*, they gathered in the galley and Jahan made the call. And got back the *unable to connect* message.

"Try Tracy," Dalea said.

Jahan nodded and keyed her ring. *Unable to connect.*

"They must both be in Fold," Ernie said.

"You know anybody else super famous and powerful?" Kielli asked.

Jahan just shook her head. She felt old, hopeless, and helpless, and she was developing an intense headache. Dalea spoke up. "It's urgent we get this information to Mercedes or Tracy. We have to keep trying. Every hour until we reach one of them."

✦ ✦ ✦

THERE WAS THAT stomach-churning twist as the ship returned to normal space. The scanners showed his ships and anything else that might be in the area. Tracy wished he could partition his brain, but he couldn't, so he checked his own forces first. It seemed all but one of them had arrived and he'd calculated the spacing properly since there weren't two ships trying to inhabit the same space. They were in the outer system where two enormous gas giants and their flock of captured moons held sway.

Tracy snapped the question to his bridge crew. "Have we got company?"

"Scanners indicate twelve enemy ships within two hundred thousand kilometers," Vaughn reported. "But the magnetosphere on those two giants is playing hell with the sensors," she added. "So, there could be more ..."

Tracy felt his sphincter tighten. "Battle stations." The alarms began to blare.

"Twelve ships against one hundred and twenty-three. They'll cut and run," Beatrisa said on his private channel.

"Probably, but they'll try to sting us first," Tracy replied.

"Weapons are hot. Targeting now." Cassutt's voice over his radio.

"Launch at will," Tracy said. He felt the ship buck a bit as missiles were launched. He turned to Luis. "Okay, let's get out of the way of the big guns." He looked to the comm station. "Order our ships to execute the withdrawal."

"They're returning fire," Vaughn reported.

"Firing chaff," came the word from the weapons deck.

Tracy checked the scanners again. Most of his understrength fleet had fired, but a distressingly large number still didn't have their countermeasures deployed, and some were slow to drop below the plane of the elliptical to allow the Blue and Gold to press the fight.

The scanners flared as the Blue and the Gold began to blink into existence to the left and right of the Green's position on the plane of the ecliptic. The Blue was on a higher and the Gold on a lower plane, which would hopefully keep them from firing into one another's positions. Of course, there were some wandering orphans, ships that were well out of position.

One ship translated right into the path of oncoming missiles from a *necrófago* ship. Tracy winced as gouts of fire erupted from the side and belly of the destroyer. His suit was jacked into the ship's onboard computer, so the name was quickly supplied—*The* Reliant, *fleet designation Blue. Crew complement three thou*—Tracy cut the link. He didn't need to know all the grisly details. Another wince as one of his slow-moving ships collided with a ship from the Gold. The damage reports weren't too bad, but it meant three ships out of the fight already.

Mercedes's voice came over the radio. "Don't get distracted. Focus. Find your positions and get there."

Engines began to flare, maneuvering jets spat fire as they came to life. The light from the distant sun glittered on the chaff being released by the League ships. The twelve enemy ships, having launched their weaponry, began burn maneuvers to evade the oncoming missiles from the Green.

✦ ✦ ✦

"MA'AM! SHIPS! LOTS of them!"

Mercedes couldn't blame her sensor officer for the nearly hysterical tone because ships, lots of them, were appearing from behind the bulk of the two gas giants that held sway at the outer edge of the *necrófago* system. And given the relative positions of the massive planets, it placed one group of ships above them and the other able to fall on them from the rear. Not that any of that would happen instantly. Space was big, and the distance between the two gas giants was large, but what had looked like an easy advance toward the system's fourth planet now seemed far more fraught.

She radioed her spouse aboard his flagship. "Boho, detach half the fleet and turn to engage the ships at …" She looked to her navigation officer who quickly provided the coordinates.

"Got it. Be careful, *mi amor.*"

A click to change channels and she had Talion. "Admiral," but before she could say more, he interrupted.

"The ships are on your flank. I suggest you engage while I divide my forces and try to get behind and above them."

"They're going to pound us until you can get here."

"I know, Majesty. We always knew this was never going to be easy."

✦ ✦ ✦

"YAY! TRACY, WE finally got you," Jahan cried. The entire crew was gathered around the comm station on the bridge of the *Selkie*. She rushed on. "Look, there's something dodgy going on at Nephilim. We almost got shanghaied and we had to leave … well, a crewman behind, and they hid the fact—" She became aware that the background noise she was hearing was the whoop of alarms and the sound of explosions.

"*Little* busy *right now!*" Tracy gritted back.

"You're in combat."

"No shit. Goodbye."

"Wait!" But he was gone.

They all exchanged glances. "He'll get back to us once they disengage," Jax said.

"Try the Empress," Dalea suggested. "You've got her private line, too."

Jahan shrugged. "Okay." She keyed the code. This time she got not only sound but image. Smoke and flames. The sound followed, alarms and explosions and an added horrible bonus—screams.

"Jahan, what is it? Is it Cypri?" Mercedes's features were distorted behind the faceplate of her battle armor. Her normally husky alto was tinged with panic.

"No, no. It was … Are you in the same battle as Tracy?"

"Yes. Why? I really don't have time—"

Dalea leaned in over Jahan's shoulder. "Majesty, is the Gold also with you?"

"Yes, we found the—"

Jahan's claws extended as she gripped the edge of the console. "Majesty, something is going on at Nephilim. You need to be careful!" But she was talking to dead air. The connection had been broken.

Once again, they exchanged glances. The alarm she saw on Dalea, Kielli, and Ernie's faces was no doubt matched on her own. Jax was shaking as if a high wind had swept through the bridge.

"Oh … shit," Kielli breathed.

✦ ✦ ✦

"OH … SHIT." Tracy stared at the place where one of his ships had previously been. It wasn't destroyed. It was just gone.

"Seven more just translated," Beatrisa yelled.

Tracy ran to the scanner station. Gripped Vaughn's shoulder. "What are you reading?"

"Half the Gold is gone." Her voice was a high squeak through his helmet radio. "Some ships have vanished out of the Blue, too."

He wanted to give a hysterical laugh at her inadvertent joke. Instead, he lunged back toward the command station. "Get me the Empress. We've got to withdraw," he bellowed at Comms.

"Sir! Tracy!" Luis yelled. Tracy whirled, torn between anger at the young man's familiarity and frightened by the terror in his voice. "The Gold's flagship is attacking one of the *exploradors*."

A suspicion became sick certainty when he saw the name of the small scout ship—the *Meteoro*. "Can we get any *infiernos* over there to help her?" Tracy asked.

Luis ran frantic calculations. "Not in time, sir. Looks like they're trying to cripple it, not destroy it," the young man offered as if that information would be somehow comforting. But Tracy knew it wasn't. Talion wasn't after one small scout ship. He wanted her captain—Mercedes's youngest sister, Princess Carisa Valentina Maite Kiara de Arango—to serve as a convenient hostage.

"Sir!" It was Vaughn. "A bunch of *infiernos* have launched from the *Meteoro*."

"She's playing the shell game," Tracy murmured. "Smart." He turned to the lieutenant at comms. "Send out a tracking signal. Let's try to bring some of them to safety." He wasn't sure how successful that would be given the fact they were in the middle of a shooting gallery.

As if Cassutt had read his mind, the weapons officer came online. "Excuse me, sir, but are we planning on just rolling along like a duck in a shooting gallery or are you planning to set us up to do some damage?"

"It seems you haven't been keeping up with current events—we just lost a third of our forces," Tracy snapped back.

"Fuck—"

He muted Cassutt and brought his *infierno* commander online. "The *Meteoro* is under attack. Some of the crew have evacuated in fighters. We need to give them cover."

"You want to pull them off the *necrós*?" came the incredulous response.

Tracy switched to privacy mode. "The Princess Carisa is aboard one of the *infiernos*. We need to get her to safety."

"Oh. Okay. On it."

✦ ✦ ✦

"WE HAVE TO translate. Get out of here." It was the first time he had ever heard abject terror in his wife's voice. "Save what we can."

Time seemed to slow, distend. Boho stared out the viewport at the carnage going on before him. The flare as missiles burned fuel seeking a target, gouts of flame belching from the sides of ships, League and *necrófago* alike, burning fiercely only to die in the cold of space as the available atmosphere was burned and dissipated into the void. He was terrified. He was facing death by fire or death in the nothingness of the Fold, for to translate without preparation in the midst of a battle was to be lost. He knew that with every fiber of his being.

What skills could he bring to bear? To save himself and his wife? He had been an indifferent student, bored with the tedium of tactics and strategy with no head for numbers. Probably why he had so often ended up overspending his allowance. Gambling, like sex, had been his passion. Perhaps because both made him feel alive. He opened his mouth to give the order to translate and then it struck him with blinding force. This was not tactics or strategy. Only one thing could save them. That single throw of the dice, that one card that would change everything.

He grasped the arm of his *necrófago* expert. "I need you to send a message to these devils." The young officer gaped at him, then nodded. Boho lunged to the comms station. "Open a channel."

"To whom, sir?"

"Everyone! But especially those bastards."

"Aye, aye, sir."

Boho turned back to the linguist. "Send this message from Admiral Prince Beauregard Honorius Sinclair Cullen, Knight of the Shells, Shareholder General of the Grand Cartel, and the 19th Duque de Argento y Pepco." His voice was gaining strength as he rolled out his titles. "You may have noticed a number of ships vanishing." The intelligence officer repeated the words in the guttural language of the *necrófago*. "That's because they will be translating into orbit around your home world. Which you have left defenseless as you sought to stop us here in the outer system. Your people are going to die. Your mates and your children. They will burn!"

"Boho, what are you doing?" Mercedes's voice on his private channel.

"Bluffing."

+ + +

"MA'AM! IT'S WORKING! They're breaking off the attack. Running for home," Gelb yelled. "We can get out of here."

The fires on the bridge had been suppressed. Repair teams were frantically ripping out fried wires and motherboards trying to get systems back online. The CSAR team was frantically ferrying the wounded off the bridge.

Mercedes stared at the screens flaring with information. The enemy fleet was losing all cohesion as they raced for the distant planet. "No. Maintain the attack. Follow them home. We can't give them time to regroup. Let's finish this!"

She jerked in surprise when her bridge crew began to cheer.

+ + +

BEATRISA HAD A faraway look. She then jerked her head down to look at Tracy. "Private, scrambled channel. I know which *infierno* is hers."

"I can't divert this flagship."

"I know." The stern, confident features twisted with grief. "However, tell her to jettison her escape pod and you take a shuttle and gather her up. I'll send an escort of fighters with you. Then burn like hell and catch up with us."

"Thank you," she breathed. He was startled when she threw her arms around him and pressed her helmet to his. She ran off the bridge.

The radio cracked to life. It was Cullen. "Belmanor, you're closest to that traitorous bastard. Engage."

"I'd love to, but with respect, sir, won't you need us at the planet?"

"I have a little surprise in mind for the *necrós*. You can join us after you dispatch Talion. You're up to the task … aren't you?"

Always the implied smear. Did he take the bait, allow Cullen's sneer to goad him, or follow Mercedes's order? Tracy hesitated, considering. Technically they held the same rank. Technically he could refuse this order, but in practice that title—*Prince*—swung a lot of weight, and he knew that many of his officers viewed the consort with respect. Only he and Luis knew what a shit Cullen truly was. He ground his jaw and then said, "As Your Highness commands." He turned to Luis, "Plot a course, and when I give the order bring us to this alignment." He leaned over and input the data.

Luis gave him a startled look. "Really?"

"Really."

The young man shrugged. "Okay, ass first it is." He began the process of swinging the ship.

Tracy brought Cassutt and Abhishek Lal online. He spoke to the engineer first. "How hot can you run the main engines?"

"How hot do you need them?"

"Hot enough to detonate incoming missiles."

"It'll tear the hell out of them, but we could sustain it for a little while."

"I'll let you know when."

"Aye, sir." He broke the connection.

Cassutt spoke up. "We're going to take damage with them detonating that close."

"I know."

"Might damage the engines."

"I know that, too. But I also know Talion. He'll throw everything at us. I want a cloud of chaff around us and every antiballistic missile and laser ready to go."

His next call was to Miller, who commanded the *infiernos*. "Keep Talion's fighters off us and do what you can to harry the flagship. Sorry I can't be more specific than that."

"That's okay, sir, my kids are creative as hell. They'll take care of the treasonous bastard."

While he was directing orders to his top commanders, he was also trying to watch the progress of Beatrisa's shuttle and her escort. He jerked in alarm when his flag captain gave a wail of despair. "Oh, Cari, no! No!" On the scanners, an *infierno* had flared into a ball of fire and died. The pursuing fighters peeled off and headed back toward Talion's flagship. He bowed his head and crossed himself, offering a quick prayer for the soul of a dead princess who he knew only as an image on the vids. Mostly he prayed for Bea who had lost a clearly beloved sister. But there was no more time for grief. Battle would soon be joined against a foe he knew to be ruthless.

+ + +

"KIELLI, HAYDEN DOESN'T know the coordinates of Freehold, does he?" Jahan asked as they gathered in the galley for dinner.

Her nephew looked down at his feet, his toes wriggling nervously. "Um … yeah, I was teaching him about astrogation, and I might have used it as an example."

Silence as they looked at each other. Jax let out a long, trilling toot which was his version of a sigh. "Well, if I were planning to break away from the League, I'd love to have some leverage, like say, a hostage."

"And the press made no secret of Hayden and the *Infante*'s closeness."

"Didn't they film them leaving together?" Kielli added.

Ernie stood and took a long pull of his beer. "Well, fuck, guess I better fire up the engines. Save me some dinner."

"I'll start laying in the coordinates," Kielli said, and he bolted for the ladder.

Jahan leaned forward and gently banged her forehead on the table. Dalea patted her on the shoulder.

+ + +

"WE'RE BEING HAILED by the Gold, sir." His comm officer's voice had drifted into the soprano range. "Do you want me to disregard?"

"No. Let's see what the traitor has to say," Tracy said coolly. That seemed to steady the boy, and he gave an emphatic nod and opened a channel and Talion's holographic image appeared in the center of the bridge.

"Belmanor, what a shame we've come to this. Once, long ago, I indicated to you that you could have served me well, and I would have rewarded you well, too. Made you a *Duque*. And I seriously thought about approaching you, but ultimately, I decided you have such bourgeois notions that it was pointless to try. So, instead, here we are on opposite sides."

"Yes, my bourgeois morality puts a premium on loyalty. Didn't peg you for a traitor though, Jasper. A psychopath, yes, a traitor, no."

Talion tsked. "Such a pejorative word … traitor. And if being willing to do what's necessary makes me a psychopath, then I'll happily accept the label. The League is weak and corrupt. I see no reason for Nephilim to go down with it."

"I'm going to beat you," Tracy said.

Talion smiled that feral expression that no normal person would associate with pleasure. "It would be interesting to see which of us is the better strategist, but now that I've lost the princess, I have more important matters to attend to. I'm sure we'll have the opportunity to match skills at some point. *Adios*, Belmanor. *Buena suerte*." The holograph flickered and vanished.

"They're translating to Fold, Admiral," Vaughn said. The flagship of the Gold vanished from their screens.

Tracy sighed. "Let's pick up our fighters and Captain Princess Beatrisa, then set a course for the planet." He looked to Luis. "Lieutenant, the bridge is yours." The look of joy and gratitude on the young man's face had Tracy blinking hard.

He left the bridge and took the lift down to the shuttle bay. He had a feeling his flag captain was going to need a drink and they could take a few minutes to mourn the dead. The wall of the elevator beckoned, and he leaned against it for a few moments, removed his helmet, and rubbed at his sweat-damp hair. Grit seemed to grind at his eyelids as he briefly closed them.

The lift arrived with a whisper and a bounce. Tracy hurried to the shuttle bay just as the doors opened and the ramp came down on the shuttle. Beatrisa emerged grinning like a maniac. It stopped Tracy in his tracks, and he looked at her in confusion. The grin grew even broader, and she stepped aside and made an elaborate gesture. A tiny figure stepped out from behind her. The bulky battle armor disguised her figure, but her helmet was off, and Tracy recognized the elfin features of Captain Princess Carisa de Arango. Sweat glistened on her face, tension had etched lines around her mouth and eyes, but now that he had met her in the flesh it was clear pictures didn't do her justice. She was breathtakingly beautiful.

"But … I thought …" he stammered.

Beatrisa threw an arm around her sister's shoulders and hugged her close. "This clever bunny set her *infierno* to self-destruct a few seconds after she ejected the cockpit capsule. The explosion hid her bailing, then she called me, I supplied the grief-stricken wail, Talion fell for it, recalled the fighters, and I was able to scoop her up."

Carisa stepped forward, gave him a sharp salute. "Admiral, thank you for facilitating my rescue."

Tracy bowed as he had been taught by his father when

greeting royalty. "Honored to do so, ma'am, but most of the thanks should be directed to your sister."

Beatrisa gave Carisa a hip bump. "Told you he'd say that."

"Admiral, did my *explorador* survive? If so, I should get back to my ship and crew."

"It did, though it has taken significant damage—"

"All the more reason I should get back aboard," Carisa shot back.

"I understand and we will see to that, Highness, but right now we need to get underway to the planet. The Empress is going to need our assistance. So, if you will accept our hospitality for a few hours ..."

"With pleasure. If I could clean up—"

"My cabin is yours, Highness." He signaled for Kallapus, who arrived within seconds. Apparently, the news of the Princess's survival had already spread through the ship and the Hajin had anticipated Tracy's order.

Before Tracy could head to the lift, Beatrisa caught his sleeve. "Admiral, we can be sure the *necrófagos* are going to scream for help. This is the logical translation point for any arriving ships. Would it make more sense for us to stay here with the remaining loyal ships of the Gold and keep them off the Empress's back?"

Tracy pondered on that. It did make sense. It was unlikely the enemy ships would arrive on the other side of the sun from the *necrófago* planet and be facing potentially weeks of travel. "Good idea, but I think we have to divide what's left of the Gold. The Empress is going to need all the firepower she can get. As for where we wait—they do have a disconcerting habit of translating deep in a system. Let's head toward their home world and take up a position at a point where they can't make a safe translation."

"Yeah, that's a better idea. Otherwise, we might risk having them appear *inside* us." Beatrisa looked queasy at the prospect.

27

WE BRING ONLY DEATH

BOHO TURNED TO his weapons officer. "Are the mines prepared?"

"Yes, sir, but I can't guarantee we'll be able to drop them exactly where you wish. Some may impact the planet or even try to translate inside the surface."

"I believe the point of this is to ensure that the *necrófagos* have a really bad day. Which is another way of me saying—I don't give a shit."

"Yes, sir." The man saluted and left the bridge.

He was exhausted but vibrating with tension. He had been on duty and on the bridge in battle armor for thirty-eight hours as they pursued the *necrófago* ships who were now within light-minutes of their home world and preparing for its defense. He didn't want to rest because the timing of this maneuver was going to be critical. He had removed his helmet when it began to look like they weren't going to be under imminent attack. It meant he could eat something and drink coffee, instead of being limited to the water in his armor and stimulant pills.

He had been frustrated when Talion failed to engage the *Sutāburezā* and instead had translated out of the system. Like

King David with Uriah, Boho had hoped to send his rival to die in a manner by which no possible blame could fall on him. Unfortunately, Talion had failed to play his part.

"We're ready, sir," weapons reported.

"On my mark." He watched the seconds tick past, then said, "Fold."

A few seconds later sensors reported explosions on the planet, but a quick read of the scanners revealed that a majority of the mines had indeed exited Fold in orbit around the planet and in the midst of the alien ships who were trying to set up a blockade. A massive cheer went up from his bridge crew as *necrófago* ships struck mines, taking massive damage.

His private channel came to life. "Boho, was this you?" It was Mercedes, and she sounded excited and baffled and thrilled.

"I thought I'd better back up the bluff with something."

"I love you."

✦ ✦ ✦

A YOUNG OFFICER replaced her oxygen canister and Mercedes barely noticed. There was that brief moment when an indrawn breath left the lungs starved for air and then the sweet flow resumed. She gave the young man a quick wave of her fingers to indicate her thanks but kept her focus on the multiple screens that flashed tactical information and damage reports from not only her own ship, but from her fleet as well. The battle had taken them past the orbits of the planet's three moons and perilously close to the planet itself.

And the closer they approached to the planet, the more frenzied the defense by the aliens became. Ships from both sides were dying all around her. Often their death throes took them into the atmosphere, where they endured a fiery funeral pyre. She had received a message from Tracy that the remnants of the Green and Gold were engaging returning enemy ships. She wished that the firepower of the *Sutābureză* was with them, also having him even a few hundred thousand kilometers nearer to her would be comforting, but his fleet was keeping enemies from falling on them from the outer system.

They were taking heavy losses, but the *necrófago* losses were worse. It could not go on much longer. But her thought felt more like a hope than a fact, because despite repeated calls to them to surrender, it had not stopped.

Mercedes's back ached and her legs were shaking. It was only the suit's power servos that were keeping her erect, and the suit's health monitoring system was dispensing stimulant injections directly into her bloodstream at far more frequent intervals. They helped, but eventually the piper would have to be paid and she would collapse.

"*Madre de Dios!*" Gelb yelled. "They're going Kamikaze! Three of their fighters just rammed the *Sun Diver*! What the fuck? Why won't they just admit they're beat?"

Panic was yammering in her skull. Mercedes felt frozen, unable to think. How can you fight an enemy that seemed to have no instinct for survival. She frantically studied the flow of information, praying that some desperate insight would strike. That she had not led them all to utter annihilation. A tiny detail caught her attention.

There had been more than a few missiles that had lost guidance control and headed for the planet. *And* necrófago *ships had moved to intercept even if it resulted in their destruction.*

She turned to the linguistic expert assigned to her and clutched the woman's arm. "What are the aliens saying when they break off an attack to intercept any missiles that are heading toward the planet? I mean, it makes no sense as a tactic." Even through the distortion of her helmet's faceplate, Mercedes could tell from the linguist's expression that she wanted to say something but was hesitating. "You're thinking about something. Please tell me." Mercedes punctuated the demand by giving her a shake.

"Well, it's not verified. It's just a theory. *My* theory, actually, but we didn't include it in the briefing reports because it's not verif—"

"Get on with it," she snapped.

"It's about their religion. It's hard to get them to talk about it, but it seemed to be closely affiliated with planets. Most races put their deity in the heavens, but that's not what we were getting from the prisoners. I think that's why they hit our worlds so hard. It wasn't just about killing civilians. *I* think they were trying to kill our God."

"Which might explain why they self-destruct rather than surrender," Mercedes muttered. "Individual lives don't matter. Why they'll ram a ship when all else fails."

A plan began to form. Was it audacious or desperate? Probably a bit of both, she concluded. She set up a private call to all the remaining captains of the Blue. "Break off attacking the ships! Direct all your fire on the planet, particularly the cities. Everything we've got, rail guns, missiles."

"Are you mad?" Boho's voice was shaking. "They'll be on us in a second and we'll be destroyed."

Mercedes hesitated, swallowed hard, offered up a small prayer, and said, "I don't think so."

"Oh, Dios mio," Boho said.

"As Her Majesty commands," Gelb said formally. The rest echoed the words.

She broke the connection and watched as her bridge crew leaped into action. Gelb relayed the order to the weapons officer. It was a junior, his superior had been killed. She watched the minutes counting down. Then the seconds. She prayed. *Mother of God! Be with them on the battlefield during life and at the hour of death, and grant that they may live and die in the grace of thy Son, amen.*

"Fuego," she ordered.

✦ ✦ ✦

"ADMIRAL BELMANOR."

"Majesty."

She was on a heavily encrypted channel set for privacy, so Tracy knew it was serious and probably not about the fact Carisa had chosen to remain with the Green after the remnants of the Gold had been divided, with half going to join the Blue at the planet and the rest staying with Tracy.

Tracy had been puzzled by the princess's choice, but Beatrisa had just smiled and shrugged. *"She knows Mercedes would fuss and fret and Cari doesn't want to be a distraction."*

"And you won't? Fuss and fret?" Tracy had asked.

"No. I know Cari's not a baby. Mer still sees the little girl she used to bring ices and cakes from the balls. I see the woman."

Mercedes continued. "I believe we may be on the cusp of victory, but I need you to tip the balance." He didn't waste time answering, just listened. "I need you to find a rock. A nice big one. Something that could potentially cause an extinction level event. Then you and your fleet will escort it to the *necrófago* home world."

The request shook him, and the charming image of a big sister bringing treats to her youngest sister vanished in the face of the vengeful reality. It was one thing to engage soldiers, but to wipe out life on a planet? Even separated by millions of kilometers she seemed to read his thoughts. "Tracy, I have no intention of actually using this. It's just for leverage."

"Do I have your word?" he asked.

"Yes. I swear I will not make you a party to genocide."

"All right. And I assume my ships are providing the escort for this leverage?"

"Yes."

"We'll start hunting."

She broke the connection, and he did some quick research on the size of rock that would cause an ELE. He wanted to locate one on the low end of that spectrum because shifting a huge asteroid would take longer and be more complex. As it was, they weren't going to be able to boost this rock at any significant speed. He could foresee several months of boredom and battle, because presumably the *necrófagos* weren't just going to sit still and wait for the humans to arrive with a planet-killing rock.

Once he had decided on a size, Tracy gave the order for the *explorador* captains of his small fleet to join him aboard the *Sutābureză* for a briefing. He didn't want this order going out over an open channel. If he were the enemy, he would be monitoring all League communications, and he sure as fuck didn't want them hearing about this and doing everything in their power to stop it.

His next call was to Kallapus to have refreshments ready in the conference room. It would take a few hours for all of them to arrive, so he turned to a task he dreaded, but had to be faced—writing condolence letters to the families of the deceased. He was grateful when his ring pinged him that it was time, and he could head for the conference room.

"I apologize for the sparse display," Kallapus said, gesturing at the table that held only a plate of small cakes and a cheese board. "But we are running rather low on fresh ingredients," he added as he laid out the final cup next to the coffee urn and the one containing hot water.

"I doubt anyone will notice," Tracy said. "Sitting in the middle of a hot war does tend to distract you from trivialities."

"Very true, sir." The Hajin bowed and left.

A few minutes later the captains assembled, and the conference room seemed suddenly very small given the presence of thirty-two men and one woman. At the last-minute Tracy had added Valada-Viers to the mix since the *Swiftsure* was the fastest ship in the fleet. He wanted the frigate to guard dog the smaller vessels.

Once they all had a beverage, a plate, and idle chitchat had been satisfied, he called them to order. He was too nervous to sit, so he stood behind his chair gripping the back.

"First, let me assure you that the Empress has no intention of making us party to a planetary genocide, but she needs a negotiating edge, so here is what she wants us to do." He then outlined the size and type of rock they needed to locate.

There was a moment of silence, then every eye in the room swiveled to focus on Carisa. It might have been unspoken, but the question hung shivering in the room like the final echo of a cathedral bell.

She didn't wilt under the scrutiny. If anything, she sat taller. "Her word is her bond. If the Empress gave Admiral Belmanor her assurance that the rock would not be used, it won't be used."

"Conversely, a bluff's no good if the opponent knows you're … well, bluffing," Valada-Viers said.

"And they know we bluffed once. When the Consort radioed that those bastards in the Gold were actually going to the planet instead of turning tail. Why will they believe us this time?" another captain added.

Carisa gave him a withering look and said with enough acid to eat through steel, "Gosh, I don't know. Maybe because we're going to be escorting a mucking big rock?"

The other captain's embarrassment was easy to read, and Tracy turned his chuckle into a cough. *So, the little princess has teeth,* he thought.

"There is a certain reality to a large asteroid approaching as opposed to invisible ships that never arrived," Tracy said.

"And they most likely don't understand human psychology all that well."

"Yeah, they're not big on that whole taking prisoners thing," Valada-Viers muttered.

"If I might continue?" Tracy said with deceptive sweetness. The murmurs subsided. "Once the rock is located, our engineers will figure the best way to boost the thing out of its orbit and onto a course that would take it ultimately to the *necrófago* home world."

"This will make them fight even harder," Valada-Viers said. "*Mierda*, I would if it was my world being threatened in this way."

"And they're going to come at us *hard*," another captain murmured.

"It's not clear that they have much left to come at us *with*," Tracy said. "And whether they do or not, we have our orders. Her Majesty feels this could end the war. So, let's give her what she needs."

✦ ✦ ✦

THE ULTIMATUM HAD been sent and now they waited tensely for a response. Vast numbers of *necrófago* ships had been lost in the attempt to prevent the League missiles from impacting the planet. After the ultimatum had been delivered, an eerie calm had fallen. The *necrófago* ships had stopped launching weaponry against the humans, giving them a chance to make repairs and rescue escape pods from destroyed ships. Despite their best efforts, the butcher's bill was going to be very high.

"Sir, something bizarre is happening," the officer seated

at the scanners called. Boho moved to his side and studied the data. "The ships that were in low orbit are no longer holding their positions. Gravity and atmospheric drag are starting to pull them down."

"What the hell?" Boho said. "Did they simultaneously lose control or are they all asleep?"

The lieutenant shook his head. "The energy readings off the ships are normal."

"Seppuku?" Boho's flag captain, Joshua Friedman suggested. Boho turned to face him, and he shrugged apologetically. "My grandfather on my mother's side had a lot of Japanese ancestors. He told me stories about how a samurai would commit suicide rather than surrender. And God knows we've seen that. They destroy their damaged ships rather than surrender."

The memory returned of a Hidden World filled with close to a hundred thousand dead people. An entire population who had all died by their own hand to avoid annexation by the League. Was this the *necrófagos* version of that? Boho watched the scanners as one by one ships became falling stars. What were these creatures that they embraced death so willingly? Apart from a few cultures, most humans fought like caged badgers to survive.

He called Mercedes on their private channel. "What's your read on this?" he asked.

"I think we … have seen this before, Boho," Mercedes said. "On Kusatsu-Shirane." Dread was a dull grey edging of lead around her words. "What are we, or what have we become, that we seem to bring only death?" Her expression was agonized.

"Not our problem if they choose to be that stupid, and may I point out the obvious—they started this. We're just finishing it," he replied. "But before we drop a big rock on them and spoil a perfectly usable planet, we might want to send down drones and see if anybody salutes, as in starts shooting at them. We've got four months before that rock arrives. Plenty of time to figure this out."

✦ ✦ ✦

HER COMM OFFICER called to her, "Admiral, incoming message from Admiral Marqués Chapman-Owiti. Tagged as urgent."

"I'll accept," she said. Her flagship was a newer design that provided her with a small room just off the bridge, which saved her having to descend to the officer deck and her more formal office. The door closed behind her, and security measures sprang automatically to life. Mercedes sank gratefully down into the chair. A diet of stimulants and coffee were starting to take their toll.

"So, what unpleasant news do you have for me, Ernesto?"

"Well, that's rather dispiriting and anticipating the worst," said his holographic image.

"Am I wrong?"

He shook his head. "No. I'll get right to it. Our remaining prisoners are dead."

"How?"

"Damned if I know. They just fell down dead. Like somebody flipped a switch."

"I think the same thing may have happened here," she

said. "All activity on their ships has stopped. We're preparing drones to scan the planet. I'll let you know once they've returned their data."

She broke the connection and sat for a few minutes. An image of a dead mother lying in a bed, poisoned children in her arms and a husband slumped in a chair with a gunshot wound to the head. On Kusatsu-Shirane, the human inhabitants had taken the drastic step of mass suicide to avoid losing their children to the League's policy of fostering any child of twelve or under. Could the *necrófagos* have known of that? But if they had been monitoring the League, they would also have known that such measures were not employed against the League's alien subjects. They had just been conquered and integrated into human society. Such would have been the fate even of the *necrófagos*. Yes, they were disturbing to human eyes, but so were the Sidone Spiders and humans had come to accept them.

She shook away the memories and returned to the bridge. "Have all ships release drones to scan the planet. It's time we had some answers."

✦ ✦ ✦

"FUCK, FUCK, FUCK, fuck, and fuck again for good measure!" Jahan was storming around the Keim's living room while the human couple, huddled on the couch, looked on with alarm. Dalea stood, hands folded at her waist, and watched. The room was a pleasant place, with a couple of overstuffed chairs to augment the couch and kid's toys on the floor and a half-completed puzzle on a table. Jahan discovered the toys because she trod on one of the plastic figures, heard it crunch, and felt a stab of pain in the sole of her foot. "Ow, fuck." She picked up the broken toy. "Sorry."

"No, we should be sorry," Mrs. Keim said. "We should have checked with the authorities—"

"They did have all the right credentials," the husband said a bit defensively. "And Elizabeth seemed to know the gentlemen—"

Jahan broke in. "No, I'm the one who should be apologizing; I shouldn't have lost my shit. It's not your fault. All these FFH assholes … uh, people, know each other, go to the right parties, etcetera, etcetera."

The wife spoke up, her tone both hesitant and apologetic. "Also, Hayden was with them."

Jahan and Dalea exchanged horrified looks. "Could he really be working with them?" Jahan asked to no one in particular.

Mrs. Keim stood and walked over to them. "I don't know if this will answer your question, but before they left Hayden hugged our girls. I found this in Lily's pocket when I was getting her ready for her bath." She handed over a data spike.

Jahan grabbed it and tapped it against her ring. The information sprang to life. It was the transponder code for the ship.

"Clever, clever boy," Dalea said. "I could kiss him."

"I'll let you, right after I wring his damn neck," Jahan growled. "What I can't figure out is why he agreed to help at all."

"Because he's fifteen and we don't know what kind of threats were used against the boy," Mr. Keim said.

"Oh, yeah, good point." Jahan sighed.

"We're so sorry," Mrs. Keim said again, and Jahan realized she was being horribly unfair.

"Really, it's okay. Well, not okay, but understandable. How could you know that we decided to have a civil war in the middle of a real war, 'cause that's just not all kinds of stupid?" She ran her hands across the top of her head trying to smooth her fur that was standing on end in her alarm.

Dalea turned to the Keims. "When did they leave?" she asked in her gentle way.

"I suppose yesterday or maybe early today. They came here late in the day," the husband said.

"We need to get to the spaceport, find out about this ship," Jahan said.

They left and returned to their rented car. Jahan beat her hands on the steering wheel. "We should never have left Hayden."

"And then we wouldn't have gotten away so we'd be right back in this situation," the Hajin said. "We should probably tell the president that a faction of the League knows about them. They should prepare their defenses."

"I expect Nephilim is going to have their own problems. Mercedes isn't going to take this lying down." Jahan sighed. "But yeah, we should let them know that we fucked up big time."

Dalea made the call while Jahan drove. It went about as well as they could have expected, and by the time they reached the spaceport Freehold's space command was scrambling. They checked in with the port authority and got the details on the ship. It wasn't a military vessel; the

Freeholders would never have allowed it to land if it had been. Instead, it was a fancy FFH pinnace.

"It's gonna be fast," Ernie grunted when they had gotten the news from Jahan and Dalea. "Faster than us."

"And neither of us are armed," Kielli offered. "So, what could we do even if we caught up with them?"

"We've got to tell the Empress," Jax said.

Jahan shook her head. "No, she's leading our forces against the enemy. We tell her that her son is in the hands of a traitor, we risk distracting her at a critical time. We tell Tracy."

Jax swayed in agreement. "Yes, he has sufficient rank to take action and ships he could assign to locate and capture the Nephilim ship."

Jahan held up the spike. "And the means to track it."

28

WITH SUFFICIENT INCENTIVE

"HE'S MY NEPHEW and my future emperor, so I damn well *am* coming with you," Beatrisa raged as they almost ran down the corridor toward the hanger bay.

Tracy had gotten the message from Jahan only minutes before and had quickly begun to plan. He stopped, grabbed the princess by the shoulders, and pushed her against the wall. "No. You are part of the royal family, and we gave the leaders of this Hidden World our word that their location would not be revealed to the League."

"But *you* know the location."

"Yes, because I'm lowborn scum who has had a … shall we say … checkered career before now. I need the fastest ship we've got, so I'm taking the *Swiftsure* and you and Valada-Viers can figure out who gets to be admiral and who's the flag while I'm gone."

"I have to tell Mercedes," Beatrisa said. Intensity and emotion had her voice shaking.

"You bloody well don't and that's an order. Once the prince is safely secured, I'll inform you and then you can tell Her Majesty. Look, we have to be ready to blow this rock into fragments once we have secured the *necrófagos* surrender, and the *Sutāburezā* is the best ship to do that."

"And if they don't surrender?" Beatrisa asked waspishly.

"Let's just say I'm glad that won't be on *my* conscience," Tracy said, and he was only half joking.

She punched him hard in the gut. *"Cabrón!"*

"Look, I expect they'll negotiate terms. I think they destroyed their ships because they wanted to deny us access to their technology and to keep us from taking any prisoners. My gut tells me they won't let their entire species die."

"Let's hope your gut is right and it's not just gas." She shrugged off his grip. "Let's go."

When they entered the hanger bay control center Cipriana, Flintoff, and Luis were all waiting. "So, you're taking my officers, too?" Beatrisa yelped.

"What's happening, Admiral?" Flintoff asked. Her pale cheeks were red with excitement. Luis looked worried and Cipriana was as expressionless as the Sphinx.

"You're from a Hidden World," Tracy said to Flintoff. "You have any problem with keeping the location of one of them secret?"

The girl's face twisted in a fleeting expression of corrosive rage. "Hell, no."

"Well, I do, so why am *I* here?" Cipriana asked.

"To help rescue your son. I figured that would be enough of an incentive."

Cipriana's blank expression was gone, and she clutched at his arm. "What's happened?"

"I'll brief you once we're aboard the *Swiftsure*." He turned to Luis, who delivered a perfect salute and then grinned at him. "And you I know I can trust. That's why you'll be navigating."

As they talked, the big outer doors opened to receive the arriving shuttle from the *Swiftsure*. Once the bay was pressurized, they went out to greet Valada-Viers, who saluted and then gripped Tracy by the forearm and gave him a clap on the back. "So, do I get to keep the flagship?" he joked.

"Sure, I hated giving you the *Swifty* anyway." In a more sober tone he added, "Thank you for this, Tony. It really is an emergency and I need a fast ship."

"I won't ask what's going on. Perhaps you'll tell me when you return."

Tracy and his handpicked officers entered the *Swiftsure*'s shuttle for the return to the frigate. During the two-hour journey he briefed them on what Jahan had told them.

"The good news is that this planet is deep inside a dust cloud. You cannot safely translate to Fold until you're well outside the nebula. That means we have a chance to get there before they can translate."

"And if we don't?" Cipriana asked harshly.

He met her gaze. "We follow them to Nephilim. We're going to get your son and the *Infante* back. I swear it."

✦ ✦ ✦

THE *SELKIE* WAS doing her best, but the trading vessel was no match for the sleek pinnace. The only advantage they had was top-of-the-line scanning equipment purchased with the reward money they had received for rescuing the Empress. Jahan suspected Tracy had spent that large amount because he was still hoping to find another derelict Cara'ot ship. They had lost the one they had found when the consort had stolen it out from under them. Whatever Tracy's reasons, the equipment was first-rate, so while they couldn't catch the Nephilim ship they could sure as hell track it.

Once Tracy reached the system, they could send him the ship's location and then haul ass to try and offer assistance. That was what she was telling Ernie and Kielli. The truth was more complicated—she needed to keep Tracy from laying eyes on the prince. He was male and a human, but he wasn't completely stupid.

Jahan covered her burning eyes with one hand and tried to find a comfortable position in the captain's chair that would ease her aching neck and head. A soft rustling and a wafting smell of greenery heralded Jax's arrival. "Please don't be coming to tell me something I don't want to hear," she mumbled.

"Difficult for me to judge since I am not a meat creature. I wanted to suggest that we should scan for more than just the pinnace. Hayden is a clever and resourceful lad. He might do something unexpected to try and free himself and the prince."

"Well, I hope to hell he doesn't. He could get himself killed. And thanks, now I have to worry about that, too!"

"I gather that is sarcasm," Jax sniffed, and he rustled his way back to the lift.

Kielli, at his station at the scanners, swung around to face her. "So, I'll calibrate to look for escape pods or humans in spacesuits."

"Let's hope Hayden isn't *that* creative," Jahan said.

✦ ✦ ✦

TRACY'S STOMACH TRIED to climb up the back of his throat. It had been years since he had had such a strong reaction to translating out of Fold. It had to be nerves and the tension that had kept him awake for much of their Fold journey to Freehold. He had assumed the Nephilim ship would pick the fastest route to the edge of the nebula and planned the *Swiftsure*'s course accordingly. He just hoped they weren't too late.

Taking the frigate to Nephilim to rescue the heir to the throne would not be his first choice. By now, Talion would have reached home and have with him the combined might of the ships and captains he had convinced to mutiny. Tracy spared a moment to wonder about the fate of any *hombres* or officers who might *not* have approved of their captain's choices. He suspected that it hadn't been a happy one.

He opened a channel to the weapons deck. "Acevedo, please have weapons hot, but make certain nobody with an itchy finger is programming fire control. And once we have a scan of the ship, I want you to personally triple check the targeting. I'm hoping they'll surrender, but if not, we have to take out the Fold engines. *Only* the Fold engines. Remember the prince is aboard that ship."

"Aye, aye, Admiral. I've got Commander Lady McKenzie on fire control. She won't miss a trick."

"Good call."

He next put in a call to Jahan and the *Selkie*. "You have the coordinates for me?"

"Yep, and hurry, because they're getting damn close to the edge of the nebula." The coordinates arrived on his ScoopRing and he beamed them over to Luis at navigation.

He had thought she would break the connection, but instead Jahan took the conversation into encrypted mode. "Uh, Captain … I mean, Admiral, you should let us take the prince and Hayden aboard the *Selkie*. Hayden's been with us for months—"

"What the hell?" At the looks from his bridge crew, Tracy modulated his volume. "What do you mean he's been with you?"

"Umm, guess that wasn't the best way to break that news to you. Look, it's a long story. I'll tell you once we have possession of the kids. Point is Dalea and I can look after a couple of traumatized kits—"

"Hayden's mother is aboard. I think Cipriana is perfectly capable of comforting her son and the prince."

"Uh … oh, didn't know that. Smart of you to add her to the crew. I mean, I know she was on your flagship … I do check the rosters. Not because it's creepy, but just to be sure you've got good people with you—"

"Jahan, why are you babbling?"

"Am I? Just nervous, I guess. I got very fond of that boy—Hayden—while he was with us. Kid is smart and super brave."

"That's great. I'll look forward to meeting him." Tracy broke the connection and moved down to stand by Luis.

The younger man gave him a sideways glance and a grin. "Gonna micromanage me, sir?"

Tracy gripped Luis's shoulder. "No, just going to tell you

to run as hot as you can and ignore any screams from engineering. We have to catch them inside the cloud."

"You got it, sir."

+ + +

BOHO WATCHED AS a gaggle of engineers studied the *necrófago* ship specs. Once the League forces had realized that their enemies were all dead—the understanding of why or how that had happened would come later—they had swarmed the ships and then the cities to seize the fruits of their conquest.

Computer experts had figured out how to access the alien's computer network, and in the process had discovered advancements that would improve computing times by thirty percent without risking unleashing any kind of AI development; because if there were two things' humans feared, it was aliens messing with their human DNA and some computer achieving sentience. Boho pulled his attention back to the briefing and discovered that the engineers had moved on to excitedly discussing how materials and building techniques from the *necrófago* shipyards would also improve League ships.

Planetary Settlement had discovered that the aliens had ruled a small cluster of planets. All of them within the proper parameters for human colonization, thus removing some of the pain over Talion and Nephilim's secession. And Ernesto had arrived with a team of exobiologists to study the corpses and try to understand why they had died and why they were decaying at such a rapid rate. Not that anyone was complaining; it saved the League the grisly task of cleaning up the remains.

It was like a fairy godmother wanted the humans to have the gift of ten habitable new worlds spread across six star systems, intact shipyards, new technology, and no truculent aliens to govern.

Instead, they were going to have to turn their attention to truculent rebellious humans, but right now the military was sighing in relief that this war was over. They could take at least a few days to enjoy the moment before they launched into another one.

Initially, Mercedes had resisted announcing that the war was over, which had made the palace press office crazy, but Boho had understood her reticence. He suspected that she shared his feeling that if things felt too good to be true then they were probably too good to be true. Eventually, though, she had given in to the increasingly hysterical demands from the communications office and Mercedes, with Boho at her side, had announced the victory.

As if his thoughts had summoned her, Mercedes entered the command center that had been established in one of the elaborate spiraled-glass buildings in the largest city on the planet. The added gravity of the planet dragged at their limbs, but it was not much worse than Kronos and well within human parameters. The humans who would eventually settle here would just develop denser bones and squatter and more muscular bodies.

Boho expected his wife to look upset, since she had been inspecting what they had believed to be schools, but instead she was frowning. "You don't look like a woman who's just seen a lot of dead children," Boho commented.

"That's because I didn't." She sighed, yanked the ribbon off the end of her braid, and let her hair fall free. "And they weren't really schools." She massaged her scalp. "Ernesto is inspecting these … incubators? I guess that's what you would call them. The *necrófagos* seem to have produced eggs that developed in a cocoon for several years, and what emerged was an almost fully grown *necrófago*."

It was Boho's turn to rub at his head. "So how do they learn if they're not being taught as children?"

"Ernesto thinks it's a bit like a hive mind—bees or ants. They emerge with a basic knowledge and then highly technical skills are taught after they emerge."

"It's certainly efficient if they can bypass all the helpless infant and screaming toddler stages of development."

"It would also explain why they seemed to have so little regard for their own lives or the lives of their companions," Mercedes said.

"So, is this mass suicide?" Boho asked. Mercedes shrugged helplessly. "I ordered the Green to pulverize that rock. Whatever fragments do reach the planet will just provide a spectacular meteor shower. And you might want to check in on your sister. She sounded … odd."

"You mean Beatrisa?"

"Yes."

"Odd how?"

"Well, for one thing, she took the call and not that *intitulado*."

"She is his flag captain."

"Yes, but even though I didn't ask she started giving me

excuses for why I was talking to her and not him. I wouldn't put it past that bastard to have joined up with Talion."

"He wouldn't do that!" she flared. "He would not betray ... us."

"With sufficient incentive, anyone ..." Boho just let it hang there. Watched her worry. Felt both enjoyment and guilt at his pettiness.

29

SECRETS COME HOME TO ROOST

THEY WERE BOOSTING with everything that Ernie could coax out of the engines. It hadn't been fun enduring the increased gee forces, but they wanted to arrive as close to the inevitable confrontation as possible. And now Kielli was reporting that they had closed to within twenty thousand kilometers of the pinnace and the frigate.

Jax was on the Comm board and whistled to her. "They still appear to be in that particularly human activity of dick waving. Tracy is demanding they hand over the prince and Hayden. The captain of the pinnace is telling him he is mistaken *and* an idiot."

"Oops, there it goes. The frigate has fired a missile," Kielli called. "And the pinnace is firing its maneuvering jets to pull the missile off course so it will hit the body of the pinnace."

"That'll force Tracy to detonate the missile. He can't risk it," Jahan said.

"And he just did," Kielli reported. "*Infiernos* have just launched. The pinnace is boosting for the edge of the nebula. They're taking fire from the fighters. Okay! A bunch of escape pods just launched."

"Why would they do that?" Jahan asked to no one in

particular. "They're a million kilometers from Freehold. Our ship and Tracy's are the only possible rescue … Oh." She leaped over to Jax and pulled him away from Comms and over to one to the scanners. "Scan those pods. I'm betting most of them are empty."

His multiple fronds swept across the screen faster than any two-armed creature could match. "Yes. Only one is occupied."

"Set a course for that pod. I'm going to take the Talon and try to grab them."

"The pinnace is also pursuing," Kielli yelled after her retreating back. "Aaaand that thing we thought was decoration—"

✦ ✦ ✦

"ADMIRAL, IT'S A rail gun. It's small, but it'll be effective against those pods," Flintoff reported. At the same time, a boy's voice came over the radio.

"Mayday! Mayday! This is Hayden McKenzie. I have the Infante *with me. We're sharing a suit. Running low on oxygen. Mayday!"*

The sound of a child sobbing and wailing could also be heard. *"Izzie, my Izzie!"*

"Cyprian, Your Highness, hush. We don't have enough air!"

Tracy stiffened as if an electric current had run up his spine. "Shit, the boy has just pinged their location. We've got to confuse the pinnace." He joined the officer at comms. "Can you bounce that signal? Make it look like it's coming from multiple pods?"

"I can try, sir."

"Do better than try." Tracy swung back to command and ordered, "Fire on the pinnace!"

"No, wait!" A new voice came over the radio. It was Jahan. *"The prince's nanny is still aboard."*

"The pinnace is firing. Two pods have been destroyed," Flintoff reported.

"We don't have an option," Tracy responded to Jahan. "*Infiernos*, fire at will. Take out that rail gun and target the engines."

✦ ✦ ✦

THE TALON WAS fast. Not as fast as the fighter that had replaced it, but it had significantly more speed than the pinnace or the pods. Jahan was closing fast. Fortunately, she had identified the correct pod before Tracy's comm officer had started playing games with the radio signal. She doubted that a rich man's craft like the pinnace had the kind of scanner that would identify life signs. Of course, most pleasure craft didn't have a rail gun either, but the thing looked like it had been jury-rigged onto the elegant fin that decorated the top of the pinnace, so maybe they hadn't upgraded their scanners. One could hope. Especially when hope was all one had.

The Talon had been outfitted with grappling clamps. The crew of the *Selkie* had rarely used them, and now she was going to attempt to deploy them on a fast flyby. The military grade computer, like the guns, had been removed before the

Talon had been sold for scrap, which meant she was programming a rather rudimentary computer for this very complex maneuver. She offered a quick prayer and crossed herself as the Talon raced past the escape pod.

"Hayden, I'm coming for you," she radioed.

"Hurry." His voice was barely audible.

"Brace yourself and check your restraints."

She fired the front thrusters in a hard braking maneuver, felt the craft jerk as the grapples were deployed. Only two caught. One line and hook were oscillating in wide arcs. She prayed it wouldn't hit anything vital on either the pod or the Talon. She then fired the engines and headed back toward the *Selkie*, towing the pod. A hard blow tumbled the fighter as one of the slugs from the rail gun hit the Talon. The heavy armor on the fighter shrugged off the hit, but the tumble had caused one of the two grapples to break loose. The pod was now literally hanging by a single thread.

The *Selkie* was swelling in the viewport. *One hundred and twenty kilometers. Ninety kilometers.* There was a flare of brilliance that caused the viewports to darken in reaction. "Bye bye, pinnace," Jahan whispered. The doors to the freight deck were open. Jahan knew she was coming in far too fast. She killed the main thrusters and began firing the front rockets to slow the craft. She felt the left landing strut collapse as she landed. The Talon was on its side sliding toward the back wall of the freight deck. She craned around to see the bay doors closing, but it seemed agonizingly slow.

Dalea, wearing her spacesuit, came running onto the deck. She was carrying a medical bag and oxygen. Ernie was right behind her. He climbed onto the side of the Talon and began to wrench open the canopy that had been bent by the rough landing. Jahan scrambled out and ran to Dalea, who had the pod open and was filtering air directly into Hayden's suit. His features were visible through the faceplate. He looked like a resting saint or an angel.

"Please wake up. Please wake up," Jahan muttered. His eyelids began to flutter, and she gave a sob of relief.

"We're pressurized," Ernie said as he removed his helmet.

Jahan and Dalea began getting Hayden out of the suit. It was an adult size, which was the only reason Hayden had been able to cram both himself and the prince inside. The prince was resting against Hayden's chest. Dalea pulled him out, laid the child flat on the deck, and began administering CPR. Jahan, her arms wrapped around Hayden, watched tensely. She was counting seconds under her breath. Then with a mewling cry the prince jerked, and his eyes flew open. He began to scream and cry.

"Izzie! Izzie, my Izzie!"

"They shot her. While we were running for the pods," Hayden said in a tone so flat and calm that Jahan knew he, too, was on the thin edge of hysterics. "He saw it happen."

Jahan swallowed hard against the tightness in her throat. "Let's get you all upstairs."

✦ ✦ ✦

IT WAS A tight fit to wedge the shuttle from the *Swiftsure* into the bay on the *Selkie*. Especially with the battered Talon lying on its side. Tracy felt a pang of sorrow for the old fighter. While they waited for the bay to repressurize, Tracy noticed that Cipriana's hands were shaking. He took her hand in his and slipped an arm around her shoulders.

"It's going to be all right," he said softly.

"He hasn't seen me since ..." She gestured at her ruined face with her free hand.

"He won't see it. He'll only see his mother."

"I abandoned him." She pulled free and covered her face with her hands. "My hate was so corrosive. I didn't want him to see that. To think that I blamed him for living when James and Fiona died."

Tracy motioned for Luis to give them privacy. Oxygen having been restored, the young man hurried to open the shuttle's door and rushed down the ramp. Tracy could hear the sound of a noisy and joyful reunion between the *Selkie*'s crew and their former crewmate.

Tracy turned Cipriana around to face him and pulled her hands away from her face. "Then tell him that. This is clearly one very bright, very tough kid. He'll understand. Now come on. They're waiting." As they left the shuttle, he asked, "The prince knows you, right?"

"No. I saw him when he was just an infant. I haven't seen him since. This"—she again gestured at her face—"would give any child nightmares."

"Then get it fixed. The war is almost over. Hell, it may *be* over for all we know. You don't have to keep the scars as an incentive to fight."

They reached the group and Tracy introduced Cipriana to his former crew. Jax swayed into a deep bow, his fronds swirling around him like green leafy ribbons. The bandy-legged human gave an awkward bow. The young Isanjo's bow was perfect, and Jahan bobbed a curtsey. She then leaped into Tracy's arms and hugged him tight. Jax wrapped a few fronds around his hand and gave it a shake.

"So *damn* glad to see you," Jahan said.

"Welcome back aboard, Captain. The ship feels properly crewed now," Jax offered.

Jahan gave the Flute a jab from her fist. "Thanks, I haven't been *that* bad a captain."

"Ehhh," said the young Isanjo, and he waggled his hand in a *not so sure* gesture then gave a barking laugh.

"That miscreant is my nephew, Kielli," Jahan said. "This is Ernie, our new engineer."

"I'm pleased to meet you all," Tracy said. "But Commander Lady McKenzie would like to see her son, and I should check on the prince."

"Of course, Hayden is in the galley," Jahan said. "And the prince is fine. He's in my … your … the captain's cabin and Dalea is with him. No need to check on him right now. Besides, he's probably asleep."

Once again, his former first officer was babbling, and Tracy could not understand why. It couldn't be the presence of Cipriana. A mere lady, even one who was the daughter of a powerful duque, would not be enough to rattle Jahan. After all, they had hosted the woman who now ruled them all and the Isanjo hadn't been this nervous.

They all squeezed into the lift and rode up the three decks to the galley and cabin level. A stunningly handsome teenager sat at the table wolfing down a bowl of chili. He leaped to his feet at their entrance, but his gaze was fixed only on his mother. Cipriana froze and gave him a twisted smile. The cool demeanor crumbled, and a child replaced the young man.

"Mummy." And he ran to her. As they hugged, Tracy noted that the boy was now taller than his mother. Tears ran down both their faces.

Tracy stretched out his arms to block everyone from entering and coaxed them all back onto the elevator. "Let's check out the bridge for a few minutes," he said.

"Sure, you're going to love the purple vinyl covers on the chairs," Kielli said. "Kidding. Kidding."

Tracy glanced over at Jahan. "He's a real cutup, this kid."

Jahan cuffed her nephew on the back of the head. "Yeah, but I'll keep him."

They wiled away a quarter of an hour in inconsequential chatter. Tracy asked Ernie about how he coaxed the extra speed out of the engines. Jax had his usual complaints about how much money the *Selkie* was losing, and how he sincerely hoped the humans had ended this war because it was damn bad for business. Jahan kept glancing about nervously and finally said, "So I guess you'll be taking Hayden back with you? I mean, he should probably be with his mother."

"Yes. And with the prince."

"Seriously, why don't you let us take him back to the capital or to Merce—the Empress."

"Because the *Swiftsure* is significantly faster than the *Selkie* once we're out of Fold and because he should with his friend. My understanding is that the child and Hayden are close," Tracy said. "Also, it's my duty."

"Yeah, okay, but with the boy's nanny being killed he might be better off with Dalea. She can mother anyone and—"

His irritation flared into anger. "Okay, what the fuck is going on? Have you sold the prince? Planning to hold him for ransom? Why are you so determined that I not take custody of the boy? Do you think I'm going to hurt him because he's the son of … of … that man?"

Jahan looked around desperately, then rolled her eyes toward heaven. "Fine! Fuck it! But please try not to … oh, never mind."

He glanced around the bridge as Jahan marched over to the access ladder. None of the other crew members were moving and they were all avoiding his gaze. A shadow of suspicion began to bloom, but to acknowledge it meant accepting that many, many people had lied to him. Tracy followed her down the ladder. Cipriana and Hayden were sitting side by side, hands entwined at the table. Tracy had a momentary pang remembering meals shared and stories read. Memory provided another image of Mercedes dressed in a tee shirt and a pair of Luis's pants seated at the table smiling at him.

"Haydy?" came a child's voice.

Tracy looked at the doorway where Dalea stood behind a little boy wearing an overly large tee shirt that based on the vid game it was promoting probably belonged to Kielli. But the shirt was not what arrested Tracy's gaze. As he gazed down into the child's face, he knew with stunning clarity that this was *his* child.

His son.

His accusing gaze raked Dalea. She gave a shrug. Apology? Acknowledgement? He couldn't tell. He also could not process his own emotions. Shock. Joy. Fury. Tracy felt a fool not to have realized sooner, but to be fair, it had taken the passage of time to begin to reveal the angular planes of a face that no longer carried his mother's Madonna-like beauty.

It was Hayden who gave voice to the situation that held them all in thrall. "Oh, great. Things are gonna get real fucked up now."

IF YOU LIKED ...

If you liked *The Currency of War*, you might also enjoy:

The Imperials Saga:
The High Ground
In Evil Times
The Hidden World
The Thucydides Trap

ABOUT THE AUTHOR

Melinda M. Snodgrass studied opera at the Conservatory of Vienna, graduated Magna cum Laude from U.N.M. with a degree in history, and went on to Law School. After 3 years as a lawyer she realized she hated lawyers and turned to writing.

In 1988 she accepted a job on Star Trek: The Next Generation and began her Hollywood career where she has worked on staff on numerous shows and has written television pilots and feature films. She currently has two television series in active development.

In the prose world she writes for and co-edits the shared world anthology series Wild Cards with George R. R. Martin.

In addition, she writes her own novels. She is working on a fourth novel in the Carolingian series and a fourth novel for her White Fang Law series.

For fun she rides her dressage horse, plays video games and spends a lot of time in the gym. (Or she did before there was a pandemic).

BOOK CLUB QUESTIONS

1. Did it make sense for Mercedes to call Tracy back into active military service? Or did she do it for more personal reasons?
2. Beatrisa and Carisa are more major players in this book. Did you like getting to see more of Mercedes's sisters?
3. Did Tracy take the right approach with his officers who are League nobility by telling them his background?
4. Tracy feels that Talion is a psychopath. When you read, that Talion had returned to the story did you see that as foreshadowing and that the author had plans for that character?
5. Was Jahan right to want to warn the Hidden Worlds about the alien threat, and Tracy was wrong to stop her?
6. Should there have been more consequence when Tracy arrested one of his captains and promoted the scholarship student?
7. What is it in Tracy's background and personality that makes him willing and able to work with aliens?
8. Given how humans react to just other humans of different, races, religions and nations do you think humans would ever accept aliens and live in peace with them?

9. Why do you think Tracy led the boarding party onto the crippled alien ship? Were you surprised when the Isanjo showed up to help?
10. Did you agree with the priest's argument that captured aliens were also children of God and deserved humane treatment?
11. Did the alien's choice of targets – financial center, political capital, and site of the state religion—as detailed by Boho make sense?
12. Would targeting those types of sites make people more or less likely to fight?
13. What historical precedent is there for Mercedes making the decision to evacuate the children?
14. If you were in charge of a Hidden World, would you ever trust The Solar League?
15. Was it smart of Talion to defect with a number of ships and avoid being in the final battle? Do you think he was hoping Mercedes would be killed?
16. What do you think is behind the mass death of the Necrafagos?
17. Was it wrong for Mercedes to deceive both Boho and Tracy about the child?
18. Why do you think Dalea lied to Tracy, and was there more to it than just maintaining Mercedes' medical privacy?
19. Do you have the feeling there are secret machinations going on under the noses of the humans? What do think might be going on?

OTHER TITLES BY MELINDA M. SNODGRASS

Circuit series:

Circuit

Circuit Breaker

Final Circuit

Queen's Gambit Declined

The Edge series:

The Edge of Reason

The Edge of Ruin

The Edge of Dawn

The Imperials Saga:

The High Ground

In Evil Times

The Hidden World

The Currency of War

The Thucydides Trap

White Fang Law:

This Case is Gonna Kill Me, Book 1

Box Office Poison, Book 2

Publish and Perish, Book 3